# Praise for *The Dea*



"Carter Wilson's *The Dead Husband* is a perfectly paced and expertly written thriller. The prose is as smooth as glass, and the pages fly by as fast as the reader can turn them. And then the ending provides a shocking jolt. This is a smashing story about families and secrets and all the things you don't want to know about the people closest to you. Read it!"

—David Bell, *USA Today* bestselling author of *The Request*

"How far would you go to protect the ones you love? Rose Yates has come home to a house and a family she'd rather forget. But what waits for her there isn't the closure she's been hoping for. Instead, her past hides in the dark corners and recesses of her mind, ready to spring out at her. Carter Wilson's writing is evocative and tense, his characters deeply flawed yet relatable. In *The Dead Husband,* he weaves a story of a woman running from her past and the detective determined to uncover her secrets."

—Julie Clark, *New York Times* bestselling author of *The Last Flight*

# Praise for *The Dead Girl in 2A*

"With a story as riveting as it is mysterious, Wilson's *The Dead Girl in 2A* is a terrifying plunge into the depths of a childhood trauma rising back into the light. Wilson's characters are as deep as the mystery that surrounds them, and the fast-paced plot doesn't disappoint. This is not to be missed."

—R. H. Herron, international bestselling author of *Stolen Things*

"Wilson provides plenty of creepy and downright disturbing moments on the way to the unexpectedly heartfelt conclusion. Psychological thriller fans will be well satisfied."

—*Publishers Weekly*

"Will grip you from the first chapter and never let go. A lightning-paced thriller reminiscent of Dean Koontz. I couldn't turn the pages fast enough!"

—Liv Constantine, international bestselling author of *The Last Mrs. Parrish*

"Dean Koontz fans in particular will find a lot to enjoy. A disturbing, propulsive, and satisfying thriller. Wilson is an author to watch."

—*Kirkus Reviews*

"Readers will be intrigued by this exploration of how scientific experimentation…goes awry, leaving a trail of bodies and few survivors behind."

—*Booklist*

"Carter Wilson's novels slip under your skin with the elegance and devastation of a surgeon's scalpel. In his latest book, Wilson weaves a gripping tale in which the present can die in a single careless moment, and the past is as unknowable as the future. *The Dead Girl in 2A* is a high-wire act, exquisitely balanced between shattering suspense and the sudden opening of our hearts. I couldn't put this book down. Bravo!"

—Barbara Nickless, author of the
award-winning Sydney Parnell series

"A deftly scripted psychological thriller of a novel, *The Dead Girl in 2A* showcases author Carter Wilson's distinctive narrative storytelling style and expertise. An original and intensely riveting read from cover to cover."

—*Midwest Book Review*

"One of those books you devour in a single sitting. *The Dead Girl in 2A* promises a lot from the start and delivers in spades."

—Alex Marwood, author of *The Wicked Girls*

"Bestselling author Wilson (*Mister Tender's Girl*) delivers a solid standalone psychological thriller with a clever premise that brings to light the devastation of memory-altering drugs in psychological warfare research."

—*Library Journal*

# Praise for *Mister Tender's Girl*

"In spare prose, Wilson ratchets up the horror spawned by obsession to a bloody end. For those who tolerate intense, sometimes graphic fiction, this is mesmerizing."

—*Booklist*, Starred Review

"Dark, unsettling, and full of surprises, *Mister Tender's Girl* takes the reader on a dangerous journey alongside a woman who must face the past she's been hiding from. A fast-paced, spine-tingling read—and a reminder that imagined dangers are just as worthy of being feared."

—Megan Miranda, *New York Times* bestselling author of *The Perfect Stranger*

"Wilson turns the creep factor up to eleven, balancing his prose on a knife's edge. A highly satisfying high-tension thriller."

—*Kirkus Reviews*

"Chapter by chapter, Carter Wilson's *Mister Tender's Girl* compels the reader forward: another question, another mystery, another fear to be dispelled or realized. Start reading this thriller and you won't stop until the end. That's how compelling, whether endearing or nefarious, the main characters are. And that's how talented a writer Carter Wilson is."

—Randall Silvis, author of *Two Days Gone*

"[A] taut, complex thriller."

—*Publishers Weekly*

"Mix the raw terror of early Stephen King with the best of Harlan Coben's small-town secrets, then add a dose of shocking current events and top generously with a heaping portion of paranoia, and you've got an idea of the kind of chiller Carter Wilson has penned in *Mister Tender's Girl.*"

—*Strand Magazine*

"This elegantly written, masterful thriller, by turns meditative and shocking, lyrical and violent, will keep you glued to the pages from start to finish."

—A. J. Banner, *USA Today* bestselling author
of *The Good Neighbor* and *After Nightfall*

"A can't-put-down thriller that will reverberate with readers. The characters are well-drawn, the plot hums, the creepiness level is high, and you won't see the ending coming. Fans of psychological suspense shouldn't miss this great thrill ride."

—*Library Journal*

"The writing is both gorgeous and gritty, and the story so enticing that I gobbled it up in one sitting. I can only humbly request that Carter Wilson hurry up and write some more."

—Sandra Block, author of *The Girl without a Name*
and *What Happened That Night*

"Make sure you don't have any other plans when you crack this book open. This first-rate thriller will consume you."

—*The Oklahoman*

"Carter Wilson hits it out of the park with *Mister Tender's Girl*—one of the most suspenseful novels I've read in a long time. This book is a true page-turner, riveting on every level."

—Allen Eskens, bestselling author of *The Life We Bury* and *Nothing More Dangerous*

"Written full of tension sharp as the edge of a razor blade, Wilson weaves together an intense story that is as chilling as it is haunting. Not for the faint of heart, *Mister Tender's Girl* is a mesmerizing, complex thriller that's impossible to put down until the very end—just make sure to keep the lights on."

—BookTrib.com

"Not since *Gone Girl*'s 'Amazing Amy' has a character from a make-believe children's book been so richly imagined and realized, and led to such a twisting, seductive tale. *Mister Tender's Girl* forces Alice Hill out of her lonely, isolated world to confront the inner demons that arose after she became the victim of a violent attack. As Alice delves into the events surrounding the crime, she finds that the fictional Mister Tender may have been a very different man from what the world believed. Carter Wilson's latest novel will have readers checking outside their windows for monsters—and, like Alice, also looking for those that lurk inside themselves."

—Jenny Milchman, *USA Today* bestselling author of *Cover of Snow*, *Wicked River*, and *The Second Mother*

"With its fierce heroine and surprises at every turn, *Mister Tender's Girl* is a thriller to devour."

—*Shelf Awareness for Readers*

## Also by Carter Wilson

*Mister Tender's Girl*

*The Dead Girl in 2A*

# THE DEAD HUSBAND

CARTER WILSON

Poisoned Pen
PRESS

For Drew

the nicest guy I know



Published by Poisoned Pen Press, an imprint of Sourcebooks
P.O. Box 4410, Naperville, Illinois 60567-4410
(630) 961-3900
sourcebooks.com

Library of Congress Cataloging-in-Publication Data is on file with the publisher.

Printed and bound in Canada.
MBP 10 9 8 7 6 5 4 3 2 1

Remind me to breathe at the end of the world,
Appreciate scenes and the love I've received,
There's always a girl at the end of the world,
The departing,
The departing.

**—JAMES, "THE GIRL AT THE END OF THE WORLD"**

# PART I

# ONE

**Bury, New Hampshire**
**August 11**

**THE NAME OF THE** town is Bury, but it hasn't always been. The local government renamed the town from Chester after a local Union soldier named William Bury did some heroic thing or another a hundred and whatever years ago.

Poor Chester. They took the name of a whole town right away from him.

Bury, New Hampshire.

Most locals pronounce it *berry*, though there's a small faction of lifers who insist it rhymes with *fury*. Doesn't matter how it sounds out loud. In my head this town always makes me think of underground things, burrowed by worms, hidden from light. Secrets.

I grew up here. Part of me has always been buried here.

Thunderheads jostle for space in the summer sky. The air is heavy enough to create a drag on my steps, or maybe it's just my natural hesitation to walk up the long stone path to my father's front door. The house in which I grew up looms, as it always has, grand but not beautiful. Rum Hill Road is filled with mansions, but none of them feel like homes.

Max grabs my right hand as we approach the door. He does this when he's scared, feeling shy, or simply wants to be somewhere else. In other words, a lot of the time. Not atypical for any eleven-year-old, much less one who's going through what Max is. What we both are.

I look down and the diffused light from the gunmetal sky makes his blue eyes glow, as if all his energy is stored right behind those irises. Max has his dad's eyes. Looking at my son, this fact haunts me, as if I'm seeing the ghost of Riley. I don't want to see any part of my dead husband in Max.

It hits me again. I'm only thirty-seven and a widow. It's both depressing and freeing.

"It's okay," I tell him. I think I've said those two words as much as I've said *I love you* to him over the past month. One phrase is the truth. The other is a hope.

"I don't like Bury," he says.

"We just got here."

He gives my arm a tug of protest. "It's not Milwaukee. It's not *home*."

I tousle his hair, which probably assures me more than him. "No, it sure isn't."

We reach the front door, a curved and heavy slab of maple reinforced with iron hinges and bands. My father told me when I was a little girl that a door like ours conveyed wealth and strength. That we needed a thick door, like a castle, because it sent a sign to all who tried to enter. I asked him who we needed to protect ourselves from, and I'll never forget his answer.

*Everyone.*

For a moment, I have the impulse to ring the bell of the house where I spent my childhood. I try the door. It's locked, so I press the doorbell and hear the muffled ring of the familiar chime inside.

I'm surprised when my father himself opens it. He stares at me, then offers a smirk that never blossoms into a smile.

The air of the house leaks out and crawls over me. Smells of the past. The aroma of time, of long-ago fear. My father is one of the reasons I left this town and never looked back. He's also one of the reasons I'm back. Now, in this moment, a time when I need to be here but am dying to be anywhere else, my past threatens to scoop me up and wash me out to sea.

Perhaps this is how it all ends.

Maybe I was always meant to drown in Bury.

# TWO

**WHEN I WAS SEVENTEEN,** my father showed me a *BusinessWeek* article about him. It was a profile of his private equity firm, Yates Capital Partners, and the reporter quoted anonymous sources labeling my father "cold-blooded" and "ruthless." My father considered those terms high praise.

Now as I look at him boxed by the mammoth doorframe, he doesn't look all that different from his picture in the decades-old magazine. Just as bald, equally wiry and lean. If you asked a stranger what color my father's eyes were, they'd probably guess wrong, because his eyes are largely hidden within a perpetual squint, the kind that makes the receiver of his gaze anxious. Logan Yates will stare at you in silence with that squint, embracing the tension, and wait until you talk first.

And you will always talk first.

The only signs of his aging are the deepened grooves forged by that squint, the dry riverbeds spider-webbing from the corners of his eyes. Etchings of time, and casualties of practiced, unwavering stares. My father would have made a hell of a professional gambler.

"Hello, Dad."

"Rosie," he says.

Only he calls me Rosie. To the rest of the world, I'm just Rose.

"Where's Abril?" The housekeeper.

"She only works part-time now. I realized I didn't need someone skulking about the house if there wasn't enough work to do."

*Skulking* is a fifty-cent Logan Yates word.

I haven't seen my father in nine years. There are no hugs. Hugs are luxuries of the weak, and the Yates family tree is carved from petrified wood.

"Maxwell."

Max squeezes my hand as if clinging to a flotation device. "Hi, Grandpa."

The last time Max stood face-to-face with his grandfather, he was two. He's only known him through phone calls and FaceTime since then. Max used to ask me why we never saw him, and I explained Grandpa didn't like to travel, and I didn't like going back to Bury. The answer never satisfied Max, but he eventually stopped asking. Children grow used to routine.

"No more Grandpa," my father says. "You're twelve, right?"

"Eleven."

"Okay, eleven. How about you just call me Logan. I call you your name, you call me mine. Agreed?"

"I go by Max, not Maxwell."

"Fine, *Max*." My father reaches a hand out to his grandson, who hesitantly takes it and gives it a feeble pump. "Son, you shake a hand like that in the real world, and you may as well yank your pants down and bend over."

"*Dad*."

My father looks at me in mock surprise, and still the squint remains.

"What? He's gotta learn these things." He turns back to Max, sticks his hand back out. "Take my hand, Max."

Max hesitates, then does.

"Now squeeze, boy." My father looks down at their joined hands. "Harder, Max. Come on."

"Dad, please."

Max grunts as he puts all his strength into his grip.

"Listen to me," my father tells him, still squeezing Max's bony hand. "A handshake isn't a sign of friendship. It's an assessment. You versus the other guy. Who would win in a fight? That's what I want you to think about. You need to show the other guy that if you absolutely had to, you could tear his throat out. Now, squeeze like you mean it, son."

"Oh, for chrissakes, Dad."

Max grunts more and his eyes narrow; his intensity as he squeezes suggests he's actually trying to inflict pain. Only then does my father allow a rare smile. "There you go," he says. "That's more like it. Now you've got me on the defensive. Good job."

Max releases but his defiant expression remains. I feel years of my parenting efforts crumbling away.

"That's not the kind of lesson he needs in his life right now," I say. "Or maybe ever."

My father puts his hands up. "Fine, by all means." He's poised to say something else, perhaps one of the quips he had loaded at all times, ready to fire. Then he appears to think better of it, saying, "You're right. You're right. You've both been through a lot. I'm sorry."

"Thank you."

He stands aside and ushers us inside.

1734 Rum Hill Road.

There's a faint current of electricity rippling through me as I enter, bringing goose bumps to my arms. Like walking through a collection of ghosts who desperately try to drive me away.

I look down at my son. If he senses a change in the atmosphere, I don't see it on his face. Why should he? This house doesn't hold the memories for him that it does for me. Max has no idea what happened here, long before he was born.

And now we're here to live. For a while, anyway.

My father lured me back to Bury after Riley's death a month ago, and against all my urges, I had to concede I couldn't do things on my own. Riley and I had always lived independently of my father's wealth, but really, it was hardly living. My husband's entrepreneurial ventures were always doomed to fail, and we'd saved up just enough cash to hold us over until he tried something new. As for me, my income from writing novels is just past the "hobby" threshold as defined by the IRS. I was hoping my third book would be my breakout, but it just hasn't happened.

Yet my father's money wasn't the only motivation for coming home. I couldn't stay in Milwaukee. Not in that apartment where the coroner whisked away Riley's body, which was cool to the touch when I placed a hand on his bare shoulder. I didn't even want to remain in the city. Too many eyes, watching. Too many shadows, long and reaching. So I left the ghosts there to come face the ones here.

See, the thing is, I need to be here. I need to face the things I ran from a long time ago. I have this idea of finding peace, but could be such a thing doesn't exist.

The goose bumps fade, and I breathe in the familiar smells of the house. The ghosts allow me to pass.

For now.

# THREE

**Whitefish Bay, Wisconsin**

**DETECTIVE COLIN PEARSON LOOKED** down at his buzzing cell phone and saw the three letters on the screen he'd hoped against.

*Mom*

By the time he decided to answer, the call was already off to voicemail. He checked the time. Nearly 9:00 p.m.

*Probably four or five drinks in by now,* Colin thought. Which meant her lips were loose and ready to spew out whatever came to her mind.

"Jackie again?" Colin's wife, Meg, rested an open book on her five-month-pregnant belly.

"Yup."

Colin would listen to his mother's voicemail, but he needed a minute. A minute, and a couple more sips of his beer.

Colin and Meg were snug on their living-room sectional, perpendicular to each other, her head on his lap. Before bedtime, they'd taken to the habit of retreating here, each with a book, reading for at least thirty minutes. It was their time to decompress, air out the day, be together silently. It had become Colin's favorite time.

Until his mother called. And she always called.

"Okay." He sighed, then thumbed the phone to the voicemail app. One new message. Fourteen seconds. He pressed Play and held the phone to his ear, not wanting Meg to hear. He wasn't hiding anything from his wife, but he knew how agitated Meg became when his mom set to drinking. Jackie Pearson was a lovely person until the evening, at which time she turned into someone else entirely. Sometimes Colin wondered if it was the other way around, and his mom's real acting chops were on display during daylight hours.

"You probably don't remember Linda Grassey," the scratchy voice on the phone said. "But she was a real slut. They lived just down the street, and she always flirted with your father. Fawned about him like a goddamn saloon whore, getting him to help her out whenever she could. *Oh, you're such a good neighbor. And so strong!* Bitch died twelve years ago."

*Saloon whore?*

His mom's foul-mouthed missives were a beacon, summoning Colin to come rescue her from her own mind.

She'd been on a steady decline since Colin's father died two years earlier. Her doctor labeled it anxiety, prescribing meds she refused to take, just as she refused so many other things. Refused to move out of the family home and into an assisted-living facility. Refused to stop driving until the state wouldn't renew her license. Refused to stop drinking, even though it was probably the thing that'd end up killing her. She was only seventy-five but whatever life remained was eating her from the inside out.

Colin and Meg had been happy in Madison, but he knew he needed to return to the town he grew up in and look after his mom, because no one else was going to. He had no siblings, no father, no relatives anywhere near Wisconsin.

Meg agreed, though Colin knew the move from Madison to Milwaukee wasn't what she wanted. By the time they'd settled into their rental home in Whitefish Bay four months ago, Meg was unexpectedly pregnant. Though they'd been trying, they'd put a pause on their plans until they had a better idea of how long they'd be in Whitefish Bay. But there was that one night they hadn't been so careful, and now Meg, at thirty-five and on the cusp of being a first-time mother, was without her Madison friends and community.

Colin hoped they could go back home in the not-too-distant future, but that, of course, would require his mother dying.

"What'd she say?" Meg asked.

"Something about a woman named Linda."

"You going over there?"

"Suppose I need to."

She sighed.

"Don't stay late."

He never did. He just made sure his mother got into bed, just as she had done for him four decades ago when he'd been the one unable to figure out the world.

Colin and Meg had rented a house only four blocks from the one he grew up in, and the walk took him less than ten minutes. It was odd being back, smelling the same summer-night air, passing the same houses he did when he walked to school as a boy. With the observational skills he'd honed as a cop, he noted the subtle changes in the old, familiar houses: new paint schemes, reconfigured landscapes, popped-out roofs accommodating new additions. But it wasn't the little changes he noticed most. Rather, it was a sense that Whitefish Bay seemed a little smaller, more frayed, and less special than Colin remembered. There was a lesson in that, he thought. Maybe the key to living was being continuously on the move, experiencing new things, so the ache of time was never acute; memories and melancholy were inextricably mixed.

One thing he knew for certain. No way in hell was he going to end up like his mom. Trapped in a house, trapped in a mind, and unwilling to attempt escape from either.

Colin walked up the path to his old house and tried the door. Locked. He took out his keys and let himself in.

"Mom?"

"Upstairs."

He exhaled, ever-so-slightly disappointed in hearing her voice. A small part of him (though larger than he'd ever confess to) was anticipating the moment no voice called back. That he'd arrive to find she'd passed on, her heart or liver having finally given out.

It was a morbid thought, but one he had nonetheless.

Colin walked around a waist-high stack of newspapers and headed to the stairs, shaking his head at how much of his old house was now brimming with piles of worthless things. The worst part of his mom's descent into her dark twilight was the hoarding. It had started years ago, but until his father died, it was more like heavy clutter than anything more serious. But in the last year, the piles grew, as if she was trying to leave layers of her life's sediment behind to be studied by future generations.

Colin's mind churned the same thought, over and over, as he navigated the crowded stairs to his mother's bedroom.

*It's all just such a goddamned shame.*

# FOUR

**Bury, New Hampshire**

**PEOPLE ASSUME I'M OF** Irish descent because of my green eyes, reddish-brown hair, and skin that will burn if I as much as look at a postcard of the beach. I'm an anomaly; the rest of my family appears as WASPy as the Yates family name implies. We are a small, Protestant family destined to keep our numbers low and our wealth growing.

I'm thankful to be the black sheep.

My mother is dead, a victim of a pulmonary embolism when I was only three. I hardly remember her, but in every photo I have, I see Grace Kelly. Elegant even in her most casual of poses. Lithe, willowy. She was a model, and I have a handful of magazine ads to prove it.

My father never remarried. All those years, and he never found the right person again. Or perhaps he was thankful to be out of his marriage and vowed never to repeat. But I hate to think that way. Despite all that is cold and calculating about Logan Yates, I like to think he's capable of love. But unlike with my mother's magazine ads, I don't have anything to prove that.

We had the Disney family, where the mom died young and the dad raised the kids. The deviation from the Disney story was we were raised by nannies and my father slept with as many women as his schedule would allow. This did not exclude the nannies.

Women buzzed in and out of our lives like mosquitoes over the years, attaching themselves to my father and sucking as much blood as they could until he grew tired and swatted them away. It wasn't uncommon to find a statuesque blond sipping coffee in our kitchen as my sister and I prepared for school, nor was it rare I'd never see that person again. Dad preferred blonds, but rarely the same one twice.

As for the rest of my family, there's only my older sister, Cora. She has my mother's looks and my father's venom. Cora still lives in Bury, and as with my father, she's part of why I left this place without any intention of ever coming back.

Still, two decades later, here I am in this house. What happened here is why I became a novelist after all.

I push bad memories away and focus on unpacking the three bags I brought. The rest of our things are in storage back in Wisconsin, hastily crammed in a small unit after I broke the lease on our apartment.

"This house is too big."

I turn and find Max standing in the doorway of my bedroom, which was a guest room when I was growing up.

"Hey, buddy. I thought you were reading."

"I finished it."

"You finished the second Harry Potter book?"

"Third. *The Prisoner of Azkaban.*"

"Wow." Max has never been a great student but the kid is smart as hell. When he was old enough to understand Mommy was a writer, he latched onto reading, working his way quickly past his class level and the level after that. He read *A Wrinkle in Time* at age eight and *The Hobbit* at nine. I could never have read Tolkien at nine. He struggles with math and is allergic to tests of any type, but he'll be devouring Joyce by fifteen. He's asked to read my books on several occasions, but I always tell him they're too adult for him right now. A few more years.

"My room is too far away from yours," he says.

"It's just one floor away," I say. "There're three floors in this house, so that's not so bad." I unfold a shirt and place it on the bed.

"I don't like it here," he says.

I nod, knowing how he feels. We could fit six or seven of our old apartments in this house, not even counting all the yard space. "I know. It's a big change. But you'll get used to it."

Max looks down, as if the world suddenly got just a little too heavy. I walk up to him.

"Hey," I say, pulling him in to me. His head fits snug against my chest, and part of me doesn't want him to grow any more so I can always cradle him just like this. "I know this is hard, but there's no easy way through this. There are no shortcuts through this kind of pain. It's not fair, but it's how it is."

He doesn't answer. Instead, he goes into this kind of fugue state where his mouth hangs a bit open and his eyes focus on some distant world. It scared me when he first started doing this after Riley's death, but I realized it was all part of him processing a major shift in his life. It happens to me, too, maybe without the complete withdrawal from the present. But that moment of getting stuck on a reality so profound you lose yourself in it. For Max, his typical de-animation lasts ten, twenty seconds.

Finally, he blinks. Says, "We could have stayed in Milwaukee."

"No," I say. "We needed a new environment. And we need help."

"No, we don't. We can do everything on our own."

I shake my head as I squeeze him harder. "No, we can't. Not yet. That's the reality of this. Your grandfather's helping us out, and we need to appreciate that."

"He could have just sent us the money."

How do I tell my son that Mommy suffers from debilitating nightmares and my only hope for relief is to face my past head-on, right here in this house? I can't tell him, just as I can't tell anyone else. So I do what I'm skilled at: changing the subject.

"He's even paying for the school you'll be going to, and it's a really nice one. Same one your cousin goes to."

"I know. You told me that already."

I release and look down at him. His gaze moves back to his toes.

"Look at me," I say.

He doesn't.

"Max, look at me."

He finally looks up and into my eyes for about two seconds before shifting his eyes to the right. Two seconds of eye contact is pretty good for Max.

"This is probably the hardest thing you'll ever have to do in your entire life," I say. "But we're going to do it together. I'm not going anywhere. You know that, right?"

He doesn't answer at first. Finally, he says, "I see his face sometimes. At night, when I'm trying to fall asleep."

"Daddy?"

He nods.

I see his face, too. Blank. Dead. One eye a quarter open, pupil dry as bone.

"Does that feel good?" I ask. "To see him?"

Not an ounce of expression. "No."

His answer tickles the back of my neck, not in a pleasant way.

"Are you missing him?" I ask.

He surprises me by not answering. Instead, he turns and plods away, dragging his feet as he leaves the room. My impulse is to go after him, comfort him by saying how much I miss Riley as well. But I can't do it.

Maybe later I will, when I build up the proper calluses allowing me to lie to my son with grace and conviction.

And what a depressing thought that is.

# FIVE

**Whitefish Bay, Wisconsin**

**COLIN WALKED UP THE** stairs inside his mother's house, stepping with care around endless towers of crap on every riser. His mother would claim each pile to be full of things with which she could never part. To Colin, it was all junk, most of it not even worth donating to the Salvation Army. Some piles were lumps of old clothing, most having belonged to Colin's father. Three shoes here, a pair of faded corduroys there, a bathrobe and collection of tighty-whities there.

But most of the piles on the stairs were rectangular and towering just enough that any forceful brush against them would topple them, like a gigantic Jenga game. Stacks of old hardcover books, tabloid magazines dating back to the eighties, shoeboxes with decades-old photos inside, and even empty Tupperware containers. *Empty containers.* Those puzzled Colin most.

The upstairs landing was no better. Nor was the hallway, nor any other area in the house. Crap was *everywhere.* Colin sometimes wondered if his father's heart attack had been a blessing for him. Easier to die than to untangle this mess.

"Where are you?"

"In my room," his mother replied.

Colin stubbed his toe on an end table lying on its side in the hallway. He cursed and was tempted to kick it in frustration but decided to let it go. The end table didn't choose to be there after all.

He rounded the corner into his mother's bedroom and saw her at her vanity, a set once owned by his mother's mother. Mahogany finish, tri-angled mirror, and a delicate, needlepoint-topped stool. His mother was facing the mirror, applying lipstick, a creamy silk robe cinched loosely around her bony frame.

Her reflected gaze caught his.

"You have to clean up all your things," Colin said. It was his usual greeting. "It's just not safe."

"You know I'm not going to have *that* conversation again." Her typical reply.

"At least the stairs," he said. "You'll kill yourself. One stumble and gravity will do the rest."

"Oh, don't be so morbid."

He noticed the cocktail glass on top of the vanity. Empty. No coaster. His grandmother was undoubtedly cursing from her grave.

"Why are you putting on makeup? It's time for bed."

She turned and her long, wiry gray hair swept across her shoulders. "Because it makes me happy. When you get to my age, doing things that make one happy is far more important than doing things that make sense."

Her crooked lipstick and slurred words didn't nullify what Colin conceded was a sound argument.

"You were ranting about some Linda person," he said. "I don't remember her."

She sighed, turned back to the mirror, and started brushing out her hair. The image that popped into Colin's head was the tail of a horse being groomed. "Oh, I'm past that," she said.

"It was only ten minutes ago."

"I suppose it was just something that needed to come out."

"How many drinks have you had?"

"One away from enough." She picked up her empty glass. "Pour me that last one, will you? The bottle's in the bathroom."

This was the part Colin hated because he always agreed. He'd put up much more of a fight when he and Meg moved back to Whitefish Bay four months ago. Back then, he'd argue with his mother, even hide her booze. Urged her to see a therapist to help with her mood swings, her compulsive hoarding (*collecting*, she called it), her need to get on some medication. But he learned he couldn't force her to do anything, much less force himself to ignore her. So they settled into a routine on these nights, the evenings where she'd rant and call him to her side. He'd lightly chastise her about the clutter, ask her how many drinks she'd had, pour her one last one, and see that she got to sleep. Maybe he was nothing more than an enabler, and when he really thought about it, Colin figured he'd become the parent in the relationship, and that was about as bittersweet as something could be.

He stepped into the bathroom and grabbed the bottle of Plymouth Gin. This was the most clutter-free area of the house, along with a four-foot berth around her vanity set. Colin wondered if it represented some kind of safe zone for her, a place that existed as it always had, a return to her past she held dear while she slowly suffocated herself in the rest of the space.

He walked back and poured her two fingers.

"Thank you."

"You need to drink less," he said.

She lifted the glass, her hand wrinkled, spotted, and quivering in a way Colin thought more typical for a person twenty years older.

She took a sip and said, "Nights are difficult for me."

"I know they are."

"I'm not as bad as I seem."

"I know, Mom."

It was mostly true. She never drank until the sun went down, and during the daytime, she led a fairly normal life. She had a small community of friends that managed to get her out and doing things, and Meg drove her when she needed to go to the store.

"How's the baby?" she asked.

"Fine. Kicking a little."

"It's a girl. I'm sure of it."

"We'll find out in December." The due date was a week before Christmas.

Colin sat on the edge of the bed. His mother pivoted in her chair and smiled at him.

"I don't know what I'd do without you."

He shrugged. "I'm not sure I do anything for you at all. We moved here, and I'm just sitting back and watching you crumble."

"Everything crumbles eventually," she said. "That's how the world makes room for new things."

"Maybe we should look into getting you help. Someone who comes by the house for a few hours every day."

"You keep suggesting that," she said. "You keep at it, and I'll keep saying no. I don't need a stranger in here milling about my things." She lifted her glass and drained the rest in a gulp. "Those people are all thieves."

"That's just not true."

"Shh, shh," she scolded him. "No more talk of that tonight. I'm going to sleep." She rose from her chair and Colin moved off the bed, allowing her to stumble into it. He thought of the lipstick smears sure to accumulate on her pillow throughout the night.

His mother pulled the covers up to her chin, closed her eyes, and soon became perfectly still, her breaths so shallow as to be unnoticeable. With her eyes closed, hair brushed, lipstick on, and arms at her side, she looked prepped for a casket viewing.

Colin tried to push the thought away but found it heavy and unyielding. He leaned down and gave his mother a peck on her forehead.

"Good night," he whispered.

As Colin turned to leave the house and return to the comfort of his wife, his mother said, "Good night, Thomas."

Colin stilled, unprepared to hear his father's name, then accepting it as the next phase of his mother's mental deterioration.

Everything crumbles.

# SIX

## Bury, New Hampshire

**"WOW, *CORA*."**

It's all I can think to say as my sister lets herself in the front door of my father's house, followed by Peter and Willow. Nine more years hasn't aged her. Cora's beauty is perfectly embalmed.

"Rose!" Her excited voice sounds forced, and as I move in to hug her, I vow not to be so cynical, that maybe she *is* happy I'm here. But if she feels how I do, then she's a wonderful bullshit artist. Nine years is a long time for sisters to go without seeing each other. Now it feels too short.

Cora's embrace is delicate, as if there's a Fabergé egg between us. She smells the way a summer afternoon in the Hamptons must.

She pulls back but keeps her hands on my shoulders, studying me. She isn't even preserved—I think she's aging in reverse. She's thirty-nine but could be twenty-five and, now that I think of it, reminds me a lot of the blonds my father always favored.

"Did you dye your hair since I last saw you?" she asks.

"No."

"Oh. It looks less red. More dull, I guess."

This is Cora.

"Well, thanks."

"Oh, I didn't mean it like that, silly. You look beautiful as always, Baby Sister. I can't believe how long it's been."

*Yes, you can,* I think. *And I'm sure you're not happy I'm invading your little world now.*

I think about the placement of her hands on my shoulders and how I would react if she were attacking me. I have these thoughts from time to time, about how I would physically control a situation if I had to. I've taken enough self-defense classes over the years that my mind can shift into a defensive mode when someone touches me.

*Parry away Cora's right arm, then seize her left hand and bend it backward toward her wrist. The pain will force her to her knees. Then finish her off with a swift knee to the bridge of her nose.*

I don't want to think these things. I want to love Cora.

Growing up, we were fiercely different in our personalities: she was always more feminine, preferring dolls and dresses, whereas I liked video games and sweatpants. In high school, she was a cheerleader and I played soccer. The boys drooled over her, as she inherited my mother's Grace Kelly looks. I inherited my looks from god-knows-whom and was the fiery, freckled redhead who looked like she'd start a bar fight, given the opportunity.

Cora and I were closest before she turned ten. Then our closeness diminished, year by year, as she grew into her own world and I sought out mine. Whatever affection we still had for each other disappeared in the course of one night, a long time ago.

Tonight, she and her family have come for dinner, and as I look at Cora in the foyer of our childhood home, I wonder if any of that affection will ever come back. The probability is low.

Cora removes her hands and whisks past me. Her husband, Peter, is close behind, carrying a bottle of red wine. Nature, grooming products, and likely Botox have finely sculpted Peter into the perfect accessory for my sister. He looks like one of those Scandinavian actors trying to play an everyman role but looking a bit too perfect to be ordinary.

I don't have anything against Peter other than he's enchanted with my sister, but admittedly, that's a pretty big character flaw. Truth is, I hardly know him, and I can only imagine what she says to him about me.

We don't hug, but Peter gives me a perfunctory kiss on the cheek. Like Cora, he smells amazing.

My niece enters the house last. I see photos of her from time to time on Cora's social-media accounts, and Willow has developed into a frail-looking, sinewy, pale teen who mothers fear and fashion editors love. Her beauty is striking, despite the fact that she'd likely snap in two if the wind picked up.

"Willow, you've grown so much," I say.

Willow lets me hug her, which is as satisfying as embracing a corpse. Like mother, like daughter.

"I was, like, four when I last saw you," she says. "So, yeah. I've grown."

I call out for Max, who shuffles his way down the winding staircase to reacquaint himself with the Yates side of the family. The McKay side is entrenched in Arizona, where Max's paternal grandparents are slowly declining in an assisted-living facility. They came to their son's funeral, and I never saw either of them cry, as if the death of their firstborn at the age of thirty-nine was almost expected.

I look at my boy, who suddenly appears so out of place and alone, like a stray dog spending its first night in a shelter.

Max mutters *hi* to everyone but avoids physical contact, and no one but Cora even attempts. She gets within a foot before she realizes his arms are staying at his sides, then opts to give him an awkward rub on his shoulder.

"And look at you," she tells him. "If I hadn't seen pictures, I wouldn't even recognize you. You're twelve now?"

"Eleven."

"Willow's thirteen," Cora says.

"No one cares."

"Willow, attitude," Peter says.

"It's just hard to believe we haven't all been together in so long," Cora says. "It's crazy, right? We're a family. We shouldn't let time slip away like that."

"You knew where we lived," I say. "You could have visited anytime." I'm careful not to say she was *welcome* anytime.

My comment registers the smallest of glancing blows on her face. "Well, as I recall, I invited you out for Thanksgiving a few years ago, and you declined."

"I wasn't ready to be here then," I say. "I am now."

Cora puts a hand on my shoulder. "Oh god, of course. And I'm so glad you're back so we can help you. I just couldn't believe when we heard about Riley." She looks only at me as she talks, as if Max has faded into the background. "I was shocked. Simply *shocked*. I mean, so young. Not even forty, right? What a terrible, terrible thing. I just can't imagine."

Riley's name slides like cold steel into my guts, and I wonder if that will always be the case.

"It's been hard," I say instead of *thanks*. I reach for Max's hand and squeeze it. I hope I'm grounding him as much as he is me.

Peter takes a small step forward and makes eye contact with me first, then with Max. "You know," he says, "I've taken sleep medication from time to time. Stress of the job and all. But I'm always careful not to mix it with alcohol. Too much risk." He seems to hear what he just said and scurries to demolish and rebuild his point. "I'm just saying I know how easy it is…you know, to overdose by mistake. Happens all the time, at least that's what my doctor says. Anything we can do to help. Seriously, anything. Just let us know."

I let out a practiced sigh. "I think being in a different place will be good for both of us."

Willow steps around her father and right up to Max. She's a good five inches taller than him. "Did you see the body?" she asks.

"*Willow Sofia*," Cora says. "How can you ask that?"

Cora is horrified, as am I, and both of us for reasons beyond the shock of the question itself. The moment produces a surge of electrical current through my body, jolting me to a sudden, surprising, and dissonant thought:

I miss my sister.

So odd I feel that right now, in this moment. It doesn't last long, but enough for Cora and me to make eye contact and have what I think is a shared moment.

Max squeezes my hand a little harder but gives no other indication he's upset. He doesn't react. He doesn't retreat.

Instead, he simply says, "Yes."

I'm amazed he answered.

Willow's eyes widen. "What was it like?"

"Okay, that's enough," I say.

"Quite enough," Peter adds. "Behave yourself, Willow."

"I was just asking."

Before Willow gets another scolding, Max says, "He looked peaceful." Max shifts his focus and looks directly at me. "He didn't look angry anymore."

His answer sucks the air out of me. Max has never talked about the few seconds he saw Riley's body in the bed, and now that he does, he describes it…this way.

*He didn't look angry anymore.*

"Did you cry?"

I turn and see my father, who's just walked into the foyer with a drink in hand. Single-malt whiskey, if habit holds true.

"No," Max mumbles. "Not right then."

"That's because you're a Yates," my father says. "And Yateses don't panic. Don't lose their nerve in a crisis."

"*Jesus,* Dad."

My father barrels right over me. "In fact, I'd wager none of us were as young as Max when we first saw a dead body. Any takers on that?"

My entire body stiffens with an old, familiar dread, one so heavy and instant it's as if I've been cast into stone.

"*Stop it,* Dad," I say.

Willow chimes in. "I've seen lots of messed-up stuff on YouTube."

"No." My father points in her direction with his drink. "I'm talking real stuff. Live, so to speak. You had to be there. See it in person." He doesn't pause long enough for anyone to interject. "I saw my first dead person when I was twenty-one. Wasn't even a funeral, though I'd been to a few of those already. But they were all closed-casket." He takes another step closer, locked in on me. "Cory Levitz. Senior year of college. I didn't know him, but his car wrapped around a lamppost right outside my apartment. After midnight on a Friday. Drunk as a skunk. I was the third or fourth person there after hearing the crash. Car was crumpled like a beer can. His blood all over the windshield. Someone had a flashlight, and I couldn't even fathom the fact his arm was no longer—"

I snap. "Dad, what the hell is *wrong* with you?"

That stops him. He doesn't look angered. He seems amused.

"Well, fair enough," he says. He reaches out and ruffles Max's hair. "I'm just saying your boy is a tough son of a bitch."

Then he turns and walks back from where he came, jingling his glass, the clinking ice the only sound among us.

My god, we haven't even made it past the foyer.

# SEVEN

**Whitefish Bay, Wisconsin**

**BACK HOME, COLIN FOUND** Meg with a book in bed, covers pulled up to her waist.

"Hey," he said.

She looked up. "How was she?"

"Numb," he said.

"Did you talk?"

He nodded. "A little. Usual stuff, mostly."

"Did you tell her we want to hire someone to check in on her?"

"Yup, as always. And as always, she said no."

Meg let out an exhale, and Colin identified it. Meg's exhales all had fingerprints on them, and Colin could gauge her state of mind by which exhale she used at any particular time. His guess was confirmed with her next sentence.

"We uprooted our lives, and all we're doing is watching her slowly kill herself. We could have done that from Madison."

"Let's give it a little more time," he said. "We haven't been here all that long. We're adjusting, she's adjusting. Besides, it's an easier conversation to have in the daytime with her."

Meg looped a strand of her shoulder-length hair behind her ear. "I just don't know what good we're doing here. And when the baby comes, we'll have even less time to spend with her."

"But maybe having the baby will help turn her around," he said. "Maybe our child is the spark she needs."

"If she makes it until then."

"We're family," Colin added. "Just being close by, it means a lot to her. We don't have to solve every problem right now. We just need to be here."

Colin walked up to the bed, leaned down, and kissed Meg on the cheek. As he did, he reached with his left hand and lightly traced his fingertips along the base of her neck, down over her breasts, and finally up and around her stomach, which was only half-covered by one of his loose-knit tank tops. He thought once again of their child, though this time, Colin didn't picture a baby but an adult, a person his own age. He pictured a man, Colin's son, forty years old and grappling with the same issues Colin faced now. Was Colin destined to end up like his mother, old and rattled, a collector of junk, alternatingly lucid and crazed?

And would Colin's child be there for him?

He hoped the answer to the first question was *no*. But if history was going to repeat itself, Colin liked to think the answer to the second was *yes*.

Meg gave him enough of a smile to let him know she didn't want an argument, either, and then went back to her book.

Colin stripped to his boxer briefs and joined Meg in bed. After leaning over and kissing her shoulder, he grabbed his own book from the nightstand. It was a novel, but although he was enjoying it, he wasn't reading it for pleasure.

He looked at the cover again.

*The Broken Child* by J. L. Sharp.

He'd never heard of the author before a couple weeks ago, though that wasn't unusual, considering he didn't pick up a whole lot of books, and when he did, they were usually of the true-crime variety. But he had to admit Sharp's books were well written, intriguing, and not too full of flowery descriptions. Colin hated flowery descriptions.

In fact, Sharp's writing was so well honed that Colin had torn through her first two books in a week before starting *The Broken Child* a couple of days ago. Each book centered on a female protagonist, Detective Jenna Black, who investigated cold-case files in Missouri, cases most often involving children.

The reason for this recent literary quest was that J. L. Sharp was the pen name for Rose Yates, a thirty-seven-year-old ex-Milwaukee resident and recent widow. Her husband, Riley McKay, had recently OD'd on alcohol and sleep medication. The coroner's report didn't rule it a suicide but rather an accidental overdose. Colin wasn't so sure; Riley McKay's toxicity levels suggested he must have had significant trouble sleeping to ingest as much as he had.

The Yates case was a small one for the Milwaukee PD and one that Colin, as a member of the Special Investigations Unit, would normally never have seen. But Riley McKay died right as the assigned detective, Bertram Cooper, was about to retire. Cooper worked the case for a week but his retirement day came before the case was closed out. Colin, with the least seniority in his new department, was told to deal with it. *Put the case to bed,* his sergeant had said.

Colin assumed it would be a matter of routine paperwork, but it hadn't taken long before he had questions.

Why was there no extensive interview with the wife?

Why wasn't the doctor who prescribed the meds consulted?

Why were there no notes about the family dynamic, any notes of mental illness or depression history, or observations from friends or family about the relationship between Riley McKay and Rose Yates?

The likely answer to all these questions was because Detective Cooper, on his way out, had seen the Riley McKay death as a simple overdose, perhaps suicide, and nothing more. Maybe in his anticipation of sailing the world or doing whatever he had planned, Cooper had been a little sloppy with the McKay case. Or, perhaps, he was just a mediocre detective.

Colin had planned to talk to Rose Yates, only to find she and her son moved to New Hampshire just a few weeks after her husband died. A little town called Bury.

Then, when Colin had discovered Rose Yates wrote novels about detectives, that piqued his interest, so he'd bought her first three books and read them. He hadn't known what, exactly, he was looking for in these books but figured he'd know when he found it. He'd read through the first two books with interest, but it was the third book that grabbed him. One chapter in particular.

Now, in his bed, he thumbed open Sharp's third book and opened to page 108.

Chapter 12. He'd just read it for the first time earlier in the day.

All in all, a seemingly inconsequential chapter, unless it ended up taking on greater importance later in the book. In the chapter, Detective Jenna Black recounted an old case of hers to a work colleague. A case she was proud to have finally solved after it had gone cold years ago.

The case involved the death of a forty-year-old man. Turned out, Black told her colleague, he'd been killed by his wife.

The colleague inquired about the method of killing.

And this was the part that sent a thousand-watt jolt right through Colin when he'd first read Jenna Black's answer in the pages of chapter 12.

*A mixture of alcohol and sleep medication.*

# EIGHT

**Bury, New Hampshire**
**August 12**

**I JOLT AWAKE, SWEAT** basting the back of my neck. It takes a few seconds to orient myself.

I'm in a bed. Nighttime. I'm at…*Dad's house.*

It was a dream.

It was *the* dream.

I throw the sheets off and jump out of bed, not wanting my mind to replay that last scene, over and over. My limbs are weak, but the horror soon releases a nice shot of adrenaline in my system. Nature's methamphetamine.

I can't. Not again.

Bedside table. I flip my phone over. It's 3:22 a.m.

Tonight's dream was worse than normal. So vivid, as if I were reliving it all over again. From experience, I know it'll take at least two hours to fall back asleep, at which point it will be close to my alarm time. And I'm not going to lie there and let the imagery eat me. Not tonight.

Into the bathroom, light on, the harshness of which hits me like high beams from an oncoming truck. I see myself in the mirror, wince against my reflection. I don't want to be real, to exist. Not right now.

God, how good it would feel to smash my fist into the glass, see my image burst in a thousand shards. I can taste it. The pain. The blood.

I resist. It's not easy.

I allow one long stare at myself, my gaze full of accusation, diminishment, maybe even hate.

I spring into action, needing to do something with this burning self-loathing, needing to sweat the toxins out of me. Hair pulled tight in a ponytail. Throw on running shorts, sports bra, Dri-FIT tank, HOKA sneakers. Down the stairs to the main level. Punch the code into the keypad, disarm the house. Out the front door. No phone, no headphones, no Fitbit, no water, no headlamp, no plan, nothing.

And I run.

Streetlights glow against my wishes. I want to run in complete darkness. Maybe then I could fall off a cliff or smash headfirst into a tree. Then they could tell my son my death was an accident.

I tire quickly, because jumping out of bed in the middle of the night and sprinting is a foolish idea.

But I keep going, wanting to puke. Wanting my heart to burst. Wanting to feel pain, longing for punishment.

Distance is immeasurable. Only not as far as I want, but farther than I should.

I reach the point where I capitulate to reason and turn around. That's the hardest part of all. Making that decision to come back. How much easier to let the night take me, swallow and digest me, and excrete me into the afterworld.

Still, I turn and begin walking toward home.

A few steps in, I see his face. That face. Helpless.

It's all I see.

"I'm sorry," I tell the night. Tell him.

I close my eyes. I see his.

There's an eternity in this moment.

*"I'm so sorry."*

# NINE

**August 30**

**I'M ON THE FOURTH** mile of my morning run. It feels good to run for exercise, not just to escape nightmares. I haven't had the dream for over two weeks, so maybe my return to Bury is starting to provide the therapy I need.

Last night's heavy downpour washed away the humidity, leaving the morning crisp, a rare hint of a fall that's still a few weeks away. Despite the cool, sweat flies off me with each step, and I'm already tapping into my second water pouch.

I know all these streets, all these houses. Little has changed since my teen years. Bury hasn't expanded or contracted; it remains trapped in a pocket of time and money, insulated from the outside world. No wonder my father loves it here. The town of Bury is nothing more than a strong front door. Steadfast and unyielding to time.

There is scarcely any lower or middle class here, and I'm reminded of that with every house I pass. Every perfect lawn, every iron gate.

All the brick is red, all the creeping vines green. Most of the residents white.

I make a right into Arlington Estates, a small neighborhood of colonials built sometime in the forties and fifties. I remember a few high school parties in this area held at Bob Sakin's house. He was a classic screwup of a kid, an only child of very rich and devoutly inattentive parents. They let him do whatever he wanted, and since he wasn't smart enough to do anything worthwhile, he spent his days in a haze of pot smoke and held huge parties on the weekends when his parents dashed off to their other house in the Hamptons.

Sometimes I wonder what happened to all these people from my past. But those times are few. I'm content keeping my past buried, which underscores the conflict with being back here. I'm sure many of the people from my past still live here, and I won't be able to avoid seeing them for long.

I round another street, intent on looping my way around this neighborhood on my way back home. Two houses up on the right, a man in a tank top is trimming back branches on a tree that towers over the sidewalk. His presence doesn't intrigue me so much because he's black, though I'd be lying if I said that didn't surprise me a little. I'm more intrigued because this man is intensely good looking, and as I approach, I realize the better term is *beautiful*.

I'm running on the sidewalk where he's working, compelling me to cross over to the street. As I close in, I cut through a strip of soaking-wet grass, and my right foot slips out from under me. It doesn't take more than a split second to realize I'm going to fall, with no ability to do anything about it other than accept my fate.

The man and I make brief eye contact as my banana-peel crash happens less than ten feet from where he's standing. I land hard on my butt, my earbuds popping out as I do, and the only thing saving me from a broken tailbone is the spongy grass. I twist on the ground in a little pain and a lot of embarrassment.

The man drops his shears and races toward me.

"Are you okay?"

My running shorts have soaked in water and my butt is now unpleasantly moist.

"I think so," I say. I struggle to rise and he reaches his hand out to help.

I buck against my Yates instincts to reject help for fear it projects weakness and take his hand. He lifts me with no effort, as if just pulling a weed from his lawn.

"I think the only thing bruised is my ego," I say.

He smiles and I'm blinded by a perfect set of teeth.

"I've done worse," he said. "I was on a first date and tried going through a revolving door that was locked in place. Walked right into the glass. Even got a bloody nose. There was no second date."

"That's definitely worse," I say. A part of me wants to know how long ago that date was. Another part of me is immensely distracted by the back of my soaking-wet shorts.

"You sure you're okay?"

"I'm fine. Thank you…" I let the last word dangle.

"Alec. Alec Wallin. This is my place here."

"Yup, I assumed that. You working in the yard and all."

"I could've been the hired help."

I'm not quite sure what to say to this. My father would instantly quip *Yard work is for Mexicans, not Blacks.*

I clear my throat. "I'm Rose. Yates."

His eyes widen just a hair. "Ah, *Rose Yates.*"

"What does that mean?"

"Only that I've heard of you. That you're back in town after having grown up here. And...oh, hell, I'm sorry. I heard about your husband. That's just awful."

"Thank you." I wonder how long the *I'm sorrys* will last. "I didn't realize I was part of the gossip mill already."

"Well, if you grew up here, you know how this place is. I've been here ten years. My name's been dragged around town its own fair share." His gaze does a quick sweep of the sky, as if he's scanning a force field trapping him here. "Actually, I think you know my ex-wife. You went to school with her. Tasha Collins."

*Bam.*

This is how Harry Potter felt hearing the name Voldemort spoken aloud.

Tasha Collins.

"Tasha?" I say. I can't even pretend to hide my distaste. "I don't even know—"

He holds a hand up. "I know. You don't have to say anything. Just don't hold it against me. I've learned my lesson."

Tasha Collins was the clichéd popular girl in high school, though everyone I knew hated her. Her popularity stemmed from her physical gorgeousness. She was hated because every other part of her was ugly. A massive flaunter of money in a place where everyone was swimming in it already. Dumb as dirt. And bitterly mean to anyone she spoke to, including her friends. Last I heard of her, she was going off to Tufts for college, though I can't imagine how she ever would have graduated.

"Tasha still lives here?"

"Oh yeah," Alec says. "Only reason I'm still here. I won't give up seeing my boy."

So Tasha Collins married an African American man. I have to admit, that's more progressive than I would have credited her with being.

"When I was twelve, she once called me Pancake Tits," I tell him. I can't believe I just said this, but the memory came back with such jarring force I couldn't help myself.

Alec looks properly taken aback for about two seconds before laughter takes over. From-the-gut laughter, and I can't help but join in.

"Yeah, that sounds like her," he says.

"Maybe she got better after high school?"

Alec wipes a film of sweat off his forehead and shakes his head. "Nope."

"But you still married her?"

He grimaces. Only word for it.

"Let's just say I didn't know Tasha well when she got pregnant. Not sure we would've ever stayed together if not for Micah—that's my boy. We made it last as long as we could. And I can't say I was the perfect husband either. Micah's better with his mom and me under different roofs, that's for sure." He shifts his footing and gives me a gaze I could get lost in.

"I can understand that."

Alec lets out another laugh, this one softer. "I'm normally not so open. Certainly not with someone I just met."

"How does it feel?" I ask.

He thinks about it for a moment, then smiles. "Good."

The ensuing silence lasts long enough to make me nervous. I brush a few stray strands of grass off the backs of my thighs and say, "I better finish my run."

"Okay, Rose. Nice to meet you. I'm sure I'll be seeing you around."

"Okay, then," I say, hearing a tiny bit of Wisconsin accent come out. I turn and carefully make my way across the grass and onto the street, where I start jogging again.

The only thing distracting me from the uncomfortable wet stain on my butt is wondering if Alec notices.

# TEN

**WHAT KIND OF WOMAN** is attracted to another man less than two months after her husband's death?

Maybe it's a defense mechanism, a way of dealing with grief. Or perhaps it was such a transient, innocent attraction that it doesn't even warrant analysis. After all, I'm just human, and a still-youngish, heterosexual female version at that. I'd challenge any others in my category to stand face-to-face with Alec Wallin without the smallest of stirrings.

But I know the true answer is altogether more fierce.

I didn't love my husband.

In the beginning, there was the facsimile of love best described as passionate infatuation. I wanted to be around Riley every hour. Share experiences together. Spend days naked in bed. Travel wherever our whims took us. I suspect the line between love and a desperate fear of loneliness is drawn in wet ink and easily smudged.

When I left Bury for college, damage seeped into every decision I made. At Northwestern, I studied both journalism and criminal justice, perhaps knowing on some level that writing about crime would someday be necessary for my conscience.

I dated boys who were the opposite of my father. I preferred the wild, the carefree, the spontaneous. I wanted smiles, not squints.

Riley was so different from my father that it was easy to think I was in love.

In those days, Riley had an adventurous spirit, a sharp intellectual curiosity, and an insatiable need to achieve. We met fourteen years ago. I was just twenty-three, two years younger than him. I was a few years out of school and was doing investigative journalism for the *Chicago Tribune,* mostly covering local crime. Riley was a friend of a friend, and I was immediately drawn to him the moment a group of us went out for drinks. His scraggly beard and mussed hair suggested a casual playfulness, yet there was also an intensity about him that drew me in. It was more than confidence. He had the air of a man who knew greatness would come to him after a mandatory waiting period. There was no arrogance, just a certainty.

My courtship with Riley was a frenzied whirl of sex and adventure, ingredients more addictive than heroin, at least until the high wears off.

Weekends away at whatever place we could afford, just for a different setting. Cheap hotels in the winter. Camping in the summer. Twice we even spent the night in our car, just because.

We moved in together after six months. He proposed after seven. I'd never met his family. He'd never met mine. I was swept away by a current I thought was called fate, but it turned out to be a riptide.

I should have known.

You know who did?

My father.

One month into our engagement, my father flew out to visit me in Chicago. He stayed at the Four Seasons, preferring that to the spare room in our apartment. Couldn't blame him.

One dinner. That's all it took.

One dinner at an expensive Italian restaurant on the Mile. I can even isolate the chunk of conversation where my father determined Riley wasn't worthy of me. It went something like:

Dad: So, Rose tells me you're an entrepreneur?

Riley: Yes, that's right.

Dad: And what the fuck does that mean?

Riley (smiles): I'm cofounding a company that will bring clean-energy products to impoverished areas of Africa and Asia.

Dad: Clean-energy products in Africa? Jesus, son, those poor countries don't even have power. They've got nothing, which means no pollution. You want the freshest breath of air you've ever tasted? Go stand in the middle of Burkina Faso and inhale. Probably give you an orgasm. They don't need clean energy, Riley. They need *energy*.

Me: *Dad*.

Riley: That's actually not true, and it's more complica—

Dad: What's your funding? How many months of burn do you have left? What's your future income stream based on? Most importantly, what's your exit strategy?

Riley tried. He answered all those questions, and looking back now, I can see how they didn't explain what, in fact, his full plan was. But Riley cared about making the world better for people other than himself, something my father couldn't comprehend. So I was more than pissed off when my father took me aside the next day and said, "Look, sweetheart, there's no easy way to say this, but your guy is a fuck-all. I've seen the type before. He's not as smart as he thinks he is, which is compounded by the fact that I think he's probably lazy. I'm guessing you've told him how much money I have?"

Then came the argument, the one that began the moment I left home for school. Logan Yates's money traveled only within a certain radius and for a designated time period. He was quite willing to pay for tuition and a comfortable lifestyle when my sister and I went away for college, but we were expected to return to Bury after school. Work for him, or at least be close to him. My father's idea of family was based on proximity, never love.

Cora returned to Bury. I didn't, knowing that I'd rather be destitute than return to that place.

My funding was cut. Black vs. white. Right vs. wrong. Yates vs. the world. My father exists in absolutes.

"Dad," I replied to him, "it doesn't matter how much money you have. I don't see any of it. And that's not important anyway."

"No?" I remember the smug, knowing look on his face. "You're still in my will, and you know you'll always have a place back in Bury if you want to be...more comfortable. I'm guessing your man knows that. Maybe he's just biding time, hoping I'll kick it in the near future."

"You're so frustra—"

"Prenup. Just have him sign a prenup. If you get any money from me, he's not entitled to it in the event...you know...he does what a typical fuck-all does. Which is fuck it all up."

I stormed away.

My father went back to Bury.

Riley and I married, and we never had a prenup. My father and my sister came to the wedding, which was a very inexpensive affair at a

DoubleTree hotel in the Chicago suburbs. My sister drank and looked bored the whole time, and my father wore a just-you-wait look on his face for most of the night. During the father-daughter dance, he predicted I'd come home to Bury, eventually. He was as sure of this as Riley was about his eventual greatness. I told him he couldn't be more wrong.

That was thirteen years ago.

Turns out he was right.

# ELEVEN

**Milwaukee, Wisconsin**
**September 8**

**TWO DAYS AGO, DETECTIVE** Colin Pearson had walked out of his sergeant's office, trying to suppress a smile. Smiling might jinx things.

He'd laid out his case against Rose Yates to Sergeant Al Brennan, Colin's direct supervisor in the Special Investigations Unit. Brennan was a fiftyish fireplug of a man who wore a scowl as his default expression. Colin hadn't been too hopeful; asking for travel funds from a tight budget to cross state lines and interview a person of interest was never an easy sell.

Colin had learned over the years to keep requests like this straightforward and to the point. No flowery language.

He'd outlined to the sergeant how thirty-nine-year-old Riley McKay died due to an overdose of diazepam, zolpidem, and alcohol. McKay commonly took both meds to help him sleep, but they were not prescribed to be taken in combination, certainly not with alcohol, and definitely not at the high levels of his final ingestion.

There were no usual hallmarks of a suicide, Colin had explained. No note, although the majority of suicide victims didn't leave notes anyway. No phone call to anyone, no red-flag social-media posts. McKay's only external communication that night was with a buddy, confirming their weekly Frisbee golf game.

Detective Cooper had taken the case shortly before his retirement and had only interviewed Rose Yates once for about fifteen minutes. Colin had told the sergeant that, in his opinion, Detective Cooper might have rushed through some of the standard procedure on his way out the door. He hadn't asked Ms. Yates about her relationship with her husband or even if she thought her husband committed suicide. There were a lot of holes left to plug, including the question of why Ms. Yates had taken her son and quickly moved to New Hampshire after her husband's death. Colin had conceded the move was not necessarily unusual for a grieving widow, but it was worth a few follow-up questions.

Capping it all off, Colin had told his sergeant about Ms. Yates's alter ego, J. L. Sharp, a mystery writer. Not that being a mystery writer carried with it inherent suspicion or even the writer's intricate knowledge of police procedure, case management, and suspect-interrogation techniques. What *was* suspicious was the scene in Yates's most recent book in which a woman killed her forty-year-old husband by grinding up eight tablets of his prescription sleep medication and stirring the powder into his whiskey nightcap.

"That's a reach," the sergeant had said. "I'm not saying it's not interesting, but you don't really think she'd commit murder in the same manner as a character in her book, do you? That's pretty blatant."

"Maybe the wife had written the scene based on watching her husband regularly mix meds and alcohol," Colin countered. "And on that night, she acted impulsively. Maybe didn't think about the connection to her book."

"Sounds like she's smarter than that. Statistically speaking, it's probably equally likely the husband offed himself in that manner to frame her."

Colin nodded. "Could be. But we don't have him around to ask. Just the wife."

"And her motive? Money?"

"Don't think so," Colin had said. "They didn't have much. Had a small life-insurance policy on him, but they'd stopped paying the premium a year ago."

"Who paid the bills? Did the wife know the policy lapsed?"

"That's one of the questions I want to ask her."

"Other assets?"

Colin shrugged. "They have, or Ms. Yates now has, about twenty grand in credit-card debt and less than three thousand in a checking account. Couple older-model cars. A small IRA, about seven thousand."

"So he wasn't worth more dead than alive."

"No. And the wife comes from money. Her father runs an investment firm in Boston. Maybe they're estranged, because Ms. Yates appears to be just getting by."

Sergeant Brennan had taken everything in and leaned back in his chair. "Maybe it was just an accident."

"It's a possibility," Colin had conceded. "But I don't think we're close enough to determining that right now."

The sergeant hadn't outright agreed, but he hadn't dismissed Colin's request either. He'd said he'd take it to the captain for review, which was the best thing Colin could have hoped for.

Now, two days later, Colin got his answer in an email from Brennan with the subject line *McKay Case*.

> Approved. Two nights max. Pick the cheapest hotel you can find. Ditto airfare.

Colin gave the top of his desk a satisfying pound with his fist. It was the first time he'd be traveling out of state to interview a person of interest, and he was going to make the most of those two days.

He tried to do what detectives were taught. Follow the facts. Don't make assumptions. Be objective.

But there was that little voice, the one all people have, and with detectives, that voice is even stronger. Louder. And Colin's voice hadn't quieted since he read J. L. Sharp's last novel.

*She did it*, the voice said, over and over again.

*The wife did it.*

# TWELVE

**Bury, New Hampshire**

**FIRST DAY OF SCHOOL** and I think I'm more nervous than Max.

We sit in silence as I drive my father's black Suburban, the tank of a car he designated for my use. It's been a month back in Bury, and I'm already regressing to my childhood. Living in my father's house, grocery shopping with his credit card, driving the car he provided for me.

I glance over as Max gazes out the window, and I see his ghostly image reflecting back, as if he's staring at me and the rest of the world at the same time.

"What are you thinking about?" I ask.

He doesn't say anything, and it looks like he's slipped into one of his fugues. Or maybe he's just nervous about today. That's to be expected. New school, and he doesn't know anyone except his cousin, with whom he shares nothing in common. Max always struggled to make friends among kids he knew for years, and I can only imagine how isolated he'll feel at Middleton Prep.

But when he answers, he doesn't voice any of these things.

"Before Dad, had you ever seen a dead person?"

My stomach knots as I grip the steering wheel until my knuckles strain. "Why are you asking me this?"

"Because of what Grandpa said. That I was the youngest to see a dead person. So I wondered if you ever had."

I feel him looking at me. I don't look back. If I do, he'll know I'm lying.

"No," I say. "I never had before."

"What about your mom?"

"I was too young to remember, but I don't think so."

Max offers a soft *mmm* and looks out his window again. "I wonder how many more I'll see in my life."

"Can we not talk about this?" I say.

"Okay."

How casual my son is about death. I sometimes wonder if the detachment with his own experiences is part of his grieving process or if it's just that. Detachment. I think of what he told Willow when she asked what it was like to see his dead father.

*He didn't look angry anymore.*

And that's true. Riley didn't look angry in death. But there're other faces of death that aren't nearly so calm. Twisted faces of rage, pain, and mind-shattering fear.

I pray my son never has to see any of those.

---

Four blocks later, we arrive.

Middleton Prep is an exclusive private school for sixth through twelfth grades, and my father insisted on Max going there as long as we live back home. I wanted to take some kind of noble stand and insist public school was just fine, but I didn't consider this for long. I won't sacrifice a better education for my son out of principle. Max struggles with school enough as it is, and I can't argue against sending him somewhere the teachers are paid fairly and the average class size is fifteen.

We bypass the drop-off lane and park; I want to escort Max in on his first day of sixth grade. I start to open my door when he says, "You don't need to come in."

"You sure? You don't want me to come inside?"

"No, I'm okay."

I want to ask him why, and I don't want to ask him why. I don't want to make him second-guess himself, make him crack this delicate shell of courage that he's apparently been able to build.

He sees my struggle and pushes his glasses up the bridge of his nose.

"Gotta grow up some time," he says.

This simple statement breaks my heart. I reach out, touch the side of his face, and force back the tears. A few still escape, but I don't break down.

"You're a strong kid, you know that?" I say.

"I suppose."

I lean in and kiss him on the head, then Max reaches down, picks up his backpack and lunch, and gets out of the car. I decide to get out anyway, if only to watch him walk inside, because driving immediately away feels too much like abandonment.

I call out after he crosses the drop-off lane and reaches the sidewalk. He turns and offers a wave, and for a moment, I think I see a trace of a smile, though perhaps the glare of the early sun is tricking me into thinking so.

"Morning, Rose."

The vaguely familiar voice comes from behind me, and I turn and see Alec. He's walking my way, packaged neatly in a crisp, blue button-down shirt and thin olive slacks. A little boy holds his hand.

"Hi, Alec."

"That your son heading in over there?"

"Yes," I say. "Max. Just starting sixth grade."

"Well, this is Micah," he says, then looks down at his son. "Looks like you'll have another friend, buddy. Max just moved here from…" Alec looks over to me.

"Wisconsin," I say.

"Wisconsin. That's right." Alec smiles, and everything around me warms a degree or two. "Micah's starting sixth grade, too. It'll be nice for him to meet Max. Micah, this is Rose."

Micah looks a lot like Alec, just with lighter skin and thoughtfully chaotic hair. Looking at this boy, I can already imagine what a striking man he will someday become. He reaches out his right hand and offers it to me.

"How do you do?" he asks.

In a thousand years, Max would never offer his hand and a *how do you do* to a stranger. I take Micah's small hand and give it a shake. His grip is stronger than I expected.

"Well, I'm just fine, Micah. Nice to meet you."

The pleasantness of this little exchange is ended by another voice, this one also distantly familiar, but not in a comforting way.

"*There* you are."

I turn and see a bullet of a woman walking with a brisk huff directly toward us. Her gaze is drilled into Alec.

Tasha Collins.

Like my sister, she hasn't aged as much as she's been maintained, like a car whose owner keeps applying wax in hopes of hiding the wear from all those miles. Her long, lush hair looks unnaturally black, as if it were dipped in a giant inkwell, and her face has a plastic sheen to it, no doubt the subject of a lengthy, daily makeup routine. But otherwise Tasha looks just like she did in high school. Tall, pale, and slim, a beautiful, brittle mannequin, ever unsmiling, as if doing so would wrinkle some of the smooth.

"You're late," she says, coming up a few feet from us and stopping with still no acknowledgment of Micah or me.

Alec sighs lightly, perhaps a micromeditation necessary before any conversation with his ex.

"Good morning to you as well," he says. His voice takes on an edge, the kind that conveys his desire to scream at Tasha were he not around others. I picture him angry, realizing it's not hard to do. Nostrils flared, forearms tensed, veins in his temples pounding. I'll bet Alec and Tasha have had some epic arguments.

"You know I wanted to talk to his teacher before class started."

"Hi, Mama," Micah says.

Tasha finally notices him, bending down and giving him a swift, almost aggressive kiss on the forehead. "Hi, sweetheart. Ready for your first day?"

"Uh-huh."

Tasha straightens and faces me. Blinks a couple of times with owl-like wonder. "I know you," she says. "How do I know you?"

"Hi, Tasha," I say. "Rose Yates." I don't extend my hand. I don't have Micah's manners, at least not in this moment.

The wonder breaks and a wave of excitement washes over her face, as if she's been told a terrible secret about one of her enemies. "*Rose Yates.* I heard you were back in town. Wow, it's been so long."

She moves in for a hug. For a half second, I consider stepping back but then realize I have no real reason to hate this person now. Sure, she called me Pancake Tits back in high school, but I don't even know the Tasha Collins of today. People change.

We hug. It's like embracing a lamppost, minus the warmth.

"I heard about your husband. I'm so, so sorry."

I've heard this enough that I can rate someone's empathy on a scale from one to ten. Alec was about an eight when he told me this. Tasha clocks in somewhere around a two. Maybe one and a half.

"Thank you," I say.

"I mean, I can't even imagine," she adds. Then Tasha throws a quick glance at Alec and adds, "Well, I can't say there weren't times I didn't fantasize about it."

She seriously says this. Right in front of her son.

Tasha follows up with "You have a child here?"

"My son, Max. Sixth grade." I nod over to the school. "He just walked in. Said he wanted to do it on his own."

Tasha puts a hand on her chest. "Bless his heart, sweet thing." Then the hand moves to the top of Micah's head, and he looks annoyed by it. "We wanted to go in with him on the first day. Meet the teacher, establish a connection, you know, make it a little more...special and supportive. But how brave for your son just to trot right in there all alone."

I glance at Alec and his eyes contain half apology, half amusement, as if he's given up trying to figure out why Tasha is so evil and now just accepts the dark humor of it all. I feel sorry for him. He still has to share raising a child with this woman, which must be like constantly scooping water out of a sinking life raft.

Even more, my heart goes out to Micah.

"He's brave all right," I say.

"Tasha, weren't we in a rush?" Alec says.

"Yes, yes. Only because you were late." Back to me. "Well, Rose, great to see you. We'll have to get together for some wine. I can introduce you to some other parents. I'm sure...social activity is important at a time like this for you." Tasha doesn't bother waiting for a response. She simply grabs Micah's hand and leads him away.

"I guess we're going in now," Alec says, leaving me with a smile that nearly lifts the haze of unpleasantness left in Tasha's wake. "See you around, Rose."

"See you," I say, watching him leave. My gaze moves from him to Tasha, from Tasha to the front door of the school, and finally to a lone window, behind which I imagine Max sitting all by himself in a classroom as other children cluster together in their pre-established friendship groups.

Goddamn me.

I should have walked in with him.

Goddamn *you*, Riley.

Why did you have to be the person you were?

# THIRTEEN

**I IMMEDIATELY KNEW MY** husband was dead.

When I touched his bare shoulder, no energy radiated from him. Not warmth, but *energy*. A sense of life we absorb around us from others but never realize its presence until it's gone.

The moment my fingertips stroked Riley's shoulder, I knew I was alone in that room.

I floated above myself, above our bed, detached completely but yet so focused, reaching over to the bedside table and grabbing Riley's phone to dial three numbers.

*911, what's your emergency?*

*Yes, hello, thank you. I think something's wrong with my husband.*

I said that. I said *thank you*. Who says *thank you* to a 911 operator at the *beginning* of a call?

That phone call started my path to where I am now.

Back here, to this house.

My fingers hover over the keyboard of my laptop, frozen. My brain doesn't know what to tell them to type, so they wait there patiently for a command.

It's been two hours since I dropped off Max at school, and I'm sitting in the covered back porch, the midmorning sunlight strong and heavy, weighing on me like a blanket. Through the open windows, I can smell the musk of the lawn, freshly cut by the landscapers, likely one of the last mows of the season. A cup of black coffee cools in a mug on the side table next to me.

My job at the moment is to inherit another world, the world of Jenna Black, Missouri detective, as imagined by J. L. Sharp. J. L. Sharp is my pen name, one chosen for the non-gender-specific initials and vaguely sinister last name.

I have three books published in the Jenna Black mystery series, all with the same boutique publisher. My fourth comes out in January, and I was about ten thousand words into my fifth when Riley died.

I need to dive into Jenna's head, see how she's planning to piece together the clues in her latest cold-case investigation, this one centering on a sixteen-year-old girl found raped and dead in a Topeka barn in the midnineties. I want to absorb Jenna's strength, be guided by her moral compass, but yet again here I sit, fingers poised, a blank canvas with no painter in sight.

Other thoughts pinball inside my head:

*I feel guilty by writing. I should be outwardly mourning. I never wear black.*

*I'm worried about Max. Maybe I made things worse by moving us here.*

*I need to find a job, a real job, just so I don't have to totally rely on Dad. I don't want to be kept by him.*

*I'm afraid of being lonely but don't want to admit that to anyone.*

*And…*

I place the laptop on the side table, stand, and walk into the kitchen.

Slowly. Up the hardwood stairs, sixteen steps I've climbed thousands of times.

Second floor. The hallway stretches before me, shorter than I remember as a child but long enough to still swallow all my courage in the middle of the night.

It was here.

This hallway.

The hallway, and then the stairs.

It ended on the stairs.

I close my eyes, as if inviting the memories back, and they come.

That night.

His face.

His fear.

This is why I'm here, isn't it? To exorcise my demons? To face my past head-on? That was the plan, but this house has so far won the battle; it continues to scare the shit out of me.

My eyes open at the distant sound of my phone ringing. It's a relief, as if the universe knew I needed to be pulled away from my thoughts.

I race down the stairs and into the kitchen where my phone is charging. The caller ID display ices my stomach.

*MIDDLETON PREP*

"Hello?" I say.

"Hello, I'm calling for Rose Yates." The tone of the woman's voice doesn't do anything to assure me.

"This is she."

"Hi, Rose. This is Sandra Halliday, assistant vice principal at Middleton."

"Is everything okay? Is Max okay?"

"He's fine. But I'm calling to tell you there's been an incident, and we need you to come down and pick him up."

My chest tightens at the word *incident*.

"What kind of incident?"

"We'll explain more face-to-face, because that's always easier. But he was involved in an altercation with another student."

"Alter—"

"I know this is stressful, Rose. But I assure you he's fine, as is the girl."

*Girl*. Oh god, what the hell happened?

"We just need you to come down," she continues. "Max will be in the front office with me."

"Yes, of course. I'll be right over."

I hang up, scramble for my purse, and rush to the garage. I back out, race through the neighborhood, then force myself to slow down as I reach the main boulevard leading to Middleton.

Red light. I bring the car to a stop and use the precious few seconds to try to center myself. Deep breath. In, then out.

It doesn't work. My pulse doesn't slow a beat.

Four words keep churning in my head. Over and over. Usually I can summon a mantra, a positive affirmation, something simple and powerful I can repeat, looping in my mind, assuring me.

But these words don't provide comfort, and though I want to think of different ones, these won't go away.

*It's all my fault.*

# FOURTEEN

**MIDDLETON PREP LOOKS A** lot more like a prison than it did this morning. The tint on the exterior windows is too dark to see through them. I suppose that's a safety feature, but I imagine each of those rooms as a solitary confinement cell.

I sign in at the front office, using the Student Absence sheet. I'm stopped when I get to the box asking for the reason I'm picking up my student. My gaze scans previous entries, which alternate between "sick" and "appointment."

I finally write "unknown." It's the truth.

I'm ushered into the administration area by a mousy woman who tries so hard to avoid eye contact it's as if she walking me down death row. We get to an office with a closed door and a nameplate reading "Ms. Halliday."

Mousy knocks, and I hear "Yes?" from inside. The woman ushers me inside Ms. Halliday's office before scurrying away. Max is sitting in a chair, hunched over, and when he turns his head, I see his tear-glazed eyes.

"Oh, sweetie," I say, rushing to him. He stands and hugs me, squeezing harder than normal.

"I didn't start it, I swear," he says.

"What happened?" I ask.

Before he gets a chance to answer, the assistant principal speaks. "Hello, Ms. Yates. I'm Ms. Halliday."

I'm immediately put off by the whole last-name convention, as if this were a congressional inquest. I straighten, keeping one hand on Max's back. Ms. Halliday is probably in her midforties but has put effort into looking older. A conservative white blouse, gray slacks, black hair in a tight bun, and glasses that look too large for her narrow face. She reaches out a hand and I shake it. Her fingers are frigid.

"I'm sorry we haven't had the opportunity to meet yet, so let me first say welcome to Middleton. We're excited to have Max here this year. Please, take a seat."

I don't, and Max remains standing at my side. "Can you just tell me what happened?" It dawns on me Max is the only child here. Where's the other kid?

Ms. Halliday scrunches her face in a look of highly practiced mock concern and says, "I'm afraid Max engaged in behavior with another student that would fall within Middleton's definition of bullying."

"Bullying? That's impossible." Max is so meek and shy that even talking to other kids has always been a struggle for him.

"I'm afraid not. We have a zero-tolerance policy when it comes to bullying, in fact, much stricter than what you'd find in the public-school system. And zero tolerance means the student is required to go home for the rest of the day, at a minimum."

My voice is louder than I want it to be, but I can't hold back my frustration. "What *happened?*"

Max bursts out. "She started it. She said stuff about Dad."

"Please, Max," Ms. Halliday says. "That's enough."

Anytime another adult talks to my son with a sharp tone, my neck muscles tighten.

"It's okay," I tell him, trying to be as calm as possible.

"We only discipline behavior we witness or are certain of," Halliday continues. "His teacher, Ms. Cathman, saw Max threatening another student with a sharpened pencil. She heard him telling the student that he would hurt her."

"*What?*"

"No!" Max shouts.

"Now, Max, you know it's true," she tells him, and the hairs on my neck stand just hearing her say his name. Then to me: "There was no physical harm done, and I'm not ruling out the possibility Max had been provoked. But we do know what we witnessed, and Max needs to go home for the rest of the day."

I turn back to him. "Is this true?" I don't want to confront him because there is so much pain in his face. I want to hold him, assure him. But I need to know. "Max," I say, "did you do this?"

He drops his gaze to the floor. "I wanted her to stop teasing me." His voice is barely a whisper. "She said…she said the only reason parents kill themselves is to get away from their kids."

"Good god," I say, turning back to Halliday. "And how is that behavior excusable? Do you know what he's been through? Why is *he* the one being punished here? What a horrible and cruel thing for any child to say to another."

Max tugs on my arm, wanting me to lower to his face. I do and he cups a hand around my ear and whispers so faintly I struggle to process the words.

"I didn't hurt her," he says. "But I wanted to."

I pull my face back and look at his, but he shifts his gaze to the floor.

Halliday didn't hear him, thank god. "I understand your concern, Ms. Yates. And I do appreciate the…circumstances of your recent move here to Bury. It must be exceptionally difficult. We have spoken with the other student, but we can't confirm she said those things."

I try to shake off what Max has just whispered to me and focus back on Halliday. "What do you mean 'confirm'? Of course she's not going to admit to it. Why would she? They're *sixth graders*."

She takes a step forward and places a hand on my shoulder. It's forced, like a tip out of a sensitivity-training seminar she was loath to take. "New schools are tough, I get that. I'm sure Max will fit in just fine. We're happy to have him back tomorrow. Clean slate."

This woman, she's just doing her job. And of course I'd want any kid who threatened my son disciplined as well. But I struggle to keep this rational mindset. What I actually feel is fury. Fury at every little circumstance that led to this moment, at every decision made by myself and others that ended with Max hauled into this room.

My *irrational* mindset tell me how delicious it would be to grab Halliday's hand and pull her wrist back until it broke.

But I do nothing.

I say nothing.

She drops her hand from my shoulder and I take a deep breath, escaping inside myself for the few seconds it takes to regain my mental footing.

"Fine," I concede. "We'll try again tomorrow. Come on, Max."

Halliday presses her lips together in a satisfied smile. I don't say anything else as I lead Max by the hand.

As we leave, I can't wash away the seething rage. Max's comment comes back to my mind, but this time, it's as relatable as it is concerning.

*I wanted to hurt her.*

# FIFTEEN

**September 29**

**I HAVE ONE HOUR.** One free hour of time to get writing done, and I've made the unspeakable mistake of leaving my phone on. A writer's worst enemy is distraction, and nothing serves that role better than the gleaming screen of my iPhone.

It buzzes. A text.

I look down. It's from Cora. Just three words.

What the fuck?

I have no idea what she means or even if I'm the one she intended to text. I reply simply:

?

Seconds later, she texts again.

The book. Your book. U at home?

I tell her I am. She says she's coming over. That we need to talk.

A slow panic begins to rise in me and I push it down.

It's fine. It'll be fine.

Laptop screen closed. I can forget about my free hour. I make another coffee and contemplate adding Kahlúa to it. I don't. Instead, I walk up to my bedroom and to the box I received a few days ago. Fifteen copies of my latest novel, *The Child of the Steps*. The book doesn't release until January, and these are just advance-reader copies intended for reviewers and the media, as well as a few copies the publisher always sends for my own use.

Cora stopped by a few days ago, saw the box, and grabbed a copy for herself. If she's read any of my other books, it would be news to me. But this book, of all of them, was the one she expressed mild curiosity over. I think it was because they were sitting there in front of her, ripe for the taking.

Or maybe because the cover shows a staircase.

Based on her text, I'm guessing she read the book.

Ten minutes later, I hear the front door open, then slam shut. I can feel my sister's presence, like a tumor my doctor told me was growing inside my guts.

"*Rose?*"

"Coming," I say.

I walk downstairs, taking slower steps than usual.

She's in the foyer, perfectly put together for whatever she does during the day. She has the copy of my book in her right hand, clutching it like a fire-and-brimstone preacher would a Bible. Weapon-like.

I don't even make it to the bottom step before she unleashes.

"What the *fuck*, Rose?"

"Yeah," I say. "That's what you texted me. I think you need to be more specific."

"I mean, what...the...*fuck*...with this book?"

"It's a novel, Cora. 'Novel' means 'fiction.'" She's still staring at me with saucer-sized eyes. "Fiction means it's *not real.*"

"I know what fiction is," she says. "This isn't fiction. This is our lives."

"No, it isn't," I say. "Not even close."

"But one element is. The main part of the story." She raps on the cover of the book, as if I don't see it in her hand. "The main fucking event is very real. It happened here. In *this* house." She glances over my shoulder, and I know what she's looking at. The stairs. The solid wooden stairs, hard and unforgiving.

I say nothing, and this enrages her.

She slams the book to the floor, as if she could shatter it. It *thunks* down unharmed, all the words in the same order as they were before.

"You can't publish this," she says. Her tone shifts from outright anger to fear, betrayed by the crack in her voice. "You have to stop this. Give the publisher something else."

I see Cora as I did twenty-two years ago, and it hits me yet again how much of my life has been dictated by what happened in this house back then.

I fled the state for college, compelled to study journalism and criminal justice. Despite being cut off from my father's money, I vowed never to return to my hometown and took a job with the *Chicago Tribune*. I worked as an investigative journalist, which, as I'm sure any psychologist would note, was no coincidence.

When I started writing books, I felt my novels creeping closer and closer to reality. In fact, I think the whole reason my character Detective Jenna Black exists has been to get to the point where she is now.

In *The Child of the Steps*, I face my past head-on, even if it's disguised as fiction. Yes, it scares the hell out of me to see those words on the printed page. But I also needed to do it. It's as if writing those scenes made up for the years of the therapy I never had.

"I can't stop it, Cora. It's just a book. It's coming out, and it'll sell maybe a few thousand copies. Nobody knows anything; there's nothing incriminating in there. It's just a story, that's all."

She's shifting back to anger. "Has Dad read it?"

"Dad? Are you kidding?"

"When he reads this, he's going to *freak* the fuck out."

"So you're going to get Dad to read my book?" I say. "Good luck. And even if he does, he won't care."

She's starting to shake, just a tremor, which moves from her shoulders down to her hands.

"He *will* care," she says. "Then you'll be back out on the street, no more support. Not even a husband to help pay your bills."

Jesus, she's cold. "Well, in that case, I'll need to sell a ton of books," I say.

Her breathing is shallow but fierce, as if she's on the verge of a panic attack. She's still in there somewhere, I think. That Cora I grew up with. My older sister, who used to laugh with me. Play games with me. That Cora still exists, and part of me wants to find her, while another part wants to just mourn her passing and move on.

"You're putting this family in harm's way," she says. "What you've done…it's completely reckless."

Her comment is saturated in irony. "*I'm* reckless? Are you even listening to yourself? Damn it, Cora." My voice is just shy of yelling. "Don't you understand? I *needed* to write it."

"And why now?" she asks. "After all this time, why *now?*"

My answer is immediate. "I never used to dream about it. I think about what happened all the time, but never in my sleep. Then the nightmares started a couple years ago, and I can't stop them. A replay of that night, every single detail, like a movie on a loop in my head. I wake up shaking, then can't fall back asleep. It's going to drive me crazy. I can't go to a shrink. I can't confide in anyone. I needed some kind of…release. So I wrote about it."

Cora considers all of what I've told her, puts a hand on her hip, and says, "Boo-fucking-hoo."

"God, you're a bitch."

"So did your scary little dream go away? After putting the family in danger, are you at least getting your beauty sleep?"

"No," I say. "It didn't stop. So I came home. I realized I need to deal with our past. I don't know how, but I have to reconcile what happened. The more I try to hide it away, the more it grows in me."

"God, you're so dramatic."

"How are you so emotionless about all this?"

"For all you know, it haunts me, too," Cora says. "But I'm smart enough not to publish an account of it in a book."

"Yes, I *wrote* about it. But I'm not crazy. I was careful. Read it again. There's nothing in there that anyone else knows about." I try to calm myself the best I can, steady my breathing. "I mean, you're telling me that after all this time, you haven't talked about it at all to anyone? Not even Peter?"

I can see in her eyes that the Cora I hoped to find is nowhere to be found. Probably doesn't even exist. "No, *Rose*. I haven't told anyone. You know why? Because that was our *fucking agreement*. You, me, Dad. We *all* agreed to it, right here." She looks around. "Exactly where we're standing. That night, we swore to each other we'd never say a word."

"That was a long time ago," I say. I'm sure I knew all along, even subconsciously, that writing about it was a risk, and now I try to convince myself everything will be fine. It's easy for Cora to spot the similarities between the chapter in my novel and the real-life event on which it was based. She was there after all. But how would anyone outside her and my father be able to piece anything together? *There's no way.*

Still…

Maybe the past should have remained there.

Cora looks to be deciding whether to keep arguing or take a swing at me. "You will not ruin my life."

"Maybe you should have thought of that before you did what you did," I reply.

"You're a mess, Rose. And I don't want to be a part of it."

"You need to—"

"Don't tell me to calm down," she says. "Don't ever tell me to calm down, I swear to god."

"I wasn't going to," I say. But Cora doesn't even allow me the chance to finish my first thought, which was to tell her to trust everything will be okay. She apparently has decided she's done with this conversation, because she kicks at the book, sending it sliding along the hardwood floor.

Then, without another word, she turns and leaves, slamming the mighty Logan Yates front door behind her. In her absence, the foyer takes on a degree of warmth.

My heart is racing; anger and fear course through my veins. My body yearns to run, and as I start calculating if I have enough time for a few miles before I pick up Max from school, it hits me.

Running.

I'm always running.

Each time I have the dream, I run. After arguments with Riley, I'd run. After taking the wrath of Cora, I want to run.

Running away. That's what I've always done, isn't it? And that's what I promised myself to stop. After Riley died and my father asked me to come back to Bury, I told myself it was time to face my past. Go back to the house. Be with it.

And still I haven't.

Here I was, thinking that moving back would stop the nightmares. But just being in this house isn't enough.

I have to *be* in this house.

So I turn, absorb the silence of the foyer, and head to the stairs.

# SIXTEEN

**I DON'T KNOW HOW** to do this or what it is I'm even doing. But I have an idea.

I step out of my shoes, peel off my socks, and feel the cool kiss of the wooden floors on my soles. It's only a few steps to reach the base of the stairs, but I take my time. I'm not scared as much as I am thoughtful. I'm not going to race through this.

When I reach the base of the stairs, I step onto a spot about three feet from the bottom of the first riser. This is the first time I've stood here in over two decades. Ever since that night, I've always approached the stairs at an angle, just to avoid standing exactly where I am.

It doesn't feel any different.

I sit, cross my legs, place my hands on top of my knees.

Close my eyes.

*No, keep them open. No more looking away.*

The color of the hardwood stairs is a golden red, the last seconds of a sunset. Glossy finish, always gleaming. I can even see where two of the steps were restained, the color very close but not exactly the same as the adjacent ones.

As I stare, the silence shifts into a hum, a rhythm of energy both soothing and overwhelming. It's as if I'm floating through space, enveloped in the vibration of all the universe.

I surrender to this hum, letting it take over my body, letting it pulse from the crown of my head to the chilled tips of my toes. Eyes open, ears attuned, and the surface of my skin poised to feel even the breath of a spider, I have become a receptor for whatever signal wants to transmit through me.

This is when I realize the hum is not a singular, steady sound. It's the collective sound of all the voices of my past. All the words of everyone in my life up to now, stitched together in a mosaic of noise. And these words, some of them are loving and soft, but many are angry. Desperate. Every decision I've made as an adult has been born of some kind of desperation, and I hear that now. My decision to leave Bury. My path to writing crime fiction. My relationship with Riley. I was chasing off a desperation each and every time. That desperation would scurry away just out of reach but, like a pack of wolves, always returned, and each time got a little closer.

I don't blink, and the steps start to melt in front of me. Dripping, oozing. They run together until they're no longer recognizable.

Deep in the recess of my mind, there's a realization that none of this is real, but I let that knowledge stay tucked away. In this moment, I'm where I need to be.

I'm transcending something.

I remain motionless, watching the melting continue.

I don't know how long I sit here, but it seems forever. With each passing minute, the hum deepens. Grows louder. Tells me it needs to be fed.

Finally, I talk. Offering the stairs what I think they need. Just two words.

"I'm sorry," I whisper, and my voice is like cannon fire. The hum protests, as if unwilling to accept my apology.

"I'm sorry," I repeat, a bit more forceful. The hum digs into my brain.

I wait a moment, take a breath, hold it for as long as I can, then release.

*"I'm sorry,"* I scream, and after I do, the hum shatters into the millions of words of which it's comprised, each flinging off into the outer edges of my mind. Whether real or imagined, the explosion causes a sharp pain to the front of my brain and I wince against it, closing my eyes for the briefest of moments.

When I open them, the stairs have returned to their normal imposing and solid state. There is only silence. A deep, dark, and lonely silence, the sound of a shipwreck sleeping for centuries within the deep silt of an ocean floor.

The silence affirms what I've known all along.

I can't change the past, and my apologies go unheard by those who need to hear them. I can't do anything to change these basic facts.

All I can do is pull my knees up, lower my head, and cry.

So I do.

# SEVENTEEN

**October 13**

**Two Weeks Later**

**FIFTEEN MORE MINUTES IN** my shift, then off to pick Max up from school.

I got a job.

I didn't need to. My father has made it very clear that as long as I'm back at home, I don't need to worry about frivolous little things like earning a living. But I felt a need to contribute *something*. My self-worth might be measured in pennies, but it's not bankrupt.

I'm working twenty-five hours a week at Tuli's, a boutique grocery store on Union Avenue, five minutes from Middleton Prep. When I was growing up, this used to be a mom-and-pop hardware store, but the demands of creeping affluence (not gentrification, since the area never sank to a depth where gentrification could occur) necessitated an independent grocery store catering to Bury's choosiest. Essentially a smaller and pricier Whole Foods, Tuli's is owned by Nathan and Joanne

Carnes, a middle-aged couple from Concord. The Bury store is their third in New England, and given how busy this one is, I imagine more are on the way. The Tuli's logo is the face of the Carnes family dog, a goofy, wide-eyed mutt.

I scan the items on the conveyor belt as I attempt to make eye contact with the shopper on the other side of the register. Each beep of my system is the sound of an obscene profit margin. Seven dollars for a single tube of "locally sourced" lip balm. Six organic limes, a dollar each. Nearly seven dollars for a half gallon of organic, naturally sweetened almond milk.

When I'm done ringing her up, the shopper nods, grabs her bag, and remains glued to her phone as she walks away. I turn to close my lane when I find one more customer waiting in line.

Alec.

"I thought that was you," he says. "I didn't know you were working here."

A thousand responses whiz through my mind, and I end up choosing the lamest.

"Yup."

He sets down an avocado. A single avocado, his entire shopping purchase.

"That's cool," he says.

I turn off the light above my register, officially closing my lane to anyone else.

"It's decent," I say, which is close enough to the truth to count. "How are you?"

"Good, good," he says, digging his hands into his pockets. "How is your son enjoying school? Max, right?"

"Yes, Max." I think about how to answer this, and a part of me has an urge to tell him everything. *Actually, Max is pretty damn miserable. He got sent home on his first day for threatening another kid, and since then, he barely talks to anyone. The only other student he even remotely knows is his Wednesday-Addams cousin, who's two years older and doesn't want anything to do with Max unless she's questioning him about his dead dad. And speaking of, I still can't figure out how he's dealing with his father's death since he never wants to talk about it. But he does go into these weird states where he seems catatonic for a few seconds here and there…*

"Fine," I say, packing all my thoughts into that meaningless word. "I mean, it's an adjustment. We're both…adjusting." I ring up his avocado, and Alec swipes his credit card to pay.

"I imagine you are," he says. "Not easy making friends in a new place, for either a kid or adult."

"Very true," I say. "Though I have a book club tonight, so that might be fun. My sister's club."

"What book are you discussing?"

I hand him his receipt and avocado. "Mine."

He takes a second to process this.

"You're a writer?"

"Yes."

"What kind of books?"

"Mysteries."

He flashes a smile. "I love mysteries. Do you write under your name? I'll have to check your books out."

"I write under the name J. L. Sharp. You might find them in the library. You can get them online for sure."

"J. L. Sharp. That's a good name. I'll keep an eye out." The moment lingers.

I untie the back of my olive-green Tuli's apron and remove it. "Okay, off to school."

"Me too," Alec says. "Have fun at your book club tonight."

"Thanks." I turn to walk away.

"Hey, wait just a sec." Alec reaches over the counter and grabs a pen, then starts writing on the back of his receipt. "Here's my number. If you ever want to talk. And…I mean it. I'm not asking you out or anything. I just imagine it's tough being in a new place."

I take the receipt from him. "A new place would be easier," I tell him. "But Bury isn't new to me at all." *It's all the old ghosts that make coming back a challenge.* "Thanks for this."

As I leave, I take a glance at the number and slide the receipt into my back pocket.

It would be nice to have someone to talk to.

The problem is, the closer you get to someone, the heavier all your secrets weigh.

# EIGHTEEN

**I'VE DONE BOOK CLUBS** before, which are really just wine clubs in disguise. I imagine this one will be no different.

My sister's house is nestled in a newer neighborhood called Dairy Farm Hills. Perhaps a dairy farm once stood here, but now it's just a collection of boxy estates that are all colored similar variants of brown. Cora's house is too big for just the three of them, but the Yates kids were raised to consume more than we needed, and she's carrying on the tradition proudly.

Peter works for my father, and last I heard, he was vice president of something or other. Judging by their house, Peter is very well paid.

"Pour you a glass?" Cora asks me. I'm the last to arrive, and the others are chatting away in the living room as my sister guides me into the kitchen. I can almost see my reflection in the gleam of the tiled floor.

"Sure, thanks."

"No, thank *you,*" she says. "The girls were so excited to have an author here to discuss the book in person."

This is typical of my sister. Gone are any signs of her rage from the other day. She's hidden away her demons, where they lurk behind a glossy veneer of civility.

"Happy to be here," I say.

She hands me the glass. "Usually we read heavier stuff. You know, more of the *literature* kind of books. It was a nice break for us to read an easy little mystery."

I sip rather than respond, which might be how this evening goes. Chances are good I'll have to get a ride home.

She takes me into the living room where about ten other women are spread across two couches and a number of chairs. They all have drinks, two of which appear to be water and the rest wine. Cora introduces me and they tell me their names, which I try to make note of though I'm likely to forget. I recognize two from Max's school.

"You work at Tuli's," one says. "I've seen you there."

"That's right," I say.

"Well, good for you," she says, as if I just learned to tie my shoes.

"The employee discount is great," I say. "I can almost afford to shop there now."

No one laughs.

I take a seat and another swig of wine. Most of them have a copy of my last novel in their laps, and I'm still amazed to see my book in the hands of strangers.

Cora asks me to tell the group a little about how I got into writing before we discuss the book. I give them my standard spiel about my journalism degree, my work at the *Chicago Tribune*, and my first stab at a novel. I describe the long search for an agent and then the subsequent rejections from a multitude of publishers and how I have several novels that never sold and likely never will.

They ask questions, mostly ones I've answered at other book clubs.

*Where do you get your ideas?*

*How long does it take you to write a book?*

*What kind of research do you do?*

*Do you know how the book will end when you start writing it?*

*How did you come up with the name J. L. Sharp?*

Cora is mostly silent, nodding and smiling. But I see her better than the others do. Her tight jawline, showing the tension in her face. Her fingertips reddening as she holds her wineglass, revealing her tight grip. I don't think she likes the attention I'm getting right now. She's the one who arranged this evening, suggested it even. But in this moment, as her friends are focused solely on me, I think Cora is jealous of her little sister. She's not used to that.

In the smallest of lulls, she finally makes her move and shifts the focus of the conversation.

"So let's talk about the book," she says, holding up a copy of *The Broken Child*, the third book in the Detective Jenna Black mystery series. "I, for one, thought it was quite good. Kept me entertained while I was on the elliptical, helped pass the time, because those workouts can be *so* boring. Though I have to say I figured out who the killer was pretty early on."

*No, you didn't*, I think. Now it's my turn to clench my jaw while offering no more than smiles and nods.

"I agree," a waif of woman says. I think her name is Jenny. "I was pretty sure who did it. And I also wanted a little romance between Jenna and Bart. It seemed like you were going there, then pulled back."

"I don't write a lot of love scenes," I say. "Violence is easier to write than sex. Though both are equally messy."

Nothing. Not a single chuckle. These women.

"Her books are more on the dark side," Cora says. "Though I have to admit, this is the first one I've read." She throws me a hard glare. "And a little bit of her upcoming book. Haven't finished that one yet, though."

I shift my gaze away as I listen to them discuss my book. They're mostly talking to one another now, and I'm just a spectator. A few remark that they liked the book, but there are several who comment it's not the type they would normally read. Some didn't finish it, and one didn't read it at all. I guess she just showed up for the wine.

The discussion lasts fifteen, twenty minutes, and I refill my glass a second time. I never ate dinner and a buzz creeps over me. It's not quite a pleasant buzz, but numbing enough to loosen me up. Maybe Cora's friends are nice people, I consider. Maybe they're not haughty Bury rich bitches who demand the world revolve around them. Maybe I'll even see some of them again. Perhaps even make a friend.

A friend would be nice.

"Your husband died of an overdose, right?"

The words strike through the numbness, jolting me. The woman who said them sits across from me, her dyed-blond hair worn in a long, straight bob, her fleshy cheeks flush from alcohol. She's leaning forward, elbows on knees, her body language more aggressive than the others.

"I'm sorry, what was your name again?" I ask.

"Sylvia."

"Yes, Sylvia, he did."

"I Googled you," she says.

"*Okay.*"

"There was an article in a Milwaukee newspaper. That's where you're from, right?"

"I'm from here," I say. "But we were living in Milwaukee. I'm not sure how that's—"

"Sorry, you must think I'm incredibly nosy," she says, half laughing and not looking the least bit sorry. "But Cora told me a bit about you, and I couldn't resist Googling you after we agreed to read your book for the club. I saw the article about your husband, and then I read the book. I was just wondering… Is it weird?"

I can only offer the blankest of stares. "Is *what* weird? Being a widow at the age of thirty-seven?"

She shakes her head. "No. The scene in the book with Connor. The fact that he also dies from an overdose of prescription drugs and alcohol. And that he was about the same age as your husband."

She sits up and purses her lips in satisfaction, as if she's just accidentally solved a Rubik's Cube.

Someone lets out the smallest of gasps. I'm not sure who.

"Jesus, Sylvia," a woman named Claire says. "What a thing to ask."

"I'm just saying. I'm curious. Life imitating art." She leans back against her chair, and it looks like she's fighting an impulse to smile. "I mean, come on. Doesn't anyone else find that strange?"

I bore a hole through her with my gaze, and my temperament and the booze work in tandem to make a decision on how to respond.

Fuck this person.

"First," I say, "yes, you're right. You *are* incredibly nosy. Not to mention highly insensitive. Second, the character in the book was murdered. So what the hell are you suggesting?"

She blanches and her smug expression evaporates.

"Look, I'm sorry, I just—"

"Just what?" I say. "You decide it's okay to bring up my recently deceased husband because you found it *strange*? And you think I killed him just because I know how to write a mystery novel?"

Her lips curl inward, and she squeezes onto the arms of the chair. "I said no such thing. And I don't appreciate your tone."

I swivel my head and scan the others, their faces frozen in the excitement of the moment. They are loving this.

"Are you kidding me?" I say. The night I didn't want to go to hell has just gone there, but I no longer care. "You don't appreciate my tone? *I* don't appreciate you stalking me online and asking me questions about a personal tragedy you have no understanding or appreciation of. Maybe I'll go and Google you. Bet I could find out a few things myself. You have no idea how much information a person can find with a little work. And trust me, I'm all about research."

She doesn't reply. I say nothing else. The tension in the room is thick, and no one says anything to break it. I expect someone to come to my side, maybe not Cora, but someone.

No one does.

"I think I'll call it a night," I say, standing. For a moment, I'm unsteady. Whether it's the adrenaline or the wine, I sway just for a second before catching myself.

I walk to the kitchen, grab my purse, and take one last gulp before setting my glass on the granite countertop.

I don't have to pass through the living room to get back to the front door, but I do. I walk slowly, giving them one last chance to say something. All their judgment. All their thousands of decisions about my existence, all calculated instantly and without error. And now they have a new decision to make about me. A big one.

*Did she kill her husband?*

They say nothing. I look over to Cora before I reach the front door. She's smirking.

Of course she is.

# NINETEEN

**BACK HOME, I WALK** into Max's room and find him on his Xbox.

"Hey," I say. "I thought we said no screens tonight."

He jerks around, surprised to see me.

"Yeah," I say for him. "I'm back early. You weren't expecting that, were you?"

"No."

"Well, that's not okay. I asked you to finish your homework, then you could read a book."

"I did finish," he says as he turns off the TV. "I read earlier, and I don't want to do that anymore. There's nothing else to do in this house."

"Where's Grandpa?"

He shrugs. "Downstairs, I guess."

"Did you spend any time with him?"

"No."

I sigh, walk over, and sit on his bed. "You can't just stay in your room all the time. I need to be able to go out every now and then with other adults, so you have to be in charge of yourself sometimes. That doesn't mean hiding in your room and playing games. Did you eat the dinner I made?"

He nods.

"Did you clean up your dishes?"

"Oh. I forgot."

"Okay, here's the plan," I tell him. "Go downstairs, clean your dishes, say hello to Grandpa, and come back and get ready for bed. Do that and I'll come say good night in a few minutes, okay?"

"It's not even that late," he protests.

"It's a school night. Besides, if you truly can't find anything to do, you might as well go to sleep."

He seems to be debating whether or not to argue but apparently decides against it. "Okay." Max starts heading for the door, then turns and says, "Did you have fun tonight?"

My shoulders sag, as if someone just placed sandbags on them.

"No," I say.

"Me either."

---

Forty-five minutes later, Max isn't quite asleep but will be soon. As I kiss him on his head before turning off his light, I briefly wonder what it is he thinks about in these moments, these minutes of stillness under the blankets, in the dark, before sleep takes over. Does he think about his father? Is he scared? Does he repeat mantras in his head like I do, something like *I want to go home?* I wonder this but do not ask, because I don't want him to say something that'll make me feel even guiltier. I can't handle that, not tonight.

Downstairs, I pass the kitchen, where the clock above the sink reads just past nine. I never did have dinner.

I continue down the dark hallway of the main level toward a faint glow. My father's study. Before I even enter, I can smell the trace of cigar smoke, which over the years has soaked into every surface of the room. I pass through the open doorway and find him sitting in one of two overstuffed leather chairs. He's not smoking, but he is drinking, a cocktail glass with two fingers of whiskey, neat, in his right hand. He's not on his phone. He's not reading his *Wall Street Journal* or a book. He's just sitting there in the silence, a solemn look on his face, as if wondering what the point of everything is anyway.

He looks over to me as I enter.

"Rosie," he says.

"Hi, Dad."

"Come join me." He points to the other chair, which hasn't had a regular occupant as long as I can remember. My father always sits in his favorite chair, and once in a while, someone's weight might bend the cushion of the chair next to it. But mostly, I'm guessing, my father sits alone.

"Okay," I say.

As I sit, he stands, walks over, and pours me the same drink as his, not asking if I want or even like whiskey. Fortunately, the answer to both these unasked questions is yes. I take the offered glass and sip. It burns deliciously, putting to shame the light tingle of the wine.

I clear my throat, barely suppressing a cough. "You know," I say, "your whiskey was the first alcohol I ever tasted."

He looks over to me without moving his head. His eyes have a look of playfulness that doesn't match the rest of his demeanor. "That so?"

"I was thirteen. Cora and I snuck some."

"What did you think?"

"I thought it was the worst thing I'd ever tasted."

He nods and considers this.

"What brand was it?"

"Jameson," I reply, remembering clearly.

"Well, that was the problem. You didn't go top shelf." He points to my glass. "What you're sipping right there is Charbay Release III. Four hundred bucks a bottle. If that was the first thing you ever drank, you'd be an alcoholic by now."

I take another sip and confirm my taste buds aren't sophisticated enough to appreciate the liquid flowing over them. It tastes good, but four hundred bucks good?

"Well, thank god for Jameson," I say.

We sit there and soak in the heavy silence. There's no tension, exactly, but it's not quite comfortable. Like being under a blanket that's both scratchy and cozy.

After a minute or so passes, he says, "What are your vices, Rose?"

"My vices?"

"Yes, your vices."

I'm stumped by the question. Not because I can't think of any answers but because my father is the one asking me. I think about it a few seconds more, then raise my glass and tilt it side to side in front of him.

"Alcohol is not your vice, Rosie. You drink, but you're not a drunk, far as I can tell. An important distinction. You don't smoke, at least not that I've ever seen. Probably don't gamble. Truth is, I don't know you very much as an adult. I'm just wondering what it is that you regret about yourself."

I push back in my chair, making myself smaller. "That's a hell of a question. Especially given our…past."

"I don't see much value in small questions."

"That I believe."

"Okay, I'll start then," he says. His voice is so calm, so smooth, just that same tone he always has. Stern and reassuring at the same time, the voice of quiet authority. "I like women too much. I see a pretty lady, and I just want to sweep her off her feet. And by that, I mean screw her."

"God, Dad."

"Just being honest with you. The thing is, I never meet an attractive woman I want to spend time with outside the bedroom. Other than those moments, I just want to be alone."

"So that's your vice?"

"That, and I have an insatiable need to conquer everyone I deal with in my business. I guess that's the pattern. I see a pretty company, I want to buy it and then sell it off in pieces. Companies and women. I just want to have my way with them. Then, the second I get what I want, I feel nothing." He takes a sip, allowing the alcohol to linger in his mouth for a few seconds before swallowing, chasing the numb. "Pretty much nothing at all."

"Well, that's depressing," I say. "So what's the point of it all, then?"

"Exactly," he answers. "What the point?" My father rises, walks over, and pours himself another. He's always been a heavy drinker, but I can't say I've ever seen him drunk. The alcohol just settles deep into his bones, fortifying rather than unsteadying him. When he sits again, he says, "It's like I'm chasing some feeling I haven't experienced in a long time, and I can't even describe what that feeling is anymore. I don't know if I'll ever catch it again, but I keep trying. I do believe that's the definition of insanity."

"You could take a cruise."

He laughs, a short, bitter bark. "Yeah, suppose I could." He flashes me another look, those eyes squinted as always. "So I've told you my vices. My weaknesses. So what about you?"

I've been thinking of my vices since the second he brought it up. How do you define a vice, exactly? At what point does something cross the line between being a simple human frailty and a significant character flaw?

There is one thing that bubbles to the surface. One thing about me I know to be true. Whether it's a flaw or not, it's the first thing I thought of when he asked.

"I'm not good at forgiving," I say.

This time, his laugh has sincere delight in it. "Are you kidding me? Rosie, that's not a vice. That's a virtue. And, by the way, you can thank me for that trait."

"And I have a hard time moving on from the past."

He considers this for a bit, nodding.

"The past is a whore," he finally says. "The present is your mistress. The future is your only true love."

I don't completely understand what he means, but the word *mistress* burns into me and makes me say what I do next without much thought.

"I was going to leave Riley."

His face freezes for a second, followed by an almost imperceptible raising of his eyebrows.

"Interesting."

I lower my voice, though I know we're far beyond earshot of Max's room.

"I told him I wanted a divorce."

"When?"

"Six months ago. I was about to move out when he died."

"Did Max know?"

"No," I say. "I don't think so. I didn't tell him. Maybe Riley did, but I doubt it."

"What was your plan?" My father is always about the plan. "Where were you going to go?"

"I don't know," I admit. "But I had to get away."

He sits up, leans forward, and cradles his glass in both hands. I have his full attention, and it's a bit unnerving. I both fear and admire his intensity.

"Why?" he asks.

I take a deep breath, hold it for a moment, then release it and tell him something I haven't told anyone else.

"He was cheating on me."

My father considers this and offers no more emotion than a feeble grimace. "Cocksucker," he says, and I'm not sure if he's referring to Riley or the bitch he slept with. "Can't say I'm not surprised, though. I always knew he wasn't good enough for you."

Men. Fucking *men*. Why is their field of vision so completely narrow? "Dad, I wasn't even good enough for *you*. You cut me off as soon as I wanted to leave Bury."

"You cut yourself off, Rosie, which was the best decision you could have made. Made you stronger, smarter. You think your sister would have made that choice?" He shakes his head. "No way."

"So why do you enable her now?" I ask. "You hired Peter. You still give money to Cora. Why do it if you think it's hurting her?"

He looks at me as if I've just asked why the sky is blue. "Because she's

Cora, and you're Rose." He takes his index finger and loops it around the rim of his rocks glass. One time. Two. "How long had he been cheating on you?" he asks.

"I don't know," I say. "I think at least six months."

"Who was it?"

"Does it matter?"

"It's always essential to know the enemy."

My stomach churns every time I think of Riley with that woman. We'd already grown apart by the time I found out, but the simmering rage that stirs in me when I think about walking in on them in our apartment makes me want to throw my glass against the wall and watch it burst into shards.

"She was one of his business partners," I say. "Also married."

He nods, as if this all makes perfect sense. "Did she go to the funeral?"

"I made it very clear she wasn't welcome."

"Does Max know about her?"

I don't know the answer to this. "I hope not," I say. "He knows there were problems. Arguments he witnessed. Riley and I said some things I wish Max hadn't heard."

My father settles back deeper into his chair, lost in thought, his gaze not on me but on the wall of books on the other end of the room. He takes a sip of his drink and says, "No matter what you think of me, I'm your father and will always do what I can to protect you. You can tell me anything. You know that. So I'm going to ask you a question, and I want you to be honest in your answer."

An inferno of dread sweeps through my chest.

He leans forward and drills that stare of his right into me.

"Did you?"

It takes more than a second for me to understand what he's asking, but not much more.

"Jesus, Dad, what kind of question is that?"

"A simple one. Couldn't be more simple. A yes-or-no question."

"You are not seriously asking me this."

"Why not?" he says. "You found out he was cheating on you. Then he ends up dead."

"I'm not having this conversation," I say.

"We can end it after you answer the question."

"What kind of person do you think I am?"

This question elicits a knowing smile, so gentle and slight, yet there's an underlying menace only another Yates could detect. "You, me, your sister. We all have a thread stitching us together. You ask me what kind of person you are? I *know* who you are. You're a Yates."

I take another sip of my drink, clinging to the glass as if it will somehow protect me, a magical amulet.

"I don't want to talk about this," I say. "About *that*. The thread."

"Don't you?"

"We said we'd never talk about it. That was our agreement."

The room is smaller, tighter, the air stale and warm. A prison cell.

"And yet," he says, "the very thing we agreed to never talk about is part of your next book."

There it is. That's what he's really getting at.

"Cora told you."

"Cora told me."

"It's not the same thing," I say, hearing the outer edge of panic in my voice. The doubt. The second-guessing. "It's different. Different circumstances. It's *fiction*."

I can see his pulse pounding in the veins of his temple. Though his voice doesn't waver in tone or volume, I know him well enough to hear the brewing anger beneath his words. "And what do you say when fans ask you how you get your ideas? What do you tell them, Rosie?"

"I think you're overestimating my readership."

"Once it's out there, it's out there. Forever. Is that the risk you want to take? You do understand there's no statute of limitations, right?"

I rise to refill my drink, not because I need it but because I don't want my father looking at my face. I don't want him reading my fear.

"Have you even read the book?" I ask.

"Not yet," he admits. "But I will. Your sister filled in the details for me."

"She's overreacting." My hand quivers as I fill my glass.

I don't hear him rise from his chair, and when I suddenly hear his voice at the back of my neck, I nearly scream.

"The name Caleb Benner is still well known around here," he whispers. "You might have left, but the mystery of what happened to that boy hasn't. People still talk about it, time to time, like they would about a local boogeyman. Once in a while, there's still an article written about his case. How the police vow to never give up figuring out what happened, despite no new leads for nearly twenty years. Your sister was interviewed back then, if you remember."

I don't turn around. "A lot of high-schoolers were interviewed."

"That doesn't change the fact that the Yates name is still part of the public police record."

"It's different," I say. "You just... You need to read the book. It's a very small part of the story."

He's closer now. I don't see him but I can sense it. "You used the name Corey Brownstein. The same initials."

"Dad, I—"

"The same *fucking* initials, Rose. How stupid are you?"

Finally, I turn. My father is inches away, and despite his stillness, I picture a thousand springs coiled inside him, ready to release at a breath of a trigger.

"Change it," he says. "Change the book."

I'm a little girl again, facing my father's anger whenever I displeased him. It never took much, sometimes as little as an eye roll when he told me to finish eating my dinner, but I could always feel the instant shift in energy as I do now, that heaviness in the air, an invisible wave washing over me. Logan Yates is an accommodating father as long as you do everything on his terms. The second you draw a line in the sand, the man no one wishes to face emerges.

"I can't just change it, Dad. The book is coming out in January. The final edits are done. The book is being printed."

"Bullshit," he says, his eyes flaring for a moment beneath his perpetual squint. "And the title, even? *Child of the Steps*? That's right on the goddamned nose. There's time. Get it changed. All of it."

"I can't."

"You will."

"Or what?" I ask. "Are you going to excommunicate me? In case you hadn't noticed, I've lived outside your bubble before."

"And look how well that turned out," he says. "You've got an autistic kid, a dead husband who cheated on you, and you're working in a fucking grocery store. You call that success?"

All those times in my life that my father intimidated me, even scared me, I never fought back. He never raised a hand to me, but sometimes I wished he had, because his towering presence and biting words were more painful than an open palm across the cheek. But I'm not the same frightened child I once was.

I've learned how to defend myself.

"First of all, *fuck you.*"

I've never said this to my father in my life.

"Second," I continue, "Max is not autistic, and if he were, that'd be just fine. He's your *grandson,* for god's sake, and he needs your love, not advice on how to dominate everyone he meets. Third, yes, I have no money. You think I don't know that? You think it doesn't stress me out? It does, but not nearly as much as taking your money does."

My voice has risen multiple decibels, and I suddenly picture Max pressing up against a wall in the hallway, eavesdropping. I walk around my father and peek out the office doorway but see nothing.

"You still have answered my question about Riley."

I walk back to him. "I don't have to. You'll continue to believe whatever narrative is burned into your brain."

He downs the last of his drink, and I can't remember if that's his second or third since I came in.

"*You* have blood on your hands," he says. "You do, I do, your sister does. That doesn't go away, and this book of yours will draw attention to it."

"I had to write it," I tell him. "There's nothing incriminating in the book, but I had to write what I did. What happened… It crushes me. The pain hasn't gone away." I think of my recurring nightmare. "If anything, it's gotten worse. I can't tell anyone. Not even Riley knew. Only you and Cora, and even just putting that one scene in my book was a relief valve. Can't you understand that?"

"No, I can't."

"Don't you feel the same thing? The guilt?"

"By the time I came home that night, the damage was done. I just cleaned up the mess."

There are moments when I wonder about my mother, what she was like, what she sounded like when she laughed, or if she ever laughed at all. I don't remember her, but in my mind, she was a beautiful, generous, gentle soul, and whatever good qualities I may have inherited I got from her. So if she really was that type of person, what did she see in Logan Yates? What was it about him that allowed her to forgive his cold shoulder to the world, his utter lack of empathy?

How did I come from this man?

"I just don't understand how you don't have any remorse," I say.

"Change the book," my father repeats. "At the very least, change the boy's name. That should be easy enough to do."

Seconds pass, and I'm left feeling unsteadied by alcohol and weak-kneed with anxiety. I don't want to admit he's right about this. But he just may be.

"I'll try," I say. "The best I can do is try."

"You will. And if you run into any problems with your publisher, you come tell me."

"And you're just going to fix everything?"

"Apparently, it's what I do best."

He sets his glass down, leaving it for the housecleaner to deal with. Then my father walks away without saying another word, and as he disappears into the hallway, I'm jealous at not having inherited his dispassionate nature.

How wonderful it must be to feel nothing at all.

# TWENTY

**Whitefish Bay, Wisconsin**

**COLIN PEARSON LAY NEXT** to his wife in bed, his breathing still elevated from sex. He reached out and touched Meg's hand, feeling her warmth spread into him.

*Anchor,* he thought. It was the word that came to him often when he thought of Meg.

*She's my anchor.*

He wasn't quite sure where he'd drift off to without her, but he knew he'd drift. All the way out to open sea.

Silence passed between them, comfortable and familiar, minutes sliding by in the dark. When she spoke, her voice jolted him from the cusp of sleep.

"I don't think she did it."

Colin turned his head to her voice. "Who?"

"The Yates woman. I don't think she did it."

He took a deep breath and sank lower into his pillow. "No?"

Colin was leaving in a couple days for his trip to Bury. He'd told Meg the high-level details of the case, and she'd even started reading the most recent J. L. Sharp book.

"I don't know what her motive would be," Meg said. "Women kill out of anger or for money. We know they didn't have money."

"Maybe she didn't know the life-insurance policy had lapsed," Colin said.

"Maybe," Meg conceded. "But I doubt it. And if it was about anger, there probably would have been evidence of a fight. Was there?"

"Not that was noted by the detective working the case," he replied. "But that's why I'm going out there. To ask the questions that weren't asked. Find out about their relationship. See what she'll be willing to tell me."

"If she talks to you at all," Meg said. "She might just shut the door in your face."

"What, on this sweet face?"

Meg laughed and Colin felt her turn in the bed, and he did the same. He suddenly felt her lips on his as she moved in toward him and then her palm on his cheek.

"You do have a sweet face," she said, extending for another kiss. "I just can't imagine not having you. You would have to screw up really badly to make me want to leave you."

The question popped into his head, and he asked it before he fully realized how morbid it was.

"What would I have to do to make you want to kill me?"

"God, Colin."

"I mean it," he said. "What kind of thing would make you want me gone forever? And not just a spur-of-the-moment killing. Something you planned for, knowing all too well the consequences of getting caught."

"I don't even want to think of it."

"It's helpful."

The ensuing silence was heavy, and Colin knew what Meg was doing. She was running through all the scenarios in her mind and trying not to make them so real as to believe they could happen. But she was thinking about it.

Finally, out of that silence, she spoke.

"I think if I found out you loved someone else," she said, a crack in her voice. "Not just having an affair but truly loved someone else. Maybe even had another family. Maybe even had a kid with her. I don't think I could handle that."

Colin knew how unlikely the scenario was. In love with someone else? A hidden family? A secret love child? That sounded like a nightmare.

"Even then, I'm not sure I could kill you," she whispered. "Or at least plan to. Maybe in the heat of the moment, but not otherwise."

Colin said nothing. These were the statements you just left there, taking up space.

She went quiet for a period longer.

Then she said, "No. The only thing that would make me kill you is if I thought you would hurt us."

*Us*. Colin squeezed his eyes shut against the dark and tried to force away the image of him hurting his wife and unborn child.

"If I thought you would hurt us, and leaving you wouldn't stop you, *then*, I think. Then I could kill you. Make a plan. Carry it out."

He couldn't remain silent any longer. "That's awful."

"I know," she said. "But you did ask."

"Yeah. I did."

"So you think he was hurting her?"

Colin had asked himself that same question many times over.

"I don't know," he replied. "There weren't any signs of it from Cooper's report, and he would've noticed anything obvious."

"But everyone is different," Meg added. "Not all women are the same, you know."

"I know."

"Maybe she has a threshold that's lower than mine. But I still don't think she did it."

He turned to her, though she couldn't see him. "Because you can't figure out motive?"

"Maybe," Meg said. "But she's also a writer. Her book seems so...well researched. Organized."

"So what, then?"

"I don't know. It's like...somebody capable of writing multiple books is too sound of mind to commit homicide."

Meg was a helluva lot smarter than that, Colin knew. Maybe she just had some kind of soft spot for the Yates woman, he thought.

"Or just the opposite," he said. "Maybe she knows a lot about killing because of what she writes. And maybe she writes what she does because she has a dark part of her trying to get out. You ever heard of Clara Tomson?"

"No."

"She's a writer," he said. "Has over thirty books or so, mysteries. Lots of them bestsellers."

"And?"

Colin thought about the articles he found on Clara Tomson after doing a simple Google search querying *writers who have killed people*.

"Formerly known as Elsa Holm. When she was sixteen, she and her boyfriend killed Clara's father. Stabbed him while he was sleeping."

"God. She must have written those books from prison."

"Nope. She went to prison, but only for about three years, over in Sweden."

"Why'd they do it?"

"Clara claimed the father was abusive. Maybe he was. Her mother denied it, as did her brother."

"Spousal denials are common."

"Yes, they are," Colin said. "Anyway, justified homicide or not, Clara did her time and now writes mystery novels. I think she's in her eighties now."

"So she writes about murder?"

"I haven't read her books, but yeah, I assume so. Wouldn't be a mystery novel without a corpse, I'd think."

He felt Meg shift in the bed, and her toes touched his.

"So are you extrapolating this Tomson's life onto the Yates woman? You think she writes what she does because she has some dark past?"

He had never formed those exact words in his head, but now that Meg had suggested it, Colin wondered if there was some truth to the idea.

"I'm not extrapolating anything," he said, stifling a yawn. "I'm just saying there might be a reason J. L. Sharp is good at writing books about violent crime."

Meg offered a *hmm* and nothing more. A few minutes passed in silence, and then Colin heard the slow and steady breaths of his sleeping wife. Sleep came easy for her, always had. But Colin's mind still churned with thoughts of Rose Yates and what might or might not have happened in that Milwaukee apartment on the night of July seventh.

As he turned to the side, gathered the pillow up in a ball beneath his head, and tried to fall asleep himself, Colin couldn't keep four words from looping in his mind. That old phrase from decades past, a basic piece of advice for authors.

*Write what you know.*

# TWENTY-ONE

**Bury, New Hampshire**
**October 15**

**MY EDITOR IS PISSED.**

I'm hunched over the laptop at the kitchen table, reading her response to my email requesting a change to the manuscript.

> Rose–
>
> As I told you very clearly, the last round of edits were the final edits. We can't make changes at this point unless they are obvious typos, etc. Certainly not the scope you are talking about. Even if we could, I wouldn't want you to change the death scene on the stairs, as it's a powerful, impactful scene. As you know, the galleys are already out and we'll be getting trade reviews

in about a month. I hate to say it, but we simply cannot accommodate your request.

Best,

Nancy

Shit.

When Cora freaked out about the scene in the book, I admit it rattled me. Made me second-guess the idea of it all. But after my father insisted I have the scene changed or removed altogether, I outright panicked. That night, I went back and read the chapter from a viewpoint of paranoia and suspicion and concluded *Oh my god, what have I done?*

My father was right. I need to change this, but I can't do it on my own. I write back.

Nancy,

I understand and it's difficult for me to explain my reasoning other than I'm fully convinced the scene doesn't work as is. I want to change the method in which the character dies and the character's name as well. I really hate the name Corey Brownstein and don't know why I used it initially. I'd like to use the name John Simms instead. I think it works much better, and just changing the name should be an easy fix. Let me know if at least this is possible, and thank you.

Rose

I've done enough police-procedural research to know many murders are never solved, and once a crime is in cold-case status, there's almost no hope of solving it unless new technology exposes a previously hidden clue or the killer makes a deathbed or prison-cell confession. If a murder has gone unsolved for twenty years, the killer (or killers) should have a high degree of confidence of never being caught, especially if that murder was the only one they committed.

But here's the thing research never reveals: if *you're* the killer, all that confidence can be shattered at the faintest shift in the wind. There's never 100 percent confidence, and rarely even half that. Odds don't mean anything to your nerves, your gut. And your conscience, if you have one.

"Miss Rose?"

I turn my head and see Abril, the housekeeper. She comes over a couple hours each day during the workweek, cooks, does light cleaning. She's pleasant enough but quiet, keeping to herself even though we've been in the house several hours alone together. I tried to strike up a conversation a few times but received very short answers to my questions.

"Yes?"

"There's a man at the door. Asking for you."

I didn't even hear the door ring. I was too entrenched in my email with Nancy.

"What does he want?" For a moment, I think maybe it's Alec. One of those flash fantasies where I picture Alec stopping by under some transparent pretense, just to say hi.

Abril shatters this daydream.

"I don't know. He says…he says he's police."

This is a word I neither expected nor wanted to hear.

"Police?"

"*Sí*. No uniform. But badge."

My immediate, irrational, horrifying thought is that Cora went to the police and told them everything. But that makes no sense, since she's much guiltier than I am. But what if she's so paranoid about the chapter in the upcoming book that she decided to get ahead of everything and craft her own version of what happened to Caleb Benner, leaving me to shoulder all the responsibility?

That would be suicide. My father would cut her off forever.

But the improbability of the thought doesn't give me comfort. Who knows what Cora is capable of doing? She's as unpredictable as a rabid dog, and just as dangerous.

"Yes, of course." I rise from the kitchen table, feeling the heat of my body rushing to my extremities. I'm certain my face is flushed, and even thinking about it is making it more so. My complexion always betrays any kind of heightened emotion: anger, embarrassment, lust, nervousness.

As I head to the foyer, Abril scurries deeper into the house. I want to hide, too.

The door is half-open, and as I reach it, I see the man.

He wears a dopey, disarming grin, as if he's a neighbor going to ask to borrow a couple of eggs.

This unnerves me more than anything else.

# TWENTY-TWO

**"HI, MA'AM. ARE YOU** Rose Yates?"

"Yes."

"I'm Detective Colin Pearson with the Milwaukee Police Department." He holds up a badge that looks authentic, but I also know how easily those can be faked.

"Milwaukee?"

"Yeah, I know. Long way from home."

My brain tries to process all the little details at once, hoping to get a step ahead of whatever it is he wants. He's plainclothes, which makes sense for a detective. Nicely dressed: khaki slacks, crisp, white button-down shirt, blue-and-gold-striped tie. All topped off with a blue blazer, cheap but serviceable, the kind a cop would buy. He's maybe upper thirties, tall and a bit lanky, fit but not muscular, and he's avoided the cop gut that usually comes with riding either a desk or patrol car.

And his face. It's so benign. So *aw shucks*. Light stubble that looks as if he's a fifteen-year-old getting his first moss of facial hair. Dark hair that's short but still manages to be a bit moppy. Eyes that convey both warmth and trust. And that grin…so light and disarming. His is the kind of face that puts someone at ease.

Except right now. With me.

"You're here to see me?" I ask.

"Yes, I am. And I won't take up much of your time. Just want to ask you a few questions, if it's not too much of a bother."

I look past him and see a Bury police sedan parked on the street. A cop in the driver's seat.

Pearson follows my gaze and then turns back to me. "Oh, that's Officer Simmons with Bury PD. He's just my ride. He'll wait out in the vehicle until we're through. Mind if I come inside?"

How many times have I talked to cops, interviewing them as necessary research for my books, asking them questions about their procedures, their psychology, their instincts? Now, it's the other way around. The way I don't want it to be, because police officers are trained to detect guilt. Some of them are exceptional at it, and some of them are barely serviceable. I don't have any idea where Colin Pearson falls on that spectrum.

My choices are limited here, and as I open the door to this man, allowing him to pass into my father's house, I briefly close my eyes and recall a mantra designed specifically for hard moments. Moments of suffocating darkness, those silent, stabbing seconds when I doubt who I am at my innermost core. Who I've been. What I've done.

*I'm stronger than I think.*

*I'm stronger than I think.*

*I'm stronger than I think.*

Minutes later, with a digital recorder placed between us, our conversation begins.

# TWENTY-THREE

**THE HOUSE WAS MASSIVE,** swallowing Colin without noticing, krill to a whale. But it wasn't the size of it that had him off-balance. The place had an energy, and not necessarily a good one. There was a sense of *occurrence* here, though everything was still. Best he could compare it to was a crime scene. A silence reverberating with aftershocks.

He sat across from the woman he'd come to see and pressed the button on his recorder.

"Okay, it's Thursday, October 15, approximately 14:30 hours," he started. "I'm at 1734 Rum Hill Road in Bury, New Hampshire, speaking with Rose Yates. I'm not being assisted in this interview. Drew Simmons, patrol officer with the Bury Police Department, is in a squad car outside the residence. Ms. Yates is not in custody and has voluntarily elected to speak with me. The subject of this interview is case 18-33456, concerning Riley McKay, Ms. Yates's late husband."

She crossed her legs. "God, this all sounds so serious."

"I know, and apologies for the formality of it all, Ms. Yates. I prefer to record conversations in conjunction with any case I'm working. Makes it easier to remember things. I'm a bit of a stickler for details and procedure."

"You can call me Rose."

"Thanks, Rose. And you can call me Colin, or Detective Pearson, whichever you prefer."

"Well, then." She leaned back and pulled a strand of hair off her face as he started asking questions.

He went light and easy, as was the plan, telling her he had a few routine follow-up questions in the matter of her husband's death. He was only a few questions in when it became clear she wasn't buying it.

"Routine things are usually handled through the phone," Rose said. "But you came all the way from Milwaukee to New Hampshire. That means you had to get approval for a travel budget from your department, which I'm sure isn't easy. And certainly not something approved for routine questions."

Colin nodded rather than smiled; that would come off as patronizing. "I suppose that's the mystery writer in you coming out. I imagine you've researched a lot of police procedure for your books."

There was a brief widening of her eyes. She was surprised he knew she was a novelist, Colin guessed. "I have. Talked to a lot of cops, a few in your own department even. But not you."

"Well, I normally don't work cases like this. But I transferred from Madison not too long ago and I'm helping the department pick up some slack."

Then followed a slight beat where Rose seemed at a loss for words, compensating by gesturing to the table between them.

"I'm sorry," she said. "I never offered you coffee. This is usually the time I have my last cup for the day. Can I get you some?"

"No, thank you, ma'am."

"Rose."

"No, thank you, Rose. But you go right ahead."

The moment she left the room was when he felt the relief. Her relief. The relief of someone who didn't want to be interviewed getting a brief reprieve. Rose didn't want coffee, Colin thought. She wanted to get away.

In her absence, he leaned back in his chair and tried to massage the bias from his brain. There was a big difference between being attuned to suspicious behavior and trying to shoehorn some narrative into a predetermined judgment of guilt. Rose Yates was innocent until someone other than Colin said otherwise. It was just his job to ask some questions.

But...goddamn it. There was guilt in the air, he was sure of it. Maybe it wasn't even her. Hell, the whole *house* felt guilty.

When she returned, cup in hand, Colin decided to be more direct with his questioning.

*How would you characterize the relationship between you and your husband?*

*Were you having issues?*

She replied with mild offense, but it had an air of desperation to it. Trying too hard, Colin thought. She said all couples had issues, and she and Riley were no exception. He poked and prodded into this as best he could, but she put up a wall he couldn't penetrate.

Then he'd told Rose he'd read all her books.

"Well, that makes an even dozen of you now," she said.

"I read them back-to-back," Colin said. "Real quick, like two days each. And each one got better. More suspenseful, you know? You can really see how you were progressing as an author. Your main character, Jenna Black, she doesn't get boring. You keep her fresh."

Rose took a moment, then leaned forward toward him. Body-language experts would deem it a subtly aggressive move. "This is the part where you tell me the thing you really came here for."

He matched her posture. "Well, now, Rose. I'm not trying to make things sound so sinister or anything. And you, having interviewed so many cops with all your research and all, I'm sure you can appreciate that something in your books made me a little curious."

"*The Broken Child*."

"Correct. Your third book. Or I guess I should say J. L. Sharp's third book. You can understand why a scene where an abusive husband is poisoned by his wife might arouse some interest."

"Riley wasn't poisoned. It was an accidental overdose."

Colin scratched the back of his hand though it didn't itch. "Still, you can see where that scene piqued my curiosity a bit. Piqued. That's the right word, isn't it?"

"Detective, if I were guilty of all the crimes my characters have committed, I'd be on death row a hundred times over."

He held eye contact and she didn't back away, though she seemed to want to look anywhere but his face. "Oh, sure. I'm well aware of that, Rose. Like I said, I'm not trying to spook you. This is pretty routine stuff. But I wouldn't be doing what the citizens of Wisconsin pay me to do if I'd not followed up with a couple of questions. Want to be thorough."

He'd tried to slip back into a folksy charm but it was too late. The cloud that passed over Rose's face assured him so.

"I'm going to say this once." Rose reached over and grabbed the recorder. Colin thought she was going to turn it off, but she actually held it to her mouth as she spoke. "I'm assuming you've never lost a spouse, so you can't understand what it's like, expecting to see them in the morning getting ready for the day only to find them still in bed. Then to go over and touch them, only to feel that unnatural cold on their skin. To know they'd been taking sleeping pills and anxiety pills for years, all the while mixing them with alcohol, and they were always fine. What they needed to sleep at night. And you...you eventually stopped protesting. Because, after all, they always got up in the morning, right? And then, one day, they don't. Gone."

Colin watched every tick of her face, every shift of her eyes. If she was lying, she was good. But he had run into more than his fair share of good liars in his work.

"I'm not offended by your questions," she continued. "I know you have a job to do. But I can see the eagerness in your face, the hope you might make some kind of name for yourself with your new department. But I can tell you this: you won't make it from this case. You won't make it from me. Whether Riley's death was accidental or maybe something he secretly wanted, I'm not sure I'll ever know. But I would never hurt someone I loved."

There were many key words in what she'd just said, and Colin would surely go over the transcript of the recording many times dissecting them, but one word stood out above all others. It stood out because it had the clearest ring of a lie, more than anything else.

"So you loved him, then?"

She rose, and that was that.

"If you need to speak with me again, you can contact my lawyer."

# TWENTY-FOUR

**THE MOMENT HE LEAVES,** a dull throb begins in my head, a manifestation of anxiety. As is the tightness in my chest and the sudden glaze of warm sweat inside my armpits. I try to calm myself with a few deep breaths, but it's like trying to meditate while drowning.

Detective Pearson didn't want to know about my distant past. I was paranoid to think he did. My distant past has nothing to do with Milwaukee, so a Milwaukee cop would know nothing about something that happened twenty-two years ago in Bury, New Hampshire.

I pull back the thick mahogany drapes from the living room window and peek outside as Pearson gets in the patrol car, where he sits and talks with the Bury cop. Who was it? Timmons? Simmons?

Our conversation didn't end the way I wanted. I didn't want to threaten getting a lawyer, but the alternative was to answer Pearson's questions, and I saw no good end to that. Every cop I've ever interviewed for my research has told me it's usually the best move for a suspect to lawyer up, but it always reinforces the perception of guilt.

*How would you characterize your relationship with your husband?*

Well, Detective, it was pretty damn bleak. We'd been growing apart for some time, and then I recently found out he was screwing his business partner, who is younger, firmer, and way richer than me. Riley wanted to save our marriage but I wasn't able to move forward emotionally with him. We continued living together while planning how best to separate.

In the final months leading up to his death, Riley grew bitter.

Bitter and angry.

Riley wasn't prone to anger, and even in his worst moments, he just tended to be sullen. But not long before he died, that changed. I'd told him I'd had enough of sharing the apartment and was going to find my own place, even though I could scarcely afford it. I needed out. We'd share Max fifty-fifty and figure out a schedule as we moved toward divorce.

Maybe Riley had still been clinging to a hope that we'd remain together, or perhaps he just didn't like me making the final decision. But the sullenness became anger.

Searing anger.

*You want to leave me? What the hell are you going to do with your life? You're incapable of making money. How're you going to pay for a place?*

Name-calling.

*You're just a selfish bitch, you know that? You're ruining our family.*

Threats over Max.

*If you think I'm going to let you take him away, you're out of your mind. In fact, I'll sue for full custody.*

Riley changed into another person in those last weeks, a desperate, needy, and hateful little boy. I should have left sooner. Should have taken Max and stayed with friends. But a part of me was convinced I could stabilize Riley, get him to accept our marriage was over and we both needed to get on with our lives. We were still going to have to raise Max together, and I wanted Riley in a more grounded place before I left.

I thought that would be the best thing for Max.

But Riley didn't stabilize. He got worse.

I should have anticipated that.

Riley started drinking earlier in the day and finishing later at night, always capped off with his prescription sleeping pills, which would knock him out until late in the morning. He stopped looking for work, hardly left the apartment, hardly spoke to either Max or me. Just brooded like a sullen child convinced the world was out to get him.

But for all his horrible behavior, he was never violent. I was never scared of him.

I should've been.

The light of my world remains blocked by the black mass of all my *should'ves.*

On that last night, the last of his life, he walked into our bedroom while I was folding laundry on the bed. I could tell he was already several drinks in on the evening. He thought I was packing, that I was leaving him that night, and he flipped out.

> What the hell are you doing?
>
> *I'm just folding laundry.*
>
> No, you're not. You want to go, Rose? Just go already. I'm sick of you. Sick of seeing your face. You're ugly, you know that? Ugly.
>
> *You don't understand the only reason I put up with this is I keep hoping you'll straighten out enough to have a rational conversation about us.*

I'm straight as an arrow, baby. So get the fuck out.

*If you want me to leave now, then I'm taking Max with me.*

No, you aren't. He doesn't go anywhere.

*Riley, I don't trust you alone with him. Not with the way you've been behaving. Not with how much you've been drinking.*

You think I'd hurt my own son? Is that what you're saying?

*I'm saying you're in no shape to be a single parent right now.*

There's only one person in this apartment I want to hurt.

With that last statement, Riley turned and slammed his fist into the wall next to the bed. *Bam.* His hand disappeared through the drywall as if it were nothing more than rice paper; I think he was even more surprised than me. He just stood there, fist still in the wall, seconds passing, until finally his shoulders slumped, his head lowered, and he began to cry. Not just cry but sob. Sob like I'd never heard him do before, a complete and total capitulation to his circumstances, an abandonment of hope. He finally pulled his fist out and slid down the wall to the floor, where he wrapped his arms around his knees and buried his forehead on top of them. He didn't bother to look up as I backed out of the room.

Max was in the hallway, just out of eyeshot of the bedroom. I didn't know if he'd been watching, but he certainly had heard everything. This couldn't continue. I had to take him out of there.

I raced into the hall and pulled Max in toward me.

"I'm sorry," I told him, not thinking of anything else to say. We had moved well past the sometimes-parents-argue phase in our family dynamic.

He squeezed me back and asked a question I couldn't make out. I leaned him back so I could see his face.

"What?" I asked.

"Did he hurt you?"

"No. He's just…just angry at the world right now. But it's not your fault. You know that, right?"

He looked up at me, his eyes fixed on mine. "Were you scared?"

And in that moment, I was honest with him, because I had no one else I could share with.

"A little," I admitted.

But that wasn't altogether true.

I was a lot scared.

Riley had changed. Now he wasn't just a man I no longer loved. He was a threat. First he hits the wall. Then what? And what would I be willing to do to secure the safety of my son and me?

*How would you characterize your relationship with your husband?*

No way I was going to tell Detective Pearson all those things. No way I was going to tell him how, after calling 911 that morning I found Riley dead, I hung a picture over the hole in the wall to avoid questions about there having been a fight. Or how I had a neighbor take Max that morning so it would be harder for the police to ask him any direct questions. And I got lucky. I got Detective Cooper assigned to the case, and he was quick to tell me he was retiring in a few days and promptly declared Riley's death an accidental overdose.

I'm not stupid. I've talked to enough cops to know the questions Cooper should have asked, the same questions Pearson is asking now. The truth about how Riley died doesn't matter. What matters is how it looks, and I'm not going to fuel more speculation by volunteering information about how my marriage had imploded.

Now, as I continue to stare out my window at the police car, I see movement to my right. It takes me a moment to focus, and at first my mind rejects who I'm seeing, but my eyes soon provide concrete evidence. It's Tasha Collins, and she's walking a dog outside my house.

Of all people. At this point in time.

Tasha Collins.

She either lives in this neighborhood or she's trolling me, and I can't decide which option is more plausible. In the moment, it doesn't matter.

She's walking a chalk-white standard poodle, its head held perfectly straight like a schoolgirl in the 1950s walking with a book on her head to perfect her posture.

Tasha slows as she moves past the police cruiser parked in front of my father's house. She lets her dog sniff around my lawn, as if hoping to find some bodies. She looks the cop car up and down, then turns her head and spies me through the open drapes. My impulse is to duck away, but I fight against it. I maintain direct eye contact with her, and Tasha's eyes narrow as she homes in on me. She nods, I don't. She turns away first, but before she does, she allows herself a little smile. A smug little grin.

I'm tempted to go out and tell her there was a suspicious person going house to house and I called the police. But I only consider the idea, and my feet never move from where they're planted.

Moments later, Tasha and her dog move on, her pace more brisk as if she's anxious to get home. The cruiser finally pulls away from the curb and rolls gently away.

As I keep staring out the window, I can't push away the feeling that a dreadful series of events has just been set in motion.

My job is to figure out how to stop it.

# TWENTY-FIVE

**October 17**

**SIX HOURS OF SLEEP** in the last two days; fatigue and anxiety battle with great ferocity to see which gets the honor of killing me.

I'm two hours into my four-hour Saturday shift at Tuli's and am desperate to get out of here. Anxiety is winning the war at the moment, and despite my exhaustion, I have energy far beyond what's needed to stock shelves, which is what I'm doing.

"Hi, Rose."

I turn and find the cause of my sleepless nights standing behind me. Detective Pearson.

He's dressed more casually than when he came to my father's home two days ago. Long-sleeved white dress shirt, jeans, sneakers, and sunglasses hooked into the vee of his shirt. I don't see any gun visible, but there's no way a detective walks around unarmed. I flick my gaze down and see the slight bulge on the lower part of his right leg. Ankle holster.

He has neither a shopping cart nor a basket.

"You're still here," I say.

"I am."

"The Milwaukee PD must have quite a budget."

"I'm not staying in luxury accommodations. I'm leaving later today."

I'm holding a jar of organic tomato sauce, which suddenly feels more like a weapon in my hand than an item to shelve.

"What do you want, Detective?"

He shifts his footing, placing his right foot back just enough to suggest a defensive stance. Subtle, but I notice.

"I'd like to talk to you one more time before I leave. A bit more formally, down at the Bury police station."

My gut tightens.

"Just to clear up a few little things?" I ask, recalling Pearson's initial approach to me on Thursday.

"Yes, exactly."

"I recall telling you if you wanted to speak to me again, you had to go through my lawyer."

"Well, I don't know who your lawyer is any more than I know who your dentist is," he says. "But if you feel you really need a lawyer, I suggest you give them a call. Have them meet us down at the station."

I lower the jar in my hand, squeezing it, the muscles in my forearm tightening.

"I'm in the middle of a shift right now," I say.

"I'm sure your boss will understand."

"I'm not sure that's true," I say. Pearson's face doesn't wear the *aw shucks* humility of a few days ago. He looks like a man unwilling to take *no* for an answer. "Am I under arrest?"

I've imagined having to ask that question before. More than once. But it's terrifying to do it, to speak those words to an actual detective.

"No, Rose, you're not. You don't have to go with me. And I suspect you know I'll tell you it's in your best interest to do as I ask. You probably think that's just a ploy to get you to talk, and sometimes it is, no doubt. But the god's honest truth is, if you don't have anything to worry about, then you *will* be helping yourself if you come in for an interview."

I look down the aisle past Pearson and spot my shift manager, John Ridley, staring at us. John's the type of boss who'd get annoyed if he thinks I'm having a personal conversation at work. He's in his fifties, unmarried, and clings to his ounces of low-grade power. I can only imagine John's reaction if he knew what Pearson and I are talking about.

I shift my gaze back to Pearson. "You're far from convinced of my innocence. Otherwise you wouldn't have come all the way out here in the first place. I have nothing to hide concerning my husband, but I have nothing to gain by talking to you. I need to get back to work."

"Did you know your life-insurance premium payments weren't up to date?" he asks. "Did you handle the bills, or did your husband?"

"I'm not answering that."

"I see," Pearson says, pushing his hands in his pockets. "Well, that's a shame, Rose, I'll tell you. I was really hoping we could get a chance to clear the air, but I guess I'll have to do a little more digging. I would've thought you'd have wanted to put all this behind you, move on with your grieving process. But it's your call, and I have to respect that."

"Thank you," I say. "Now, if you don't mind."

"Nope, nope. I'll let you be. Probably be contacting you again. Or, if the cards play out in your favor, maybe you'll never hear another word from me."

*Let's hope for that option,* I think.

"Bye, Rose," he says. "I'll be keeping any eye out for your next book. I'm sure it'll be as good as the others."

I nearly lose my grip on the tomato sauce. A jar crashing to the floor is not the reaction I'd want to give him, or my boss.

Pearson walks a few feet down the aisle before turning back.

"You said 'concerning my husband,'" he says.

"Excuse me?"

"You said you had nothing to hide 'concerning your husband.' It's just that most people wouldn't have used a modifier. They'd have just said they had nothing to hide. Period."

I turn to the shelf and finally place the jar of tomato sauce next to all the others, hiding my face from Pearson.

"You're reaching now," I say with my back to him.

I picture him cracking a gentle grin, a cop smirk, the kind that's supposed to be disarming.

"Maybe I am," he says. "Can I ask one last question? Just about being an author. I was curious about something."

"Fine," I say, turning back to him and crossing my arms.

He nods as if to say thanks and says, "I was thinking of that old piece of advice for authors and was wondering if it is really true."

"What advice?"

"Write what you know," he says. "Is that really a thing? Do authors write what they know?"

If Pearson is trying to unnerve me, it's working. I compose my thoughts the best I can and answer.

"Doesn't really allow much room for imagination," I say. "Some of the best parts about writing are discovering new worlds."

He scans my face, and I keep mine as still as possible. Cops are trained to identify signs of a person being deceitful, simple physical tells. Averting of the eyes. Biting of the lips. Touching the face.

If Pearson registers something about my face, I can't tell.

"Yeah, that makes sense," he says. "Imagination." He dwells over the word like a distant memory, then snaps his attention back to me and adds, "Say, you ever read Clara Tomson? Mystery writer, like you."

The name sounds vaguely familiar but I can't place it. "No," I say. Pearson certainly asked me this for a very specific reason, and because of that, I say nothing else, not wanting to go wherever it is he's hoping to lure me. I do, however, etch the author's name in my mind, because I sure as hell am looking this person up when I get home. *Clara Thompson.*

"Oh, okay. Just thought I'd ask." He holds a beat but I remain steadfast in my silence. Pearson then thanks me again and walks away. As I return to stocking the jars, I notice the tremors in my hands.

Maybe ten seconds elapse before John, my manager, scurries up from behind.

"He said he was with the Milwaukee police." John comes around to the side and I look at him. His salt-and-pepper mustache twitches, and his eyes are wide with weird, nervous excitement, like a cat that doesn't know what to do with the bird it's just maimed. "What'd he want with you?"

*It's none of your goddamn business,* I want to scream. *Why can't everyone just leave me alone? Why do you all have to ask so many questions? I came here to escape my life, not be suffocated by it.*

But I don't say anything, because there's a rope still tethering me to social convention. The rope is well frayed and may only have the tensile strength of dental floss, but for now, it holds.

"He's just closing out the case on my late husband," I say, jaw tensed, voice monotone, offering no more. I've never told John my backstory, but I'm assuming he knows about Riley. I simply assume everyone knows because this is Bury.

John nods. "I see." Assumption confirmed. "Well, I suppose that's good," he adds. "But…he came all the way here just to close out a case?"

"Everything's fine," I tell him.

"Okay." Based on the fact that he doesn't leave, I'm guessing it's not really okay to him. He just hovers around a few more seconds until I finally reach out and put a hand on his arm.

"John, everything's good. I appreciate your concern, but this is a private matter. If it's all the same to you, I don't want to talk about it. Things have been hard enough."

He nods, the mustache twitches a little more, and he gives me another nod before turning and walking back down the aisle.

I exhale, as if I could simply breathe out all the things that are eating me from the inside out.

But those things stay inside, burrowing and devouring, until there is nothing left to be had.

# TWENTY-SIX

**I MAKE IT AS** far as the front seat of my car before I search *Clara Thompson* on my phone.

The first Google result tells me she was a prominent psychoanalyst who died in the 1950s. I look at the Wikipedia page and see nothing about her being a mystery writer.

I return to my search, scroll down, and realize I had the last name wrong. It's Tomson, not Thompson. I find a link for her website.

*International Bestselling Novelist*

I click on it and scour through all her titles, none of which are familiar. That's hardly surprising; I don't read many cozy mysteries. Her bio page shows the face of an elderly woman, coiffed brunette hair, striking blue eyes, and an expression that conveys a mild displeasure at having her picture taken.

The bio is long but hardly revealing. Born in Norway just before World War II, moved to Sweden as a child. Started her writing career in her twenties, and her work mostly consists of light, cozy mysteries and includes what appears to be a very successful series featuring a character named Victoria Landon. And cats. Lots of cats.

The final bit of her bio states she's been an evangelical Christian for over forty years. I try to find some significance in that, some tie-in to Pearson's interest in me, but come up empty.

Back to Google, type the name in properly. First entry is her website again, but the second is what I was hoping to find. A Wikipedia page for Clara Tomson. If there's something about her that Detective Pearson wants me to know, I'll find it here.

The page loads, and the first thing I notice is a table of contents on the left side of the entry.

The next thing I notice is the second heading in that table of contents, the one immediately following *Early Life*.

It says *Murder and Trial*.

I thumb the hyperlink and jump to this part of her bio. A part not mentioned at all in her official website.

"Holy shit," I say, my own voice startling me.

In dry language, Wikipedia tells me that Tomson (born Elsa Holm), committed murder when she was only sixteen. In Gothenburg, Sweden, she and her seventeen-year-old boyfriend, Liam Persson, killed Clara's father, with Clara claiming he'd raped her numerous times from ages twelve through fifteen.

If I'm still breathing, I'm not aware of it.

They stabbed him while he slept and the mother was out of town. The worst sentence is this: *The attackers presumed one blow would kill him but it took more than twenty*.

Oh my god. Oh my god.

Pearson just casually dropped the name of a mystery novelist who committed murder as a teenager.

I furiously read the rest of the page, then a second time. It never states who actually did the stabbing. Maybe Tomson was just complicit but didn't commit the act. It didn't make a difference because both went to prison in Sweden. Tomson for just over three years, Persson for five. When they got out, Elsa Holm changed her name to Clara Tomson and started writing books. Now, she has more than thirty of them.

This woman is highly successful.

But she paid her debt to society. She never had to keep a secret. She might not detail this part of her past on her own bio, but she knows it's not a secret.

I don't have that luxury, if you want to call it that. I have a weight that gets heavier every day, as all secrets do.

And Pearson.

He suspects something.

*Write what you know,* he said.

This is about more than Riley.

This is about Bury.

# TWENTY-SEVEN

**COLIN WALKED AT A** slow pace as he left the grocery store, as if Rose Yates might still rush out and tell him she'd changed her mind. That she did want to talk after all. Clear the air.

But he knew that wasn't going to happen, and his pace had less to do with a hope of talking to her and more with a reluctance to return to Milwaukee just as clueless as when he'd arrived. He'd shot the moon getting permission to come here, and his sergeant's expectation was he'd return with evidence to either arrest or exonerate her.

Colin had neither.

He barely even had a sense of Rose Yates. Before the trip, he found as much as he could about her online. There had been a handful of blogs by and about her, a couple of podcast interviews, and even a brief local TV news interview from a few years ago when her second book had come out.

Colin thought he had a good picture of the woman. How to approach her. How to act to get her to trust him.

But he'd been wrong.

Rose Yates was a fortress wall, smooth and solid, with no place for handholds.

Colin paused for one last moment before getting in the cruiser waiting for him. One breath. Three seconds of silence. Then he opened the passenger-side door and slid in.

"No go?" Officer Drew Simmons—Colin's local PD escort while he was in Bury—started the ignition, and cool air blew from the Dodge Charger's air vents. Colin hadn't been expecting seventy-degree weather in New Hampshire in the second half of October.

"Negative," Colin said.

"So now what?"

" I go back to Milwaukee tonight."

"That's a shame," Simmons said.

"Yeah." Colin sighed. "It is."

Simmons pulled the cruiser from Tuli's parking lot and turned right on Bryson Street toward the police station, about a mile away. He kept to the speed limit, bringing all other cars around theirs to the exact same speed. *Everyone's cautious around a cop,* Colin thought. Some of the folks in traffic just didn't want a ticket. Others perhaps really had something to hide, maybe the kind of crime that only gets discovered after a routine traffic stop.

Colin scanned the rows of houses along the boulevard, sensing he was staring at a Norman Rockwell painting. After taking in the town for a few seconds, he turned to Simmons. "How old are you?"

"Twenty-five."

"And you said you grew up here?"

"That's right."

"What was that like? I mean, this place seems so perfect."

Simmons shrugged, as if he had never considered his childhood before. "It was okay. Boring, I suppose. I'm sure my parents hoped I'd do something other than be a cop, but it's what I wanted."

"Boring," Colin repeated. "Nothing exciting ever happened?"

Simmons turned to him. "Exciting like how?"

Ever since Colin had found out about Clara Tomson, he couldn't get the write-what-you-know notion out of his head. It was an overly simplified and ignorant notion, of course. Writers didn't only write what they knew. There would never be a *Game of Thrones* or *Pet Sematary* if wild imagination didn't come into play.

But Colin had also learned to listen to himself. When an idea struck him in a certain way, as obtuse as it might be, he'd learned how to nurture that idea until it yielded something of substance. The idea that Clara Tomson committed murder when she was a teen and then lived the rest of her life writing mystery novels… Well, that struck Colin in a certain way, especially when he added Rose Yates into that same thought process.

"Crime," Colin said. "What kind of crime you have here?"

"What, growing up or now?"

"Has it changed?"

Simmons allowed a grin. "Not really. Nothing here much changes. You've seen the board at the station. Not a lot on it."

"Pretty quiet town."

"We're in the top three safest cities in New Hampshire. Truth is, it's just that kind of area. Was the same way when I was a kid. Never really had to worry about being out at night, things like that."

The Pleasantville metaphor was becoming even more apt. "But you have crime," Colin said. "Every place has crime."

"Sure, of course we do. Had a rape a couple of years ago."

In Madison, they had over a hundred rapes in Colin's last year there before he'd transferred to Milwaukee. That was a much bigger city with a large university population, but still.

"Okay, what else?" Colin asked.

Simmons thought about it. "Car break-ins. The occasional DUI. Maybe three or four legit house burglaries a year. A couple of months ago, a guy torched his self-storage unit. Turned out he was going through a nasty divorce and wanted to burn all his wife's stuff."

Colin processed this. He supposed given Bury's size—just about seven thousand—it wasn't unusual to have such a low crime rate. He also knew the socioeconomic profile of the town had a lot to do with it. Affluent white folks were less inclined to commit crimes warranting a 911 call. The crimes likely being committed in Bury were the less obvious ones. Those involving offshore accounts, routing numbers, and shell corporations.

Then there were the vices of the rich.

"Does Bury have a drug problem?"

"Nah," Simmons said. "Not like Manchester or anything like that. Some heroin issues, some opioid abuse. Nothing off the charts. Other than that, yeah, we've busted some kids with coke at parties. Some pot. Nothing more than recreational. No large-scale dealers or anything."

"And murder?"

Simmons shook his head. "No, sir. At least not since I've been on the force the last two years. Had three suicides. One vehicular manslaughter. But no murders."

*Not that you know of,* Colin thought, not really knowing why that thought popped into his head.

"When was the last murder in Bury?"

Simmons thought about it a minute, then shook his head. "Can't say I know. Like I said, it's just not that kind of place."

Moments later, they arrived at the station. Colin had a couple hours before he had to leave for the airport, so he worked at an open desk and caught up with paperwork. He also spent some time chatting with Wallace Sike, the Bury chief of police. Sike had been around about a decade and mostly confirmed what Simmons had said.

"Ayuh, Bury's pretty quiet. Lower crime rate than Hillsborough County as a whole, that's for sure. We assist the other jurisdictions more than they assist us." Sike appeared on the edge of fifty and had a mustache as bushy as a raccoon tail, completely hiding his upper lip. His pronounced gut affirmed the fact that he didn't spend a lot of his day running down suspects. "But there've been murders over the years, no doubt about it. Can't think of any place without a murder every now and then. But ours are extremely few and far between."

"When was the last one?" Colin asked.

"Been seven years. Manchester is the murder capital of the county, but they only average about one homicide a year up there. Though a few years back, they had that whole Mister Tender mess. Not sure if you heard about that, but made national news."

Colin indeed remembered.

"Did you assist with that?" he asked.

"Nah. But I have a couple of buddies on the job up there. Said it was a major shit-show. Never seen anything like it."

"But the Bury murder, seven years ago?"

The expression on Sike's face passed from mild excitement to disappointment, as if he was embarrassed Bury didn't ever get its sensational killing spree.

"Drug deal gone bad. Out-of-town dealer meeting with his well-to-do Bury user. Dealer pumped three in the chest. Caught him a few hours later."

"And before that?"

"Before that what?"

"Other murders."

Sike leaned back in his chair, which squeaked in a violent protest to the assault. "Long before my time in the department."

Colin went with his gut, knowing there was something. There was *something* about Bury. If not outright malevolent, then at least mysterious. Suspicious. There are no perfect communities. Every town has a stain.

"How about way back, say ten or twenty years ago?" Colin asked. "Any major crimes in Bury? Any…I don't know…anything that got Bury a little attention beyond the town borders?"

Sike peered up into the acoustic ceiling tiles of the station, as if all the answers he ever wanted could be found in their thousands of craters. After taking a moment's reflection, he directed his gaze back to Colin.

"Missing kid. Back in the nineties. Sixteen-year-old boy named Caleb Benner. Never found him."

"A sixteen-year-old boy?" Colin said. "That's not a missing kid. That's a runaway."

"Ayuh, that's what most say. Not his family, though. Not his friends."

Colin crossed his arms over his chest, tucking his fingers into his armpits. "Were you here then?"

"Manchester. But we came down to help search. Mike Patterson was the lead on the case."

"Is he still on the job?"

Sike shook his head. "Heart attack killed him back in oh-nine."

"Do you remember the details of the case?"

"I do indeed."

Colin nodded over to the coffee machine in the back corner of their room.

"Buy you a cup of coffee if you tell me everything you know about it," he said.

"Coffee's free here," Sike said.

"It's the gesture that counts."

Sike grunted, which Colin took as an affirmation. Colin walked over to the pot, still half-full, and filled two paper cups. He took a sip from one, surprised that it tasted decent.

He walked back over and handed a cup to Sike, who offered another grunt.

Sike took his own sip, tilted back in his chair, and said, "Kid went missing on a Friday night."

It took about twenty minutes for Sike to tell Colin the story of a missing boy named Caleb Benner.

Afterward, Colin couldn't stop thinking about it.

# TWENTY-EIGHT

**October 25**

**IT'S SUNDAY NIGHT AND** I yearn for unconsciousness.

Over a week has passed since Pearson confronted me at Tuli's, which earned me two more sleepless nights and only a few hours a night since then. Now I've reached a point of such extreme anxiety and fatigue that I can barely hold a conversation, which is okay, since I don't want to talk to anyone anyway. But Max is wondering what's wrong with me, and all I can manage to tell him is I'm not feeling well. It didn't take long before my mood seeped into his, causing him to act out more than normal, lashing out whenever I asked him to do anything, even just putting on his shoes.

I can't write. I can't hold any attention at work, struggling to make it through my shifts. I canceled dinner plans with Cora last night and have been avoiding my father as much as possible.

After dinner, I slogged through a round of Sorry! with Max on the floor of his bedroom, happy to lose. He protested when I made him go to bed by nine (*Mom, it's Sunday!*), but I told him he could either read a book or go to sleep, and he chose to get under the covers with the final Harry Potter volume of the series. The world just might run out of books for him to read.

It's nearly ten now, and my thoughts drift beyond the mere need for sleep. To the wonder of what Riley felt as he slipped off for the last time. Probably nothing at all. But maybe there was a release, sweet and pure, that gave peace to his troubled soul. Maybe in those last seconds, he became a child again, innocent and uncorrupted.

I like to think so.

In my bathroom, I dig out two pill bottles from beneath my bathroom sink. Riley had a second stash of his sleep medications in his sock drawer and I kept them. How macabre is that?

I scrutinize the labels for the first time. One bottle is labeled diazepam, which I know is Valium. The pills are tiny and the blue of a robin's egg. The other bottle holds zolpidem—Ambien. The pills are a chalky yellow.

I take a pill from each bottle and sit on the bathroom floor, studying them. I've never taken any kind of medication like these before, though Riley had suggested it every now and then whenever I had trouble sleeping. But I recall what the meds did to him, making him fade into the night, slipstreaming into unconsciousness. He used to take one of each, saying the Ambien knocked him out and the Valium kept him there. I asked if the doctor said he should take them together, and Riley simply told me it was fine. That he'd done it enough times to know it was what worked for him.

Until it worked more than he expected.

I suppose everyone has these thoughts now and then. Moments

when we think about how easy it would be to make all our troubles go away. A shrink would likely tell me I was normal.

But what if I confessed I think about death more often than "every now and then"? That it comes to mind a few times each week, sometimes just as passing thoughts, dark clouds that float by after a minute or two. Other times sticking around longer. An hour. Maybe two. And all I can do is contemplate what it would be like to die. *To be in a state of death.*

Is that normal?

And here's the thing. I don't think of it as an escape from pain.

I think of it as a fantasy.

In those times when the thought lingers, I find myself imagining death as a long walk in a vast cornfield to find the edge of a late-afternoon rainbow. It's right after a summer rain, and there I am, barefoot and curious. Excited even. It's all so clear in my mind. In this image, my feet squish on the wet soil, and my nostrils take in the musty, earthy aroma of damp cornstalks. I push through perfect rows of army green, my arms wet with the raindrops coming off the husks, and the only sounds I hear are my own gentle movements as I ghost through the field.

In this image, the sky in front of me is purple-black, the color of a punishing bruise, and holds within it the storm that just passed over. Behind me, the sky is cloudless, and the brilliant sun illuminates the rainbow toward which I'm walking. The rainbow arches at the intersection of these two opposite skies, between the light and the dark, between the storm and the calm. There is such a defined crispness to this rainbow that it is impossible for it to be anything but tangible.

I'll be able to touch it. Seize it. I imagine it having a slightly spongy texture, as if made out of taffy that's been stretched for miles.

In this fantasy, death occurs the moment I touch the rainbow. I dissolve into it, am absorbed by it, and I become all those colors, the entire spectrum, forever.

I don't know why death occurs to me as such a beautiful thing, but this imagery appears in my mind each time I consider it, and it's always the same. Maybe there's so much guilt welled inside me that death represents a relief valve, something to take all that pressure away forever.

However, in my fantasy, I never allow myself to touch that candy rainbow. Even in my mind, I resist.

And now, sitting on this bathroom floor, staring at the two different-colored pills in the palm of my hand, my fantasy is to pour a few more from the vials and wash the lot of them down with that four-hundred-dollar whiskey, the top-shelf stuff. I want what Riley experienced, that beautiful drifting, a raft in the middle of a vast sea, the lightest of breezes carrying me slowly, softly, away. In this moment, I'm jealous of Riley. I envy him his death.

I think about it.

I can taste it almost.

And then I do what I always do. I force my thoughts to Max.

It needs to be about him. Him before me. Always.

So I take a deep breath, count to three, then exhale. I put the two pills back, place the vials back under the sink, then make my way to my bedroom.

Under the covers.

Close my eyes.

Wait for a sleep that may not come.

# TWENTY-NINE

**MY EYES STRAIN TO** see within the dark of the room. I may have been screaming.

Sweat covers me in a hot, thick glaze, as if my bed's just given birth to me. I'm not confused as to where I am—I'm here, in this house. And I'm not thankful to be awake after a nightmare—wakefulness is no shield from memory.

I reach back and wipe a layer of moisture from the back of my neck. Touch my pillow; it's soaked. Every time I have this dream, I must lose two pounds of water.

Whatever self-prescribed therapy I thought would work isn't. Writing about what happened only created more problems. Coming back to this house has only made the memories more vivid. Even sitting there, at the base of the stairs, apologizing to any ghosts willing to listen, hasn't made me whole. Still the dream comes.

There's too much guilt.

I reach over to the bedside table and grab my phone, squinting at the time. Just before three.

Grasp for my water bottle, take four huge gulps, replace some of what I lost.

I shimmy to the other side of the bed, where the sheets and pillow are as cool and dry as moonlight. I'm too awake to fall asleep, and I'm too physically drained to do anything but let my mind have its way with me. I won't be falling asleep again tonight. I rarely do when this happens, and never when the dream is as vivid as it just was.

So I lie here and silently scream as the claws of two decades ago reach around and tear me open.

# PART II

# THIRTY

**September 18**
**Twenty-Two Years Earlier**

**FRIDAY NIGHT. THE DIGITAL** clock on the kitchen microwave reads 8:19.

I'm fifteen years old and too exhausted to think about going out.

I've just been dropped off home from a later-than-usual JV soccer practice. I unload my school backpack and soccer gear in the kitchen and set about heating up the homemade mac and cheese left for us by Lucinda, our part-time housekeeper. The house is silent. I know Dad's not here... His car wasn't in the garage, and he usually doesn't even leave his office in Boston until after eight. Cora's car was in the driveway, but I don't hear her. Could be out with friends. The front door was locked when I arrived, though the security alarm hadn't been set. That's a little unusual.

All the sweat from the soccer drills has dried, leaving my skin with a salty top layer. My hair remains in a tight ponytail, the matted tip swishing against the back of my neck as I grab a Coke from the fridge. I need to shower, but food takes priority. Dinner, shower, TV, bed. Not an exciting Friday night, but it's what I want and need.

I scarf the meal in minutes, going for a second helping. Lucinda always adds bacon to the mac and cheese.

I've eaten too much too fast and sit for a good ten minutes in the kitchen doing nothing but silently digesting. A wave of fatigue washes over me, and I force myself upstairs to shower before I lose all motivation.

After the shower, I brush my hair out, knowing I'll sleep on it wet and it'll be a tangled mess in the morning. I put on an oversize Nirvana T-shirt and heavy sweatpants with the Tufts logo on the left leg. Tufts is Cora's first-choice college, and Dad bought us both a pair. Cora wants to stay close to home. My ideal school is located anywhere that requires a flight from here.

I end up choosing a book over a TV show. Stephen King's *Insomnia*, which is the latest in my collection of his. Another beast of a novel, nearly seven hundred pages. I'm a hundred in and like it but don't love it. There's plenty of story left for that to change.

The house is silent, and as happens every now and then, I might not see any of my family tonight. I'm completely comfortable all alone, often preferring it that way. I sometimes think I'm going to be like my father when I'm an adult. A solitary animal.

I've read about thirty more pages when that comforting sense of solitude turns into fear, without warning or reason. Nothing has changed except the thoughts in my mind. My coziness is now a chill. The silence has become a weight on my chest.

Why does my brain have to become a weapon against me?

I cast an eye down at the book in my lap.

*Damn you, Stephen King.*

I close the book.

The clock tells me it's a few minutes after nine.

I get up, knowing everything is fine but realizing I never set the house alarm. If I'm going to be alone as I fall asleep, I'm setting the alarm. Bury is safe, but I'm not jinxing anything.

I trot down the stairs from the third floor past the second, my feet cool against the hardwood steps. I catch a sudden scent on the final flight of stairs, a wisp of perfume.

Cora. She's wearing Calvin Klein's CK One, and its aroma is unmistakable.

Her room is on the second floor. My father's, on the main level. The fact that we all live on different levels of the house sums up our family perfectly. Comfortable. Distant. Wasteful.

I stop my descent.

"Cora?"

No response. Just the heavy silence from before. Maybe even heavier.

I wait for a moment. Two. Three. Four.

I'll check her room on the way back up.

Down to the first floor. Night has finally arrived, so I flip the switch for the chandelier that hangs over the foyer. Light pierces, cold and harsh. I make my way to the alarm keypad, just on the inside of the massive front door.

The alarm. It's on. Set to *Stay*.

I don't know why this unnerves me. Clearly either my dad or Cora came home and set the alarm when I was in the shower. No one called upstairs or came to my room to say hello, but that's not a shock. Sometimes I go two or three days without seeing my father.

I'll go and see if Cora's here. Must be her.

I turn around and start heading back up, leaving the chandelier light on. Someone else can turn it off later; I don't want to be in the dark anymore.

Halfway up the first flight of steps, it happens.

The scream.

An awful, primal, visceral scream.

It's not Cora. The tone is deeper.

It...it sounds like a man.

I'm frozen in total and absolute fear. The sound of the doorbell would have been enough to set me off, but the scream exists beyond my ability to reason. This must be a dream. I fell asleep with that stupid King book, and now I'm having a nightmare.

But I know that's not really true, which is the worst part of all.

No dream is as real as this.

The scream stops as quickly as it started, but it echoes in my mind. I don't know which way to go. Up the stairs? That's where the scream came from. Or down?

*Cora.*

Oh my god, something's happening to Cora.

I have to move. *I have to do something.*

But my limbs are locked, a rigor mortis of fear.

I squeeze my eyes closed for a second and tell myself this: *Push through the fear. This is the kind of moment that defines who you are. Who you'll be for the rest of your life, no matter how long or short it may be.*

My legs suddenly unlock, as if I suddenly touched a live electrical wire and reanimated. I race up the stairs to the second floor. I pause and flip on the hallway light switch. Five can lights blaze from above, illuminating the long second-floor hallway that ends at Cora's bedroom.

I'm thirty feet away from her closed door but can hear a fresh volley of noises coming from behind it. Groaning mixed with short, staccato shouting. It doesn't sound like Cora. It sounds like...

Like a monster.

My fear of opening that door is only quelled by my need to help my sister. I'm just about to race down the hallway when Cora's bedroom door opens.

A man.

No, not a man.

A boy. Teenager.

And...I know him. His face is distorted in terror, but I still recognize him.

He goes to my school. A senior, like Cora.

He spots me and his eyes widen, then he extends his arms as if he's bobbing in a stormy sea and I'm a life raft just out of reach.

His name is Caleb. Caleb Benner.

His body is soaked in blood. White T-shirt. Bare arms. Crotch of his jeans.

All blood.

He lunges toward me. Stumbling on unsteady feet. Bloodied right hand printing the wall as he tries to keep from falling.

"Help me."

His voice is a gurgle.

The rigor mortis sets in again. I'm unable to move as he scrambles down the hallway toward me.

Then I see her.

Cora, in the doorway. Materializes like a ghost.

And this thing. This tiny little thing that's scarier than the blood or the gurgling, the lunging or the prints. Even more horrifying than the scream.

It's the smile.

Cora's smiling. Gentle, genuine.

As if posing for her yearbook photo.

# THIRTY-ONE

**October 31**
**Present Day**

**I'M NOT IN A** festive mood, but when you're a single parent of an eleven-year-old who has no friends and a passion for Halloween, you can't escape trick-or-treating responsibilities.

In Milwaukee, we always decorated the inside of our apartment and then trick-or-treated in a nearby neighborhood. Max always loved running up to each house and inspecting their decorations. He was fascinated by any kind of special effects, even if it was just a cheap Walmart fog machine. But his favorite thing was a person on their front porch dressed up as a prop who'd suddenly animate and terrify the approaching kids.

My father doesn't decorate for Halloween. He never has. Nor does he ever hand out candy. When I was a little girl, I asked him why he didn't. I was maybe five years old, but his answer stays with me.

*Fuck 'em.*

I think it was the first time in my life I'd ever heard the word *fuck*. I had to ask Cora what it meant. Somehow, she knew.

Tonight, we're again visiting another neighborhood for our Halloween festivities. Cora and Willow are joining, and she suggested Arlington Estates, which she said has become the Halloween go-to area in Bury. I didn't object. Arlington Estates is where Alec lives, and the thought of him makes me happy. Not giddy, just happy. A simple, pleasant, smell-of-fresh-baked-bread kind of happiness.

Max is dressed as a classic vampire, and he chews on his plastic fangs as we wait at the agreed-upon street corner in Arlington Estates. Cora finally shows up with Willow in tow. Max and I get out of our car, and the night instantly chills me. The air is so distinct on Halloween night here in Bury. Isn't that strange? My childhood comes rushing back. Going house to house with Cora, screaming, laughing, screaming more.

The realization of how we all change injects me with bitter nostalgia, making me wish I couldn't recall my past.

Cora rushes up, pulling her coat tighter around her shoulders. "We would have been here earlier if Willow hadn't been so dramatic about wanting to go out with friends."

"Jesus, Mom, I'm thirteen," Willow says, who, if I had to guess, I'd say is dressed as a zombie slut. Dark makeup around the eyes, mussed hair, and a thin, bloodstained T-shirt that has strategic tears in it, allowing me to see her bra and belly button. "We had *plans*."

"Your plans changed," Cora snaps.

Willow rolls her eyes and belts out a huff. Then she looks at Max. "Vampire, huh? Super creative."

Max doesn't respond but just stares at and beyond her, and I realize he's drifted off again. I wonder what the cause is this time. When he's had these moments before, I've asked him afterward what he was thinking about, and he always mumbles *nothing*. It's almost as if he loses time for a few seconds, his brain fast-forwarding past a bad memory.

"What's up with you, freak?" Willow says.

"Don't talk to him like that," I say to my niece. Then I touch Max's arm. "Hey, buddy, you okay?"

When he doesn't reply, I give his arm a little squeeze, just short of a pinch. This stirs him from his reverie and he looks up to me. "Her blood looks real."

"You know it's not, though, right? It's all make believe."

He blinks, and in his eyes, I don't see reassurance. I see fear. "I know," he says.

This is not usual for him. Max loves Halloween, gory costumes and all. But somehow the sight of Willow's weak attempt at horror has him on edge.

Cora claps her gloved hands together and beams a plastic smile. "Well, then, this should be fun. Shall we start?"

I kneel in front of my son. "You okay?"

"Yes."

This is the first Halloween without his father, a reality that has to be swirling inside him.

"Okay, let's go get some candy," I say.

"You don't need to come," he says, and before I can even argue, he runs off to the nearest house, his plastic pumpkin candy pail jostling in his right hand. One moment, he seems scared; the next, he runs off into the night without me. I try so hard to understand him, and just as I think I'm getting close, something happens to make us feel more disconnected than ever.

Willow starts to follow Max when Cora says, "Did you even bring anything to put candy in?"

Willow turns to her mom, cups her hands together for a second, then continues after Max.

Cora watches her walk up to the house and says to me, "If she's this bad at thirteen, what will the next five years be like?"

"Hell," I say, meaning it. Kind of hoping it.

It's just after seven and trick-or-treating is in full force in Arlington Estates. Squeals, screams, and laughter come from all directions and distances, and roving packs of costumed kids litter the streets and sidewalks. About half the packs have adults with them, many of whom have wineglasses.

"Did you bring anything to drink?" Cora asks.

"No, I didn't even think about it."

"Great."

The air is still but cold on my cheeks. I tug on my wool hat, bringing it further down over my ears.

Max comes racing back from the house and nearly runs into me. His fangs are bared, which is good because that means he's smiling.

"What'ya get?" I ask.

With a heavy lisp from his fake teeth, he mumbles, "Full-size Snickers."

"Wow," I say. "Good stuff." He seems to be past whatever fear he was having a few minutes ago.

Willow comes up holding her own candy bar, and I think I see a trace of a smile on her face. She's trying hard not to admit having fun, but there's still a child inside her.

"Aren't you cold, Willow?" I ask.

She shrugs. "Not really."

"She refused to wear a coat, and I got sick of arguing," Cora says.

Max races away while we follow on the sidewalk. Willow stays with us on the sidewalk for a couple of houses before finally joining him.

As soon as Cora and I are alone, she starts in on me.

"So people are talking about you," she says.

"What?"

"You know what," she says. "Apparently some cop from Milwaukee came here to talk to you?"

*Tasha*. I was wondering when this moment was going to come.

"He's just closing out the case on Riley," I say. "It's nothing."

"Nothing?" Cora's voice is sharp. Piercing. "A cop comes all the way out from Milwaukee, and you don't even think to tell me?"

"It has nothing to do with you."

Max comes suddenly bounding back like a golden retriever puppy, updates me on his loot, then slips back into the night. I don't know where Willow is.

Once he's out of earshot, Cora says, "Anything that involves this family and the police affects me. Affects Dad."

"Cora, I—"

She whips her face toward me. "First, you lose your mind at the book club. And now some cop is here asking questions? People are saying all sorts of things."

"Things like what?"

She leans in and lowers her voice. "What do you think, Rose? That you *did it*. That you killed Riley."

"I didn't—"

She cuts me off. "I don't want to know. Don't even tell me, because I don't want to have to lie for you. But that's what people are saying. I know personally of three people who went out and bought your book after all this talk started. They wanted to read the scene where the husband is killed by the wife. So good for you. More sales."

My head is swimming. How did this all spiral out of control so quickly?

"Tasha," I say.

"What?"

"Tasha Collins."

"That horrible girl from high school?"

"Yeah, she's still horrible," I say. "And I think she lives near Dad, because she walked her dog in front of the house."

The impatience is obvious on Cora's face.

"So?"

"So this was right after the cop left the house, after he interviewed me. He was sitting in his cruiser with local PD when she walked by."

"Great," Cora says. "She's probably fueling all this. Between that and the book club freak-out, everyone thinks you're a killer."

"I can't control what people think."

"Don't act so helpless," she snaps. "The Riley situation is not my problem. Your last book doesn't concern me. What *does* concern me is your new one. Did you change it?"

I clench my gloved fists into balls, then release, over and over. It doesn't relieve any tension.

"My editor said it was too late."

"*Fuck.*"

Willow appears out of nowhere, more like a ghost rather than a zombie. It's clear she just heard her mother.

"Geez, what's your problem?" she asks.

"Nothing." Cora sucks in a breath and holds it, as if trying to ground herself. After she releases it into a sigh, she says, "How's trick-or-treating?"

"Lame. I'm too old for this."

"But you were planning to do this very thing with your friends," Cora says.

Willow shrugs. "That's different."

"Well, why don't you hit a few more houses? Your aunt and I need to finish a conversation."

"Whatever," Willow says. "Sorry to *intrude*." She turns and walks away into the street and away from the houses, and it strikes me how vulnerable my niece is. That she's too young to be dressed like that and just walking away into the night. I want to call her back, tell her to stay with us, but I don't. I watch her drift away as Cora launches another volley at me.

"Maybe you're not understanding all this, so let me break it down for you." Cora stops walking and pulls my arm so I turn and face her. Her breath fogs my face as she talks. "There are rumors about how your husband might have died because of a scene in your current book. Those rumors are now viral in this town because a cop is talking to you about Riley."

"I said it was nothing."

Cora bulldozes over my comment. "And now your next book comes out in a few months, and in that book, there's a scene in which a teenage boy dies in the house of two teenage sisters. At the base of the fucking stairs. And you don't think that's a problem?"

"You're overreacting," I say, not because it's true but because I know it'll piss her off even more, which I can't help but want in this moment.

"Either you're an idiot or playing the part exceptionally well," she says.

Something shifts inside me where I no longer care about crafting a perfect argument. I don't want to hurt Cora with words. I want something more. I reach down and grab her wrist. She tries to pull away, but my grip tightens, squeezing her bones through my glove as hard as I can.

"Ow, *Jesus*. Let go."

"Don't talk to me like that," I say. "I've had enough of you telling me what to do."

She yanks again and gets nowhere. I keep my fingers in their vise grip, and I know it still hurts, though she's not giving me the satisfaction of admitting to it anymore.

For a moment, I think she's going to hit me. I can see it in her face, her darting eyes full of fight-or-flight indecision. And in this moment, I want her to. I want her to take a swing, because I'll take her down. I will take my sister right to the ground, and I won't shed a tear.

I see the moment she realizes this very thing, because her gaze lowers to the ground and her arm goes limp. I let go of her wrist and she immediately takes a step back.

"We all know you were always the violent one, Rose." Cora manages a feeble smirk.

"That's not true at all."

"Sure, it is. After all, you were the one who killed Caleb Benner."

The name smashes into me, and I think it's the first time I've heard it from my sister's mouth in at least ten years. I turn my head to see if anyone is in eavesdropping range, but no one is. Still, what a foolish thing to say out loud. Foolish, and a lie.

"You know that's not true," I say. "*You* were the one."

Now the feeble smirk blossoms into a hearty smile. "That's not how I remember it. And that's not the way I'm going to describe it to the police once they come asking questions after your book comes out." She must be certain I'm not going to attack, because she takes a step closer. "You're the one putting us all at risk," she adds. "I need to take measures to protect myself."

The desire to hurt my own sister almost overpowers me, and for a moment, I see our similarities more than our differences. I resist my primal urges but stand my ground. Then I lean in closer, because I want her to smell the fury on me.

"How goddamn dare you," I whisper. "What *you* did that night has bled onto every part of my life. Every decision I've made since then has been influenced by what you did. You think I studied criminal justice on a whim? That I became a mystery writer because I love plotting out fictional murders? That I came home because I missed my morally bankrupt family? Every fucking thing I do in this world is done to either avoid or confront my past, but I can never just *be*. All I want to do is just *be*, and I can't. That's what you've done to me. I know you don't understand because you have no conscience, much less a soul. I can't change the past, but I sure as hell won't let you change the story about what happened that night. No. Fucking. Way."

Max comes up again, startling me to the point that I almost scream. I look down at him, not even getting the satisfaction of seeing Cora's reaction to my words.

"I want to go home," he says, tugging my arm.

"Max, quit pulling on me." My voice is harsher than I want it to be, but I'm not in a gentle space right now.

"I don't like it here," he says.

"You just started. What's wrong?"

"Everything is stupid."

His plastic teeth are missing, likely spit onto someone's lawn. And nothing's stupid. It's a code word he uses when he's uncomfortable, overwhelmed, or scared. The brief joy he had at trick-or-treating has vanished.

But I need to finish this conversation with Cora. Otherwise, it'll burn into my skin all night, like acid. I reach out and spin him around until he's facing the opposite side of the street. "Can you do one last house? Have you done this house yet?" I point, and as I do, I suddenly realize it's Alec's house that Cora and I have been arguing across the street from. My gaze wanders from the patch of grass where I tripped and fell, then to the front porch, which is adorned with at least a dozen jack-o'-lanterns.

"Okay, last one, but it looks stupid, too," Max says and starts crossing the street.

"Wait," I say. "I'll go with you."

He turns. "Why?"

Because the only thing more important than skewering my sister is seeing someone who makes me smile. "Alec lives there. Micah's dad. I want to say hi."

Alec probably isn't even home. Most likely, he's out with Micah doing the same thing I am, minus the horrifying familial argument.

Cora waits back on the far sidewalk, looking up and down the dark street. I walk a step behind Max, as if treating him like a shield. Up the sidewalk, to the door. We're the only ones here, though I spy a group of four kids coming from the house next door.

Max rings the bell and it's only seconds before it opens.

Alec.

A wave of comfort washes over me, and it's something I cannot explain. It's as if I've found the one good person in Bury, the one person who won't judge, won't blame, won't gossip, and won't look at me for anyone else than who I am. I have no idea if any of that is true, but his energy conveys that, and I don't want to argue myself out of it.

Especially now, when I'm still so frazzled from what Cora just said. How she's actively planning to blame me for what happened to Caleb.

He looks at me first, and the second the recognition hits, the smile comes out, wide and genuine.

"Rose," he says.

"Trick or treat."

Alec's gaze is pulled away by Max's voice. He looks down at my son and says, "Well, hey there, Max. You just missed Micah. He went out with some of the other sixth graders." Alec steps out onto the porch and looks down the street. "They're probably not too far. You could catch up to them pretty easily."

Max shrugs. "We're going home after your house."

"So early?" Alec steps back into his house, grabs a couple of candy bars, and drops them into Max's pail. "If I'm your last house, then I'll give you two. How's that sound?"

"Okay."

Alec turns to me and leans against his doorframe.

"So, Rose, how are—"

"Do you want to go out sometime?"

I don't know how it happened. The words just came out, sure as if I was just speaking them in my head. But I heard them, and clearly he did, too, because Alec's eyes widen and humiliation threatens to buckle my legs.

I try to recover, throwing out words as fast as I can. Certainly more than the situation needs. "Not like that," I say. "I mean, not *not* like that, but really not like that. I don't know why I even asked you. I'm so sorry. I just thought, I don't know, you seem like you'd be easy to talk to. But I hardly know you. But you *did* give me your number, so I was just thinking..."

I look down at Max and he stares at me, wide-eyed, more confused than even I probably am.

If there's ever a moment for a deep, grounding breath, it's now, so I take it. Even close my eyes for a second. After I let it go and open my eyes, I force myself to look Alec directly in his eyes.

"I could use a friend," I tell him. "That's all I was trying to say. You have no idea how much I could use a friend."

He says nothing for a few agonizing seconds, after which he offers a gentle smile.

Finally, he says, "Yeah, I'd like that. I could use a friend, too."

# THIRTY-TWO

**Whitefish Bay, Wisconsin**
**November 1**

**WHEN COLIN CAME OVER** to his mother's house, she wasn't nearly done with her ranting. He'd let himself in, expecting her to be upstairs in her bedroom, medicated by gin and edging close to sleep. But she was in a small carpeted alcove next to the dining room, the spot where his parents always sat after his father came home from work. The place where they had a drink and discussed their respective days. This was a fixture as Colin grew up, and as a boy, he often joined them, munching on the homemade Chex Mix his mom always had out. As he grew older, Colin was less likely to be part of the weeknight ritual and more apt to be up in his room doing homework or out with friends. But he always had good memories, thinking of his parents together in this room, sometimes talking, other times sitting silently and just being together in a harmonious way that only happens when no one says a word.

Now, those memories felt like they belonged to someone else. It was just after eight in the evening, and the house had just enough lights on so Colin could navigate around the piles of junk. There was his mother, pacing back and forth in the alcove like a caged panther, all tension and no space, the ambient light rendering her ghostlike. She figure-eighted around stacks of magazines, an old lamp, and three barstools, muttering to herself as she paced, not even acknowledging Colin's arrival.

"Goddamn fucking Bryson," she said. "Bryson took our money." She repeated variants of this same thing three times before Colin flicked on the alcove light, stopping her in her tracks.

"Who's Bryson?" he asked. It didn't really matter to him, but Colin had learned sometimes having her tell him about the subject of her latest outrage was enough to calm her down.

She looked at him with wide eyes and an accusatory look, as if not knowing Bryson was a crime.

"Jerry Fucking Bryson, that's who," she said. "Your father worked with him for a few years before Bryson left to start some shithole company decades ago. What did he call it?" She looked around, as if the answer were painted on one of the walls. Then she snapped her head back to Colin. "Craytronics. Yes, that was it. He thought he was *so* smart. Smart enough to convince your father to invest ten thousand dollars. Bryson promised we'd be millionaires within a decade."

Colin had never heard this story before, but it didn't take a detective to see where it was headed.

"Wasn't even five years before that goddamn company was out of business and our money gone with it. Fucking Bryson didn't even apologize to us. Said we knew what we were getting into."

"That's terrible," Colin said.

"It's a crime," she replied.

"How many drinks have you had?"

"Not enough."

He sighed, expecting that answer.

"Pour me one more, will you, sweetie?" Her voice was suddenly sweet and light. Her daytime voice. "That'll calm these nerves, I'm certain."

"What you need is medication," Colin said.

"I'm not a junkie," she snapped, falling back into the anger she had unleashed for the memory of Bryson. She steadied herself, took a breath, and said, "Just one more. Sit with me for one more. Then I'll go to bed."

Colin wrestled with his conscience one more time, and once again, he did as he was asked. He would pour her a drink, just as he'd surely give her morphine were she dying of cancer.

"One more," he said. "Where's your glass?"

"Kitchen counter."

Colin burrowed his way to the kitchen, found the glass, and grabbed the gin from the counter. Then he grabbed a beer out of the refrigerator, one of a twelve-pack he'd brought for himself last week. She didn't touch his booze, and he didn't touch hers.

They sat in the alcove, in the chairs where his parents sat together thousands of times, sipping their drinks in silence. Over a period of several minutes, Jackie settled her bones deeper into the well-worn fabric chair, slipping into what appeared a numbness, a memory, and a fog all rolled together. Her gaze fixed on the far wall, and a hint of a lazy smile grew on her lips.

Finally, she said, "Tell me about your day, Thomas."

His father's name rang odd to his ears, but not as much as it used to. She'd referred to Colin by her dead husband's name a half-dozen times by now.

Unsure at first how to respond, Colin choose to simply answer her question.

"I'm investigating this woman. Rose Yates. She's the reason I had to leave town a couple of weeks ago, remember?"

His mother continued to stare straight ahead but shook her head. "No, I don't remember you traveling for work."

He'd spoken in bits and pieces about Rose Yates to his mother, but she always had trouble recalling things at night. Were they having this conversation in the morning, Colin was sure she'd know exactly who he was talking about.

So he started from the beginning, from the moment he was assigned the Riley McKay case. He took his time, filling in all the details, as he knew she was comforted by the company. It also benefited him, because hashing the case out aloud helped him identify weaknesses and potential opportunities.

She said nothing, and Colin briefly wondered if she thought she was listening to her husband speak about his day at work and why on earth he was investigating a potential murder. Or maybe she was already lost in some other world, one Colin would someday know but couldn't comprehend now, a world of spiderwebs and smoke, a mind lost.

All he knew was he was talking to himself, and that was okay. Colin finished his beer and grabbed another. His mother was still nursing her last drink, a good sign she was done for the night.

Sitting back down, he said, "Truth is, I don't have enough to warrant extradition back to Wisconsin. And no, I don't really believe she'd be so bold as to directly mimic a murder scene from one of her books. I'm not even as convinced as I was before that she did it. But the amount of Ambien and Valium in Riley McKay's system was clearly enough to put someone at the very least in a coma, even without alcohol. And I'm having a hard time seeing this as suicide. Especially given that he confirmed weekend plans with a friend that same night."

Her voice jolted Colin from his thoughts. "Only idiots and junkies mix alcohol and medications." She sipped her gin.

"And murderers," Colin added.

She fell silent for a good thirty seconds before remarking, "It's the Day of the Dead."

"What?"

His mother finally looked over at him, her eyes now only half-open. "Today. It's Day of the Dead. November 1."

"Oh. Okay."

"The dead all rise today."

He took her creepy statement in stride. "Well, there're just a few hours left in the day. They better get to it."

"Cheers to that," she said, taking another sip of her drink.

The idea of the rising dead made Colin think of Caleb Benner, the sixteen-year-old who went missing in Bury over twenty years ago. Caleb was certainly dead, Colin figured. There'd been no trace of him, no real leads, and it had been so long. Caleb Benner was surely one of the rising dead today.

Colin began telling his mother about that case and how it was the only unsolved missing-persons case in the past half century in Bury.

"High-school senior. Jock. Popular kid, a bit of a reputation, but sounds like he was well liked overall. Went to a party on a Friday night and left early. He was never seen again." He rubbed the back of his neck, easing the tension that'd been building up more and more over the past few weeks. "All the kids who had been at the party were interviewed, but no one remembered much of anything. The police thought maybe he left early with someone else, but no one could say for sure. Or maybe he left alone and just ran into the wrong person on his way home. But Caleb didn't sound like the kind of kid just to leave a party early."

He turned to his mother, whose eyes were now closed, drink still in hand. "And here's the thing," he said, "the only thing that stands out to me on this. There were fifteen kids at that party, all of them interviewed. And one of them was Cora Yates, the sister of Rose."

That thought bounced around in his brain as it had been ever since he learned of that fact. Seventeen-year-old Cora Yates was interviewed in connection with the disappearance of Caleb Benner over two decades ago. Now, the younger sister, Rose, was a person of interest in the overdose death of Riley McKay. Rose wrote about a similar overdose murder in one of her novels.

Was there a connection, or just mere coincidence?

Then something clicked in Colin's mind. Something that hadn't clicked until this very moment.

Had Rose Yates, *J. L. Sharp*, ever written about a sixteen-year-old boy? One who went missing or was murdered?

Before he could mull over this question any longer, he heard the front door opening.

A voice called out, "Hello?"

Meg.

"In the dining room," Colin called out. He expected his voice to jolt his mother, but her eyes remained closed. He reached over and grabbed the drink out of her hand, setting it on a coaster. She mumbled a soft and sleepy *thank you*.

Colin's wife walked into the dining room, nearly knocking over a stack of boxes.

"Didn't expect you to come over," Colin said. He glanced at her seven-month-pregnant belly. "Everything okay?"

"Everything's fine. I just felt like getting some air."

Colin nodded at his mother. "Just about to get her to bed. You ready to go up, Mom?"

She sighed. "I suppose so." She fluttered her eyes open and looked at Meg. "Well, hello."

It was such a distant-sounding greeting, Colin thought. He wondered if, in this moment, she even knew who Meg was.

"Hi, Jackie."

"Okay, Mom, let's get you upstairs," Colin said.

Jackie began to stir as Meg looked around, taking in the house and seeming to sense the true chaos of it for the first time.

"We need to get this place cleaned up," Meg said.

Colin thought the comment a pebble in a canyon. "Ya think?"

"I mean it. Even just a little bit." She turned her head to her mother-in-law. "Jackie, how about I help you organize your place. How does that sound?"

His mother walked past her and slowly ambled up the stairs, carefully stepping around the obstacles on each riser. She never answered Meg's question.

Colin turned to Meg. "What're you doing? You can't help her clean up this place. You're almost eight months pregnant."

"Not me. I mean, I could help direct things, but maybe she'll let me bring a cleaning crew in. You know, like those Got Junk? guys."

"She tells me no every time I suggest it," Colin said.

"Which is maybe why I should be the one making the suggestion. Maybe she'll respond better to me."

"I don't know, Meg. I don't think you should—"

"She needs her dignity," Meg said. "She's lucid in the day. Do you know how awful it must be when she's sober and lucid and sees what her life's become? It's not safe with all this mess, but moreover, it's no way for the woman to spend the last part of her life."

Colin let her words sink in, and after he did, he felt a good degree of shame that he'd never considered his mother's dignity as part of the whole equation.

"Well, I suppose if you can convince her, that'd be great," he said. "And very appreciated."

"I'll talk to her tomorrow." Meg nodded at the staircase. "Make sure she gets to bed. I'll wait here… I'm not navigating those stairs."

"Agreed."

"Then let's walk around the neighborhood," she said. "I just want the air and…I don't know. The stars. I don't want to just sit on the couch tonight. I'm feeling…"

"Feeling what?" he asked.

"I'm not sure." She walked up to him and kissed him. "There aren't that many days left we can walk around the neighborhood, just the two of us."

He felt himself smiling. "There are such things as babysitters, you know."

"I don't mean like that," she said. "I mean soon we're going to be parents. And then we'll never *not* be parents. I still want to do some things as not-parents. I don't know why, but that's important."

"A walk sounds nice," Colin said.

As he climbed the stairs and made his way to his mother's room, Colin thought about what Meg said, about how they would soon never be not-parents.

So much permanence attached to it.

But this thought was transient, and by the top riser, he'd returned to what had been swirling through his mind when Meg walked in. His thoughts about Rose Yates.

There were two things he needed to read, Colin thought.

Just two things.

One: the decades-old transcript of Cora Yates's interview in the aftermath of Caleb Benner's disappearance.

And two: anything written by J. L. Sharp that he hadn't already read.

# THIRTY-THREE

**TRANSCRIPT OF INTERVIEW—(SC)**

Interviewee: Cora Davis Yates (minor)
Investigator: Det. Michael Patterson
Bury Police Dept.
In attendance: Logan Yates (father of interviewee)
Date of interview: September 20, 1995
Re: Case 76887-A

MP: Okay, for the record, today is Sunday, September 20, 14:37 hours. I'm at 1734 Rum Hill Road in Bury, New Hampshire, speaking with Cora Yates. Logan Yates, Cora's father, is also in attendance. After this interview, I'll be speaking with Cora's younger sister, Rose. Cora, I just want to remind you you're not in any trouble, okay?

CY: Okay.

MP: Our only focus here is finding Caleb. That's the goal. We're talking to everyone who was at the party Friday night, and I want you to tell me everything you remember. And I'm not going to care about underage drinking or anything like that.

LY: Were you drinking?

MP: Mr. Yates, please, this will go much faster if you let me ask the questions.

LY: *(unintelligible)* a question.

MP: I understand. Cora, can you tell me where you were Friday night?

CY: I was at Ron Finch's house.

MP: Why were you there?

CY: He was having some kids over.

MP: How many kids?

CY: I don't know, maybe fifteen of us. Twenty.

MP: What time did you arrive?

CY: Maybe seven. A little after.

MP: How did you get there?

CY: I walked. It's just a couple blocks away.

MP: Did you arrive with anyone?

CY: No. I was going to meet my friend Debbie there. She didn't show up.

MP: Why not?

CY: *(four seconds of silence)* I think her parents didn't let her. Not really sure.

MP: Was Caleb Benner at the house when you arrived?

CY: Yeah, I think so. Yeah, he was. For sure.

MP: You think so, or he was for sure?

CY: For sure.

MP: What was he doing?

CY: *(six seconds of silence)* I don't know. Hanging out. Talking with people.

MP: Drinking?

CY: Yeah. Everyone was.

LY: Detective, they're just kids. It was just a regular party.

MP: Please, Mr. Yates. Cora, did you notice anything unusual about Caleb? Was he in a weird mood? Did he seem angry? Scared? Drunk?

CY: *(eight seconds of silence)* No.

MP: Okay, I see. That's good, thank you. Now, a few other kids said they saw you and Caleb talking. What were you talking about?

CY: I don't know. Just stuff.

MP: What kind of stuff?

LY: She said she didn't know.

MP: Mr. Yates, I'm going to ask you again to not interrupt, please. I know this interview is only happening at your discretion, and I appreciate that. But the focus here is finding Caleb. Your daughter isn't in any kind of trouble. Cora, anything you can remember about your conversation would be helpful.

CY: I need some water. *(unintelligible)* I'm going to go get some and I'll be back, okay?

MP: Of course. We can take a little break.

*(eleven seconds of silence)*

LY: Detective, this just feels wrong. It's like she's being interrogated.

MP: I know what you're feeling, Mr. Yates. I don't know how else to assure you she's not. Look at it this way: If she were the one missing, wouldn't you want us talking to every person she interacted with the night she disappeared?

LY: Yes. Yes, of course. It's just that—

MP: It's fine, Mr. Yates. I don't have too many more questions. We'll wrap up soon. *(seven seconds of silence)* You mind if we move this somewhere else? Maybe the kitchen? The fumes are getting to me a little. What is that, paint?

LY: *(four seconds of silence)* Wood stain.

MP: House projects?

LY: We had some contractors touching up some of the worn parts of the flooring yesterday. Some of the stairs. Sorry about the smell. I guess I've gotten used to it.

MP: No need to apologize. I've always had a sensitive nose.

*End of transcript*

# THIRTY-FOUR

**Milwaukee, Wisconsin**
**November 3**

**THAT WAS IT. FOR** some reason, the transcript just ended with Cora going to the kitchen and getting some water while Detective Patterson and Logan Yates discussed house projects. Maybe the battery died on the recorder. Perhaps Logan Yates used his power of persuasion to keep the rest of the conversation off the record. Whatever the reason, Colin felt like he'd read the first half of a mystery story and was denied the satisfaction of an ending.

But what he had read pulsed tiny bursts of electricity through his skin. To a lay person, the transcript was dull. But to Colin, someone who'd become increasingly intrigued with the Yates family history, it was like unveiling an entombed artifact, one that would surely provide clues about who these people were.

The first thing to hit Colin was the odd fact that he and Detective Michael Patterson each conducted interviews of the separate Yates sisters twenty-two years apart in the Bury family home. That itself didn't yield any new information, but what were the odds? They'd both sat in the living room and asked the women about their involvement with a potential crime.

Of course, it was clear Cora Yates wasn't a suspect, just a witness. Patterson outright stated that, and there was nothing in the transcript to infer otherwise.

What *had* struck Colin as a red flag was how quickly Cora stopped the interview and left the room within just minutes. Patterson would have made sure the interviewee was comfortable when they began, likely suggesting she get something to eat or drink. Anything to relax her. So Cora leaving the room to get a drink was clearly a chance to regroup. And it came right after Patterson asked her what she and Caleb Benner had discussed.

No one would likely ever know the answer to that. Cora was probably the only person still alive who could say. But through his conversation with Chief Sike from the Bury PD and after reading the transcripts from some of the other kids at the party that night, Colin had pieced together the last known hours of Caleb Benner's contact with anyone.

Caleb Benner, sixteen, was one of eighteen kids to show up at Ron Finch's house for an impromptu Friday-night party. Finch's parents were only out for dinner and a game night with friends, so all the kids knew the party was going to start and end early, and Finch had enlisted Caleb's help in cleaning up any trace of the party before the parents came home. But Caleb had started drinking, and Finch said he knew early on he couldn't rely on him to help, so he asked another friend instead.

After a few drinks, Caleb apparently told his friend Rick Mastington he wanted to try to get alone with Cora. That he was attracted to her and thought she felt the same way. Mastington didn't think Cora and Caleb knew each other well and figured it was the alcohol talking. But sure enough, Mastington (and others) witnessed Caleb walk up to Cora, pull her away from the friends she was talking to, and lean in as they had a private, side conversation. This lasted until just before 8:00 p.m., at which point Caleb abruptly left the party alone. In his interview, Mastington told the police that wasn't necessarily unusual. Caleb was known to be aloof and often would break away from a group to be alone. Mastington figured he'd struck out with Cora and left the party sulking.

Without any further transcripts from Cora, Colin could only assume whatever else she'd told the police didn't shed any further light on where Caleb went after the party. If Cora and Caleb had gotten together after the party, that would likely have made her the last person to see him alive. That fact would certainly have been noted in the cold-case file, which it wasn't.

Caleb wasn't reported as seen by anyone else after he left Ron Finch's house. He was reported missing by his parents around eight the following morning. Twelve hours after that, the search parties commenced. Over the following weeks, volunteers—many of them high-school students—searched parks, fields, and the vast woods that encased large swaths of the town. Divers from a search-and-rescue team checked the Bury reservoir. Flyers printed and posted. Nightly TV coverage from the Manchester network affiliates. Caleb's case even earned a segment on *America's Most Wanted*.

But nothing.

Not a single clue. Not a substantive lead. Nothing.

Caleb Benner vanished as completely as if he'd never existed in the first place. Four months later, the police announced they would be keeping the case open but suspected the teen was more likely a runaway than a victim.

After all his research into the case, Colin didn't necessarily agree with the assessment. Usually there was a telltale sign of a runaway. Kids talk, and at least one of Caleb's friends would have known something. But every single person expressed genuine shock at Caleb's disappearance.

Colin checked—Caleb's parents still lived in Bury, though they'd moved to a different house. Outskirts of town. What an awful thing, Colin thought. All those years. Just wondering. Waiting. Hoping for as long as you could, then losing hope along with your child.

Through all his research, Colin kept coming back in his mind to Cora Yates. And that made him think of Rose Yates.

These two.

Sisters of Bury.

Their protective father.

A disappearance twenty-two years ago.

A possible homicide four months ago.

All connected by the Yates name.

Without too much difficulty, Colin had been able to download the advance reader's copy of J. L. Sharp's upcoming book, *The Child of the Steps*. This was the only one of Rose Yates's books he hadn't read, and he planned to start reading it on his Kindle that night.

*Step*, Colin thought.

The word made him flash back to the end of Cora's transcript, where Logan Yates mentioned having parts of the wood flooring and stairs refinished. It made him remember his brief time in the sprawling house on Rum Hill Road and how the energy inside its walls unsettled him, like a low wave of radiation.

Then he thought, *Who only refinishes* part *of a floor?*

# THIRTY-FIVE

**Bury, New Hampshire**
**November 6**

**I'VE REACHED ENOUGH OF** a buzz to calm my nerves. It's taken almost two whiskeys. Alec is still on his first beer.

A half hour ago, I walked into Rust, a tapas bar on the west side of Bury. Such an ugly name. *Rust*. Especially when combined with *Bury*.

Alec was waiting for me at the bar. Thin gray sweater, snug. Black denim jeans, spotless leather shoes. I hugged him like an old friend, and when I did, I had a moment of wanting to never let go. I forced myself to push the moment away rather than let it escape from me, just to give myself a little control over something.

On Halloween night, I told Alec I could use a friend to talk to, but the truth is I almost canceled tonight. I had the dream again last night, and with everything else in my head, I'm being turned inside out. I'm not sleeping well, have lost a good bit of my appetite, and am trying to quell my anxiety by running miles on end, the combination of which is threatening to crumble my sanity and my bones into dust.

At the last minute, I opted to keep the date. *The hell with it,* I thought. *I look like shit and am barely keeping things together. I need someone to see the real me.*

So here I am with this man who is little more than a stranger, and I have this incessant, looping thought that he's the only person in the world who can save me from myself. I don't even know what that means, but the irrationality of the thought does nothing to keep it from fading.

We've spent the last thirty minutes with pleasant small talk, of which I've been letting him do the most. During a brief lull in the conversation, he clears his throat and asks, "How are you, Rose?"

Such a simple question. In fact, one he even asked when we first saw each other tonight, and I replied with my usual *fine*. But how he just asked it was different from before. This time, his words were laced with concern.

I exhale, as if accepting I've been caught in a lie.

"Life is hard," I say.

"Yeah. Yeah, it is. Anything in particular?"

I want to tell him nothing. I want to tell him everything. I start somewhere in between.

"I'm sure you've heard about the Milwaukee cop coming to visit me."

He nods, his gaze steady and assuring. "I might've heard something about that. Small town and all."

*Yeah,* I think. *And Tasha Collins makes sure word travels fast.*

"Something about your husband's death?" he adds.

"Yeah."

"We don't have to talk about it."

I look around the bar, which is three-quarters full on a Friday night. It's loud enough in here no one can overhear us, and I don't recognize any of the other faces. Still, we're exposed.

Turning back to him I say, "I… They have questions about his death."

"What kind of questions?"

Exhale. Close my eyes. Get the words out while trying to keep my heart from racing. "They aren't convinced it was accidental."

I don't open my eyes. It's safer in here.

"But you already know this, don't you?" I add.

I hear him say *mmm-hmm*.

"Because of your horrible ex-wife, right?"

He chuckles, and that gets me to open my eyes. "She mentioned something about a book club where you got upset. And then she saw the cops at your place. Add that to the fact that she's friends with Lisa Simmons, who's the wife of a Bury cop, and she probably figured out more than you want people to know."

"I really hate her," I say.

He lifts his beer bottle, and I clink my glass against it. "Here's to things we have in common," he says.

"Cheers." I sip and know I'll be wanting a third whiskey before too long. "So tell me what she thinks she knows."

Alec shrugs. "Well, since you asked. In short, she thinks they might be treating the case as a murder."

This is the first time I've talked about this with someone outside my family, and there's relief with it. Relief and horror, like a Catholic teen's first confession.

"And so, knowing this, you still decided to come here tonight?" I ask. "You weren't concerned about having a drink with a murderer?"

He smiles. "It's why I chose a public place."

"Seriously," I say. "Why would you want anything to do with me?"

Alec sips. "You didn't kill anyone, Rose."

The words rip open my chest and squeeze my heart, a horrible, beautiful pain.

"What…what makes you say that?"

Then he puts his hands on the table, palms up, on either side of the solitary burning candle.

"Give me your hands," he says.

I don't. I just stare at him, feeling the stinging glisten in my eyes.

"It's okay," he says. His voice is deep, calm. Confident.

I hesitate a moment, then place my hands on top of his. He gently grasps them, enveloping my fingers with his.

"These aren't the hands of a killer. No…" He looks down at my hands for just a second and then locks into my gaze. "I don't think you'd hurt anyone."

And with that, I lose it. Right there, in this classy tapas bar named after decay, I sob. I can't control it, and after the first few gasps, I don't even care. It's as if my ability to maintain control has been a balloon filling with water and Alec just added that one final drop, the one that made me burst. I pull my hands from his and cover my eyes, feeling the heat radiating from my face.

"Oh my god, I'm sorry," he says. "I didn't mean to—"

"You didn't," I choke. "Just…give me…"

I cry under the weight of all I've carried for so long. The weight of this town, of Cora and my father. The weight of Riley. And, the heaviest of all, the weight of Caleb Benner's ghost.

To his credit, Alec gives me my space and time, saying nothing else.

I'm not loud, but I'm certain anyone at a nearby table notices this scene. Again, I don't care, and I don't think I could stop this if I wanted. It has to come out.

I don't know how much time passes. An eternity in minutes. At last, I pull my hands down and look at Alec through burning eyes.

"Can we get out of here?" I ask.

He nods.

# THIRTY-SIX

**WE'RE SITTING IN THE** front seat of his car, engine on, heat blowing, seat warmers blazing, going nowhere. When we left Rust, he started driving, and when he asked *where to,* I said *nowhere,* followed by *anywhere*. So we're cruising gently through the night, up and down the streets of Bury, like cops on a patrol. He isn't asking questions. He isn't trying to give advice. Alec is silent, just being the person I need him to be in this moment.

Ten minutes pass. I wipe my eyes again and break the silence.

"I could hurt someone if I had to."

He glances over. "'Scuse me?"

I stare directly out the windshield, watching the headlight beams sweep the empty residential street in front of us.

"You held my hands and said you didn't think I could hurt anyone. But you don't know me. You don't know what I'm capable of doing."

He takes this in for a moment. "And why would you have to? Hurt someone, I mean."

"If I felt threatened. Or if I had to protect Max. Or both."

"Why are you telling me this?"

A thousand reasons swirl in my head. "Because I was always the little girl," I say. "The runt no one paid attention to, the plain Jane living in the shadow of her cover-girl sister. The girl who left town, married someone she realized she didn't love, and couldn't find the strength to leave her husband as soon as she found out he was cheating on her. Looking from the outside, I look so weak." I turn to him, watching his silhouette glow and dissolve in the passing streetlight. "But I'm not weak. I don't know why that's so important for you to understand, but it is. I'm not weak."

"I believe you. And you never seemed weak to me."

"Thank you."

"And you're not a runt. Also, you're much better looking than your sister."

He sounds sincere, but I don't even really care if he's not. This is the first time in my life anyone told me I was better looking than Cora, and I'll soak in the warmth of those words for however long they radiate.

"I'm not saying these things to fish for compliments," I say.

"And I'm not saying anything that isn't true."

"Just because I'm not weak doesn't mean I don't have faults. I've got history."

"Everyone has a history. Good and bad."

An easy answer, I think. Yes, everyone has a history, but I doubt he has a history like mine.

"I suppose," I say.

He glances over. "So what, then?"

"What do you mean?"

"Fault-wise. You say you have faults. What's your worst fault? If you want to talk, let's talk. Tell me what you think your worst fault is."

My mind rushes back to the evening after the book club in my father's study. The smell of cigar smoke and taste of whiskey. My father asked me what my vices were, and now Alec is asking me my worst faults.

"You go first," I say.

He leans back, moves his gaze away. "So many to choose from," he says.

"I'm sure. What, you leave dirty dishes in the sink at night?"

He shakes his head, smiles. Closes his eyes, as if remembering something distant and sweet.

"Maybe I'm not better than your late husband, because I cheated on Tasha," he says. It's so sudden and dissonant with what I was expecting that I have to replay his words in my mind.

"She was trying," he says. "She was really trying. After Micah was born. I have to give her credit, she wanted to make it work, and I didn't. I wanted to blow things up. I thought I could be a perfect dad without her help. But I was wrong. I cheated on her… I think just to get caught. God, I was so arrogant."

"Wow," I say.

Now he looks at me. "You know what? You're the first person I've ever told that to. Ever."

"I don't know what to say to that."

"I don't need you to say anything," he says. "But it feels good for me to tell you."

I appreciate his honesty, but there's a tinge of a stain to Alec now. We are all weak in some way or another, but the pain of infidelity is particularly acute with me.

"I have a hard time moving on from the past," I say, not wanting to hear more about his faults.

"No fair. That's too vague. Look at what I just told you."

"It's true."

"So that's it, then?" he asks. "That's your worst fault?"

God, I want to open up to him, and maybe my inability to fully do so is truly my defining fault. My whole life is a secret, and I'm too scared to have it any other way. I want to tell him how I think of death as touching a rainbow, one appearing in a cornfield after a summer storm. I want to tell him how I'm so scared Max will grow up like anyone in my family and I have no idea if I'm able to parent him away from that. I want to tell him about my books and the place I go in my head when I write, a soft darkness that's both a sanctuary of comfort and horror all at once, and maybe the only place I'm truly myself.

I want to tell him about Riley, about what he became in the end and what that did to me.

But more than anything, I want to tell him about Caleb Benner.

But I won't.

And that is my biggest fault.

I don't answer his question. Instead, I tell him the things I'm able to say, which is still more than I've told anyone else.

"I came back to Bury to…try to face up to some things from my past and to give Max some stability I didn't think he could have back in Milwaukee. But now this detective shows up and starts questioning me about Riley's death, like I had something to do with it. Just because there's a scene…" I pause, searching for the right words.

"A scene what?"

He probably already knows this, but I tell him anyway.

"A scene in my last book where a husband is murdered by his wife. He dies the same general way Riley died—overdose. That's why the detective was out here asking questions."

"But that's just fiction."

I look at him, flames searing my guts. "Is that a question or a statement?"

"A statement, I think. I mean, that's just fiction, right?"

"Of course," I say.

"So that doesn't sound like any kind of real evidence."

"It's not," I tell him. "And I didn't do anything anyway. Which is why the detective went back to Wisconsin without me. But now the gossip is spreading and I don't know where it's going to end. Max doesn't know about it, but that's probably just a matter of time."

Alec leaves the neighborhood and heads in the general direction leading back to the restaurant.

"Hell," he says, "maybe there's an upside. Maybe your book will start taking off." He tells me this with the lightest chuckle attached to it, and I know he's trying to be helpful, but Alec doesn't understand that's not a potential upside. The idea of selling more books because people think I'm a murderer is horrifying. I think of Clara Tomson, the past she had to fight to leave behind, and yet her truth is forever attached to each and every one of her novels. I don't want notoriety. In this moment, I don't even want success. I don't want anyone to have ever heard of me, and I want *The Child of the Steps* pulled from publication.

But I know there's a current here, a powerful one sweeping me out to sea. If I do nothing, it will take me. I can't swim against it, but I can swim *with* it and at least try to make it to some distant shore.

I need to be an agent of change in my life, not just a victim of its forces.

This realization is so suddenly forceful that it ripples through me, causing me to shake. Here, in this car, crawling the streets of the town where so many lives have changed, I realize I'm doing nothing to change my own. I'm just letting everything happen to me.

I vow to myself that starting now, I take control. I don't even know what that means, but I'm ready for a transformation.

I never respond to Alec's comment about my book, and he glides his sedan gently into the restaurant parking lot, where my car sits. He pulls into a space but doesn't turn off the engine. Soft heat from the vents huffs at my face.

"Do you want to go back in?" he asks.

"No," I say, then turn to him. I unbuckle my belt. "Right now, I just want this." I lean over and kiss him, which is so unlike me it's as if I'm watching a movie. He's surprised, his mouth stiff, but after a second, he kisses me back, powerfully, his lips full, his mouth taking in mine. A wave of heat washes over me, much hotter and stronger than what's coming through the air vents. It's dizzying and doubles the impact of the drinks in my system. His lips are the first I've tasted since Riley's, and the first in a long time where I feel actual passion. A connection. Maybe even a future.

I finish the kiss as quickly as I started it, leaning back in my seat and steadying myself.

"That was unexpected," he said. "And amazing."

I say what I'm thinking, without filtering any words. "I needed to prove to myself I can still get what I want."

"So you kissed me on a bet with yourself?"

I look over, then place my left hand on his arm. "Kind of. But it's what I wanted. I hope it's what you wanted, too."

"Yeah, it was."

"Good." I stroke his arm for a moment. "My mind is all over the place, so I think I'm going to call it a night. And I left Max over at his cousin's house, which he wasn't crazy about, and I don't want him over there too long."

"You okay to drive?" he asks.

"Yes," I say, not knowing if it's the truth or not. I'm still a little dizzy, but I'm not sure that's the alcohol.

"I'd like to see you again."

"You will." I reach forward for a last, light kiss, breathing him in just enough to unsteady myself all over again. I open the door, tell him good night, and get out of the car. The night is cool and crisp, swallowing me.

*No,* I tell the night. *You don't swallow me.*

I suck in a deep breath, bringing the cold and dark into my lungs, filling me up. Then I release the air back into the night, a part of me forever attached to it.

I swallow *you.*

# THIRTY-SEVEN

**AN INTRICATE FALL WREATH** adorns the door of my sister's house. Woven branches festooned with fiery-red and muted-yellow leaves, and it's even large enough to accommodate four miniature pumpkins. Cora loves to decorate for holidays, if for nothing other than to showcase on social media. This is one of her Thanksgiving decorations, and many more are inside. Artificial cheer.

I knock, and when no one hears me, I walk in.

I had a sitter lined up who canceled at the last moment, so I asked Cora if Max could hang out with Willow for a few hours. I almost canceled plans with Alec rather than rely on Cora but then figured it would be good to make another attempt, a soft approach at establishing some kind of normal family relations.

Though I'm still not sure that's even what I want.

I call out at half volume.

"Hello?"

No answer. There's something alluring about them not knowing I'm here, as if I might see Cora and her family in their natural habitat and not hidden behind plastic smiles and ceramic cornucopias. I walk into the empty kitchen. The book Max brought over is on the counter, a two-hundred pager I'd never heard of before but is a collection of short nonfiction stories about famous criminals. Al Capone, John Dillinger, Lee Harvey Oswald, and the like. It's written for a young audience, and he told me he wanted to know more about criminal cases since I was a mystery writer, so I allowed it.

I stop and listen, hearing some faint noises upstairs. I head up without announcing myself, lightly grasping the cold and black stair railing. At the top, I hear the noise again, and it sounds like someone talking. Maybe it's Cora and Peter, or just a television, but in this moment, all I can think of is that scene twenty-two years ago when Caleb Benner burst from Cora's room, bloodied and desperate, stumbling down the hallway toward me.

The master bedroom door at the end of this hallway is closed. I take a few more steps and pass Willow's bedroom on the right. Her door is open, light on. No one's inside, and the room is a maelstrom of dirty clothes, rumpled sheets and blankets, makeup supplies, and schoolwork papers. Curiously, her walls are nearly bare—just two mirrors and a poster. The poster catches my eye because it looks so out of place in a teenage girl's room. I step inside to get a better look.

I'm utterly chilled as the image comes into better focus. It's a line drawing, quite well done, of a woman sitting at the bottom of a staircase. Her face is severe, her expression a controlled rage, ink-black hair pulled tightly back into a bun. She's wearing a black, puritanical dress buttoned to the neck, white collar circling her neck. I think *Hester Prynne*, but I know that's not right. I know because Hester Prynne wasn't known for clutching a hatchet in her hands, which this woman is doing. There's a single word in bold type at the bottom of the poster: *Lizzie*.

Jesus Christ. My niece has only one poster on her bedroom walls, and it's a drawing of Lizzie Borden?

I'm now less intrigued by snooping in this house and am much more concerned about finding Max. I leave Willow's room and walk quickly down the hallway to the master bedroom. I'm about to knock on the door when I pause and listen a moment.

The sounds from behind the door leave no doubt as to what I'm listening to: sex. Either Peter and Cora are in there together or someone is watching porn. My immediate discomfort is quickly supplanted by anger; I leave Max for a few hours with my family, and instead of spending time with him, they disappear to screw? I look at my watch. It's not even eight thirty.

I don't knock. I just can't bring myself to do it. Not yet at least.

I turn and head back downstairs.

Living room. No one. Same goes for family room. Basement. Laundry room and even the garage.

Then, as I'm in the garage, I notice a glow through the glass of the door leading from the garage to the back patio. I thread my way along the wall until I reach the door, and as I peer through, I see Max.

Max and Willow. They're sitting in chairs on the back patio, each of the kids bundled in a fleece blanket. Their backs face me and they're hunching toward the flames rising from a large stone firepit in the center of the patio. After my eyes take a few seconds to adjust to the dark, I recognize what they're doing. Roasting marshmallows.

For a moment, my body warms as if I were sitting next to them, facing the flames. This sullen teen with the Lizzie Borden poster is hanging out with Max on a Friday night, roasting marshmallows. Improbable as I would have thought, perhaps she's the most redeeming one of the family.

I watch from the darkness of the garage, my boy hanging out with his cousin. They're talking but I can't make out their words.

For a moment, this feels like a normal family.

After I moved away for college, it would have been forgivable for someone with my history to have never spoken to their family again. Forgivable, understandable, and probably what I should have done. But there's that tiny ember that never quite leaves you, that minuscule source of heat that burns inside, telling you that, no matter who your family is, they are special and shouldn't be cut from your life like some malignant tumor. *Nothing is more important than family.* That's what my father said the night Caleb Benner bled in our house. *Without family, we have nothing.* It's so easy to dismiss such clichéd phrases, but clichés only exist because of the truth on which they're based. In all my years away from Bury, all the years with Riley, a small part of me always missed my family. It's so messed up. Borderline Stockholm syndrome. But without that tiny ember smoldering inside me, I don't think I ever would have come back here. But now, watching my son and niece, I see it for what it is. I didn't come back here just for my father's financial support. I came here because of an illogical desire to be with my family. To be a Yates, grotesque, cancerous warts and all.

And seeing these two, roasting marshmallows, it's almost a validation of that desire. That maybe we can share a closeness that's always been just out of reach.

I crack the garage door open, not necessarily trying to remain silent but not announcing myself either. I want to hear a bit of their conversation, mostly because I love hearing Max talk when he doesn't know I'm around. Observing him in the wild.

"—you mean by that?"

His voice. He sounds anxious. Not what I was expecting.

"It's true," Willow says. "I'm surprised you didn't know that already. It's a good thing I'm here to tell you."

"It's *not* true."

I know that voice. Max is stressing out. My instinct is to go to him, but I resist. I want to know what exactly she's telling him.

"My mom told me everything, and she knows because your mom told her. Sisters, you know. They share everything."

"You're lying."

I grip the door handle, my stomach clenching. Nausea rising. Whatever Willow is talking about, it's clear she's already told him, so interrupting her now wouldn't do any good. Max has already heard something I'm sure I didn't want him to hear.

So I listen, fingers squeezing the cold door handle, heart in my throat.

"But my mom didn't do anything," Max says.

"That's not what the cops think." Willow's voice is calm, coy, and the perfect pitch to extract maximum pain. Now I understand why she has that poster on her wall. Lizzie Borden isn't some kind of ironic *fuck-you* to Willow's parents. She's Willow's idol. "They think she killed your dad."

"Shut up."

"What happened that night?" she asks. "What really happened? I mean, you were there. Were your parents fighting? Was it a normal night?"

"I don't want to talk about it anymore."

"It's okay, Max. You can tell me. You can trust me."

My body heat rises a few degrees, fueled by anger.

"I said I don't want to talk about it."

She shrugs, as if the subject isn't important. "Fine, we don't have to." She pauses a few seconds, then adds, "They'll take her away for a long time. Then you won't have any parents left, and you'll probably have to live with Grandpa."

It's all I can do not to race over and whisk Max into my arms, but I want to see his reaction. He says only one more thing. Mutters it in a monotone voice, free from tears.

"She didn't do *anything*."

"Okay," Willow says, her voice still chipper. Then they fall into a silence, and I realize if this were the moment in which I eavesdropped, I would have been warmed by their bonding.

A minute passes and I open the door.

"There you are," I say.

Both heads snap toward me. Max drops his marshmallow stick into the fire and rushes at me, hugging me tight.

"Well, good to see you, too," I say, hugging him back and kissing the top of his head. The heat from the fire on his clothes radiates into me, and I melt into my son.

"I thought you were going to be back later," he says. His voice has a crack of emotion in it.

"I missed you, so I came back early." I tussle his hair. "Now go into the house and get your book and anything else you brought over. I'll meet you in the car in a moment."

"You're not coming now?"

"I want to warm up by the fire for a second."

He pulls back and gives me a look of confusion, but I tell him, "Go." He obeys, walking around the porch and back into the house through the back door.

Willow looks up at me from her chair, the firelight moving across her face.

"How was your *date?*" she asks.

I'm certain she means this as some kind of barb, but I answer truthfully. "Unexpected. Nice. And needed."

I sit next to her in Max's chair and pick his broken tree branch out of the fire. The marshmallow is long scarified, and the end of the branch glows in flame. I blow it out and study the smoldering tip, bringing it close enough to my eyes that they sting from the heat.

"You know," I say, looking at the stick and not at her. "Most people think, under the right circumstances, anyone could kill. Self-defense, or to save someone they loved. That everyone is capable of taking a life. But it's not true, you know." Now I look over and the smug expression on her face hasn't left, but it's cooled. "I've talked to a lot of cops researching my books, and they say most people, even in those circumstances, still can't do it. They freeze up out of sheer terror, or their brains simply can't execute such an extreme command. A lot of people choose to lose their own lives instead of fighting to save them." I put the stick back in the fire, igniting it. "But this family. Our family. *Your* family, Willow. We're fighters. We are absolutely capable of killing."

She says nothing in the brief silence that follows, and I didn't expect her to.

"If we feel threatened at a primal level," I continue. "If someone is trying to fundamentally change our way of life. The Yateses can kill." I turn one more time to her, and Willow's face is corpse blank. "And not just me. All of us. You come from a family of killers. It's important you know that, because someday you might have to save yourself against someone trying to do you harm. Know you have it in you. It's a terrible, primal thing to have in your blood, Willow. But it's there. Like a virus. And your mom? There's a reason she didn't change her name after marrying. Just like me. She wants to be a Yates forever."

I drop the stick entirely in the fire, wait long enough to see the flames consume it entirely, then get up and walk back into the darkness of the garage.

# THIRTY-EIGHT

**IN THE CAR, I** don't want to mince words or take time extracting the evening's events from Max. I need to perform emergency surgery, even if it's messy.

"I overheard you and Willow," I tell him.

He looks out his window as we drive the short distance home.

"Max, look at me."

He doesn't.

"*Look* at me."

He waits a few seconds, then turns his head.

"Everything's okay," I tell him.

"But she said the police were talking to you. Is that true?"

"Yes, but there's nothing to worry about."

This quiets him for about a block and then he says, "That's not true."

"What?"

"That there's nothing to worry about," he says. "But they could still put you in jail for something you didn't do."

All I want to do is ease the suffering of my boy, but I can't even do that for myself.

"I'm not going anywhere, Max."

As soon as the words leave my lips, I picture them permanently seared in his brain as he visits me years later in prison. It's a horrible image I can't shake, along with the sound of his forever-eleven voice saying *She promised me.*

I think I'd rather see him cry than the calculating stare he's now giving me. He's trying to see if I'm lying.

"I promise you I'm not going anywhere," I repeat, deciding to go all-in on the belief. Manifest your future. "You believe me, right?"

He doesn't answer. He's drifted to his other world again, the one I can't penetrate.

As we drive, I don't repeat my question. Don't say anything.

Max stares straight through the windshield, his gaze heavy and fixed. It makes me think of that scene from the movie *The Shining*. Little Danny, staring transfixed into the mirror, just before he starts screaming "Redrum!"

I'm desperate to know how Max will turn out in life. I just want to know he's going to be okay. That he'll be a caring, compassionate man who will love and be loved.

That's all I want to know.

Will he be okay?

As I drive, and as he stares, and as my headlight beams sweep along the Bury streets as we make our way back to Rum Hill Road, I just want to know the answer to that one question.

Will Max be okay?

And try as I might, I can't turn off the little voice that laughs at me. Deep in my brain, deep in my heart.

Laughs and says:

*Don't be silly. He's just like the rest of you.*

# THIRTY-NINE

**Milwaukee, Wisconsin**
**November 9**

**COLIN'S ATTENTION WANDERED AGAIN,** as it had been doing all morning. The paperwork felt endless, and he still had to finish his phone-tap warrant request for a suspected meth dealer. He was working several other cases along with Riley McKay's, and though it was becoming more and more likely there wouldn't be enough evidence to consider McKay a murder victim, Colin couldn't get Rose Yates out of his mind.

He'd finished her upcoming book over the weekend.

First thing he did yesterday morning when he got to work was put a call into Chief Sike in Bury. Sike called back this morning, but Colin had missed it. Knowing he had to make a dent in the paperwork for his other cases, Colin vowed not to return the call until he at least got the warrant request done.

It ended up being the fastest he'd ever written one. An hour later, he called Sike and was glad not to get the man's voicemail.

"Chief Sike."

"Hi, Chief. Colin Pearson, Milwaukee PD."

"Hey, Pearson, good to connect."

"Things busy out there in Bury?"

Sike grumbled. "Yeah, a bit. You know, for a sleepy town anyway."

"Anything interesting?"

Sike took a couple seconds before answering. "We had a murder yesterday."

Colin sat up straight in his chair. "A murder?" His mind raced through all the people from Bury he'd met. "Who?"

"Not who. *What*. A dog."

"Dog?"

"Poodle. But you know, not the little yippy kind. Big one, like you see in the dog-award shows."

"A poodle was murdered?"

"Ayuh. Looks like it. Throat slit. Someone took it from its backyard and killed it out on a green belt."

"God, that's terrible. Who would do that?"

"Well, that's what I spent my day yesterday trying to figure out. Still no clue. Owner is out of her mind."

"I can imagine," Colin said. "Sounds like a warning."

"Yeah, that's what I thought," Sike replied. "Dog wasn't known to be a noisy one, and if a neighbor had an issue, there would've been a history of complaints, but nope. And using a knife on a dog? That's pretty brutal. My guess is it has nothing to do with the dog." He cleared his throat with enough force that Colin recoiled from his handset. "So that's what's going on here. Now, what can I do for you?"

Colin leaned back in his chair and looked around the department.

He didn't know why he felt guilty for talking to Sike about something not related to the McKay case. Maybe because Colin knew he was grasping at straws and his sergeant would certainly admonish him for wasting his time.

"Well, here's the thing, Chief, and it's going to sound a little *out there.*"

"You have some new theory about the Yates woman offing her husband?"

"No. This is about Caleb Benner."

"Benner kid? Don't tell me that's your new pet project, 'cause I'm sure you got plenty other work to do there. Best to leave Bury crimes to us."

Colin tried to swallow but found his throat dry. "I agree, Chief. I'm not trying to step on any toes. But worlds are colliding and I'm just trying to make sense of things."

The sigh of a man with little patience and a backlog of work came through the phone. "Okay," Sike said. "I got a few minutes. But just a few. I know how you Midwesterners like to drag on, so I'm asking you not to. So go on now, tell me."

And so Colin did.

With great efficiency, Colin told Sike everything that intersected about the Riley McKay death and the Caleb Benner disappearance. The connective threads were few and frayed but strong enough to make shape of something, even if Colin didn't quite know what that something was. His main points were:

1. Riley McKay's death was too suspicious to be ruled an accident, in Colin's opinion. The man died of an overdose of alcohol and sleep medication, the same way a character died

in one of Rose Yates's books. When he approached Yates, she quickly became defensive and uncooperative.

2. Twenty-two years earlier, Caleb Benner disappeared in Bury. The last person he was seen talking to that night was Cora Yates, sister of Rose. The transcript of her interview with the police felt oddly abridged, ending at the point in which the Yates patriarch, Logan Yates (in attendance), mentioned some of the flooring and stairs in his house had just been restained.
3. In her upcoming novel, Rose Yates writes about a sixteen-year-old boy who is murdered in a struggle with his girlfriend. He's stabbed and then falls down a flight of stairs, breaking his neck. The character's name is Corey Brownstein. Same initials as Caleb Benner.

Colin barely got these points out before Sike interjected.

"You trying to pull my pud here, Detective?"

"Sorry?"

"You are a detective, right? I'm just trying to confirm I'm talking to Milwaukee PD Detective Colin Pearson and not an eight-year-old with a junior G-man badge."

Colin had no idea what that meant. Sike didn't wait for a reaction.

"Because this is Conspiracy Theory Bullshit 101," he said. "And you want me to do something with this? What am I supposed to do with this?"

Colin heated up, a bit due to anger, another bit due to embarrassment. But he pushed through, trying to keep his voice steady.

"Excuse me, sir, but I wasn't done."

"Oh?" Sike said. "Do tell. I have another thirty seconds to spare."

"I called her publisher," Colin said. "Her editor."

"Yeah?"

"I told her we were just looking to confirm that the story wasn't based on any actual open-case investigations," Colin said, "given Yates's history of working with the police in her stories. I mentioned the upcoming book, the one with the murder on the stairs. I asked if she knew if any of that book was based on fact. The editor didn't have anything helpful there. But she did say about a few weeks ago, Yates wrote her asking to remove the Brownstein murder from the book entirely, or at least change the character's name. I asked if that kind of request was unusual, and she said it was, mostly because of how close they are to releasing the book."

Colin paused, tried to swallow again, but found only sand in his mouth.

Sike filled the silence. "Okay, goddamn it, I'll admit it. That's kinda interesting. Did they change the book?"

"Nope. The publisher said it was too late, and they didn't want to anyway. They said the scene is crucial to the book. Which, I agree, it is."

Sike let out a tired groan. "So you think the Yates woman you're already looking at for the McKay death and her sister had something to do with Caleb Benner?"

"I think it's worth asking some questions. You have a unit for cold cases?"

"Nope. It's just us."

Colin had one more piece of information he saved for last. "Michael Patterson, the lead on the case at the time, had transcripts on each of the kids he talked to, all the kids from the party. They seemed like complete interviews except for Cora's, which ended abruptly. Almost as if the tape recorder died or something." Colin knew he had to tread carefully with this next question. "Now, you said Patterson died back in oh-nine, right?"

"Heart attack."

"And for all you knew, he was a good cop?"

Sike didn't answer immediately. "Didn't know him all that well. What're you getting at?"

"I'm just wondering if Patterson followed all the leads he could have," Colin said. "Talked to Cora a second time."

"Are you saying Patterson intentionally backed off of Cora Yates?"

"Her father has a lot of money. Maybe he made it worth Patterson's while to focus his attention elsewhere."

Colin wasn't sure how Sike would react to his hunch, but he was glad he'd finally said it. He wanted a second opinion. Was Colin just a bit too obsessed with the Yates family, or was there something here?

"Look," Sike said. "I'm not saying this is all completely without merit. Maybe it is. But the case has been buried for some time."

"Maybe it's time to dig it up."

"Easier said than done. Budget's tight and cold cases don't get much priority. If Benner's body had ever been found, then we'd have a murder case, and the argument for continued investigation would be easier. But no body, no murder. As far as the state's concerned, Caleb Benner is still just a missing person."

This was about what Colin had expected to hear, but that didn't make it any less disappointing.

Seeming to read this disappointment, Sike added, "Look, I'll do a little poking around. Maybe you weren't sent the entire case file."

"That'd be helpful. Thank you."

"You plan on coming back here anytime soon?"

"Not on the department's budget," Colin said. "There's just not enough evidence to bring Rose Yates back to Wisconsin."

"Ayuh. 'Bout what I figured."

Helplessness overcame Colin, manifesting itself in a long, slow exhale. "It's just…"

"Just what, Detective?"

"There's just something here, I know it. Something about that Yates family. There's…I don't know. A rot there."

This time, Sike laughed, the throaty chuckle of a smoker. "Well, Detective, there's rottenness everywhere. So put your big-boy pants on and accept people do bad shit all the time, and we only see a fraction of it, much less bring justice to those evildoers. Always been that way, always will be. And on that note, I need to go figure out who nearly decapitated this poodle."

Sike disconnected the call, leaving Colin wondering how many more years he'd need on the job to reach the mental ease associated with such acute cynicism.

He hoped never, but knew that was unlikely.

# FORTY

**Bury, New Hampshire**
**November 10**

**THE HARBINGER OF MY** apocalypse is a dead poodle.

The moment I hear about the slaughter of the dog, something clicks into place in my mind, and not in a good way. A sudden certainty that my life path—carved from billions of decisions and actions—is now on an ineluctable course toward doom.

I'm working checkout at Tuli's when a familiar customer leapfrogs past the small talk as I ring up her groceries.

"Did you hear about that awful incident?"

My mind goes to something national. A shooting somewhere. Maybe some worse-than-normal political story. I intake the news in small doses, and not daily ones, trying to keep the balance between being informed and overwhelmed by the ugliness of the world. In the last few months, I've hardly paid attention. My life has enough of its own dark melodrama.

"No," I say, hoping she won't tell me. But she does.

"Do you know Tasha Collins?"

Bury is small, but it still has several thousand residents. Maybe Tasha Collins is more popular than I realize, but the odds in this situation are I wouldn't know her.

"Yeah, actually, I do. What about her?"

The woman shakes her head, her salt-and-pepper hair shimmying against her shoulders. She casts her gaze down.

"It's just so awful. So, so awful."

And in that split second, I'm thinking Tasha is dead. It has to be that. Tasha had some terrible accident. Car crash, maybe. And then I think of her boy. Oh god, let Micah be okay. My mind races with possibilities. I need to call Alec. See if he's—

"Someone killed her dog," the woman says.

"*What?*"

She looks up, the excitement of the story betrayed in the gleam of her eyes.

"Killed. Like, with a knife."

I stop scanning her groceries. "What are you talking about?"

She places a hand on the laminate counter separating us, as if she needs to hold on for the ride.

"It happened the day before yesterday. It was in the online version of the *Bury Gazette* this morning, and I know someone who's friends with her. Acquaintances at least. Neighbors, but they aren't really that—"

"What *happened?*"

She purses her lips and gives a surreptitious glance to each side. There's no one else in my checkout line.

"Somehow the dog got out of the backyard. The gate was found open, so maybe someone just came and took the thing. But whatever happened, they found the dog on the green belt behind the elementary school, over a mile away." She leans forward and whispers the next part. "The poor thing's throat had been cut."

"Oh my god."

She nods. "It must have been awful. With all that white fur and... Well, I just can't imagine. But now, everyone is freaking out. Rumors about animal sacrifice. Satanic things. *Here*, in Bury. I don't even understand it. I mean, who would do such a thing?"

It comes to me immediately, without thought or consideration. Just enters my consciousness and burrows like a bad memory I can't turn off.

Cora would do this.

I ball my fists because I have to squeeze something.

"What...what are the police saying?" I ask.

"I have no idea," she says. "I can't imagine they're saying much at all right now. All I know is, if you have a dog, keep it inside the house. That's what I'm doing. It's all just so horrible."

I force myself to finish ringing her groceries, then close down my lane. I'm the only checker working at the moment, so I head into the back office and find Erika, a new employee, working on inventory sheets. I ask her to cover me for five minutes, telling her I'm not feeling well and need some air. It's the truth.

I walk out of the back of the store and suck in dumpster air. The chilled air is wet, snow to come. My mind spins and, with it, my body. I turn slowly around, not even aware why, like a dancing figurine set atop a music box. Scanning my surroundings, three hundred sixty degrees, as if looking for holes in my reality.

John, my manager, comes scurrying through the back door and joins me outside, his salt-and-pepper mustache twitching faster than normal. He has the nervous look of a gerbil burrowing through wood shavings.

"Rose, you can't take a break now. Erika's not properly trained to work the register yet."

I stop turning and face him, a sudden wave of nausea washing over me.

"She's fine, John. She's done it before, and I just need five minutes."

He sucks in his face, as if allergic to logic. "You need to ask me before taking breaks. You don't just leave your post."

*Post.* Like we're taking turns keeping watch for zombies in some postapocalyptic world.

"Fine, John." I don't hide the attitude in my voice.

He keeps looking at me, but with only rapid-fire bursts of eye contact. His agitation is apparent and disproportionate to the minor infraction I've committed.

"I just need a minute," I say, my stomach still unsteady.

He doesn't leave. He just twitches more.

"What?" I ask him.

"You know, Nate called me up, asking about you."

Nate. Nathan Carnes, owner of the store.

"What about?" I'm not sure I want the answer.

"All these...all these rumors." He waves his arms as if the rumors could be seen, swirling about in toxic clouds.

I take a step toward him. "What rumors?" I ask.

"You know."

"I don't know, John. I want to hear you say it. *What* rumors?"

I'm calmer, the nausea subsiding as I take another step. I'm only a couple feet away, and all that is going sideways in my life has manifested itself here in John, a mid-level manager of a gourmet grocery store. He is the embodiment of every mistake I've made, of every wrong done to me, whether I caused it or not. And as I bask in his nervousness, my control kicks in, something I haven't savored in some time.

He looks away. At the ground. In the sky.

"What rumors, John?"

John clears his throat. "About the cops talking to you about…you know. Your husband."

"What about my husband?" I inch closer. This has turned into a sociology experiment. I've become the alpha, absent of fear, and I'm measuring the impact of my aggression on the beta.

John doesn't answer. Eye contact is no longer a thing.

"What, the rumors that I loved my husband?" I ask. "Or that we were living happily ever after until he accidentally overdosed? You have to say it, John. I won't know what you're talking about unless you say it."

His shoulders hunch forward, a flower wilting in extreme heat. God, how easy. I never knew it was so damn easy to be dominant. All I ever had to do was shed my fear and stop caring, and then I become the one to be feared. If only I'd know this earlier in my life, how many different paths would I have taken? Where would I be now? Certainly not here, in the back of this grocery store, arguing with this man about taking an unauthorized break.

He mumbles, but I give John credit for finally saying it. "About… whether or not your husband was murdered." He waits, swallows, then spits the next two words out like poison. "By you."

Now I'm in his face, and less than six inches separate our noses. John doesn't back away, but his eyes dart everywhere to avoid contact with mine.

"That's some rumor," I say. "I mean, that's just crazy, right? And Nate... He doesn't even live in Bury. How do you suppose he heard some kind of insane thing like that?" I lean just an inch closer, and only the thinnest of a children's book could be slipped between our faces. I smell him, that sweet tang of middle-aged mediocrity, basted over with Old Spice and accented by halitosis. "Did he really call you? Or was it you who called him?"

He closes his eyes, swallows, then summons a modicum of resolve. "You really need to get back to work now, Rose."

I pull my face back, almost feeling high. Dizzy and delightful. I untie the back of my work apron and then take it off.

"I like to consider myself a nice person," I say. "Sometimes even too nice for my own good. That person was working checkout five minutes ago and just needed a break. Just a short break. A mental-health break, really. But you couldn't even let me have that. Now that person is gone, and this one is here." I drop the apron to the ground. "So fuck you, John. And fuck this job."

"You're quitting?"

His sublimely stupid remark makes me laugh out loud, pulling me back an inch from my anger.

"Yes, that's what happening here. If you didn't help spread those rumors, then no hard feelings, okay? But if you did, you're a god-awful person."

John turns and walks back inside, no other words spoken between us.

I look down at the apron on the ground.

*Tuli's Gourmet Grocer*

*Bury, NH*

*Est. 2008*

Next to the words is a cartoonish rendering of the actual Tuli, the owner's dog. Just the animal's big, dopey face, wide-eyed, mouth open. I always thought that dog looked so happy in the company's logo, but now I think it looks dead. Those eyes have no life in them, the mouth only open because the muscles to close it no longer function. I picture that dog with a slit throat. Or worse, headless.

The nausea is back, and this time, it wins. I double over and retch onto the apron. The little that comes up lands on the poor dog's face.

I stand, wipe my mouth, and walk to my car. As I glance up and spy the menacing snow clouds closing in, my world has suddenly never felt so suffocating.

# FORTY-ONE

**THE SNOW BEGINS AN** hour later as I wait in the school car line for Max. Heavy, wet flakes, melting as they hit my windshield. But if this pace keeps up, the roads will soon be a mess. It would be a perfect night to be cozy at home, maybe play a few board games with Max by the fire, do a little writing after he's in bed, then go to sleep early. Those are all things a person not riddled with stress might do. Mine will be a different evening altogether, because I need to talk to Cora.

Two minutes until the school bell. A red blur to my right, and I look over and see Tasha Collins walking up along the car line sidewalk. She's ensconced in a cardinal-red winter coat that extends to her knees, and thousands of snowflakes swirl about her, jostling as if they're trying to avoid her path.

She never has a smile on her face, but her expression now is even more severe than usual. Eyes focused straight ahead, hands in pockets, head tilted forward.

I see her and shrink into my seat, thinking of her dog. What that must have looked like. The horror of finding such a thing. Of having to tell your child what happened to the family pet. I wonder if she—

Tasha suddenly stops just as she reaches the front of my car. She tilts her head, and that deathly gaze bores right into me. All awareness of the cold and snow has surely left her consciousness; the only thing that registers with her is my presence.

The way she looks at me.

She thinks I did it.

Of course she does. She spread rumors about me and thinks I killed her dog as some kind of retaliation. *She killed her husband,* Tasha is thinking, *so it must be nothing to kill a dog.*

This, of course, is what Cora wants.

Tasha finally breaks her glare and continues walking, leaving me with a chill that doesn't warm. If she does think I did it, she must have shared that with the police. Is it just a matter of time before I get another knock on my front door?

A minute later, Max hops in the car. He's big enough for the front seat, but ever since Riley's death, he's chosen the back. When I asked him about this, he said he just felt safer back there. I had no reason to argue the point. It's always safer in back.

"You see the snow?" he asks.

"Hard to miss it," I say. "How was your day?" I lean my head back, and he leans forward and gives me a kiss on the cheek.

"Okay. Can we go sledding?"

"Not today, sweetie. The sun sets early this time of year. Only going to be a couple of hours of light left today."

"That's plenty of time."

"But it just started snowing," I say, pointing at the patchwork of white and green on the nearby field. "Nothing to sled on yet."

"Oh yeah," he says, surveying the landscape. "I'm dumb."

"No, you're not," I say. "You need to love yourself. All the time."

"What? I am dumb, you know."

"No, Max, you're not."

"With some things I am."

This incessant argument. The low self-esteem has been particularly pronounced in the last couple of months. The kid will be reading Faulkner by age thirteen, and he can't give himself a break.

I don't respond. Instead, I pull away from the car line and from Tasha Collins, easing into the snowy afternoon.

At home, things turn ugly. After a quick snack, Max falls into a mood, and now instead of himself being the target, it's me. We're in the living room and he refuses to do his homework, even though he has all of five math problems to complete. Normally, that would take ten minutes. Now, he acts as though I'm asking him to explain string theory to me. I reason with him. *You know this stuff, Max. It'll take no time at all.* I threaten him. *No screens or books until you've finished.* I promise a reward. *We can play a game before dinner if you finish it.*

After an hour, I plead with him. *Can you just do this? I really need you to do this.* Ninety minutes later, I give up on him. *I don't know what to do with you. I'm trying my best, but you're not letting me help you, and I can't do this anymore. Not tonight.*

Perhaps this was the stage he was waiting for me to reach, because the moment I give up on him, the assault launches. And Max doesn't fire warning shots. He goes straight to nuclear.

"Sometimes I wish you were also dead."

What. The. Fuck.

His verbal attacks have worsened since Riley's death—understandable—but he has *never* said this to me before, and as patient as I am, and as much as I love him with all that's left of my soul, his words stab as if I were being knifed by a back-alley assailant. And I respond in kind.

I hit him.

In his life, I've never laid a hand on my boy. My beautiful son.

But now, when he says what he does, staring directly in my face and only a foot away, I react. I'm not even aware I'm doing it. I'm watching from above as this crazy woman reaches out and open-palm slaps Max's face so hard he falls to the floor. *Falls to the floor*. He catches himself, catlike, landing on his hands and knees, and the *thunking* of his bony kneecaps against the hardwood is gut-twisting.

I immediately crouch next to him on the floor, touch his shoulder. Max looks up to me with wide eyes that narrow after a second.

He doesn't cry.

I think that's the worst part.

Max is a crier, always has been. Always held his emotions on his sleeve. But in this moment, as he looks up at me from the floor, his face tells me nothing. No anger, no fear, no sadness. Just like Tasha Collins earlier today, just an emotionless stare, an assessment. He's judging me in an entirely new light, as if suddenly realizing he's been raised by a monster.

"I'm…I'm sorry," I say, wanting to cry the tears he doesn't. "I didn't mean that. It just happened. But what you said. Max, you can't talk to me like that. I can't hit you, and you can't talk to me like that. Ever. Okay?"

He says nothing, and now it's scaring me a little, as if I've knocked him into some kind of new reality. I sit on the floor and pull him in toward me. He doesn't resist, but he doesn't hug back. Limp as a puppet.

"Are you listening to me?" I whisper, and the first tear falls down my cheek. "Did you hear what I said?"

"Yes," he says.

"I didn't mean to hurt you. I'm so sorry. You know that, right?"

"I know." His voice is robotic.

"Look at me," I say. I pull back and he makes eye contact. It usually takes me asking him a few times before he does, but not now. A faint red glow blossoms on his left cheek, deepening my shame.

"Are you okay?" I ask.

He nods, keeping his gaze fixed.

"Did you mean it?" I say. "What you said. Did you really mean that?"

He doesn't answer. He's somewhere else now, far distant, but inches away.

"Sometimes our anger gets the best of us," I say. "We say or do things we don't really mean, and then it's too late to take it back. We're both wrong here. All we can do is promise to be better with each other and move on."

Max remains silent, gaze both at and beyond me.

The housekeeper, Abril, walks into the room and looks over to us on the floor. I forgot she was even in the house and wonder what she's heard.

"Oh, hello, Miss Rose."

"Hi, Abril."

Max moves his gaze from me to the floor.

"I'm leaving for the evening," she says. "Anything else you need?"

*So many things*, I think.

"No, thank you. Have a good night."

"You too."

She swishes out of the room, and I run my hand through Max's hair. "What just happened was awful," I say. "For both of us. I want to make sure you're okay."

Now he speaks. "I've been through worse."

That one hurts.

"I know you have."

Then he turns to me, and there's a bit of fresh life in his face. His eyes glisten enough to show me some emotion, which is a relief.

"It's not supposed to be this way," he says.

"What do you mean?"

"It's just us now. We can be whatever we want. But I don't like how we are."

"Me neither," I say. "We just have to keep on being there for each other. Working with each other, not against." I give him another squeeze, let go, then stand.

"I just want us to be okay," Max says, his voice squeaking. He shouldn't have to say such a thing, and it guts me that he does. I reply with a mantra I've used before during meditation, one that calms me, assures me, instills me with a confidence that doesn't usually last long but comforts me in the moment. When I say this mantra to my son, I change it from the singular to plural, making it encompass us as a family.

"Our lives belong to us."

He swallows, looks at me, so desperately wanting to believe those five words. Then he nods. "Okay."

"If you want," I say, "you can postpone your math homework. You still have to do those five problems, but not until tomorrow, okay?"

Max stands and walks over to the table where his homework binder rests closed. "I'll do them now." He then causally opens the binder, picks up his pencil, and starts doing exactly that.

This produces a mixture of emotions. Pride that we got through this horrible moment and he's taking responsibility. Anger that we had to go through all *that* just for five stupid math problems. For the millionth time, I project my son into the future and wonder how he'll cope as an adult with real responsibility and real problems.

I push the conflict away. He's working through the present the best he can. The future can wait.

I leave the room and head into the kitchen, nerves still raw. I pour a glass of Chianti and do the one thing I've been needing to do all afternoon.

I text Cora.

We need to talk, I write.

Seconds later, a ding.

*About what?*

You know, I reply.

It takes a few minutes, long enough that I think she's not going to respond at all. Then she does, encapsulating everything she needs to convey in a single word.

*Woof.*

# FORTY-TWO

**IT'S JUST AFTER 8:00** p.m. and I'm sitting in my car, ignition running, the only vehicle in the parking lot of the Chester Woodall trailhead. Oh, *right,* I think. Chester Woodall, that's his last name. The guy Bury was originally named for. They took away the town name and gave him a hiking trail.

Snow swirls and coils around my car, and I think this is perhaps what the inside of a genie bottle looks like. The outside winds make this short of a blizzard but more than just a snowfall. The dashboard tells me it's twenty-three degrees, and I wonder for another time why Cora wanted to meet out here.

Moments later, headlights slice through the falling snow and illuminate the inside of my car. Seconds after that, Cora eases her Land Rover into the space next to mine. Ours are the only two vehicles in the lot.

She turns off her car, kills her lights.

For a moment, I'm watching this as I would a movie. Trying to understand the motivation of the character in the adjacent car. Why are we meeting out here, in this weather, at night? Is it for the privacy, or something else?

*Woof.*

I do a mental inventory of everything in this car. My father keeps it clean, so there aren't random items lying about, but I don't know what could be in the closed-off areas. I quickly check the center console and the glove compartment, finding them empty save the car registration and manual. Typical for my father, who despises anything considered clutter.

I check the pockets behind the front seats. Again, empty. In the trunk, there has to be a spare tire, and thus a tire iron.

If I need a weapon, that's my only hope.

Weapon. Against my sister. This is where we are in our lives.

She raps on my window, making me jump. I didn't even see her out there. My fingers find the button on the door and I lower the window. A burst of snowflakes immediately seeks asylum in the car, only to meet their deaths by the heated air vents.

"Outside," she says. The scent of her perfume yanks me back twenty-two years. Smell is the most powerful memory, and I know with certainty she's wearing Calvin Klein's CK One, just as she did as a teenager. Just as she did that night.

"It's awful out there."

"It's perfect," she says.

If a character in one of my books didn't want to talk inside a car, it would be because they were afraid the car was bugged. And though I'm pretty sure Cora doesn't suspect this, the thought does spark an idea. I *should* be recording our conversation. In fact, I'd be crazy not to.

I roll up the window and wait until the interior light dims, then quickly unlock my phone and launch the voice recorder app, which I use for story notes. I press Record and then slide the phone into the snug front pocket of my jeans.

Deep breath. Then I get out of the car.

She's standing a few feet away. Three halogen lamps account for all the light in the lot. Beyond that and onto the trail, darkness reigns. It's snowing harder now and the flakes are dense and wet, the kind that bring down trees with enough accumulation. I flip up the hood of my jacket against the onslaught.

"I wanted to talk, not catch pneumonia," I say. "Why are we out here?"

"You don't like it here?"

"No, not particularly. Not in the moment."

"So you don't know what's special about this place, then."

"Should I?"

She doesn't answer. Instead, my sister says, "I think you want to be careful how you talk to my family. Willow told me what you said to her. You said things you had no right saying."

If this is what she wants to talk about, I'm happy to engage, because my ammunition stockpile dwarfs hers. "*You* told her I killed Riley. And she was telling Max that while you were upstairs having sex."

This catches her off guard, but only for a moment. "Did you like what you heard?"

"Don't be disgusting."

"He likes to be dominated, you know." With her bright eyes gleaming in the amber streetlight, her smooth skin, perfect blond hair, and freckles of snow collecting on her baby-blue wool hat, Cora looks right out of an L.L. Bean Christmas catalog. "You wouldn't think it," she continues. "So tall. So strong. Confident. But he's not happy unless he's bleeding. You know, just a little." She winks. "It's a symbiotic relationship."

"Your family is so messed up."

"*Our* family," she corrects.

I know my sister isn't right. I've known that for a long time. She's a broken toy glued and painted over so it still gleams from the outside, but if you were to shake her, you'd hear the loose parts rattle within. "Cora, did you really kill that dog?"

She looks me up and down, smiling. "Now why on earth would I do something like that?"

"That's what I'm trying to figure out."

"*I* don't have anything against Tasha. I mean, I hardly know her. It seems to me the only person who would want to threaten her is you, Little Sister."

This was what I expected her to say and what I hoped she wouldn't. I wipe a thin layer of melted snow out of my eyes. "You killed her dog so she'd suspect me. Everything you're doing is to set me up. Make me look guilty for Riley." I lean in, whispering in the absence of any others. "For *Caleb*. Jesus, Cora, after all I did for you. For all the secrets I've kept."

"I don't think you have anything to be afraid of," she says. "Unless, of course, your prints are on a missing steak knife from Dad's kitchen."

This hits me with an unexpected right hook. "You used one of Dad's knives and left it at the scene?"

"Oh, no. I'm sure whoever did such a terrible thing would've kept the knife as insurance. Ready to plant it at any time."

"There's a higher likelihood Dad's prints are on there than mine."

She shrugs. "All I know is *mine* aren't on it."

I take a small step back, almost expecting a flash of that same knife thrusting into my stomach. "You lured that animal out of its yard and slit its throat. You're a monster."

"No, sweetie. I'm a survivor. And everything was fine until you moved back to town. Now bad things are happening, and it's all your fault."

As I stare at my sister, I try once again to reconcile this woman with the little girl I knew. My big sister, who I can remember smiling as a child. Cora didn't change overnight. It was a gradual shift, one I didn't notice, until the seventeen-year-old version was the person she was meant to be all along. This person standing in front of me is the true Cora. I don't understand it, don't like it, but I can't change that simple fact. Imagining my sister as an adult version of the sweet, happy child I once knew is like picturing Hitler dying of old age after an uneventful life as a painter.

"Why are you doing this?" I ask her. "Do you want me to move away? Is that it?"

"I don't really care what you do, Rose, as long as it doesn't involve disrupting all I have here."

"And what is it you have? Some vapid, plastic existence? Your daughter has a poster of Lizzie Borden on her bedroom wall. Does that make you happy?"

"I'm letting her be the person she wants to be," Cora says.

"And what if she turns into you?" I ask. "Is that what you want? Are you counting the days until she's seventeen? Are you waiting to see if she's capable of doing what you did? What would you do then?"

This lands a punch, but her reaction is subtle. A couple blinks, a tighter smile. But rather than answer me, she turns and walks a few steps away, closer to the trailhead and the surrounding woods.

Her figure is backlit by a solitary streetlight, and she glows like some kind of fallen angel. The snowfall is lighter now, and through the flakes, I watch as she reaches into her purse and retrieves something. Facing away from me, she lowers her right hand and I see the silhouette of what she's holding. A knife. Thin and long. She just holds it at her side in her gloved hand, loose. Stares out into the dark, into the distance, as still as a mannequin gathering dust.

I have no idea if the knife is for effect, but she's surprised me, which is the last thing I wanted. Cora is ten feet away and I ease a few steps backward. This scene should be as improbable as a bad horror movie, but if I drew a line through all the moments of our collective past, it's obvious that this is where it all leads.

"This place is special because he's out there, somewhere," Cora says to the night.

That statement alone chills me more than the snow. Scares me more than the knife.

"Caleb?" I say.

"Daddy told me once. Said this is where he brought him."

Revulsion of the memory of that night overcomes me, but I can't back away. In fact, I reverse course, start walking toward Cora because I don't know if the recorder on my phone is picking up what's she's saying. I slide the phone out of my front pocket and palm it against my thigh.

"Dad buried Caleb out on this trail?"

She answers my question with one of her own. "Don't you remember that morning when he finally came back home? It was nearly daylight. We hadn't slept. You pissed yourself, just another stain we had to clean."

"No," I tell her. "I don't remember that."

"Daddy walked in the house, nearly passed out from exhaustion. Covered in dirt and sweat. Grabbed a drink and collapsed in the big leather chair. Didn't even change out of his clothes."

This part is all blank to me. I remember my father telling us to go get a tarp, and the next thing I recall is waking up in my bed sometime the next day.

"I must have blocked that out," I tell her.

She turns and the sudden movement startles me, causing me to drop my phone, which clunks on the parking-lot asphalt. Instead of reaching for it, I remain upright. Cora is a few fast strides away.

"You were nearly catatonic at that point," she says. "Daddy told us to sit on the floor next to his chair, and we did." The hand holding the knife sways like a sunflower in a gentle wind. "He patted us on the heads, like dogs. Said he'd been out on the Chester Woodall trail, and what he'd done was the hardest thing in his life. Physically, emotionally. But he said he did it because we were a family, and no matter how sideways families got, they stuck together."

I remember none of this. I glance at the ground and see my phone, screen pointing up. I'm horrified to see the recorder app visible, counting away the seconds as it captures our conversation.

"He never supported me," I say.

"That's because you left, Rose. Sticking together means being together, *all* the time."

I almost ask what happened to her to make her who she is, but the moment I part my lips to speak, they are shut by a horrible, blinding thought. A thought so distorted and perverse it can't be tethered to reality, but it invades my brain as if planted there in a microchip.

The thought is this:

My father molested Cora.

Maybe for years. And this is why she's who she is. Why she did that to Caleb Benner. I have no evidence of this, or even an inkling of it, but it's forcefully real and possible.

I gasp. She takes a step closer. I hold out my arm and kneel to the ground, scooping up my phone.

"You're overcome," she says, taking another step closer.

"Stay away from me." I rise.

"Daddy was so loyal to us. How he protected us when the police came and asked us questions."

I'm dizzy with fear and adrenaline. "I barely remember talking to them."

"You didn't talk to them for long. Neither did I. And Daddy was there the whole time, putting an end to things before we said anything stupid."

"God, stop calling him Daddy," I say. "You never call him that."

She moves closer. Slow, like a statue animating. "You never appreciated him like I do. You never saw all he did for us." Another step.

"Stay back," I say.

"Why? What do you think I'm going to do?"

"Just stay back."

Cora brings the knife in front of her, takes one more stride forward, and stops. She's now ensconced in shadows, as all boogeymen are.

"I'm not like him," she says. "Not as loyal. I'll do whatever I need to, to whomever I need to, in order to make sure secrets remain secrets. Even if that means family."

I take three steps back, sliding the phone back in my pocket, wanting both hands free. My car is unlocked, and I'm guessing I'm faster than Cora. But would I have enough time to pop the trunk and search for the tire iron before she attacks?

I decide the best move, if it comes to it, is to just get to the car, get inside, lock the doors, and get the hell out of here. Out of the park. Out of my father's home.

Out of Bury.

"Don't be so skittish, Rose. I'm not going to hurt you."

"You have a knife," I say.

"This isn't for you. I'm leaving this here, out on the trail, somewhere in a safe hiding space. Safe, like Caleb. This is the knife you don't want found."

"That's what you used to kill the dog?" I ask.

"I'm just saying you don't want this knife turning up with the police. Nor do you want the police talking to me, because I have a very distinct memory of that night that's probably very different from yours. I can be pretty convincing, you know. And when they realize what you were capable of when you were only fifteen, they'll easily believe you killed your husband, too. It all fits together."

I'm horrified by how right she is, but I don't want to give her the satisfaction of showing it.

"You're the one who wrote about these very coincidental things in your books," she continues. "And you and I know the scene about the boy is true, so why wouldn't the wife-killing-husband scene also be true?" Cora tilts her head to one side. "That's your weakness, Rose. Your ego. You just had to write about the past, didn't you? You had to brag about it."

"*Brag?* Do you know how many nights I wake up in horror because I dream about what happened?" My voice is far from a whisper now. "I wrote that to help release it from my brain. I'm not like you, Cora. I live in constant shame and guilt over that night."

"Well, then, I'm surprised in the last twenty years you never went to the police."

"There's still time for that."

She walks up to me but I hold my ground. The simmering fear I've had all night suddenly vanishes, replaced by a desire to inflict pain. This is what soldiers must feel at the brink of a battle, the moment they finally push forward through fear and into the fray. Violent destiny.

"I don't think so, Rose. You're more like me than you care to admit. We're sisters, after all. Raised in the same environment together. Same stimuli."

I swallow, then ask the question I'm not sure I want an answer to.

"Did he touch you? When we were kids, did he touch you?"

Her face is stone cold, and I notice for the first time it's stopped snowing. For a moment, everything is still and silent, a funeral home at midnight.

"We grew up in the same house," she says. "You tell me."

"I...I never saw." I try to think of my childhood, of any time I felt there might have been something off at home. Amiss. "He never did anything to me," I tell her.

"So why would you think that about me?"

"Because I'm trying to understand what it was that made you..." I glance down at the knife in her hand, the tip pointing to the ground. "What you are."

She leans in and I can smell her. Smelling like adolescence.

"A dog is just a dog," she whispers. "No one asks why it tears the rabbit apart."

With that, she turns and starts walking away, down the parking lot and toward a trail covered in a thin layer of snow. After she disappears into the night, a glow emanates and I realize it's the flashlight on her phone. She navigates the trail into the distance, disappearing into the trees, her light distant and intermittent. Firefly.

I head back to my car, where inside I find an ounce of warmth. I leave my sister to the dark, absorbed by the cold, the wet. Leave her to this place of bones.

Perhaps it's the one place she finds peace.

# FORTY-THREE

**Whitefish Bay, Wisconsin**
**November 12**

**COLIN DROVE HOME LATER** than usual, already two hours past sunset. He navigated the streets of Whitefish Bay, guessing he had two minutes left before he was in his house. Three until he was on his couch, beer in hand, fire turned on. It was his night to cook, but he wanted to sit for a little while. Fifteen, twenty minutes. Sit and do nothing. Allow his brain to slow down.

But he wasn't home yet, so on the drive from downtown, he'd allowed himself a few thoughts about Rose Yates. He considered her the way someone would a brain teaser they couldn't solve. A little bit every day, hoping the answer would suddenly reveal itself. He had no solution for Rose Yates. He had theories but no answer, and theories didn't do him a lot of good.

On the drive, he also pondered the Yates family in totality, which led to him thinking about *family* in general. How there are some good families in the world, some bad ones, but mostly all those in between, the mixtures, the good kids and the black sheep. Which one was Rose? he wondered. Did the Yates family all share the same characteristics, or was there something about Rose that deviated from the others?

*And what,* Colin wondered, *will my family be like? Will my baby grow up to be like me, like Meg? Neither? And after seven or eight decades of my own life, will I become like my mother, gentle during the daylight, confused and vitriolic after sunset?*

The more time Colin spent ruminating about the past and fearing the future, the more he realized there wasn't a damn thing tos be done about either of them. Why, then, waste so much energy dwelling on both?

Perhaps that was the real puzzle to solve. How to be in the now. The here. Maybe owning the present was really the key to happiness.

Later, months later, years later, Colin would remember this thought. He'd remember back to this specific moment, driving the streets of Whitefish Bay, two minutes from home, three minutes from his beer and couch. This thought about the dwelling on the past and the future he'd remember with equal doses of irony and pain. And then, when he was much, much older, with a sad and crushing acceptance. Only with this acceptance would he ever finally own the present.

His cell phone buzzed. The display on the dashboard showed Meg's face, a picture he'd taken two years earlier on their trip to Bermuda. Meg had been standing in their hotel room, getting ready for dinner, putting her earrings in when Colin told her for the millionth time he loved her. When she'd turned and smiled, he'd taken her picture, capturing a look on her face that he wanted to always remember. The way she looked at him with such a subtle understanding that only he could see it.

He pressed the Answer button on the screen.

"Hi, baby. Almost home."

The voice that came back wasn't Meg's. It was female, older, and carved with confusion.

"There's been an…oh, just something horrible. An accident," his mother said.

"Wait, what…Mom? What accident? Where's Meg?"

His mother didn't reply.

"Put her on the phone," Colin said.

"Oh, dear. It's just terrible. She can't talk."

Every nerve ending in Colin's body burned. He'd had plenty of moments of pure adrenaline as a cop, but he never knew what it felt like when it was simultaneously steeped in dread. Now he did.

"Mom, where are you?"

"At the house. Oh, it's so terrible. She was just helping me clean up."

Colin hit the gas. "Listen to me. Don't move. I'll be right there. Tell her I'm coming. Just tell her I'll be there in a minute. Less." He didn't wait for a reply. Colin disconnected and called into dispatch, requesting emergency medical services at his mother's address. He didn't even know what had happened, but all his mind could picture was Meg having gone into labor early. Maybe she tried to lift something too heavy. Damn it, he told her she shouldn't be moving things around at his mother's house. But Meg had insisted, saying she wouldn't carry any big boxes. Saying she just wanted Jackie's home a little more in order by the time the baby came, and she knew Jackie wasn't going to clean anything herself.

Oh god, he thought. Oh please god. Let the baby be okay. Meg would never get over losing the baby.

Colin wasn't sure he could, either, but he knew it would destroy his wife.

As he tore down his mother's street and came to a skidding stop in front of her house, all Colin could picture was Meg in the bathroom, sobbing, blood on the floor.

Not the baby. Not the baby. Not the baby.

That was all he could ask.

Up the sidewalk. Hurdled the three steps to the porch. The door was unlocked and he burst through it.

And there was Meg.

Right at the bottom of the stairs, boxes spilled next to her body. Those fucking empty Tupperware containers, a plastic red lid next to her face.

Colin knew his wife was dead the moment he saw her face. Her contorted body. He'd seen a lot of death in his life, death that came in just about every form it could. He knew what a person looked like once all life had evaporated, and Meg was that person now.

Eyes half open, glazed. Hair spilled like cream cola on the hardwood floor. Chest down, right arm awkwardly splayed, lower torso at an angle that just shouldn't be. Everything Colin had learned about death was on display right there, on the floor of his mother's house, the house Colin had grown up in, embodied in the woman who had been his anchor, and now no one would be able to stop Colin from drifting out to sea.

Colin broke in that moment. Broke so much he couldn't even comprehend how many pieces to him there were. He collapsed next to Meg on the floor, his blood pumping so violently within, thinking if he could only give his heat to her, bring her back, if only she could absorb him. Distantly aware of his mother, broken in her own way, saying how Meg had tripped and fallen, so sudden. Tripped on a silly box of empty Tupperware, a container holding more containers, and was that ironic or just stupid for such a thing to cause a fall. As she told Colin of his wife's death, his mother picked up the Tupperware and placed the containers on a nearby heap of magazines, too late to do any good.

Colin was aware how cold Meg was, that she must have been dead for some time, and why didn't his mother call for help earlier? He heard himself shouting *the baby the baby* and how maybe their child was still alive, kicking, gasping, and clutching to the death around it, like a young child suffocating inside a dry-cleaning bag. Colin saw his hand reach for Meg's phone on the first riser of the staircase, and as that finger dialed 911, he heard the sirens outside.

Of all the times he'd responded to an emergency over his career, of all the control he had to exude as he walked into the tragedies of others, Colin, in that moment, did indeed drift away, yielding all responsibility, all control. There was a sickening relief to it, not to be in charge, and trusting others to sweep in and manage the scene. Maybe time would pass and he'd come out of his fugue and be told everything was fine. The baby was fine. Meg was fine. Looked worse than it was.

But the drop of logic he still possessed told him that wouldn't be the case. There would be no good news. Not now. Maybe never again.

Shaking. Someone was shaking him. Arms.

Lights.

Sirens.

None of it mattered. Colin kept drifting, and soon the sea in front of him became vast, flat, and endless. No breeze. No movement. A world above, a world below, and just the speck of him in between.

His second-to-last thought as he floated into some other consciousness was of Rose Yates. No specific thought, just her. *What a fucking shame to have that woman's face come to my mind in a time like this*, he thought. *A goddamn, fucking shame.*

His last thought was that his baby was a girl. He didn't know how he knew it, but Colin was certain. A girl. Little girl.

That was the thought shattering the very last piece of him, smashing it into a fine powder and blowing it up into the sky, where it drifted, becoming a part of everything else.

Everything and nothing, all at once.

# PART III

# FORTY-FOUR

**Bury, New Hampshire**
**September 18**
**Twenty-Two Years Earlier**

**THEN I SEE HER.**

Cora, in the doorway. Materializes like a ghost.

And this thing. This tiny little thing that's scarier than the blood or the gurgling, the lunging or the prints. Even more horrifying than the scream.

It's the smile.

Cora's smiling. Gentle, genuine.

As if posing for her yearbook photo.

Caleb stumbles toward me and falls over just a few feet away. My fifteen-year-old brain can't do the math, can't derive the logic of the situation. Therefore, this must not exist. Must not be happening.

But when Caleb reaches forward and grabs onto my ankle with his right hand—nearly toppling me—there's no pretending this is simply a bad dream.

"Please," he gasps, "she's c-crazy."

Then I scream. Loud and fierce.

"Shut up!" Cora yells at me. "The neighbors will hear you."

But I can't stop. I yank away from Caleb's grip and back against the hallway wall. It doesn't occur to me to try to help him. All I can do is scream.

With just a few swift strides, Cora is on me. Right forearm across my chest, pinning me to the wall. Left hand over my mouth. I shriek a second longer, the sound muffled against her palm. Her skin is wet and salty, and in this moment, I realize I'm tasting blood. Caleb's blood. I look down at her forearm pressed against my chest. My gaze scans the length of it until I see the Swiss Army knife clutched in her fist, daggerlike, the longest of its blades unhoused and angled just slightly away from my breast. I recognize the knife because I have a matching one. They were in our Christmas stockings five or six years ago, because Santa knows every little girl wants a multi-tool pocketknife.

The blade is dark with blood.

"Shut the fuck up," she says. "We need to think. Gotta figure this out, Rose. You and me. He attacked me. He attacked me and I was defending myself."

"No," Caleb manages. "She…she's lying. Please…"

Cora lets go of me, turns, and delivers a harsh kick to Caleb's head, which snaps upward for a split second before his jaw crashes back to the floor.

He moans as Cora returns her attention to me.

"You're a part of this now."

"What's happening?" I manage to say. My throat is on fire, as if I've just swallowed a cup of hot sand. "We have to call for help."

"We will." Her voice is steady. How is she so calm? "You just need to understand. Caleb attacked me. In my room. Tried to rape me."

"No!" he screams, which turns into a sob. "It's not true. I didn't… do anything." He gets up to one knee before falling back to the floor, slipping on his own blood.

"*Shut up!*" Cora howls, the calm vanished. Turning to me, she says, "I had to do it. I didn't have a choice. You need to believe me, Rose. I thought he was going to kill me."

A movement to my right. Caleb is finally standing at the edge of the stairs, facing us. His upper body hunched, breaths shallow and erratic.

"Please…" His labored huffs are painful to hear. "She st-stabbed me." He looks down at his crimson T-shirt and pats his chest, then sobs again. "Oh god. Oh my god. I need help." He inserts a finger through his shirt and touches what I'm guessing is open flesh, his eyes in disbelief.

Cora takes a step and faces him. Her body is rigid, taut. He is unstable, weakened, his legs shaking in an effort to remain upright. Caleb is a strong kid and has three or four inches on my sister, but right now, she is the only threat in the house.

"Please…" He reaches a hand out and places it on her right shoulder. Not in aggression but for support. "I don't…I don't understand why—"

He doesn't finish his sentence. Cora arcs her right hand—the clutched fist holding the open blade—high above her head, then brings the knife directly into the flesh above Caleb's clavicle, the soft area between his neck and shoulder. It makes a sound I've never heard before and know will never leave me for the rest of my life.

She releases her hand, leaving the knife inside him.

Caleb's eyes bulge, a mix of surprise and horror.

"How does that feel?" she asks him. Her voice isn't even angry. If anything, it's flirty.

Caleb stumbles, loses his balance, then falls backward down the flight of hardwood stairs. It sounds like a bowling ball being rolled down the steps, and as he reaches the landing, there's a nauseating crunch that can only be some part of him breaking in two.

Silence. Desperate, painful silence, interrupted only by my own breaths. I'm still pressing my back against the wall, wishing I could disappear within it, transport to anywhere but here. Cora stands at the top of the stairs, her back to me, arms lifted by her side, a scarecrow.

Maybe two minutes have passed since Caleb first emerged from the bedroom.

Cora descends, slowly, one stair at a time, until her figure disappears from my view.

That's when I hear the distant sound of the motorized garage door opening and then, a few seconds later, closing.

Dad's home.

# FORTY-FIVE

**November 13**
**Present Day**

**I WAKE SCREAMING. THIS** isn't unusual after I have the dream, but Max is in my bed and my shriek startles him to tears. It's his habit to come into my bed after I've fallen asleep about once a week, and I hadn't even known he was in here tonight.

"It's okay," I tell him. "I was just having a dream." I reach out to rub his back but he pulls away from me, angry. "You know that I have bad dreams from time to time."

"You *scared* me," he says, his voice muffled into his pillow.

"I'm sorry. I didn't mean to."

He says nothing. I reach out and touch his shoulder, and he pulls away.

I'm so tired of trying.

I'm so tired of everything.

I fall back into my pillow knowing sleep won't come easily, if at all.

The sweat cools on my neck, and I see Cora in my mind as I saw her hours ago at the trailhead, arms spread, knife grasped in her right hand, facing the woods as if praying to some god who listens only to her.

My mind races. I focus on my breathing and repeat a mantra, hoping it will help.

*I am.*

*I am.*

*I am.*

My heartbeat slows and, after time, sleep tugs at me, but there's the problem with all this. I'm too exhausted to do anything but stay in bed, yet I don't *want* to sleep. I don't want to return to the place I just was, the world of my past. I'd rather go through my day torpid and dizzy with fatigue than keep reliving that horror.

*I am.*

*I am.*

*I am.*

A voice tears into my head. She sounds an awful lot like me, but there's no bullshit about her. She's the part of me that forces my eyes open when all I want to do is look away.

You are WHAT, exactly?

*I don't know,* I tell her, this reasoning Rose. *I just am.*

Wrong. Everyone can be defined as something. Let's start basic, Rose. Are you a good person or bad person?

*I'm a good person.*

This Rose isn't buying it. She says, I'll let you believe that. But would you agree that good people are capable of doing things society considers bad?

*Yes, of course.*

So here's a more specific question, and I don't want you to think about good or bad, right or wrong. Just facts. The question is this: Are you a killer?

I don't answer but rather repeat my mantra, telling this Rose my words have nothing to do with her question.

*I am.*

*I am.*

*I am.*

Okay, fine, ignore me. Let's talk about someone else. Let's talk about Cora.

This is easier. *Okay.*

Is Cora a killer? she asks me.

*Yes.*

But is she a good person?

I don't hesitate. *No.*

How about this one...a question you've thought about before, more so tonight than ever before. Has Cora killed again?

*Yes,* I reply. *The dog.*

No, not the dog. People. People like Caleb. Innocent people.

*Caleb wasn't innocent,* I tell her, hearing the weakness of my argument in my own thoughts.

You don't really know that. Based on everything you remember from that night, do you truly believe he was trying to hurt Cora?

*It's what I've always let myself believe, because it's the only way to rationalize what happened. He must have been trying to hurt her. Maybe she overreacted, maybe she—*

Cut the shit, Rose. You're still rationalizing. Answer without thinking. Answer from your soul. Answer from the place you've been unwilling to explore for twenty-two years. Do you think Caleb was trying to hurt Cora?

*No.*

Do you think she enjoyed killing him?

*Yes.*

Do you know why she did it?

*Because she's broken. She's different and she's broken.*

Good, Rose, we're making progress here. You won't sleep and you'll feel like hell tomorrow, but we're making progress. So given all you know about her, all your interactions from the past and present, do you think Cora has killed again?

*I have no idea.*

What if she has, Rose? What are you going to do about it?

*I can't change the past.*

She's still young. She's got a lot of years ahead of her. Just think what she's capable of. Not to mention the influence she's passing down to that little Lizzie Borden of hers.

*I never really thought it was—*

WHAT ARE YOU GOING TO DO, ROSE?

I give my own mind one final answer. One answer, as I lie here in the dark, listening to the soft snores of Max, to whom sleep comes with ease and he doesn't even realize what a gift that is.

In the dead of this night, I answer.

*I have to stop her.*

# FORTY-SIX

**Whitefish Bay, Wisconsin**
**November 15**

**COLIN NEVER APPRECIATED THE** dark as much as he did now. In his living room, ten o'clock at night, all things silent, all lights off. He'd spied stray ambient light from the digital thermostat and put duct tape over it.

Curtains drawn, taped flush to the wall.

Darkness, like a womb.

A delicate, fertile womb. It was Colin's world now. Maybe just for tonight. Maybe for the rest of his life. But in this womb, Colin felt some kind of relief. Certainly not happiness. But relief. Like pain being transferred from one body part to another.

Also, he was drunk.

He stumbled in the darkness to the refrigerator and opened it. Brilliant light flooded him, causing him to recoil. He reached inside and grabbed an eighth beer. Twisted the cap off, then closed the door, entombing himself in the blackness once again.

Comfort in the void, he thought. Colin tipped the bottle back and spilled as much as he drank, but it didn't matter. Nothing mattered in the void—that was how voids worked.

He stumbled back to the couch and collapsed onto it. Maybe he'd sleep tonight, but probably not. Not for more than a few minutes at a burst, just like the last few nights. How the fuck does a person ever get a real sleep after their wife and baby die? Seems sacrilegious. If Colin ever got a peaceful eight-hour sleep again, he'd slit his wrists out of sheer guilt.

Sleep made him think of Riley McKay, who slept so hard he never came out of it. And Riley McKay made him think of Rose Yates. Colin had become obsessed with her, something more easily admitted in the pitch-black of his house. Obsessed with needing to know what she was guilty of, if anything. Since Meg's death, Rose Yates had occupied a disproportionate chunk of Colin's thoughts. He hadn't wanted this, but he had no power to fight the way his synapses fired.

And that led to tonight, where Colin, deep in the dark, seven and a half beers in his bloodstream, wearing nothing but underwear and a thousand-pound suit of grief, powered on his phone, bringing a digital spotlight into the void. He searched his contacts for Rose Yates, whom he'd added in his list before his trip to Bury.

Colin thumbed the Call button.

*Fuck it,* he thought, bringing the phone to his ear. *Fuck everything.*

Four rings, then voicemail. It was an hour later in Bury.

He dialed again.

Voicemail.

One more time, and on the third ring, an answer. The voice was tired and hardened, dried soil sown with bitter seeds.

"Hello?"

"Hello, Rose."

"Who is this?"

"Colin Pearson." He tried to keep his voice from slurring.

The sleep cleared from Yates's voice, replaced by anger. "It's late, Detective. Why are you calling me?"

"Because I figured the case out," Colin said. The darkness, drink, and desolation allowed him to do this. A week ago, Colin couldn't have imagined making a call like this. But life is nothing if not unpredictable.

"We've been over this," Yates said, and now Colin thought he heard a little fear creep in alongside the anger. "Do you know what time it is?"

"I'm not talking about your husband," Colin said. He heard the slurring now but didn't care. "I'm talking about Caleb Benner."

He could hear her breaths but nothing else. Nothing for maybe ten, twelve seconds.

"Have you been drinking?" she asked.

"You remember Caleb Benner, right? Disappeared back when you were in high school?"

She didn't reply.

"Last seen by your sister," Colin continued. "Cops talked to one Cora Yates right there in your house. Same house I interviewed you in, matter of fact. And just like with us, her interview was cut short. So I'm kinda curious to know what conversations went on in the Yates house after the detective left."

There was a slight tremble in her voice as she spoke, but she managed to keep her composure. Not everyone could, Colin knew. Some suspects just lost their shit entirely when a cop cut close to the bone. But not Rose Yates. She knew cops. Knew everything about the inner workings of police. Or maybe Colin wasn't in any shape to mount a proper interrogation technique.

"This is a serious breach of protocol," she said. "Calling me up in the middle of the night, drunk. Harassing me. Accusing me of...of I don't even know what. But something far beyond your jurisdiction, I know that much. So you can be assured I'll be contacting your department in the morning."

"I would expect nothing less," Colin replied. "They'll be upset. Maybe I'll get fired. Probably not. I'm on bereavement leave. Probably just get a reprimand."

"Bereavement leave?"

"Wife and child," he said, adding, for no reason he could think of, "Unborn child." The tears didn't come this time, probably because he'd released so many of them earlier. Between the alcohol and the crying, Colin was dehydrated, his skin scratchy, his eyes full of burn. "Died a few days ago. So we have that in common, Rose. We each lost a spouse."

"Oh my god. I'm sorry. I...I don't know what to say. But that's still no reason to—"

"Turned out I was right," he interrupted. "A baby girl. Little girl."

"Detective, that's terrible. I think maybe you should go to sleep. Please leave me alone, and I won't report this call."

"You want to know what I think, Rose? I think you know what happened to Caleb Benner. 'Cause you wrote about it, didn't you? In your book. *Child of the Steps*. So I wanna ask you something." Colin went from sitting to lying on the couch, staring up at nothing. "What happened on those steps? Your dad mentioned to the cop back then he was having some of them refinished."

Rose said, "I don't have a clue what you're talking about."

Every suspect said that at some point. Some sort of denial. The words were meaningless, Colin knew. It was how they were said that mattered. And there, in Rose's voice, he heard a crack.

"I think you do," he told her. "I think your family has a big secret. Maybe the biggest secret in all of Bury."

"Leave me alone. You can't be doing this."

"You're right," he conceded. "This is a completely inappropriate phone call, and let it be known..." Colin subdued a belch. "Be known I'm acting on my own, not as a member of Milwaukee's finest."

"I'm hanging up now," Rose said. "I have nothing to say to you."

"One more thing," Colin said, hoping to keep her attention for one more moment. He nuzzled the phone between his cheek and couch cushion, and it hit him how tired he was. Tired as if he were living a dozen lifetimes simultaneously, all of them hard. "Just know you can talk to me," he continued. "I understand family bonds. Hell, I'll even tell you something about me related to your book. My wife? She fell down the stairs, too. Right the fuck down the stairs, just like the character in your book. Corey Brownstein. Same initials as Caleb Benner. How 'bout that?"

"Detective—"

"My mom's a hoarder. Has shit all over the house. Meg just wanted to help her organize, just a little. Though that's like throwing a pebble into the Grand Canyon. Is that how the saying goes? But she just wanted to help. And Meg, despite being as pregnant as she was, went over to help. First few minutes she was there, she tripped on a box of Tupperware at the top of the stairs. Fell down the steps. Hardwood. Head over heels. Snapped her neck." Colin listened and watched himself from a distance. Analytically. This man on the couch in the dark, processing what had happened for the first time. Without judgment. Without emotion. "My mom has dementia, which gets worse starting in the afternoon. Sundowner's syndrome, or some such. And this was in the evening.

"So Meg falls, dies. Baby...baby dies, I'm guessing. Soon after. Little girl, I said that, right? Little girl. Dies. And my mom... She does nothing for, like, two hours. Just sits there with Meg. Can't process it, so just sits there. Maybe if she called for help right away, my little girl could've lived. But my mom? She called me two hours after it happened. And by then, there was no saving anyone." Colin was close to sleep and, strangely, almost at peace. "It just happened a few days ago. But I've already forgiven my mom, because that's what families do. She's not a bad person, she just has brain rot. I suppose everything rots eventually."

Silence on the other end of the phone.

"My point is, Rose, that I know all about families. I get it. And if you ever want to talk to me about your family, you'll find someone who understands."

Colin stopped talking. He had nothing more to say on the matter.

Then he pulled the phone out from under his cheek and saw the line had disconnected. Rose had hung up at some point.

He liked to think she heard what he'd said.

The bit about family. He hoped she'd heard that, because it was all true.

Seconds later, Colin was asleep, dreaming terrible things.

# FORTY-SEVEN

**Bury, New Hampshire**
**November 16**
**6:03 a.m.**

**SIX IN THE MORNING,** my phone buzzes. The text doesn't wake me. I've been up for hours.

I slept fitfully for a couple hours after Pearson's call, but by one thirty, I conceded defeat to any further rest. I put on my robe, grabbed my laptop and phone, and went downstairs into my father's study. Poured myself a cognac and then eased into his chair. I wanted to be Logan Yates for a little while, if only to see what he would do in my position.

Bleary-eyed, sipping a drink I didn't even enjoy, I summoned the mindset of my father. It didn't take long before I realized exactly what he would do. He'd fight with every ounce of his being. He'd use his money and ego to rage against anyone posing a threat to him. He'd lie, he'd misdirect, he'd sue. Logan Yates wouldn't be satisfied until he not only won the battle but humiliated his enemy in the process.

At what point would Logan Yates take off and run? The situation would have to be hopeless.

I don't want to be like my father, and sitting there in the room smelling of cigar smoke and bitter years, I knew I had to do the exact opposite of him. The moment I came to my decision, a tremendous weight lifted, as if I'd been held captive for years and I woke one morning to find my cell door wide open.

After this decision, I wrote. Wrote like I never had before. Not in fits and bursts, but a marathon of words, hour after hour, getting up only to pee and refresh my drink. I didn't even know where my current story was headed until I began typing, but it unveiled itself to me as I wrote, as if I were driving a hundred miles an hour at night and could just see enough of the road ahead to keep from crashing.

I exhausted myself after four thousand words. I've never written anywhere close to that amount in one sitting. For the past hour, I've sat here, staring at nothing, still marginally drunk, wondering how I will get through this day.

I reach over and lift my phone from the mahogany side table, a piece of furniture that hasn't moved from this spot as long as I've been alive.

The text message is from the Bury School District. All schools closed due to weather. I'm completely disoriented, trying to remember any weather at all. There was snow a few nights ago, though it wasn't bad. The night at the trailhead with Cora. A dozen lifetimes ago.

I can't wrap my mind around what day it is, never mind the weather. I look back to my phone.

Monday.

How is it Monday already?

A year ago, I was on top of everything. Had to know the news.

The temperatures for the coming week. People's social-media tidbits. I consumed everything, but now my brain is so overloaded I can't even remember the last time I showered.

I stand, aching from hours hunched over a laptop. Blood drains from my head, threatening to topple me. I fight it, steady myself, and walk over to the window and pull back the heavy gold drapes.

Under the pink wash of dawn, an unexpected foot of snow suffocates the landscape. The sight of so much transcendent white causes me to stare for minutes on end, mesmerized. More than mesmerized. In absolute awe.

I've experienced this one other time: freshman year of high school, a ten-day trip to Italy with my school. We had three days in Rome, and my friends and I were much more concerned with Italian boys than Italian culture. One morning was dedicated to touring the Vatican, which promised to be boring in addition to hot and crowded. I had no reason to be interested in anything religious; the only time my father mentioned God was in using his last name, *damn it*. Within the sea of worshipping humanity that morning, our tour group finally inched inside St. Peter's Basilica. Self-absorbed fourteen-year-old that I was, I was impressed at only a minimal level. Another big cathedral. So. What.

But then we scuffled over to one side of the vast room, which was so packed you could nearly taste the mix of sweat, perfume, and body odor. I couldn't even see over the tourists in front of me and was approaching claustrophobia and at the brink of losing my mind when something happened. All of a sudden, there was no one in front of me, and I was staring into a glass wall with a sculpture behind it.

It was the first and only time I've seen Michelangelo's *La Pietà*. It took a moment to realize what it was, but then it clicked. This was Mary holding the body of her son. I had seen a thousand images of Jesus on the trip, but this sculpture grabbed my heart and squeezed so hard I stopped breathing. At that age, I cared little for art and had no connection with Jesus, but in that moment, I was so transfixed by this sculpture—*how could it be so smooth?*—that I began to weep. Right there. Tears fell, and I thought I was having some kind of religious experience.

But it wasn't that. It was the combination of profound beauty and sadness at such an exquisite level that it left me no option other than to cry. I hadn't experienced anything like that again.

Until now.

This snowfall.

The beauty enveloping the sadness.

With the tears welling in my eyes, I think once again about death. The rainbow in the cornfield. It's all so gorgeous, and it's all so tragic. The extremes of human emotion and how ironic that thoughts of dying fill me with such life.

I'm still staring transfixed at the world outside when my father's voice resonates behind me.

"What a fuckhole of a mess out there."

And the beauty is gone.

The sadness, however, remains.

# FORTY-EIGHT

**I TURN TO MY** father, who's dressed for work; he wears three-thousand dollar suits like a second skin. He's always known how to package himself: crisp and clean, almost vintage. Even in these autumn years of his life, my father remains attractive on the outside, despite whatever ugliness festers within.

"Bobby just called. Said he can't drive me. Can't even get out of his own driveway."

Bobby is my father's driver, who for years has taken him and Peter to the Yates Capital office in Boston every weekday. I can't even picture my father behind the wheel of a car anymore. It would be beneath him.

"They just closed the schools," I say.

"I hate working from home." He steps into the office and stares out at the landscape. I don't imagine he sees what I do. He sees only inconvenience. "It's lonely."

"So take a day off," I tell him. "Go back to bed. Enjoy some quiet."

He looks at me as if I've just casually suggested he kill himself.

"I don't think so."

"Why not? Can't you just enjoy the things you have? Or do you want to work until you die, dropping dead during a conference call?"

A grunt. "There're worse ways to go." He takes a step toward me and sniffs. "Jesus, you already drinking? I can smell it on you."

"I haven't stopped," I say. "I've been up all night."

"Doing what?"

"Losing my mind."

His glance scans me up and down, as if looking for cracks. "That's pretty dramatic."

I don't argue the point.

"You were right," I tell him. "I shouldn't have written what I did. And now it's too late. Whatever's going to happen, I can't change it now."

He lets his gaze rest on me a moment longer before walking to the door and closing it. He tells me to sit, which I do. In his chair. I expect a reaction from him, even just a subtle narrowing of the eyes at this infraction, but there's nothing. He takes the other chair and leans back.

"Tell me," he says.

And I do.

I tell my father everything.

About Detective Pearson's first visit to Bury. About Cora and what I suspected she did to Tasha Collins's poodle. What Willow said to Max, and even her creepy Lizzie Borden poster. I tell my father that Cora is both unhinged and dangerous and could be a threat to the rest of the family. I tell him about the drunken call from Pearson and what he said about Cora's interview with the police.

Through all this, his face is ice. I've never spoken to him this honestly in my life, and there's a comfort to his steely gaze, as if his tensile strength can withstand all the pressure I'm putting on him in the moment.

I reveal to my father my recurring nightmares. How I relive that night from two decades ago and can't take it anymore. The final thing I confess is that the weight of the secrets has broken me and how I think about the allure of death more often than I should. Really think about it.

Some indeterminate amount of time later, I finish, drained of everything. I slump in my chair, thinking I could sleep a year and it wouldn't be enough.

My father is quiet, contemplative. After a silence that stretches for minutes, the first thing he says is "I think you killed Riley."

"*What?*"

"You heard me."

I force myself to look into his eyes, gaze past the perpetual squint and lock in on him with resolve. I would do this as a kid, in those times he showed enough interest to chastise me about something. I'd lock eyes with him and take his barrage, focusing as deeply as I could into his pupils, those black orbs behind the squint, nearly hypnotizing myself in the process. He could belabor his verbal abuse, never yelling (and never needing to), but as long as I kept my focus, his words lost their impact. He'd eventually run out of steam, and that felt like a victory for me.

I keep my focus on those pupils, just as I did as a kid.

"I've stopped caring what you think," I say.

He doesn't blink. He looks at me with a fierce intensity.

"The truth doesn't matter," he says. "*I* think you did, and I'm your father. So of course the cops think you did. They're going to keep coming after you for that, and that's already led to this Milwaukee detective sniffing around the Benner disappearance." His left cheek twitches for a split second, the only sign of anger he's allowed. "You said you can't change what happens next, but you're wrong. I've spent my life figuring out how to change inevitable destinies." He leans in and jabs a finger to the sky, as if all the world's answers are housed there. "And you can only change the future by doing something unexpected. Something the other guy never expects you're going to do."

I ask, "Who's the other guy?"

"Whoever's trying to fuck you."

I break eye contact first. Damn it.

"How?" I ask. "How is it you've lived your life all these years in this way? You can't be happy. Not with how you make everything a competition to win. A battle to survive."

"I think you and I have very different definitions of happiness."

"We're different in every way," I say.

"But are we really, Rosie?"

I choose another path, asking him something I've thought of many times but never voiced. "Did you ever love another woman after Mom?"

This jolts him, breaks his focus. I see it in his face.

"What the hell kind of question is that?"

"Because I'm trying to figure out how much capacity for being a human you have. If any."

His reaction is stunning. Logan Yates, the man of ice, the man who'll come at you with biting words but no emotion, picks up the glass I'd been drinking from all night and throws it against the office door. It bursts, sending shards of Irish crystal raining through the room.

The sound of it is deafening.

The silence that follows is louder.

*Do something the other guy never expects you'll do.*

His squint turns into a momentary pained scowl. Once his expression returns to its normal, indecipherable form, he says, "You don't tell me about love. You don't talk to me about your mother. You don't say one more fucking thing about happiness, because with all my money, that's the one thing I can't afford. When she died, she took all that away. Don't you see that?" He's struggling so hard to maintain composure. "I'd be *happier* if I'd never known her at all. And if you tell me the shit about 'better to have loved and lost,' I'll slap you right in the goddamn mouth."

He's never laid a hand on me in his life, but given the energy he's radiating in the moment, I don't doubt his words.

Still, I'm well past the point of fear.

"If you'd never known her," I say, "then you'd have no daughters."

Not even a pause. "Exactly."

I'm not so numb that this doesn't sting, even coming from a man who means less to me by the day.

"I have to leave here," I say. "We're going back to Milwaukee."

"What good will that do?" he asks.

"I won't be running away anymore."

"But you will be," he counters. "You've got problems there, you've got problems here. No matter which direction you run, you're still running."

My fingertips dig into the leather of the chair's arms. "And what would Logan Yates do?"

"Confront your problems face on. Your sister is who you have to deal with immediately. Both of us do, really. Cora, she's..." He turns and glances out the window; the sun's reflection off the snow paints him into a ghost. "She's unpredictable."

It's my turn to accuse, the desire fierce and consuming. I rise from my chair, lean over his, placing my face close to his ear. His sandalwood aftershave hits me, whisks me back thirty years, a time machine I wasn't expecting. Tucking me in bed at night, I'd smell that exact scent, and how specific that memory is and what a narrow window in which it exists. He barely ever showed me affection, but I remember it now. How at one point he was somewhat sweet, or at least pretending to be.

"What did you do to her?" I ask.

"What?"

"Cora. What did you do to her?"

"Meaning what, exactly?"

"You always liked her more than me. Paid her more attention. By the time I was ten, you didn't seem to know I existed unless you were pissed off at me. And yet she turned into a monster." It hits me that I've been trying to ask him this for over twenty years but never realized it. "What did you do to her?"

He leans in, jaw tight, face inches from mine. "You're too soft, Rose. Cut the shit. Ask me what you're really thinking."

I swallow, finding the question hard to say aloud. Maybe it's because I don't know if I really want the answer. Deep breath. Close my eyes. That makes it easier.

"Did you touch her?"

I half expect him to hit me, denying my accusation with an open palm. The other half of me expects him to collapse into himself, a defeated man, admitting his guilt for the first time in his life.

Instead, he holds the straightest poker face the world has ever seen and says, "Did you kill your husband?"

The game continues.

I don't answer. Neither does he.

"Well, then," he says. "There you go."

"I don't want to be a part of this anymore," I tell him. "This family. This...this life."

He raises a hand, not to strike me but to touch my cheek, the kindest, coldest thing he's offered me in a long time. "You can't choose your family, Rose." He removes his hand and my cheek warms. "Tonight," he says. "Get Max out of the house. I don't care how. Sleepover."

"What? Why? It's a school night."

"I don't give a shit. Just figure it out."

"What are you talking about?"

"We're going to have a family meeting," he says. "You, me, Cora. We're going to figure this all out. Once and for all. No more loose ends."

I start to protest, ready to launch into a verbal attack. He cuts me off with a raised hand.

"There is *nothing* more important than this right now," he says. "You hear me? This requires our full attention."

I want to defy him, tell him things are on my terms now. Tell him I don't want to take his orders. But I don't say any of these things.

Because he's right.

If I have any chance of reaching the sister I used to love, of tapping into that tiny bit of humanity I know she still has left, it has to happen now.

Reach her, or stop her.

Tonight.

# FORTY-NINE

**12:14 p.m.**

**THE DAY FILLS, THREATENING** to rise over my head and drown me.

Max slept in after I told him school was canceled, then bundled up and played outside long enough to make a snow fort. When he realized there were no other kids to play with, he came back inside and stuck his nose in a book.

A snowplow service came and dug out our driveway while municipal crews plowed the streets. Few cars have ventured out; it's as if we're all hunkering down and waiting for some threat to pass.

More snow from the same system is due this afternoon, lasting into the evening. As much as another ten inches. The Weather Channel has named the storm Jayden, but given its timing, it feels a lot more like a Cora.

I call Alec and ask him if he has Micah tonight. He says he does, and when I ask if Max can have a sleepover, he agrees before even asking why. I'm poised to tell him my prepared excuse about my father being ill and not wanting Max to be exposed but instead say nothing. It feels good not lying.

I fix Max grilled cheese for lunch and tell him about the sleepover. His reaction is what I expect.

"What? Why? I barely know Micah."

"Well, this is a good chance to change that," I tell him.

"But why?"

"Because I have a meeting tonight." This is the truth after all.

"Can't I just stay here?"

"No," I say, using a tone that's firm but calm. "You guys can maybe watch a movie. Stay up a little later than usual. Could be another snow day tomorrow."

He studies my face, knowing something's wrong, something's different, but he can't figure out what. Normally this is the point where he'd start whining about having to do something he doesn't want, and maybe that's coming, but in the moment, he's silent and observational.

I decide to tell him more. Not about tonight but about the future beyond that.

"I'm thinking maybe we should go back to Wisconsin."

Max's eyes grow wide. "To visit?"

"No, to live. Move back there. Back home."

"Really?" He smiles but holds something back, as if I might tell him I'm just kidding. The thought of doing something like that breaks my heart.

"Yeah, really. Would you like that?"

"*Yes.*"

"Not the same place," I say. "Not the apartment. But back to the same area. To your regular school."

He leaps out of his chair and starts jumping around like a cartoon character. There's not much subtlety about Max. When he's sad, he'll sometimes throw himself on the floor in despair. Often when he's happy, he'll literally jump up and down for joy.

He stops for a moment. "When? When can we go?"

"Soon. Real soon."

Another Snoopy happy dance and I'm smiling, my cheeks stretching. A sensation I've grown too accustomed to living without.

I reach out and pull him in toward me. In my ear, he says, "Just you and me. Back home. That's all I wanted."

That's enough for the tears to start spilling. Silent tears he can't see. In this moment, I see a future. A life beyond tomorrow. Even happiness.

I found out Riley was cheating on me in January, and thoughts of a happy future have eluded me until now. What a long and wearisome abstinence.

Max gives me an extra squeeze, one so hard it hurts, but I don't complain.

"Why?" he asks.

"What do you mean?"

"Why are we going back?"

I pull back and look at him. He sees my tears now. "Because we're not happy here. That's all that matters."

He thinks about this, then a cloud passes over his face. "Are you still in trouble? Like about the stuff Willow said. The stuff with…Daddy?"

I shake my head. "There might be a few more questions I have to answer, but that's it."

The cloud becomes a thunderstorm. "What if they don't believe you? What if they take you away?" He looks at the ground, his default position.

"Max, look at me." He doesn't. "I'm not going anywhere. It's you and me from here on out. We have to take care of each other, and the best way I can take care of you is for you to listen to me. *Really* listen to me, Max, and do what I say, okay?"

He mumbles.

"Max, look at me."

It takes a moment, but he does.

"This is really important. Just because we're going back doesn't mean life will suddenly be easy. There'll be some tough times ahead, and that's why I need you to always listen to me. More than ever, okay?"

"Okay," he says.

"Good. Now, I need you to have a sleepover tonight with Micah with no complaining. Got it?"

His face scrunches in the way it always does before an argument, but then he relaxes it again. "Got it."

I want to bottle this moment up in a leakproof container, because there's magic here. There's hope, which I've all but abandoned since a detective from Milwaukee sat down in my father's living room and asked me if I loved my husband.

But I can't bottle this. Can't cage it. Can't contain it in any fashion. Because hope, like everything that lives in the wild, dies if it's not given the space to thrive.

# FIFTY

**2:47 p.m.**

**I'M THE ONLY ONE** on the road, driving inside a snow globe. The second round of flurries promised by the late afternoon has arrived early, coming down in large, puffy flakes that pile on top of those already fallen. Alec's house is only a mile away but the going is slow.

Everything looks gentle in Bury. A few houses already have Christmas decorations up, the owners not even bothering to wait for Thanksgiving to pass. Bury has always been a festive town. I've always struggled to appreciate Bury's superficial beauty because I know the ugliness beneath.

We pull into Alec's driveway, freshly plowed but already collecting a new layer of snow. It's coming down harder now, and as much as I want to stay with Alec for a little while, I don't think the storm has my schedule preferences in mind.

I ring the bell, Max a foot behind me. He was quiet on the way over, but he wasn't complaining, so I'm counting that as a success.

Alec opens the door, wrapped in a cashmere sweater and a smile, and at the sight of him, I think he's the only thing genuinely beautiful in this town. I want to disappear into his chest and shut the rest of the world away.

"Hi," I say.

"Hi, there. Hey, Max. Micah's excited for the sleepover."

Max's voice is cotton soft. "Hi."

Alec ushers us into the house, and I tell Max to take off his boots.

"Thanks again," I tell Alec. "And sorry this was so…last minute."

"No problem. It'll be good for the boys to have some time together. Micah's got a movie or two in mind. Popcorn. Hot chocolate, of course. Assuming that's okay with you."

"That sounds great. I wish I could be here, too."

"Yeah, so do I," he says. Alec looks down at Max. "Hey, buddy, feel free to head into the living room. Micah's putting together a LEGO set. You like LEGOs?"

Max shrugs. "I guess."

"Give me a hug," I say to Max. "Then go play with Micah."

Max shuffles over and gives me a weak embrace. I bend down and look him in the eyes. "Have a good time, sweetie, okay?"

His expression is somewhere between apathetic and miserable. "Okay."

"And remember what we talked about. We're a team."

"I don't like this," he whispers.

I whisper back, "I know. But you need to do this. I'm sorry." I rise. "Now, go play."

Alec directs him. "Right in there, little man."

Max disappears around the corner and Alec steps closer to me. "Can't you stay for a little while?"

I shake my head.

He gives my shoulder a glancing stroke with his fingertips. "You okay?"

How would I even go about answering this question?

"No," I say. "But I'm not going to break down like the last time I saw you."

"You can if you want."

I nod, knowing the chances of me doing so increase every second I stay. Every extra moment I might have someone to lean on increases my vulnerability, and I don't want to be vulnerable. Not now, not tonight. I have no idea what's going to happen over the next few hours, but I need Teflon skin for the occasion.

"I know," I tell him. "Thank you."

"Do you want Max to call you tonight before he goes to bed?"

"I'd love that, if he wants to. If he doesn't, that's fine, too."

"Got it."

I point at Max's backpack on the floor. "He has everything he needs for tonight and for school tomorrow, assuming they don't cancel again. He'll eat anything, but don't be offended if he picks at his food. He just does that. Maybe no soft drinks... A lot of sugar isn't great for his mood."

"Sure."

"And speaking of, he might get moody. Ever since his dad... You know. He might zone out all of a sudden, and he's not always comfortable around people he doesn't know that well."

"We'll make sure we give him the space he needs."

"And..." Vulnerability leans in again and I push it away. The bitch is heavy, though. "Just...thank you."

He leans down to get closer but stops short of contact. "Seriously, Rose. I'm happy to help."

I reach up and pull him in to me, not for a kiss but a hug. He wraps his arms around me, and I press my forehead against his chest, hoping to transfer some of his strength to me. I allow myself this moment, five seconds of support, and when I let go, it's like stepping off the roof of a skyscraper.

I blink away a blossoming tear and look at the floor. I like picturing us together, but the high likelihood we'll never end up together keeps me from admitting this to him.

What a world.

I don't look at him as I head to the door. I open it, and the snowy world outside has darkened to a soft gray, promising an early and long night.

I turn to say goodbye when a thought hits me.

"Hey," I say. "I…I heard about Tasha's dog. That's just horrible."

He nods. "I still can't believe it."

I swallow dry. "Any idea of who did it?"

He shakes his head. "I don't know who'd do something like that," he says. "I can't even begin to wrap my mind around it. Wouldn't wish that on my worst enemy, which…hell, Tasha's not far from that category." He almost smiles, then pulls back. "Micah. Man, that just about killed him. I mean, how do you explain that to a kid? No child should have to go through a trauma like that." His expression changes, a flash of nervousness. "I'm sorry, I mean, clearly what Max has gone through—"

"You're right," I say. "No kid should have to go through anything traumatic, whether it's losing a pet or a parent. And you can't explain it to them. I've tried. The best you can do is love them. Promise them you'll always be there, whether you can keep that promise or not. It's all you can do." I lean toward the open doorway, into the cold and growing dark. "Anyway, I just wanted to say I'm sorry."

"Thank you. I'm sorry, too." He slides his hands in his pockets and squares his shoulders. "And whatever you're going through, whatever you have going on tonight. It'll be okay. You'll be okay."

"Is that a promise you can't keep?" I ask.

He thinks about it, sighs, and to my surprise says, "Yeah, maybe it is. I've had a few of those in my life."

I say nothing else before turning, walking outside, and pulling the door closed behind me.

I stare out at the car, the roads, the billions of flakes, and I'm swept up in painful desperation. A sudden and insatiable desire for everything to just be...over.

Before I can put up my defense shield, a dark and hungry thought swoops in.

*How wonderful it would be to drive into a tree. Head-on. Seat belt unfastened. Headfirst, through the windshield, a jagged shard slicing right through my carotid artery. The blood. So much blood, draining in such a hurry from my body I'd feel nothing more than a surge of dizziness, then fatigue, and then a soft and beautiful drifting away. Surrounded by snow, all that blood. Like a piece of performance art.*

I have to shake my head to keep the fantasy from growing.

"Let go," I say aloud.

I trudge to the car, wanting to let go of everything, but still the world clings to my back.

# FIFTY-ONE

**Boston, Massachusetts**
**4:15 p.m.**

**COLIN NAVIGATED HIS RENTAL** car out of the facility and did everything the woman inside the Google Maps app told him to do. *Turn right, turn left. Merge onto the highway, continue for five miles.* He happily relinquished all decision-making to her.

The last decision Colin had actively made was this morning when he booked a last-minute flight to Boston. After that, the rest of the day he'd spent in a trance.

He was exhausted and headed directly into a brutal snowstorm, not a good combination. He'd driven through some bad storms in Wisconsin, surely worse than what he'd encounter here, but his fatigue was probably the equivalent of blowing a point-oh-seven on the breathalyzer. Not legally impaired but enough where a responsible citizen wouldn't have driven.

One hour, seven minutes to Bury. Eight-minute slowdown twenty miles ahead due to road conditions.

Colin had slept perhaps an hour after he talked to Rose last night, a conversation he struggled to recall. And sleep wasn't even the right word for it. It was more like his brain just overloaded and shut off, a circuit breaker flipping. But after that hour of sleep, his brain went straight back into panic-and-desperation mode. He'd lain in bed all night, praying for more rest, finding none.

Instead, a singular thought had begun looping in his mind.

*Go back to Bury.*

There was no context for the thought. No plan. Nothing other than a sense he had to return and confront Rose. That she wasn't allowed to get away with what she did, even if Colin didn't know what exactly that was. But she was guilty of something. Rose. Her sister. Her father.

Someone had to pay for something. For all the shit in the world. Someone had to pay.

By four in the morning, Colin gave up, turned on the bedroom light, then downed the first of many cups of black coffee as he searched for flights to Boston. There were a few options, none of them cheap, which was to be expected when booking to leave the same day. Boston had gotten snow last night with more to come later in the day, and while some flights had been canceled, there was one option available. Seven hundred bucks got him a direct flight on one of those little Embraer jets, landing at three in the afternoon. Seven hundred goddamned bucks. That was what tragedy did for you; you lost all perspective.

He hadn't known what to put in for the return date, so he just made it for a few days later, giving it little serious thought. Maybe he'd want to come home tomorrow, maybe never. Perhaps Bury was supposed to be his final destination in life. After all, Bury called to him. He cared about nothing else. Not his mother (who'd left him several voicemails), not his job, and certainly not the surprising amount of paperwork generated by the death of a spouse.

He'd get to those things. Probably. His mom had to be cared for. It was time for a nurse, and Colin would have to be the one to make those arrangements. But she'd have to drink alone and tuck herself in at least another night, because Colin was singularly focused.

Focused, but with no plan.

He settled onto I-93 North and eased his back against the car seat, now aware of how much tension he'd been carrying. The snow was already falling and it took only a couple of minutes before it became mesmerizing, wrangling Colin's overtired brain. At one point, he caught himself drifting into the other lane and corrected, but not before earning a honk from another car. He waved to the offended driver, then powered his window down an inch, letting the cold air whip his senses back to attention.

Then he thought, what would be so bad if he just ran off the interstate? Maybe veer right into a ditch. Or the concrete support pillars of an underpass. Wouldn't that just solve everything?

The thought of it became more hypnotizing than the snow. It was all so simple, as if he'd just made one random move and solved a Rubik's Cube.

No more worries. No more pain.

He knew thoughts of suicide were common for people like him... young widows and widowers. But it was different knowing about these thoughts and having them. Knowing about them was like reading a bland brochure about signs of depression. Having these thoughts... Well, there was just a comfort to them he couldn't rationalize. It was like winning Powerball. All his problems would be gone.

All it would take was a flick of the steering wheel. He'd want to take his seat belt off first, of course. The airbags might be meddlesome, but if he accelerated to seventy or eighty, they wouldn't be enough to save him.

There was an overpass coming up. Maybe a half mile away. Less, even.

Colin put his foot on the gas, passing the rest of the cars that were taking the snow with caution. Once he had a clear shot, he swerved into the right lane, nearly losing control of the car before he wanted.

Sweat breached the surface of his forehead, which was strange, because he felt as calm as he'd been in years.

Sixty-five.

Seventy.

Seventy-five.

The overpass loomed, closing in fast.

*How strange,* he thought. *That could be the place I die. Right there. Just ahead. Seconds from now. Right there.*

*I wonder if someone will put a cross there for me and if there will be flowers?*

Some distant pocket of his brain raised a feeble protest, yanking the luring thoughts away for a split second. Long enough for Colin to force himself into a decision.

*Consider the options. Don't just kill yourself. You have to* choose *to kill yourself.*

He didn't ask God what he should do. He asked the next biggest thing.

"Okay, Google, what should I do?"

The app's answer was immediate and her voice sounded different from before. Lower. Commanding.

"Fifty-nine minutes to Bury, New Hampshire."

Colin laughed. Laughed like a lunatic inadvertently released from forced psychiatric observation. Laughed until it hurt, which was long enough to whiz by the underpass, careening into none of it.

When his laughing eased and he became more comfortable with the idea that he was likely losing his mind, Colin eased his foot off the gas and drove like everyone else on the road. Cautious and conservative.

*Well, hell,* he thought.

*Might as well see this thing through. Got the whole rest of my life to kill myself.*

# FIFTY-TWO

**Bury, New Hampshire**
**September 18**
**Twenty-Two Years Ago**

**CALEB BENNER STRUGGLES TO** breathe at the bottom of our staircase, the wheezing wet and muddled, the exhales more successful than the inhales. I've made it as far as the third step from the bottom before I'm unable to will myself any closer.

I don't know if this is real. I have nothing to compare it to.

The knife is no longer inside him, having scattered a few feet away. Caleb tries to extend his arm, stretching his fingers toward the blade, but it's only a futile gesture, a waste of whatever energy he has left. The knife is out of reach, and his strength has long since left him. Blood pools around his torso, his back twisted at an angle I've only seen on a broken doll.

"We have to call 911," I whisper.

"No, we don't," Cora says. She's sitting on the floor next to Caleb, stroking his hair, as if simply petting a cat.

"I don't understand what's happening." I can't stop looking at Caleb. His face. His desperate face. "Please tell me what's happening."

"This is happening," she answers. "It doesn't have to be complicated."

She pats his cheek as I hear the sound of the door from the garage to the kitchen open and close.

Dad.

My father walks into the foyer, briefcase in hand, his suit as razor-sharp as when he'd left the house in the morning. He stops when he sees the scene before him. The dying boy not even twenty feet away at the base of the steps. His older daughter, stroking the hair of the victim. His younger, paralyzed with fear, mouth hanging open, refusing to move beyond the third step.

"Jesus Christ," he says. He drops the briefcase and sheds his jacket, letting it fall to the floor. He walks over, eyes fixed, jaw tight, arms swaying. My father reaches Caleb and grabs his face.

Caleb's eyes widen just a touch and then he settles back into a dreamy state. He's going fast, I think.

I plead with my father. "*Help him.*"

My father ignores me and speaks only to Cora.

"What happened?"

"He tried to rape me," she says, her voice devoid of any emotion. "It was self-defense."

"Look at me," he says. Not to Caleb but to Cora.

She does.

He leans closer and whispers into her ear. There's something shared between them I can't know about. But whatever it is he says, at the end of it, Cora does nothing but offer a casual shrug, as if he asked her what she wanted for dinner.

I can't do the math that solves any of what I'm seeing. Cora's an unconvincing liar, my father doesn't care, and a sixteen-year-old boy is dying in between them.

My brain snaps and I suddenly find volume to go along with my words. "*HELP HIM!*" My voice is shrill, piercing, scaring me.

This gets my father's attention. He leaps toward me and seizes my arm.

"Keep your voice down," he says. Then he takes a breath, tries to compose himself. "Rose, there *is* no helping him. He's too far gone."

"Call...call 911. He's still breathing!"

The hand around my upper arm squeezes tighter. "You don't understand. I said there's no helping him." He releases me, rolls up his shirtsleeves, then addresses us.

"It doesn't matter if we love, hate, or are indifferent to each other," he says. "We're family. We're the fucking *Yates* family, and that's more meaningful than anything you'll ever achieve in life. Your family name."

I glance at Cora. She's grinning.

"We aren't perfect," he continues. "And when we make mistakes...we make them together." He points to Caleb. "This is a mistake, and we can't change it. Cora didn't do this. We *all* did it."

My voice takes on a rasp. "*What?*"

"This is us," he says. "This moment. This mistake. We are all part of this. And that's why no one will ever know about this except us."

Caleb releases a soft moan, and it sounds so feeble I'm convinced it's his last.

"He's alive," I say. "He can be—"

"No, he *can't*. He's going to die. That's a fact, Rose."

"But we have to call the police. It was self-defense, like she said. We can't just—"

"We can," my father says, cutting me off. "And we will. *No. One. Knows.* That's all that matters. One rule, the rest of your life. No. One. Knows. I'm not saying it'll be easy, but you protect your family. Above all else, family."

This whole time, Cora has said nothing. But she loses her grin and nods her head at our father, an obedient student. He looks down at her and says, "I'll deal with you later. What you've done. The jeopardy you put our family in."

"I'm sorry, Daddy."

"Fuck you," he says to her, jarring me even more. "You aren't sorry, and that's the problem. I've known it for years. *You've* known it. You are incapable of 'sorry.' And it's led to here. To this."

She returns his gaze, wild-eyed in muted defiance, saying nothing.

"You two...you will listen to me." He's pointing now, first to Cora, then me. "This night is going to be hard, and you're going to do every goddamn thing I tell you to do. There will be no questions. There will be no refusals. You do *exactly* everything I say, and if we're lucky, we might be able to move past this. Now I'm going to ask you if you have any questions. Here's a clue to the answer: if you ask me a question, I'm going to have a big fucking problem." He pauses, and in the silence, I hear nothing from Caleb. "So, girls, do you have any questions?"

This is the moment my bladder releases, and warm pee runs down the insides of my thighs. I can't help it. My entire being is nothing more than a mix of horror, confusion, and shame. I say nothing, but I do allow myself one final look at Caleb. His neck craned, his eyes angled upward, his gaze both at and beyond me. I can't even tell if he's still alive or not, and I'm hoping he isn't simply because I don't want to watch it happen.

Or, worse, witness what I think my father will do if Caleb labors on. Snap his neck like a bird that's flown into our window.

But witnessing his death is exactly what happens, because just as I'm about to avert my eyes, Caleb smiles. Not a wide smile, hardly even a little one. Almost imperceptible. A gentle pull of the mouth, a look of satisfaction, as if he just realized everything in the world is going to be okay. That look is followed seconds later by his death, which I realize only because there is a sudden, indescribable absence of energy in the room. He doesn't change, his gaze still fixed in my direction, but there is no more life in those eyes. I don't know how I can tell this. I just know.

I turn my head and look at the wall on the staircase behind, to the exact spot where Caleb had his final view of anything in his ephemeral world.

There's a painting wrapped in an ornate golden frame. The painting depicts a cornfield, and the sunlight from behind lights up the stalks in transcendent shades of green and yellow. In the distance, the sky is black, the color of a deep and painful bruise. A thunderstorm that's just passed by, leaving the field wet and fresh, alive. And in the middle of the painting, a rainbow. It looks close but just out of reach. A thing to touch, if one could ever manage such a thing. It looks solid enough to be real. I picture it soft, spongy, like a long piece of taffy stretched out for miles.

The rainbow is the last thing Caleb Benner saw.

I like to think it made him smile.

"Cora," my father says, breaking the silence. "Go to the garage and get a tarp."

# FIFTY-THREE

**November 16**
**Present Day, 7:43 p.m.**

**I WAKE IN A** jolt, slick with sweat. Disoriented, with a sickening pit in my stomach, like I'm coming down with the flu. I blink. Two, three times. Push myself up.

My world comes back after a moment, and I regret it does. Early evening. I'm on the couch in the living room, where I'd lain down to rest my eyes after getting home from Alec's house. I must've fallen asleep. What once was a threat of night is now a reality. One lamp shines on a side table, but everything else is dark.

I get up, stumbling in the hangover of a too-long late-afternoon nap. Head to the window. The gleaming, sublime view of the white morning snow is replaced by the sight of swirls of flakes streaming in the orange haze of the streetlamp, like a swarm of locusts delivering plague.

I shake my head, as if that will dispatch the sticky remnants of the dream. This time, it took me all the way to the end. The horrible, suffocating end.

And that picture. The cornfield and the rainbow. That part was new, and as far as I can recall, the only bit of the dream I've ever had that wasn't true to life. We never had a picture like that growing up. It was just inserted there by my subconscious, a safety valve to relieve the pressure on my brain. To convince me that maybe Caleb really was happy at the very end.

"It's nearly eight."

I spin, almost falling over. My father stands at the entrance to the living room, his figure silhouetted by light coming from the hallway behind him. He flicks on the overhead lights.

"You look like shit," he says.

He's in a suit. It's eight at night and he worked from home all day, and my father is still wearing a suit. The knot of his bloodred tie is still tight and cinched to the neck.

"I fell asleep."

"I noticed. Your sister will be here soon."

I'd nearly forgotten. The family meeting. A whole new wave of unpleasant washes over me.

"Can...can she even drive in this? I had a hard time getting home several hours ago."

He shrugs. "We'll find out."

I rub my eyes. "I need to eat something."

"Or you can just head straight to drinking. I'll fix you something."

It's both a horrible and great idea. Wine will give me a headache. Whiskey will wreck me.

"Vodka," I say. "Something with vodka. Not too strong."

"Okay."

I move into the kitchen, aware I'm barefoot. Open the refrigerator door and look at everything in there. The only reason it's even stocked is because of Abril, and I scour the offerings of leftovers. What would be appealing on most days creates zero desire in me now. I shut the door, knowing I'll be drinking my dinner.

The jolting shrill of Cora stiffens my spine.

"It's a fucking nightmare out there," she yells from the foyer.

In the diffused reflection of the refrigerator's stainless steel I see none of my features, just a faint glowing outline. A ghost.

I turn and leave the kitchen.

Time for the family meeting.

# FIFTY-FOUR

**5:18 p.m.**

**COLIN FORWENT THE SHITTY** motel on the outskirts of town for a bed-and-breakfast in the center of Bury. The Oak Street Inn was charging him one-seventy-five a night, and he couldn't care less. He'd been comfortable enough at the seventy-dollar place where he'd stayed on the department's budget, but Colin wanted to spend money. Not on comfort. Just for the sake of spending money. Maybe that was what happened when you lost everything. You got the urge to keep it going. Spend every last penny in frivolity, wipe the slate clean. Start all over again. Or maybe not.

The storm saved its biggest punch until after Colin arrived in the afternoon. He pulled into a six-space parking lot that had been shoveled from a previous round of snow but was filling up again. Just one other car sat in the lot, several inches blanketing it.

The proprietors of the inn were a middle-aged couple, Franklin and Keith, who said they'd bought the four-room B and B eight years ago and invested considerable time and money into renovations and upkeep. It looked it, Colin thought. The Queen Anne Victorian was colorful, ornate, and detailed enough to let Colin imagine he'd walked into a gingerbread house. That'd been a pleasant thought for a few seconds, until the idea of gingerbread houses made him think of Hansel and Gretel, which in turn got him in the mindset of dead children. That was the moment Colin realized he could never escape his own mind.

He told the couple it was his first time in Bury, and he was visiting some family friends. He didn't have his badge, gun, or anything else that might indicate he was PD. Neither his own nor Bury's police department knew he was here. As far as his sergeant was concerned, Colin was on leave until he could figure out how to put his life back together.

*Is that what I'm doing here?* he thought. *Putting my life back together?*

He didn't have an answer for that. He had nothing. No plan, no idea of his next move. No sense of a way to heal. All Colin had was a profound urge to know the truth about the Yates family, and he thought the best way to start that was by looking Rose Yates in the eyes again, this time with his own fresh perspective on death and suffering. Colin didn't know what came after that, but that would be a start. An expensive trip for a solitary, fleeting moment, but everything began somewhere.

Eight o'clock, and after a pot-roast dinner that was surely better than his diminished appetite allowed for, Colin found himself sitting in the octagonal living room with his hosts. He was the only guest that night, another couple having canceled their plans due to the storm.

Colin sipped a glass of port, a drink he'd never tasted before. It was sickly sweet. He managed a weak smile and toasted his new friends, thanking them for their hospitality. One last sip, then Colin knew he'd hit his wall. Sleep was coming at last, whether he was ready for it or not. Beautiful sleep.

He said good night to Franklin and Keith, then lumbered to his room on the second floor. Inside, he collapsed onto a puffy queen-size bed that had two quilt blankets and at least a half-dozen pillows. After a few seconds of stillness, he summoned enough energy to take off his clothes, get under the covers, and plug in his phone.

The last thing he did was set his alarm. Eight in the morning. Twelve hours away. Colin had no idea of what he didn't want to be late for, but something was going to happen tomorrow.

It just had to.

# FIFTY-FIVE

**7:55 p.m.**

**I WALK INTO THE** foyer and Cora's standing there, snow melting on the arms of her black fleece jacket. She's disheveled, a look she doesn't wear often.

"Where's Dad?" she says.

"Here," he says, appearing from the hallway. His jacket is off, hands in pockets. No drinks anywhere to be seen.

She looks to him. "I don't like being summoned, especially when I have to drive in this shit. I nearly lost control of the car."

"Calm down," my father says. "You made it, didn't you?"

"Barely."

I'm hardly able to process it was just this morning I asked my father if he molested her. I scan back and forth between the two of them, searching for some kind of link, some kind of indication of damage. How do you find evidence of more damage in things long broken?

"In the study," he says. "We'll talk there."

"Why there?" Cora asks, just to argue.

"Because that's where the booze is. We'll be needing it."

"I can't drink and drive back out in this."

"No," he says. "You can't. I want you staying here tonight."

"What?" She releases her purse and lets it fall to the floor. "I can't just stay here. Peter's waiting for me. I don't have any of my things with me. You can't just expect—"

"Cora." My father sighs. "Just shut up, will you? Now, get into the study."

He turns and heads down the hallway and I follow. I enter the study after him, and he hands me an already-poured drink.

"Vodka tonic," he says. "Twist of lime. Simple. Classic."

"Thanks," I say. The crystal is ice-cold; the chill needles my forearm.

Cora hasn't joined us, and my father and I sit in the two chairs we used this morning. A couple of minutes pass before I say, "Where is she?"

"She's coming," he replies. "In her own time. She doesn't like to be told what to do."

Sure enough, not thirty seconds later, she appears in the doorway, purse back in hand.

"Where the fuck am I supposed to sit?"

My father narrows his eyes. "You have a hell of a mouth on you."

"Wonder where I got *that* from?"

"Take the desk chair and bring it over here."

"I don't like that chair. It's too hard."

She's a child, I think. She's a volatile and dangerous child trapped in a woman's body.

"Take my seat," I say, getting up. "I don't mind the desk chair."

Cora immediately slides into the leather chair without saying a word. I bring the desk chair and position it facing the two of them so we form a triangle in the center of the study.

My father stands and walks over to the wet bar. "What can I get you, Cora?"

"Cab sauv."

"I have a merlot here."

"Whatever."

He returns, hands her the glass, and takes his seat again.

"Well, then," he says. "Here we are. Just like old times."

The second he says this, I remember I wanted to record this conversation. Ever since I recorded Cora at the trailhead, I told myself to do the same thing with every subsequent conversation. It could be the only thing that saves me.

"Hang on," I say. "I need my phone."

"Why?"

I think fast. "Max is having a sleepover. He's supposed to call at some point."

My father waves his hand at me, gesturing me to hurry. I head out of the study and back to the living room. My phone is on the table next to the couch where I slept, and I grab it and swipe it open. No calls, no texts, twenty-eight percent battery. I select the audio recorder and turn it on, then shut off the display.

Back in the study, I place the phone faceup on the small table between our chairs. Trying to appear as casual as possible, I turn it so the phone's microphone faces Cora's direction.

"All right," my father says. "Everyone has what they need? Drinks? Phones? Canapés?"

"Yes," Cora says. "We're *fine*. Other than the fact that I don't know why I'm here."

"You're here," he says, "because you're a problem. And we need to figure out what to do with you."

There is no easing into this conversation. No soft opening jabs.

I take a sip of my drink, let the vodka settle on my tongue, and then it all begins.

# FIFTY-SIX

**"I'M THE PROBLEM? OH,** I don't think so. Not at all."

"You are," my father says. "The way you've reacted to…all *this* is unacceptable."

Cora's perched to launch a verbal assault but instead stops herself, sips her wine, and leans back into her chair. I see the change wash over her. She's shifting away from her petulant-child persona and slipping into the coolness she wore at the trailhead. Calm and chilling.

"Funny," she says. "And here I thought I was trying to save all of us from Rose's terrible decisions."

"By slitting a dog's throat?" I say.

She shifts her gaze to mine. "I don't know anything about that."

"Yes," I say, "you do. You know what you did. You're trying to set me up for what's happened."

"Oh? And what has happened, Rose? I want to hear you say it. Because all I know is the police were out here talking to you about your dear departed Riley."

I think about what's being recorded on my phone. It's not like it's only selectively capturing what Cora says.

"I didn't kill him," I say. "And I'm through talking about it. That's my problem, and I'm dealing with it."

"Oh, and how are you doing that?"

"I'm leaving Bury. Going back to Milwaukee."

My father snaps his attention to me. "Why would you want to do something like that? You've got everything you need here."

"All I'm doing here is hiding from my life. I'm not happy. Max isn't happy. I don't want to raise him here."

Cora crosses her legs. "You mean in a good private school and in a house rather than a hovel? Yeah, that sounds like a great idea."

"When are you leaving?" my father asks.

"Soon as I can. Hopefully within a week."

"I'm trying to help you, Rosie. How am I supposed to protect you when you're not here?"

"Dad, you have this idea we need to hide behind that huge front door. That we're only safe inside this house. Yet the worst thing that's ever happened to me happened right here." I nod toward the foyer. "Right over there."

He takes a drink. "Yes, it did. And I took care of the problem. You girls did what I told you to do, and I took care of the rest."

"Until now," Cora says to me. "Until you wrote that fucking book."

"Exactly what I wanted to talk about." My father sips with conviction, and he's nearly finished with his drink. "Why I called this family meeting. So let's stay focused. Back then, we worked together, and we've made it this far. Now we need to do it again. Renew our vows, as it were."

Cora jabs a finger at me. "She broke our vows. We were doing fine. I hadn't told anyone. And now she decides to tell the world about all the horrible things she's done in her books. First, her husband and now… now what happened in this house. She's the problem, not me."

As calm and reasoned as I want to be, my brain has other plans. It tells me to stand and tower over Cora, assume a threatening stance. So I do.

"You have no idea what you're talking about." My hands are shaking, fury, not nerves.

"Sit down," my father says.

"I don't?" she says. "You think you're innocent? Oh, I don't think so."

I want to smash my fist right into her cheekbone, batter that perfect face.

"You can pretend you didn't kill Riley, but how about *The Child of the Steps?*" Cora continues. "I suppose that's also a coincidence?"

"Rose, *sit*," my father commands.

I do not sit. "I'm human, Cora. A human with a conscience. With guilt and regrets. But neither of you know what that's like because you don't seem bothered by it at all." I place my hands on each arm of her chair and lean closer to her face. "We never talked about it. After that night, we all pretended like it never happened. So let me ask you." I can smell her, CK One mixed with a feral musk. "Caleb was never trying to rape you, was he? You lured him here. You wanted to hurt him all along."

Her expression doesn't change. "I think you don't know what my thoughts have ever been, Little Sister."

I'm not going to let her talk in ambiguities. "I know what I saw that night, and we're going to talk about it. Caleb Benner was begging for help, and you didn't have an ounce of fear or concern on your face. He was bleeding. You were smiling."

"Fuck off," she says.

"If he was trying to rape you and you fought back, we'd have gone to the police. Self-defense. The only reason not to do that is if you attacked him first." I rise up, point to my father. "He even knew it. Dad made the call right there, decided no one was going to know about it. Why would he have done that and jeopardized our family by covering everything up?"

"He was protecting us."

"No, it was because he knew your story was bullshit. Knew what you were capable of all along. He even said it that night. Something like, 'I've known it for years.' What was it, Cora? What had he known for years about you?"

"You don't understand anything," she says. "You write your little detective stories with no clue what really goes on in the minds of the people in your stories. You think you know, but you don't."

I pause, take a breath. "Tell me."

"Tell you *what?*"

"Tell me what it's like to be you. Tell me what happened to you. Tell me..." I try to get her to make eye contact, and when she does, it lasts only a second. Just like Max, I think. "Tell me who you are."

Cora softly shakes her head. "It doesn't matter who I am. What matters is what you've done to destroy twenty-two years of silence." Then she stands, and when she does, she doesn't look like my sister. She looks like the girl who came out of the bedroom while Caleb frantically tried to distance himself from her. "And what needs to be done about it."

She's in my face, my father is seated behind me, and sandwiched in their presence, a new disturbing thought hits me.

What if this family meeting isn't at all about what to do with Cora?

What if it's about what should be done with *me?*

# FIFTY-SEVEN

**CORA LOOKS AT ME** with a simple gaze, almost one of kindness. Or pity. Our noses are inches from each other. I stand my ground.

Ice clinks in my father's glass as he sips. "Cora was always different," he says to my back. "Quick to be cruel. Struggled with kindness. I wasn't so worried, not at first. After all, the same thing could be said about me." He lets out the softest of chuckles.

"No," I say, struggling to reconcile my father's words with distant memories. "We got along when we were little. We played all the time. You liked me, Cora. And I liked you."

Cora tilts her head and purses her lips. "Aw, aren't you fucking sweet?"

"You didn't see it, Rose," my father says. "You were too young to notice the differences between you and your sister, but you weren't like her. Not in any way. In fact, you were so dissimilar from either of us, I sometimes wondered if you were even mine."

I want to turn to him, to see my father's face, but I'm scared to turn away from my sister.

"What the hell kind of thing is that to say?" I ask him.

"Just the truth."

Several heartbeats pass. "*And?*" I say.

"I don't know," he admits. "I assume you're my kid, but who's to know the truth? I suppose it doesn't really much matter, does it?"

Cora finally speaks. "Maybe Mom fucked some bartender because she was bored. Maybe that's where you came from."

"Watch your goddamned tongue," my father says. "All I know is you two were never alike. I had to work harder with Cora, give her extra attention."

My stomach lurches at the way he said that. I pull back a few inches from her face, taking her all in at once. "Cora, did he..."

"You're so simple-minded," she snaps. "Not everything has a reason, Rose. Some things just *are*."

"Are what?" I ask. "What *are* you, Cora?"

I hear my father rise from his chair.

"Despite what I knew about her impulses," he says, "I didn't think your sister was ever capable of..." He clears his throat instead of finishing his sentence. "But I was wrong. I knew I was wrong the moment I came home that night. But what was I going to do? She was my child. My firstborn. I wasn't just going to let the wolves take her away."

I take a step to my side and pivot to face both of them. My father stands just to my right, my sister to my left, each only a couple feet away. The door to the hallway is behind me, painfully distant. The small table holding my phone rests between us. They each look at me with some kind of desire. A desire to control, maybe to harm.

I'm not safe here, but I can't leave. Things are unfinished.

"What else have you done?" I ask Cora. "Who else have you hurt?"

My father answers before she can. "I knew your sister needed my help after PJ died."

The words take me a moment to process, but suddenly I'm there, transported back to my ten-year-old self. PJ was our only pet. A black cat, long hair, shy and sweet. He'd come into my lap when I would watch TV. My lap, no one else's. The preponderance of my PJ memories are of him being old, slow, and unfailingly sweet.

I almost ask *What about PJ?* But I know better. The urge to throw up hits me hard.

"You said he just died," I say. "Old age."

My father shakes his head.

"I wanted to see what it was like," Cora says. "But I didn't do a good job cleaning up the mess. Dad found the blood in the garage, made me tell him what I did."

"You were what…twelve?"

She shrugs.

I take a step back, bumping into my chair. "You're sick. I can't believe I let Max go to your house. How could I have ever come back here?"

Everything I've ever known about Cora but wouldn't admit to myself unleashes at me with tsunami force. Am I so stupid or just always hopeful the truth is better than my perception of the world? Just like with Riley. I'd hoped he'd come to his senses. Calm down enough to see things were over and we'd be better off apart. But no. I stayed until it was too late, until the truth revealed itself with tragedy.

And here I am, back in Bury. Back in the very house where I've always denied who I suspected my sister really was.

"What about…" I start, then move around my chair until it's between us.

"Where are you going?" Cora says.

"What about any others?" I ask. "After Caleb. Where there others?"

Cora smiles, no teeth. "Are you asking if, in the last two decades, I've somehow managed to completely control the desire that possesses me? Well, sure, Rose. Of course I've controlled it. Easier than quitting smoking. Is that what you want to hear?"

That answer is enough for the vomit to finally release from my stomach. I bend over and heave vodka and bile onto the thick and undoubtedly expensive area rug.

"Oh, for chrissakes," my father says. "You and your puking. Just like when you were a baby."

I wipe my mouth, rise, and immediately get in his face. "Are you kidding me? Are you even listening to what she's saying?"

"You need to calm down," he says.

"No, I won't calm down. Your daughter...my sister...just admitted she's a killer." I'm only vaguely aware how loud my voice is getting. With each notch of volume, I'm increasingly unsatisfied, like an itch that gets worse the more you scratch it. So I keep getting louder. "She *murdered* Caleb Benner. She *murdered* that dog. And our family cat. And she... Who knows what else she's done. Who else she's killed." My father seems the craziest one here because his face is as calm as it was when we began the discussion. "Your daughter is a fucking murderer and you...you act like it doesn't matter."

Cora's voice breaks my focus on my father. "I never said any of those things."

I turn to her. "Then say it now. Admit what you've done."

She narrows her eyes for a split second. "Why? Why is it so important you hear me say what you want me to say?"

We lock gazes and I break first, and consciously or not, the first place I redirect my attention is to the phone on the table.

"What is it?" Cora asks.

"What?"

I'm incapable of hiding the guilt on my face. I lean down to reach for my phone, but Cora beats me to it. She swipes it off the table and takes a step away from me.

"That's mine!"

"I don't care," she says, dragging her finger across the screen. "God, not even a pass code, aren't you just..."

She stops talking, and I know it's now too late for me to do anything. The app I was using to record was the last thing I viewed before turning off the screen, which means it's the first thing to display.

"You little bitch," she says.

My father says, "What is it?"

She flashes the screen to him. "The little cunt is recording us."

"Oh god, Rose." My father sounds more disappointed than angry, which digs into my bones. From an early age, I was conditioned to not disappoint him, and even if I don't truly care what he thinks, it still triggers a reaction in me I can't avoid. "Why would you do something like that? We're family. Families don't break trust like that."

It's his voice. His tone. His simple statement of admonishment. This is what finally breaks me. Snaps my mind as easily as the most brittle and smallest of branches of a long-fallen tree. I'm not just loud anymore. I'm an explosion.

"Stop talking about family! Our family is shit, and you act like it is the only thing keeping the world together." I jab a finger at my sister. "She's trying to frame me for what *she* did to Caleb! She's a criminal, Dad. A *murderer*. And apparently you knew it the whole time, so what does that make you?"

Remnants of puke in my mouth, the bite of tears in my eyes. I try to fight the heat roiling my face. And my father. He's as cold as the snow outside.

"You could have said something for the last twenty-two years," he says. "But you didn't. So don't tell me how innocent you are."

"I was *fifteen*. Can you imagine what that was like for me?"

"You're not fifteen anymore, Rosie. Haven't been in a long time. So where's your conscience now?"

I want to tell him he's right and that I've already asked myself the same thing, and I've already come up with an answer. I want to tell him the reason I'm going back to Milwaukee is to stop all this hiding. That's all Bury is, after all. A place to hide. A fortress of my past. I'm done.

*I'm done.*

I'm about to tell him these things when I'm jolted by a horrible noise.

I look over. Cora's left my peripheral vision and walked ten feet over to the far side of the study, next to the unlit fireplace. She's swinging an iron fireplace poker with both hands, smashing it against the floor. I can't comprehend why she's doing this until I see what it is she's striking.

My phone.

She's shattering my phone into a thousand pieces.

All my recordings are gone.

All my innocence erased.

All I have left is my anger. Twenty-two years of rage. A lifetime of guilt. And a sense of needing to put the universe back into place.

For the first time in my life, I am my sister.

The monster with an unquenchable desire.

The desire to kill.

I launch at her.

# FIFTY-EIGHT

**SHE PIVOTS TOO LATE.** Cora's unable to raise the poker again before I plow into her, crushing her into the floor-to-ceiling bookshelves. Tolstoy, Melville, and others scatter to the floor, spines cracked open, probably for the first time. We fall with the books, Cora landing on top of them, and I on top of her.

The poker leaves her hand and clangs against the hardwood floor. I'm dizzy and confused, scared and elated. I want to kill my sister, but I also want to hold her tight, squeeze the crazy out of her, tell her I love her. My arms are wrapped around her in a bear hug, and the battle of my emotions rages in my head, unable to make a next move.

Cora has no such problem. From beneath, she begins hitting me with tight, balled fists, alternating blows to each side of my rib cage. They aren't desperate flails but rather measured attacks, each punch dealing swift, efficient pain.

*She's trained,* I think. Why this thought overrides all others in the moment I don't know. But my delicate sister who's never worked hard for anything in her life knows what she's doing.

How to fight. How to hurt.

I try to punch back but can't get any momentum. She keeps hitting me, sapping more of my strength with each contact. I have to get off her, regroup.

I start to push up and she grabs my hair and yanks back, opening my neck to her. She bares her teeth, and for a moment, I picture them tearing into my skin, my jugular, gnashing, blood spraying.

She doesn't bite. Instead, she grips the back of my head with both hands and crashes our skulls together.

The pain is blinding as everything goes dark for a second. I think I'm screaming. I don't know. Someone is.

She releases her grip and I roll off, scrambling as fast as my rubbery muscles allow. I look at her and Cora's grabbing her head, the impact just as debilitating for her.

I look over and see my father standing there, watching us from across the study. His expression hasn't changed, that perpetual squint locked in place, analyzing us as he would a financial statement. He still has his goddamned drink in his hand.

Then I realize that's all this is.

This fight. It's an analysis to him.

Now I understand what all this means to my father. What this point in time represents.

This is a decision being made for him.

If Cora kills me, everything can be laid to blame on awful Rose. They'll craft a posthumous narrative in which I was the girl who did a terrible thing as a teenager and tried to tell the world about it through her books.

But if I kill Cora, the liability of the family is finally removed. The daughter who can't control her urges, the girl whose past mistakes were always sure to be revealed will be gone, her terrible acts buried deep along with her.

Either way, my father wins. Which is why he's standing there, holding his drink, watching his offspring try to annihilate each other.

Logan Yates always wins.

I reach and grab the fallen iron poker, then lift myself up. As I get to my feet, my back is to my father as I face Cora, who scrambles to stand.

I raise the poker over my head, now grasping it with both hands.

Cora gets onto one knee before losing her balance and falling onto her back.

Now's the moment. She's vulnerable. I'm not. I have only seconds to make my move, and they might be the only seconds I'll have.

She'll kill me if I don't kill her.

Max. Think about Max. Both parents gone.

*Attack, Rose.*

*Attack with all you have.*

And still.

Still, I don't know how.

Don't know how to swing this heavy poker and smash it into my sister's skull. Don't know how to keep hitting her with it after the initial blow incapacitates her. Over and over, blood spraying, bone crunching, skin and face turning into lifeless goo.

I don't know how to do that, because I'm not Cora.

I can't.

I just can't.

The seconds pass, my body frozen, the poker held high and immobile. Cora manages to get to her feet.

She stares at me, a purple welt rising on her forehead, that toothless grin back in place.

She knows I can't do it. Knows I'll never be like her.

Her right hand slides into the back pocket of her jeans, and from it, she pulls out a folded knife. Black rubber grip. Like someone who's practiced for this very moment a hundred times, she deftly thumbs the three-inch blade from its home.

It clicks into locked position with horrifying authority.

My father, behind me, still says nothing.

"Are you ready for this?" Cora asks. Her voice is gentle, as if she's a young mother placing her child on the merry-go-round for the first time.

I don't answer her. Instead, I keep my gaze on Cora but address my father.

"Everything was always about family." I put more weight on my back leg and raise the poker higher. "We could have made things right twenty years ago, but we had to have secrets because that's how *families* take care of themselves, right? We could've brought peace to Caleb's family." My voice grows louder. Beads of sweat run from my forehead and down my nose. "But you kept insisting that families keep their secrets. Families protect each other. Well, what about now? Who's protecting us now?"

I direct the words at my father but keep my intense focus on my sister, watching her every twitch, every eye blink. Cora is half-crouched, knife in her right hand, coiled on the tightest of springs. I try not to think how I could be dead one minute from now. How my promise never to leave my son would be broken in the most painful way possible. I try to suppress the fear, work to calm myself, find a place of inner focus within this horrifying chaos. No guru could envision meditating during a life-or-death fight, but that's exactly what I do. A three-second meditation.

A single deep and purposeful breath, appreciating it could be one of my very last. A simple mantra, repeated only once.

*I am.*

This steadies me, giving me strength.

"You are," my father answers, his voice a graveled monotone. "You're both protecting yourselves now. You're my family, but this fight isn't mine."

My voice matches his, calm and unwavering. "I don't want to be part of this family anymore."

"Okay," Cora says.

She lunges with the blade.

# FIFTY-NINE

**I'VE TALKED TO A** lot of cops. Talked to both victims and criminals. Researched my books to great lengths, knowing that no matter how few people may read my novels, I'm giving my audience accurate portrayals of intense and life-threatening situations. What it's really like to face danger, push through to the other side, whatever side that may be.

There are many clichés said about such situations, but one I've been told dozens of times is how time slows down when danger is at its peak.

This happens for me now.

I see the knife coming at me. I have a thousand years to react. A thousand years all crammed into the space of maybe two seconds, but it's all I need.

I begin my downward swing with the iron poker at Cora's first movement, a push off her left foot. The arc of my weapon is in motion before that foot even leaves the ground. The blade has its own trajectory, extending out to the side, then circling in as Cora descends upon me.

In these thousand years, I see a math equation. A question of physics and geometry. Time and distance, speed and motion. Either I'll strike her first with the poker, or she'll slice though my belly, unprotected and stretched outward toward the knife, inviting disembowelment.

I have so much time but I struggle to solve the equation. I was never very good with math. Cora was better, another way we're different. Right-brained versus left-brained. Emotional versus calculating. Empathy versus sociopathy.

I can't do the math, so I have to rely on faith. Faith that I deserve life more than her.

I keep swinging, Cora keeps lunging.

And then the thousand years comes to a sudden end. Her swipe ends with her blade whooshing centimeters from my stomach. My swing ends with the iron poker shattering my big sister's skull. Shock waves through my arms, a million needles.

The sound is grotesque, like stepping on a swarm of roaches.

I let go of the poker, but the poker doesn't let go of Cora.

It's lodged in her head, the fleur-de-lis tip buried in the upper hemisphere of her brain.

She falls, first to her knees. The blood hasn't even begun to spill, but the opening in her head is clear and irreversible. For a moment, a whisk of a moment, I think how she'd hate to see herself like this. Not beautiful. Not perfect. Yet, in the strangest of ways, it's the most human she's ever looked.

The knife falls to the floor, scattering.

Cora falls next, face-first, the impact almost dislodging the weapon from her skull.

Almost.

The bleeding now starts, furious.

She breathes. She breathes. Not with ease, not with comfort.

My father says nothing.

I kneel next to her, grab her hand. I squeeze, she squeezes back.

"Call 911," I say numbly, not even sure if I mean it but knowing it was what I said twenty-two years ago, when another life was on the brink of permanent departure.

"No," my father replies.

I don't argue, and that's why I'm still a Yates.

I hold my sister's hand and feel the grip loosen. Listen to her breath become shallow and distant. Watch her eyes flutter before settling.

And then, that grin on her face, the wan smile worn by Caleb Benner. Assurances of something better in the distance.

"Touch it," I whisper, thinking of the rainbow in the cornfield, the storm in the distance, the sun brilliant and affirming. "It's like taffy."

The smile remains, but seconds later, the energy is gone. Just like with Caleb. With Riley. The fruit of my sister is gone, and just the husk remains.

This is when I cry. Cry for all I've done and all I haven't done.

And cry for what I still need to do.

# SIXTY

**November 17**
**8:24 a.m.**

**I WAKE.**

Brilliant sunlight streams in the room, filtered through white-lace sheers, rendering my surroundings like the inside of a cloud. The room is familiar, but my brain is so heavy it can't place it. I stretch, roll onto my side, blink a few times. For a moment, it's peaceful.

The moment lasts just for these few blinks, and then the horror of memory rips through my guts. Rips through with rusted metal teeth.

I'm in my bedroom at my father's house.

Cora's dead.

I killed her.

It's…it's daytime.

Think back, I tell myself. What happened last night? I remember crying next to my sister's body. Crying so hard I couldn't stop. I don't remember coming upstairs. I don't have any memory of what happened with…

I bolt up in bed.

Is she still down there? Is my sister's body still crumpled on the floor of my father's study?

My stomach's imploding, reminding me of how I felt the moment I realized Cora was a killer. I retch again. This time, nothing comes out of my mouth, but the bile in my throat burns like acid.

The aches come alive. Pain throughout my core, where my sister punched me repeatedly. Soreness on my right shoulder, and I remember slamming into the bookshelves as I attacked her.

I reach for my phone on the bedside table, suddenly desperate to know the time. When I fumble and find it's not there, the image of Cora smashing it into bits replays in my mind.

I'm untethered, a particularly unsettling sensation knowing Max isn't with me. Maybe he's been calling.

My laptop is on the table where my phone should have been. I wake it and log in to my email account.

The only new message of consequence is from the school district, declaring another snow day.

I begin writing a message to Alec when I realize I don't have his email address. In fact, I don't even know his number. It only existed on my phone, which I hadn't backed up since before I met him.

I go to Facebook and log in, hoping I can find him on there. I haven't looked at Facebook in nearly a year, having abandoned social media after I discovered my husband's infidelity.

I'm immediately assaulted with an outpouring of grief on my wall, scores of messages from friends expressing utter disbelief about Riley's death. I have forty-eight unread messages and two hundred and twelve notifications. A quick scroll reveals a Bible's worth of sentiments (*praying for you, thoughts and prayers*) and more heart and sad-face emojis than my mind can count. The postings are all from July.

After a few moments, I shake myself out of the stupor and search Alec's name. I find him quickly—his beautiful smile radiating from the tiny profile photo—and friend-request him. Three minutes and a lifetime pass, and he accepts. Thank god.

*My phone is dead,* I write in a private message. *I didn't know how else to contact you. How did Max do last night? Did he try to call me?*

Pulsing dots tell me he's writing back.

*Morning. Assume you saw school's closed. All good here. Max had a couple rough moments last night but did okay overall. He tried calling but it went straight to voicemail. Making breakfast now. Pick him up whenever. No rush.*

Another shovelful of guilt piles on top of the mountain I've already created.

My fingers hover over the keyboard, ready to reply, but I hesitate. I have a haunting suspicion anything else I say will sound guilty, something that would be potentially damning evidence in a trial.

I don't answer. Instead, I delete the message thread, knowing how meaningless the act is. Nothing disappears on the internet.

I throw the sheet and blanket off me, realizing how weak I am for the first time. Swing my legs over, stand, then brace against a wave of dizziness. I'm not even hungover. More like still drunk. I didn't have more than half of that first drink…vodka something.

Steadying myself, I look down at my clothes. Same thing I was wearing last night, and there's a small but not insignificant splatter of blood on my jeans.

I close my eyes against the sight of it, but I can't close my memory. Of Cora's head splitting open.

I'm frantic to divert my thoughts so I lumber to the window, pull back the curtain, and rest my forehead against the cold glass, grateful for the chill. White everywhere, easily another six inches of snow. The world outside is beautiful. The world inside is a chamber of horrors.

My urge is to rush to Max, but I need something else first. I need to understand what happened last night. After Cora.

I attempt a deep breath but end up coughing. Open the bedroom door, walk down the hallway, pause at the top of the stairs. The wooden steps appear sharp. Treacherous.

I descend. One flight, then two.

I look over to the wall at the bottom of the staircase, where in my dream I saw the painting of the rainbow and the field. There's nothing there. Nothing has ever been there.

Through the foyer, down the hallway toward the study. The house is as silent as a house could be. A tomb.

*Abril,* I think, panicking. What if Abril shows up?

I see the entrance to the study, twenty feet away.

I don't want to go in there.

I have to go in there.

My steps grow smaller.

As I close in, there's a smell. The aroma of chemicals. Bleach.

Ten feet away. Five.

I reach the entrance. It's dark, the wooden shutters pulled closed. There's a diffused glow from the outside light escaping through cracks, but not enough to see what I need to see.

I reach in, flick on the lights, clench my stomach.

Breathe out. Breathe in.

Nothing.

Well, except the smell of chemicals. And *there*, I notice. The area rug is gone. And…the set of fireplace tools. Also gone.

Otherwise, the room is normal and immaculate. Not a book out of place. Not a drink glass touched. I walk inside, not wanting to. The chair I was sitting in is back in place. A few more steps, over to…to where it happened.

No trace of my sister. No blood on the floor. Nothing but the smell, which is stronger here. I lower to my knees, lean over, and sniff the hardwood floor where she died.

The acrid fumes bolt up my nostrils, making me jerk back.

"Took me all night."

I scream. I can't help it.

My father is standing in the doorway. He's not in a suit. Jeans, polo shirt. Sneakers. As if he's going out to watch the regatta.

He leans against the doorframe. Folds his arms and studies me.

"What…" I struggle to focus. "What happened? I don't remember."

"You were hysterical," he says. "I gave you something to sleep."

"You did?"

He nods. "Knocked you out. You needed it."

Jesus. My father drugged me. Sleep meds and alcohol. The symbolism of it all.

"Where is she?" I ask.

"The less you know, the better."

"I know a lot already." I'm still on my knees and lean back to sit on my heels. "I didn't want to do it."

"I know. We went through this last night. You were inconsolable." He sweeps his gaze along the floor where Cora died. "I'm not sure she would've felt the same way."

The tears start to come again but I can't. I just can't. I've pushed through to some other side where crying doesn't even provide relief.

Still on my knees, I lower my head for a moment, the weight of the last twelve hours overtaking me. Then I look to him. To Logan Yates, the man behind the curtain of everything.

"I didn't want to kill her," I say.

"I know, Rosie."

"No, I don't think you do."

This elicits a deeper squint, a flex of the arms.

"You work so hard to protect a family of poison," I say. "I loved Cora, I think. In a weird way. A nostalgic way." I stare into him, deep into him. I don't dare look away. I don't dare blink. "But I never loved you."

He absorbs this, processes this in whatever way his soul is capable of doing such a thing.

And then he says, "Love is weak."

"No, it's not. You loved Mom. You must have loved her."

"And look what that got me."

I shake my head. "So you just go through the rest of your life like that? Emotionless?"

He unfolds his arms and walks into the room, then settles in his favorite chair. "I guess I'm more like your sister than you." He looks over to the liquor bottles, considering but not moving. "You asked me last night about family."

"I don't remember that."

"You asked how I could sit there and just let…let everything happen, when all I've ever talked about is protecting us." He slouches down in his stuffed chair, and I don't think I've ever seen my father slouch in his life. Logan Yates is a man who always sits up straight, an iron spine, always ready for action. Now he looks tired and beaten, finally appearing as old as he is. Maybe older. "I thought about that a lot last night. All through the night, through everything I had to do, I thought about family. And sometime this morning, around sunrise, I realized something." He looks over at me. "Maybe she would've hurt you, but I think what happened…the outcome…is what she wanted. I think it's what we all wanted. I never had the strength to do it, and you did. When I was standing there watching you two last night, all I wanted to do was keep you both safe. But then I saw there was this chance to finally solve the Yates family problem. The problem of Cora."

"I could have died," I say.

"Yes. You could have."

I rise, and as I stand over him, he doesn't seem so big anymore. He's more pitiful than evil.

"You can't protect me," I say. "You never could. Safety is an illusion."

"You know that's not true."

"There's no getting out of this. I don't even know what you did last night…where you…where *she* is. But Peter and Willow must be missing her. They must have called."

"Peter called," my father says. "I told him she left here angry, but I assumed she drove back home." He looks up at me, fatigue wearing heavy on his face. "And you're right, there may be no getting out of this one." He shakes his head. "I don't know. I just don't know."

There're things I want to ask him. I want to ask what he did with Cora, if she's buried in the same place as Caleb. I want to know why Cora became who she became and if he had anything to do with it.

But my need to understand is overpowered by my burning desire to remove Max and me from this family forever. I don't want to run from the law. I want to run from my name.

"I'm done with this family," I say. "Forever."

The squint, the perpetual squint, for once softens and his eyes widen, like a baby taking in the world for the first time. His pupils are dark, nearly charcoal. But there is an ounce of emotion in my father's face. Maybe it's a mirage induced by all the stress heaped on my system, but I think I see emotion.

Sadness.

A soft, poignant, painful sadness, one unable to hide behind his usual mask of resolve. The look of a man who's fought for everything all his life, only to find death still ultimately comes. And comes hard.

"Is that really what you want, Rosie?"

I don't hesitate with my answer. "So bad I can taste it."

"Do you dream of disappearing?"

A strange question, but easy to answer. "Like I dream of selling a million books."

"You can't have both," he says. "You can't be a famous author and be off the grid."

"I'm not selling a million books anytime soon."

He stands, using obvious effort. Takes a step, leans into me. I don't pull away. He kisses my forehead. Once. Then pulls back.

I think, just maybe, that's the only kiss he's ever given me.

"If that's the case," he says, "then I want you to run. Take your boy and run."

"What?"

"I haven't led the cleanest life, Rose. Obviously you know some substantial reasons why, others you don't. But I always had a plan for us. A way to get out."

"I don't know what you're talking about."

"You, me, Cora. A parachute cord set up for each of us."

"What the hell is a parachute cord?"

"A phone number," he says. "Actually, three phone numbers. One for each of us. Three different agents, each unrelated to the other."

"Agents for what?"

He shrugs. "A new life."

# SIXTY-ONE

**MY FATHER WALKS OVER** to the bookshelves, pulls out a volume that sits at eye level. A hardcover of *Gone with the Wind*. He opens it and removes three slips of paper, looks at them, puts two slips back, then shelves the book.

"I've had these numbers for twenty-two years and pay annual retainers to keep them active. There was always something…comforting about knowing I could up and disappear without a trace if I wanted. A complete sense of freedom." He turns, walks over, stands eye to eye with me. "Funny thing is, whenever I think there might be a need to use these numbers, I don't want to go anywhere. I always want to stay and fight whatever threat I'm facing."

He hands me the slip of paper. There's a phone number typed on it. Long number, international. Above the number is a single word, written in my father's hand.

*Rosie.*

"If you stay and everything comes out," I say, "you'll go to prison."

He smiles, such a rare and unsettling thing. "No, no. I won't be going to prison. Even if I get arrested, I can afford a lawyer who will get me out on bail. I'll put a gun in my mouth long before I do any jail time. Maybe in my favorite chair."

My father isn't prone to hyperbole. I believe everything he's telling me, and I can't find the empathy to argue against his plan.

"And who knows?" he continues. "Maybe I'll use my phone number. Maybe I'll end up running after all."

I shake the slip of paper. "So you expect me to call this number and disappear?"

He nods. "I do. You and Max. I have no actual idea what happens when you call, but whoever answers that phone will tell you everything you need to do. Their job is to make sure your history as Rose Yates will end, and no one will ever find you unless you want them to. You'll be set up with enough money to be comfortable for at least twenty years, if you're sensible about it."

"I don't want to disappear," I say. "And I don't even have a phone to call with if I wanted to."

"Get a burner phone," he says. "Then make the call."

"But I didn't do anything wrong."

He sees right through my naivete. "We've all done something wrong."

"I didn't kill Caleb. And Cora...that was self-defense. That's not how I wanted that to end." I believe my words, so why does it feel like I'm lying?

"I know. But there are other wrongs. There's Riley."

He catches my gaze, daring me to look away. I don't. What does he see? Guilt or innocence? The truth or obfuscation?

He doesn't even bother to wait for an answer. "I suppose only you know the truth about your husband. Still, Rosie, you stayed silent about a lot of things, and that's conspiracy. With the storm that's going to be coming over your sister's disappearance, I imagine it's only a matter of time before all your excuses add up to jack shit in the eyes of the law."

"I'm *not* disappearing."

"Oh, no one ever wants to disappear. Everyone wants to be in control of their own fate. It's very difficult to concede the innate powerlessness we all have. It's far better to manage your lack of control rather than to deny it exists."

This is Logan Yates, *Art of War*, talking now.

"Tell me something," he continues. "Back after the Caleb incident."

"It was more than a fucking incident, Dad."

He waves this off. "The day after the incident, your sister was questioned. Here. In this house. What do you remember?"

I think back, but it's like trying to discern shapes through foot-thick glass. "It's blurry."

"You were nearly catatonic. I cut Cora's interview off before it was over, and I thanked god the cop didn't talk to you. At one point, you ran off to the bathroom and vomited."

That I remember.

"I yelled at the detective," he says, "complaining he was harassing my daughter after she was already upset about the disappearance of a classmate. He backed off because, well, let's face it, I've always been good at intimidation. But I thought he'd be back, which is the reason I set up those three phone numbers to begin with."

"But the cops didn't come back."

He shrugs his shoulders. "I think I overestimated how guilty your sister looked during her interview. No, he didn't come back. But murder never goes away. Not ever."

The word *murder* crawls all over my skin, looking for an opening to get deeper inside.

"But now I think we have run out of time and luck," he says. "If you want a chance to be free, you need to make that call."

Silence settles. Here we are, looking at each other, daughter and father, and I feel a profound certainty I'm never going to see him again. I can see it in his eyes, and I'm sure he sees it in mine.

"Pack a bag," he says. "One for you, one for Max, no more than that. Then take the car. I put some cash in the glove compartment. Get Max, drive to Boston, and park in the Central Parking Garage at Logan Airport. Those are the only instructions I have. Once you're parked, call the number. Do what they instruct you to do."

I don't tell him again I have no intention of disappearing. I don't think my father can comprehend a person's willingness to face the consequences for things they've done. It's taken me twenty-two years to understand it myself, but this is where I am. However I think I can justify my past, I *have* done things. Bad things. Worse than some people, not as awful as others. Yet I see a future for myself. A future where I've paid for my wrongs and live life free from prolonged guilt.

Like Clara Tomson, I think.

Free from thoughts of the suicide rainbow. Maybe even free from the dreams that haunt me.

And maybe this is some chemical in my brain, some compound the body generates to battle extreme anxiety, but standing here in this room of death, staring at the man who raised me and now wants me to disappear forever, I have a sudden, irrational, and blissful belief everything will be fine. The truth about Caleb and Cora will come out, and it will be months or even years of stressful legal and emotional struggles, but in the end, I'll be fine. Cora will be revealed for the person she was, and maybe even more of her crimes will be unearthed. I won't be taken away from Max. We'll be the people we've always wanted to be.

I'm not even worried about Detective Pearson and his quixotic obsession with Riley's death. There's nothing they can prove. If there were, I'd be arrested by now.

I could be completely delusional, but I cling to this fantasy for as long as it agrees to swirl inside my head.

"So what are you going to do?" I ask my father. "Right now. Today."

He looks around, as if the answer is supposed to be written on the wall for him. Then he turns and says, "You know what? I think I'm going to sleep. I'm going to have a drink and then go to bed. Fuck work."

"Good for you," I say.

As he turns and reaches for the bottle of single-malt whiskey and pours a splash into the shimmering crystal glass, a little of Logan Yates crumbles away, like a once-impenetrable fortress eroding with time and neglect.

"Pretty early in the morning," I say.

"I never slept," he answers. "Far as I'm concerned, it's still night."

He walks back and sits in his chair, this time fully upright. In command. He takes a sip of his drink, closes his eyes for a moment, and a faint rush of color comes to his cheeks.

"Mmm," he says.

"Don't leave this room until I'm gone," I say.

"Why?"

I look him up and down. Logan Yates. My father. Drink in hand, in his favorite chair, surrounded by books he's never read but desperately wants people to think he has.

"Because this is how I want to remember you. Just like this."

"Rosie, I'm not going anywhere." With that, he raises his glass to me. I hate him but want to tell him I love him. But there are no *I love you's* in this house. Not even if it might be the last thing you ever say to each other.

Petrified wood, this Yates family tree.

I turn and walk away.

Once I'm out of the study, I have a sudden and altogether different energy. Frantic, mixed with a bit of excitement. Freedom.

I'm getting the hell out of here.

# SIXTY-TWO

**UP THE STAIRS, FIRST** to Max's room, then to mine. I throw things into our suitcases, packing them tight. Rush back to the kitchen to grab a couple of Hefty bags for the overflow, the things we've acquired since being back in Bury. There's no order to anything, and it doesn't bother me in the least.

Finished.

I take everything to the garage, load up the black Suburban. The keys are already in the ignition. I go to the passenger side and open the glove compartment.

There's not just a little money inside. There are four rubber-banded stacks, each at least an inch and a half thick. I take the top one and flip through them. All hundreds.

Christ. I don't know how much is here, but more than I've ever held.

In the driver's seat, I place my hands on the steering wheel and take a few deep breaths. Do I have everything? Purse, keys, and all our bags thrown in the back. And money. Lots of money.

My pulse pounds like I'm running away, but I'm not. I just want to get away from this house. I'll go pick up Max, and then we'll start the long drive to Milwaukee. What happens from there? The only certainty I have is I'll finally be done running away.

I back out over the soft padding of snow in the driveway and into the street.

One last look at 1734 Rum Hill Road. The place I grew up too fast.

Good riddance.

I shift into drive and lurch forward, and as I roll along the blanketed street, I don't even look in the mirror.

The driving is slow; the quiet residential streets haven't yet been plowed. All the rooftops breathe steam into the freezing morning air. I want to push the pedal down, race as fast as I can to Max, but I'll do my son little good if I kill myself trying to reach him.

I make it to Alec's house in one piece, park in the street next to the patch of grass where three months ago I tripped and fell in front of him. The grass is now dormant, covered in snow, and the tree Alec was pruning that day has only a few remaining leaves, holdouts that will lose their grips before too long.

I ring the bell, my stomach doing flips.

Alec opens the door, flannel pants and a baby-blue V-neck T-shirt, the picture of softness and warmth. We all live our own inner turmoil, but if Alec has any, I cannot see it, not now, not here. I see a man who has a snow day, just like his boy. I picture them playing board games by the fire after downing a stack of pancakes and, when they get the energy, donning layers to venture out and make a snow fort. I see a man who's my friend and maybe could have been my lover. I see a human being with whom I could share the truth.

For once, I just want to tell the truth.

But I won't, not now, not yet, so I don't, and the weight of that must show on my face, for he looks at me with questioning eyes and asks if I'm okay.

No, I tell him. I'm not. Not now, not yet.

I walk inside, making no small talk because the idea of wasted words is unbearable in the moment. If I can't confide in him, I at least won't diminish whatever relationship we have with idle chatter. He lets the silence last, and I'm awash with a belief that this is a man with whom I could have shared a forever love.

The beauty and the sadness of it all.

Max races from the living room and hugs me.

"I called last night," he says. "You didn't answer."

*Because Cora shattered my phone before I shattered her.* Another torch of bile rises in my throat, and I swallow it down.

"I know. I'm sorry."

"I was scared."

I don't console him as I normally would because I'm already holding enough fear for both of us. "I'm sure there was nothing to be scared of," I say.

"I...I just don't like it when you're away."

"I'm here now, and we need to get going."

Winter jacket zipped up over pajamas. Boots pulled over bare feet. Max thinks we're going back to Rum Hill Road, and I say nothing to him yet. A fresh outfit waits for him in the Suburban.

I tell him to go out and get into the car, that I'll be there in just a moment. He doesn't argue.

At the front doorway of Alec's house, I hear cartoons from the other room, knowing Micah must be plopped in front of a screen, zoned out, happy and safe.

I have one foot inside the house and one foot out, and if that's not some kind of metaphor for my life, then I don't know what is. Alec stands a few feet inside the foyer, smiling, though his eyes betray concern. He asks me if his promise held. That things would turn out okay for me.

I tell him I don't yet know the answer to that, but I hope so.

He asks if I want to talk about anything.

Yes, I tell him. But I can't. Not right now.

I step back in and kiss him, lightly, a brush of the lips, for if I pressed any harder, I might not ever leave. I thank him for letting Max stay here.

*No worries*, he says.

I almost laugh. Every molecule of my being is some kind of worry. I struggle to remind myself that just before coming here, I was convinced everything would be okay.

I stare at Alec a moment longer, reach out, and grab his hand. He grabs me back.

I take a deep breath, and when I let it out, I tell Alec I'm leaving and never coming back.

If this surprises him, I don't see it.

I ask him if he'd ever think about getting into a car and driving west. The Midwest, specifically. Maybe to visit me, or if he could ever figure out some kind of custody plan, maybe to move there with Micah. I say I know it's a selfish thing to ask, but all I'm looking for is an answer, not a promise. I just want to know if I'm allowed to hold on to that little bit of hope, something to cling to during the upcoming time of struggle.

He answers with just two words, and ones that don't form an empty promise.

*Anything's possible*.

I soak in his response for a few seconds, letting it warm me.

Then I say goodbye and leave, because I simply have to.

I don't want to leave Alec, but god knows I'm ready to leave this town.

Just one more stop first.

# SIXTY-THREE

**9:31 a.m.**

**COLIN SLEPT IN, A** luxury he rarely allowed himself, though there was no pleasure in it today. Extra sleep didn't much help when it was riddled with nightmares. Or, worse, fleeting bursts of hope that everything was okay, only to have reality kick him in the groin and tell him in no uncertain terms that his world was, in fact, completely fucked.

He missed the hot-breakfast hours at the inn, but Franklin and Keith had left some coffee out along with an assortment of pastries. Colin drank three cups and picked at a blueberry muffin. Then he shaved, showered, and dressed, wishing he had a uniform to put on. He missed the days when he wore a uniform. If he had his blues, a gun on his hip, and the hard brim of a trooper hat over his face, he'd be a lot more confident about the visit he was planning to make.

On his way out, he found Franklin reading the newspaper on a love seat in a small sitting room at the front of the house. A fat cat—long, white fur and eyes squinted deep in happiness—lazed on the neighboring cushion. Colin didn't remember there being a cat.

"You're surely not going out in this mess," Franklin said.

"Yeah, planning to."

"Roads still being worked on. Heck, I didn't even get today's paper yet. This is yesterday's. Driving's going to be tough."

"I've seen worse in Wisconsin," Colin said.

"But you haven't dealt with New Hampshire drivers. The only folks who are going to be out on the road are emergency services and stubborn fools convinced they can drive in anything."

Colin managed a weak smile. "Got someone to visit."

"Must be someone special."

Colin nodded. "Yeah. I suppose so. Thanks for the coffee."

"Our pleasure. Be seeing you later?"

Franklin said this in a way that surprised Colin. As if there was a strong possibility Colin would never be seen by anyone ever again.

"I wouldn't miss your dinner," Colin said. "If it's going to be anything like last night."

Franklin smiled. "It will be."

"Okay then."

"Okay then."

Colin walked outside and spent ten minutes getting the snow off his car. Then he got inside, turned on the ignition, and breathed a fog of frost into the air.

It was cold.

It was so goddamned cold.

# SIXTY-FOUR

**10:34 a.m.**

**IT TAKES TWENTY MINUTES** and some slippery turns, but I make it to the house at the edge of the town. Seems appropriate that this place is in a distant orbit of Bury. Far enough outside the ecosystem of the town, but still just within the weakest pull of its gravity.

I navigate the Suburban down a long road that's probably dirt but currently snow. I pass only two other houses, each set back down its own lengthy stretch of driveway. Unlike the planned neighborhoods in most of Bury, the houses out here sit on several acres of land, but they aren't farms. Just a smattering of homes with ample land and enough trees to feel cut off from the world.

"Where are we going?" Max asks, and the question is bigger than he could possibly imagine.

I want to tell him that once we leave Bury, we're headed back to Wisconsin, toward a hard life but the life we're supposed to have. Free from lies and deceit. Free from the crushing weight of the past. That he'll finally know his real mother, and in my blistering vulnerability, in the light of my shame and self-forgiveness, I will be fully present for him for the first time in my life.

I don't say these things. Soon.

"Just one last stop," I say, summarizing all my thoughts of the future in those four little words.

It's the third and last house on the road I seek. As I creep closer, it unfolds into view.

It's a pretty house, in a simple way. A two-story front-gabled farmhouse, white-slatted siding matching the snow and camouflaging the house so much that the only dominant feature is the pitched roof, gray and steep, with a brick chimney rising from one side of the distant end. No smoke comes from it.

On the outside, it's a pleasant house. But I suspect there's no lack of sadness and despair on the inside.

I don't dare pull down the driveway; it's taken enough overcoming of my fears just to get this far. I pull over in front of the black-metal mailbox at the entrance to the drive. The faded, weatherworn family name is displayed in a series of gold-and-black adhesive letters, one of them missing.

*BEN ER*

James and Maggie Benner live here, or so a search of the county records told me. Both their names are on the title, and they moved out here three years after Caleb, their only son, went missing.

A strange thing. Parents of missing kids tend not to move, keeping hope their child will one day walk back through the front door. But the Benners did move, and in relatively short order. They must have had a sense Caleb was never coming home, and I don't know if that gave them any relief or not.

Relief.

Is that why I'm here? To tell them I know their son is dead because I watched it happen?

I can't imagine those words coming out of my mouth, and certainly not in front of Max. Truth is, I don't have a plan at all. I thought maybe I'd come here and then know what to do. But I don't. I'm as lost as ever.

"What are we doing?" Max asks.

"Climb into the back seat," I tell him. "There's some fresh clothes in a grocery bag. Get changed."

"Why?"

"Because I said so."

He unbuckles his belt and scampers over the second row and all the way back into the third.

"Why are our suitcases here?" he asks.

"Because we're leaving."

"Leaving Bury?"

"Yes."

"For good?"

"For good."

I expect either a scream of happiness or an angry protest. But he remains silent, and as I flick my gaze to the rearview mirror, I see him processing the information.

"No more school here?" he asks.

"No, sweetie."

"Are we ever coming back?"

I start to lie but force myself away from old habits.

"No."

A little more silent processing followed by a simple "Okay."

And the world spins on.

I just stare up the driveway as Max changes. No fresh tracks. A Ford truck is parked near the garage, but there's enough snow piled on it to tell me it hasn't been moved anytime in the recent past.

I wonder if they're inside. If so, I wonder what they're doing. Are they retired? What do they do with their time? What did they do with all Caleb's things? Did they give him his own room in a house he's never seen, or are all his things in boxes, cardboard time capsules that will likely be thrown away before ever being reopened?

I could spend my life wondering. Just, I suppose, as they have.

Max makes his way into the second row and sits directly behind me.

"Who lives here?"

"Some people I don't know. I knew their son, though. A long time ago."

"Was he nice?"

I never thought about Caleb as being nice or not. I can only picture him scared. Scared and desperate.

"I don't know," I say. "I guess so."

"So how come we—"

"Their son disappeared," I interrupt, needing the words to come out before I get into a back-and-forth with Max. "Back when I was in high school. He was around my age, maybe a year or two older."

"What happened to him?"

This is a question I would normally answer by saying *He disappeared, so no one knows*. But I can't say that, because I *do* know.

"He died," I say.

"What happened to him?"

"He died, Max. That's all I want to say about it."

"Did they find him?"

"No."

"So how do you know?"

I unbuckle my belt and turn to look at him, and as my eyes connect with his, tears fill mine. "I just can't imagine," I tell him. "These people. What they've been through. What they're still going through. I just… It's just so sad, Max. Do you understand that?"

"Not really," he says.

"You lost Dad," I say.

"I know." His tone is so normal. So matter-of-fact. "But that's different."

I reach back and touch his cheek, having to fully stretch to do so. "Yes. It's true. It's different."

I turn back around and look at the house, thinking how I could put to rest two decades of wondering in three minutes. Isn't that what I want?

The practicality of it all is unnerving. What am I going to do, leave Max in the car while I have the most painful conversation of my life?

I'm itching to do *something*. The fear slips away, the adrenaline kicks in, the thirst to do something right overwhelms me.

My hands start to shake. I place them on the steering wheel; the shake travels up my arms to my shoulders. That, in turn, starts my teeth chattering.

I'm going to do it.

I have to. It's the right thing.

They need to know the truth.

I'll tell them, then I'll drive away. Drive west to Wisconsin. Not running away, just driving toward my future. And whatever happens after that, happens.

*Everything will be okay.*

I'm just about to tell Max to stay in the car when something catches my eyes. Movement in the mirror.

A Jeep. White, coming up the lane behind me. Lights on.

It slows as it reaches me, then finally comes to a halt right next to my car.

Is it them?

It has to be them.

The Jeep's tinted front passenger window is streaked with melted snow, allowing me only the faintest definition of a shape inside.

My heart races, my throat clogged to the point of asphyxia, wondering if their window is going to roll down.

And then, it does.

There's only one person in the car, and it's the last person I expect to see.

He looks right at me, his gaze soul-searching, as if we've known each other in so many different lives that there's nothing I can do to hide from him. Not his presence, his thoughts, his accusations, his truth. In his look, he knows everything.

Detective Colin Pearson.

# SIXTY-FIVE

**10:42 a.m.**

**COLIN HAD THOUGHT ABOUT** visiting James and Maggie Benner ever since Chief Sike told him about Caleb's disappearance twenty-two years ago, but he knew the pain he'd cause would outweigh any good. You never wanted to rip open old wounds if you weren't bringing any recent developments on the cold case.

And Colin knew better. There were no old wounds for those who'd lost a child. There were just wounds, forever open and festering, with no promise of even a crusty scab, much less any real healing.

So he drove out to the Benners' place on this day of cold and snow, a day of such quiet he felt as if he were navigating the lunar landscape, desolate in its isolation, painful in its beauty.

Colin didn't know what he was going to ask them. Maybe he wouldn't ask them anything. Maybe he'd just tell them he was someone with information about their son and preferred to remain anonymous. Perhaps he'd tell them what he suspected about the Yates family and then just slip away, leaving them to their own devices.

That kind of thing would get him fired, no doubt.

But moreover, it was just wrong. He only knew what he knew, and all that knowledge stopped short of certainty. Maybe Cora Yates was just unfortunate in that she was one of the last to see Caleb. Perhaps the floor repairs Logan Yates rushed to complete the day after Caleb disappeared had been needed for years. Maybe Rose Yates truly mourned the death of her husband, who died accidentally when his desire for deep sleep outweighed his common sense.

But when Colin thought about it, really thought about it, it wasn't information he wanted to impart to the Benner family. He wanted advice.

*How do you do it?*

How do you push on, day by day, with such blackness covering your every thought? Does laughing make you feel guilty? Were you ever intimate again after your son disappeared, and if so, was that an act of love or just sheer desperation for touch, a need to feel *something*?

Colin knew a lot about survivors and their coping mechanisms… You couldn't be a detective and not know such things. But all he'd learned couldn't reconcile how he felt, which was that he didn't think he could last another week.

So maybe the Benners could tell him how they did it. How they lasted. Or just how to make it that one more week.

Whether or not he'd even summon the strength to knock on their door remained to be seen. All he knew was some invisible and indefinable source had told him to come here. Whatever unfolded would be unplanned, as were the best and worst things that happen to anyone.

As he neared their house, his attention was drawn to the curb at the end of the Benners' driveway. A Suburban idled in front of the house, its exhaust rising into the air like ghosts escaping into the wild.

Colin slowed, squinted his eyes. Focused on the license plate.

He knew that plate. Knew it by heart.

It was the car Rose Yates drove. Registered to Logan Yates.

"Holy hell," Colin said, crouching over his steering wheel.

He pulled up alongside the Suburban. Through his snow-streaked tinted window, he saw her.

Rose Yates.

Parked in front of the Benners' house.

Colin had been so sure something was going to happen today. And whatever that something was, it was going to happen now.

Right now.

He rolled down his window.

# SIXTY-SIX

**I ROLL MY WINDOW** down, because what else is there to do?

I don't have to explain anything. I'm not doing anything wrong. I don't have to say a word.

But I want to tell him everything.

"Detective Pearson," I say. I try to say it with the ease of meeting an old friend, but I can barely hear my words over the sound of the blood pumping through my head.

"Rose," he says.

"You're back."

"I am."

"Are you following me?"

He shakes his head. "No. I believe this is one of those strange moments in life when things just line up."

"Do you believe in such things?"

"I do now," he says.

He's a hundred years older than when I last saw him, and it's not just the heavy weariness on his face. It's his soul. His energy. It's 10 percent of what I saw just a month ago, an EKG close to flatlining.

"I'm sorry about your wife," I say. "And your…your baby."

"Thank you."

There's nothing thankful about any of this.

"Why are you here?" I ask.

He thinks about this a moment, taking his time. "Well, I suppose I came to see you. And then, in the moment, I thought I'd come to see them." He nods at the house. "But I guess I'm really just doing what you did. Running away after tragedy. Back to Bury."

*Back to Bury*. How that phrase hits me in the moment. I did come here to bury things, mostly my past. But the past doesn't lie six feet underground. It's a zombie, relentless in its need to feast.

"I'm not running away," I say. "I'm going back to Milwaukee. Driving there today."

"That so?"

"It is."

"Still, we should talk. Long as I'm here."

I look back at Max, who's staring at me with wide eyes. The back windows of the Suburban are tinted so dark I doubt Pearson even sees my son.

"Who is he?" Max whispers.

I roll up my window. "No one to be concerned about," I say. I hate dismissing his question, but I don't really know how else to answer. "Someone I know," I add.

I see him processing, and then all his calculations get stuck as his mouth hangs open half an inch and his gaze goes out to the beyond. Max is having one of his moments, one of his fugues.

"You in there?" I ask.

He doesn't reply, just stares out the windshield. Three months ago, this would have concerned me. Now, after a number of these spells, I know he'll snap out of it in a moment or two. Were we at home, I'd sit next to him until he became responsive again.

Now I don't. Now I have to talk to Pearson. Max will be fine.

I tell him to wait in the car and I'll just be a few moments.

I get out, leaving the ignition running, heat blowing.

The Jeep is only feet away, and after I close the door of my car, I open the passenger door of Pearson's.

Now I'm sitting next to him for no reason other than I made a promise to myself, and it needs to start now.

# SIXTY-SEVEN

**PEARSON LOOKS WORN, LIKE** he's been a beat cop for thirty years and has seen the worst of humanity.

"Rose," he says. "I'm on leave. Maybe I'm done with the department… I don't know. But…but the point is, right now, I'm just a civilian. I can't arrest you. I have no jurisdiction here. And I won't blame you if you don't believe this, but I'm more interested in the truth than any kind of justice. I just need some goddamned truth in my life. Some sense of black and white. Does that make sense?"

He looks at me with some kind of weak and anemic hope. It's gut-wrenching.

"What are you trying to ask me, Colin?"

He thinks a bit, then says, "That's the only time you've called me by my first name."

"If not now, when?"

He bows his head a moment, nods it slowly up and down in agreement, then raises it again and locks in on me. His eyes are as bloodshot as an alcoholic on a three-day binge.

"I just need to know, Rose. Did you kill your husband?"

# SIXTY-EIGHT

**MAX ICED FOR A** time, as he'd been doing for months. He'd come to call these moments *icing*. He only called them this to himself. He didn't talk about icing to anyone, not even his mom.

Icing was what happened when the darkness got so black he couldn't do anything but be consumed by it. Didn't matter time of day, didn't matter sunlight or starlight. When it came on, somewhere deep inside, a cold blackness crawled out and devoured him, a billion ants bursting from a hole and covering him as completely as wraps on a mummy. It took only a second to happen, and then he'd be lost in it, unable to hear, speak, or even move. On the outside, he was paralyzed. On the inside, he was thrashing in terror.

The icing was bad now. As bad as ever, and Max had to tell his brain there was a world out there where he needed to be. It was like trying to wake yourself up from a bad dream, but you weren't sure if you were even asleep. Maybe the terror was real. Maybe it would last forever.

This time, he came back, but with great effort. Maybe thirty seconds passed, but it felt like he'd been buried alive for days.

His mom had left the safety of their car and climbed inside with the man. She just sat there next to that man, chatting, like it wasn't a problem at all.

But Max knew. He knew because that man had triggered the icing.

*It's not safe. The man isn't safe.*

He was a detective. His mom had called him that. Detective Something.

Max's thoughts raced back to the night at the firepit. Back to roasting marshmallows with his cousin. To the moment Willow had told him about a cop investigating his mom over his dad's death.

*They think she did it,* Willow had said. *What do you think?*

The memory scared him almost as much as seeing his mom in that car with the unsafe man. Max had worked hard to forget that night with Willow, worked so hard he'd come close to convincing himself it never happened. A dream. A mind-demon that sprouted up after all he'd been through. It couldn't have happened, because the idea of what Willow had told him *(mind-demon, that's all it was!)* was the worst thing he could think of. And he could think of plenty of awful things.

*They'll take her away for a long time,* Willow had said. *Then you wouldn't have any parents left.*

And now he was here. The unsafe man was here. Came all the way back in the snow to take his mom away. And look at her. Just getting into his car like it was okay. It wasn't okay. She'd promised to never leave him, and she'd just jumped into the mouth of the monster. Just like that.

That made him so mad.

Mad to him felt like the sting of a burn, fingertips on a hot light bulb.

*He's going to take her away,* Max thought. *Right here. Just leave me in here with the car running, all the way until the gas runs out. Then I'll die in Grandpa's car. Frozen to death.*

Max knew fury. He didn't think others could see when it happened to him, but he sure felt it. It felt like this. This scramble in his brain. This need to smash and cut and burn and stomp.

The last time it was this bad was the night Dad died. But it had been bad enough a few times even before then. Enough to give Max ideas he knew he shouldn't be having but couldn't control even when he tried. And he tried so hard.

Pretty hard, anyway.

He'd read all his mom's books. She didn't know that, but it wasn't hard to sneak them into his room. She said they were for grown-ups, but he'd read plenty of grown-up books. Plenty. And he'd wanted to read hers, because she was…well…*Mom*. Max wanted to see how she thought. How she used words. How she made stories.

He didn't understand everything in her books. But he could tell she made good stories.

But most of all Max remembered the crimes. All the crimes in her books. All the work she did to make them realistic. And scary.

And Max remembered the killing of the man in one of her books. The husband who would hit his wife just because he was bored. He remembered how that man died.

Alcohol and sleeping pills.

Max knew his father liked both of those things.

He also knew his father had turned into someone mean. Mean and fierce.

Like a ghost suddenly stepping inside his body, Max felt his muscles move. His muscles were talking, and soon his brain got the message.

*You have to do something.*

*You have to tell the truth.*

*Because the unsafe man's going to take her away.*

*Forever.*

*And you'll be alone.*

Max opened his car door and stepped out, his boot plunging deep into the snow.

The moment he was outside the car, the cold air taking him into its arms, Max descended into a fog.

One step out. Then another.

He seemed to float through the snow. To the unsafe man's car. To the man's window.

Directly to the mouth of the monster.

He was hardly aware of his movements. Or of the sun. Of the exhaust of the two cars spiraling into the cold morning. He did hear a bird, just in that moment, a bird that didn't escape the storm, a short cry, lonely and unreturned, then repeated.

It was maybe the saddest sound Max had ever heard. And it took a little of the fury away. Enough for him to get the courage to do what he needed to do. To think straight, at least long enough.

Max rapped on the glass of the unsafe man's window.

The man rolled it down.

# SIXTY-NINE

**OVER ROSE'S SHOULDER, COLIN** saw the back door of the Suburban open. He'd thought Rose had been alone.

Her son emerged from the car, looked first at the ground, then swiveled his head to them. Pale skin, moppy brown-blond hair. A cute kid, but there was nothing light and airy about the expression he wore.

Rose turned her head, following Colin's distracted attention.

"Max, oh my god."

"I didn't know he was with you," Colin said.

Colin expected the boy to go to his mother, but he didn't. He and Rose watched in silence as Max trudged along the snowy country road, around the front of the Jeep, then stood directly next to Colin's window, looking in. Then the boy knocked on the glass.

Colin lowered his window; a chill seemed to flow off the boy and swept inside the car. The kid just stood there, unblinking.

"Max," Rose said, "you need to get back in the car. It's cold out. We're almost done talking."

"So you're Max," Colin said to the boy, trying to put any cheer he could into his voice. He reached a hand out the open window. Max didn't take it. "I'm Colin."

"I know who you are." The way Max said this unnerved Colin. Deep and slow, a boy possessed by something ancient and malevolent. "You came here to take my mom away."

Had Colin been standing, those words might've buckled his legs. He'd come to Bury with few ideas of what he'd hoped to achieve, but ripping a parent away from a child was the last of his intentions. That didn't suppress the reality of what would happen if Rose was ever convicted of Riley McKay's murder, but seeing that possibility—right here, right in the face of this already traumatized boy—tore into Colin.

"No, Max. That's not what I'm here to do."

"Max," Rose said, her voice firm. "Get back in the car. Right *now*."

"No," Max said, not moving his gaze from Colin's.

A few seconds passed, an eternity as Colin and the boy stared at each other.

"What is it, Max?" Colin asked.

Finally Max blinked. And then he answered.

# SEVENTY

**I HAVEN'T SEEN THAT** expression on Max's face since the moment I told him about his father. Smooth on the surface, a torrent behind the eyes, as if there's a whole universe inside his head. Galaxies upon galaxies, captured in a fragile shell, ready to burst.

"What it is, Max?" Pearson says.

I'm immediately angered; how dare he ask my son any questions? It's bad enough Detective Pearson keeps hounding *me*, but he has no right to say a single word to Max.

But then Max answers, and the universe explodes.

"I did it," he says.

"What?"

My one-word question falls out of my mouth in a raspy breath, but it's just a placeholder, a pause, a moment to try to redirect time on any path other than the one it's on. It'll be of no use.

"I killed him," Max says, his voice colder than the air around him.

"No, no, no."

Pearson says nothing; the words are mine. More placeholders, simple stutters. A primal response to something that here, in this shattering moment, I know is true.

Maybe I've known it all along. Somewhere, in the deep recesses of my mind, those dark pockets I tap into whenever I think of the rainbow in the cornfield, there's a spot held for questions about Max. Why he never really cried over his father's death. Why he sometimes talked about wanting it to be just him and me together. And questions about which of the family traits he carried. Specifically, the Yates ability to kill.

"Tell me," Pearson says. Calm, like a counselor who deals with troubled children all the time. "It's okay, Max. Are you telling me the truth?"

I scream. "Max, don't say anything!" Then I clutch onto Pearson's arm, not even sure why, but I want to rip it out of its socket. He turns to me and there's a swirl of emotions in his eyes, but confusion reigns above all.

"*You don't get to talk to him,*" I tell Pearson.

His tone remains gentle but commanding. "Let go of me."

I do. But the rage and fear remain. "Max, we're leaving now. Right now. Get back in the car."

Max looks directly at me and says only one more thing. The words chill me more than the air spilling from the outside.

"It was always just supposed to be the two of us."

"*Go back to the car.*"

This time, he listens, circling a path behind the Jeep. I turn my head just long enough to see him climb into the passenger seat of the Suburban before whipping back around to Pearson.

Time slows. Before saying anything, I perform a two-second meditation. One deep breath. A single mantra, spoken once inside my head.

*Protect your child.*

# SEVENTY-ONE

**WHEN I SPEAK, I'M** surprised how suddenly calm I am. Maybe this is what it's like on the cusp of slipping into shock.

"You don't have jurisdiction here," I say. "You aren't even on active duty. You can't do anything."

"You know it doesn't work that way. You can't just run, Rose."

"That's my decision. Mine and Max's. No one else's."

He puts his hand on my arm but doesn't grab. It's light, as if to comfort, but I'm also aware he's larger and stronger than me. If he tries to restrain me, I'll fight like hell. Fight with everything I have.

"Is it true?" he asks.

My instinct is to scream *no* as loud as I can, but I don't. And that pause, my little hesitation, is probably all Pearson needs to know with certainty that I didn't kill Riley.

"I...I can't even..." I turn my head to the Suburban. To where my son waits for me. "I just need to go."

"Go where?"

"Away from here," I say.

"You can't hide forever," he says. "And Max is a minor. A case could be made about why he did it. Abuse. Self-defense. Protecting you."

I look back to Pearson. "He'll never confess to anything. As long as I live, I'm protecting him. He's my only family. I'm the only one he has."

Pearson nods, eyes heavy.

"Are you going to try to stop me from leaving this car?" I ask.

"No, Rose. I'm not."

"Are you going to call Bury PD as soon as I drive away?"

He thinks on this a moment, face full of sorrow.

"There's no way I can stop you from running?" he asks.

"Not a chance in hell."

"In that case, I want to know the truth."

"I already told you; I didn't kill my husband."

He lifts his hand from my arm, and in a strange way, I wish he hadn't. His touch grounded me.

"Not about that. About Caleb." Pearson nods to the house down the driveway. "The reason we're here. We both showed up at the same house on the same snowy day. If you're running for good, I want to know what happened. You owe me that."

"I don't owe you anything," I say.

"Then you owe it to yourself."

He's right. How many times in twenty-two years have I wanted this? This chance to tell someone about what happened. To confess my sins. To confess all our sins. It's the promise I made to myself just this morning.

I glance briefly at the clock, the digital time glowing blue and bold, the car's heat still pumping into my face from the vents. I take this pit of shame, this thing that has done nothing but grow like a cancer in me for the last two decades, and I choose to take a scalpel and cut it out of my body, right here in this car, hoping I'll be strong enough to survive the operation.

"Cora killed him," I say. I don't even let him react or ask questions. I just talk. I tell Pearson everything I've always wanted to say. Everything that happened back then, every gory detail that I relive in my endless nightmares. Everything about Riley, his affair, his unraveling, and the night he died. About my books and how the scene with the husband dying from alcohol and sleep meds was no more than a simple chapter in a mystery novel, but I couldn't say for sure that Max hadn't read the book. I admit I did write my new novel hoping to confess my complicity through fiction, but that backfired.

I tell him about my move back to this horrible little town. My father and his insistence on family above everything, a trait I have quite clearly inherited.

I talk about Cora. Our relationship, the sisters of Bury. I pass the point of worrying about what I'm saying, and it's the most beautiful feeling I've ever experienced. Maybe it's my moment of touching the rainbow, a release, followed by freedom.

I tell him I think she might have killed others. Perhaps many. Undoubtedly a poodle and a long-ago family pet. I tell Pearson that Cora is dead, and I killed her, an act of self-defense, inasmuch as that even matters. That my father buried her.

He takes all this in, saying nothing. I want to cry, but perhaps like him, I have nothing left to give.

I look at the clock.

Eleven minutes have passed.

Eleven minutes. The weight of all I carried for so long only took eleven minutes to unload. That alone is singularly painful.

"Where is Caleb?" From all the things I've just told him, this is the only question Pearson asks me.

"I don't know. I think in the woods leading from the Chester Woodall trailhead. Maybe…maybe Cora is there, too."

"Do you have anything else to say?"

"No. I've told you everything. I have to go. My son…"

The digital clock counts off another passing minute. Pearson says, "I'm going to get out of this car and go up and knock on the door of that house. Maybe they'll answer, maybe they won't. If they do, I'm going to ask for a bit of their time. If they're kind enough to let me in and hear me out, I'm going to tell them a long story. One that ends with where I think their boy is buried. Once I leave that house, I'm going to drive directly to the Bury Police Department and tell Chief Sike everything I know. So, Rose, by my best estimate, you have anywhere between ten minutes and ninety to get going."

He pauses. My stomach's about to come up through my mouth.

"You'll never have proof," I say. "Everything I've told you. You can't prove it."

"Maybe not, but I have to do something. I took an oath."

"Okay," I say, hardly breathing.

"That's the best I can do, and more than I should. You need to protect your family, and I understand that with more heartache than I would ever wish on my worst enemy. But I can't just let this go, Rose. Someone has to pay. Time doesn't erase murder, never will."

"I understand," I whisper. "Thank you."

He nods. "You're welcome." Pearson inhales deeply, as if he's about to explore the bottom of the ocean on one lungful of air. The exhale is resigned. "You ready?"

"I'm ready," I say.

I've never been less certain of being ready in my life.

Then follows a simple mantra, repeated in my head, just as I've done thousands of times before. A mantra to which I never truly connected but still repeated, hoping to understand. But now, as I repeat the two words—a total of three letters—there's a clarity that's eluded me for thirty-seven years. There's a beauty in the words. A beauty and a sadness. And an absolute, stunning revelation.

*I am.*

*I am.*

*I am.*

"Goodbye, Rose."

"Goodbye, Colin."

He opens his door.

I open mine.

# SEVENTY-TWO

**THIS WORLD IS NO** longer a familiar one. The landscape is a blazing white; the reflection of the sun off the snow sears my eyes. I blink. Tears gather, run halfway down my cheeks, then freeze in place.

I've walked a few feet toward my car when I stop and follow Pearson's shuffle up to the house, watch as his boots plunge into the soft snow, leaving behind deep, dark imprints. Between ten and ninety minutes, he said. Ten minutes does no good. Ninety is probably enough to get me to the airport without being hunted down. I touch the front pocket of my jeans, feel the folded paper inside. The single phone number, my get-out-of-jail-free card. For all I know, whoever is supposed to answer the phone is long dead. The number no longer in service.

Pearson reaches the porch, and I can't move. I should be back in my car, at least making the most of any few minutes I have. I should be fishtailing though this snow to Boston Logan, hoping not to see a swarm of blazing red-and-blue lights in my rearview mirror.

But I can't. I have to watch.

I wipe my eyes, squint to focus. I haven't breathed in a hundred years.

My future depends on if the Benners are at home. Everything that happens next results from whether or not they open that door.

Pearson stands and waits. Waits some more, gloved hands tapping against his thighs. Frosted breath, tight little clouds.

I can't look away.

And then.

Then it hits me, and when it does, it releases me from my unwavering stare and I turn my head and look over to the Suburban. To where my son sits, waiting for me, the weight of the world on top of him.

My future doesn't depend on the Benners being home. Nor does it depend on some unknown person paid to help me disappear. Those things are pieces of the puzzle, not the puzzle itself.

My future depends on one thing only.

I walk the last few feet to the car door.

When I climb into the Suburban, I look back to Max. He holds my gaze, strong and confident. Doesn't drop his eyes, not once. It's as if his confession ushered him into a manhood from which he can never turn back, which is both beautiful and achingly sad.

I start the car and turn around in the street, avoiding looking over at the Benners' house as I crawl through untouched snow. As I drive back down the street and away from this lonely place, I think all I have to do is flick my gaze to the rearview mirror to see if Pearson is inside the house or headed back to his Jeep. Ten minutes or ninety minutes. A split-second movement and I could find out.

But I don't, because the answer won't change my direction.

A deep, focused breath. I try as hard as I can to stay in the present moment, because living in the past or wondering about the future doesn't serve me any longer. It can only be about the now.

"What now?" Max asks, his voice deeper than I think I've ever heard. Those two words will be the only ones he'll say for the rest of the drive.

And the five I answer with will be my only ones.

"Our lives belong to us."

I press down on the accelerator. The Suburban responds, busting through the snow, barreling toward whatever is next.

Ten minutes or ninety minutes.

The clock starts.

**READ ON FOR A LOOK AT**

# THE DEAD GIRL IN 2A

BY CARTER WILSON

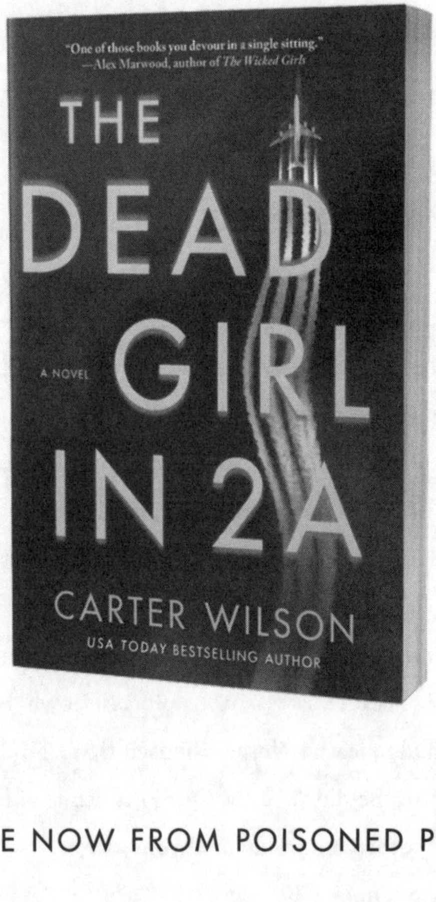


AVAILABLE NOW FROM POISONED PEN PRESS

# ONE

## The Day Of

**JAKE BUCHANNAN PLACED HIS** palm on his eight-year-old daughter's cheek, hooked a strand of chestnut hair behind her ear, and wished again that he could change the past. Em lay on top of her bed in her room, beneath a ceiling light needing two of its three bulbs replaced, and Jake thought her scar seemed a deeper shade of purple than usual.

Thirty-seven stitches. That was how many it had taken to sew his little girl up again. The scar wound from just above her right eye across her temple, then up over her ear, looking like a millipede forever crawling on her face.

*I'm sorry,* Jake thought. His therapist had told him to stop apologizing out loud, because it wasn't helping his own healing process. Apparently, he had to learn to forgive himself first, and though Jake said he understood this, he didn't really. Or didn't want to. He wasn't ready for forgiveness. Not from himself, or anyone else.

"I gotta go now, honey," he said.

"For how long?"

"Just a few days."

"I wish you didn't have to." Em's words were better, but not perfect. The word *didn't* came out slurred, as if she were just coming out of anesthesia.

"I know, me too. But this is a good job. Good money."

"How much?"

*More than it should be,* Jake thought.

"A lot," he said.

"Enough?" she asked.

That one word caught Jake off guard. There was only one way his young daughter could have an understanding of how much money was "enough," and that was because she'd overheard the arguments. Arguments about the accident, arguments about the medical costs, and...god...arguments over whether their little girl had permanent cognitive damage. Em had certainly overheard things neither Jake nor his wife wanted her to hear.

They had argued less since Jake moved out a month ago.

"Let me worry about money, and you take care of your homework," he said.

"Okay."

He reached down and kissed her forehead, and his lips could feel the tight, rippled skin along her scar. "I love you to the moon," he said.

"I love you to Mars."

"I love you to Jupiter," he said.

Jake knew what was coming next.

"I love you to Ur-*anus*." Em burst out giggling, which always ended in the most wonderful snort.

He leaned in, smiling, and she wrapped her arms around his neck.

"Come home soon."

*Come home.*

"I will, love. I'll call you from Denver. Now finish your homework."

"Okay."

One last kiss, then Jake stood and left her bedroom, stealing a final glance of Em as he passed into the hallway. He instinctively began to head to the master bedroom to finish packing—until he remembered he was already packed and his clothes no longer existed in that bedroom anyway. His bag was in his car, outside.

Another memory fog. Perhaps this one was excusable... He and Abby hadn't been separated long. But his memories *were* slipping, and whenever it happened, it filled his stomach with ice. He'd always been unable to recall his early childhood, but now his mind fuzzed over recent things. Conversations he had only days before, or appointments he was supposed to attend and simply forgot. At thirty-five, Jake knew he was too young for these memory slips to be occurring as frequently as they were, so whenever this happened, he'd stop himself and force a memory to the surface, as if to retrain the muscle inside his skull.

*Yesterday's outfit?* he asked himself. A few seconds passed, then it came to the surface. *Jeans, Ecco loafers, blue oxford shirt.*

His therapist had suggested the memory loss could be stress related, or due to his poor sleep habits, adding he should see a specialist if he was truly concerned. Jake never did. He knew he could only get answers if he told the specialist *everything* that was happening in his life. This would mean Jake would have to admit it wasn't just the memory loss that was different.

There were other things. Mood swings. Heightened emotions. Even…moments of enlightenment.

He wasn't ready to tell anyone those things.

Jake had secrets.

He continued into the kitchen. Abby was there, her back to him, intentionally or not. She wasn't quite his wife at the moment, and she wasn't his ex-wife. She was, he supposed, just Abby.

"I'm taking off," he said.

She turned to face him. That helped.

"Okay. Have a safe trip."

He tried to read her and struggled. *Ironic,* he thought. *Suddenly I can read the emotions of strangers, but Abby is a brick wall.*

"Thanks."

They locked gazes, and a thousand words died unspoken between them.

Jake walked over and gave her a hug. She squeezed back, but not as hard as he wanted.

He let go, left the house, and drove to the airport as the first few drops of rain spittled from the Massachusetts sky.

Jake had to accept he was a different man now. Different for so many reasons, and still changing every day. He might not be able to forgive himself, but he was starting to learn to accept.

*I'm going to make things better, baby. I promise.*

Inside the airport terminal, a sea of people swirled around him, and for a moment, Jake fought against breaking down and crying. He managed to keep it together.

Still, one tear escaped.

# TWO
# JAKE

**Wednesday, October 10**
**Boston, Massachusetts**

**GODDAMN IF IT ISN'T** happening again.

Right here in the airport terminal, a sudden burst of emotion, coming from nowhere. I have no idea what triggers it, if anything at all, but here it is, spidering up my chest and flushing my face. A wave of heat, and a moment, always just a moment, where I have to force back tears. A single tear snakes down my cheek, and I wipe it away.

I rarely used to cry. Maybe once a year? And now...I'm a mess.

The thing is, it's not even sadness. Not exactly. It's more like a sudden, profound understanding of something, a sense the universe just contracted a fraction smaller around me, and in the process, I become larger within it and have more of a sense of place. Of purpose.

I remember taking a Psych 101 class in college and learning about Maslow's hierarchy of needs. We learned the ultimate goal, the greatest need, was self-actualization. Its definition always resonated with me: *The realization or fulfillment of one's talents and potentialities*. I remember thinking for so long, how is it possible to completely fulfill all of your potential? How would you even know?

But now, in the moments where sudden emotion threatens to buckle my legs, it's exactly how I feel. As if I'm reaching my potential, even when I can't point to anything that's changed about me. Like I'm standing at the podium, having a gold medal hung around my neck as the anthem plays, but I haven't even gotten up off the couch.

*Steady yourself, Jake.*

I board the 757, giving the outside of the plane a light tap as I pass through the doorway. Superstition of mine. Touch the plane gently, pay a little respect, and she'll get me to my destination in one piece.

Today, that destination is Denver.

The flight attendant at the front of the plane nods and smiles, but there's exhaustion behind her well-worn smile, desperation just behind her blazing, sea-blue eyes. She's in some kind of struggle. I don't know what it is, of course. But I know it as certain as I'm breathing.

Last year, I wouldn't have noticed anything about the woman beyond the half second she smiled at me.

A lot has changed in the last year.

First class, seat 2B. I haven't flown first class in years, but my client insisted. I didn't argue.

I place my leather bag in the overhead bin, slide it to the left, then reach for my noise-canceling Bose headphones. After slipping them on, I take my seat.

I thumb on the headphones, and the ambient sound around me is sucked away, as if I've just been dropped inside a snow globe. Then I navigate my phone to a playlist containing only the recordings of thunderstorms. I know each track and can almost predict the violent thunderclaps as easily as the hook from a song. My go-to is a tropical storm, where nestled within the hiss of a rain-forest downpour are the metronomic calls of some exotic, lonely bird. In my mind, the bird is telling his mate to find shelter because the rain is exceptionally fierce and unrelenting.

The pang of emotion has subsided, but I know it sits close to the surface. I wait for it as I would a hiccup, in anxious anticipation. Nothing comes. Breathe in, hold, breathe out, then glance around me. Passengers file in, and each who passes leaves a trace of energy behind, like a dust mote of dried skin, clinging to me. Collecting. This woman is pleased with something. That man is frustrated. A child is scared.

All this emotional noise. I can't escape it.

Last year, I wouldn't have noticed a thing.

A sudden flash of Em's face in my mind. Strange, in my mind, I don't see the scar.

Thunder rumbles deep in my ears. The sound of a steady, digital downpour. I look out the window at the tarmac, where actual lighter rain falls. Cold, steady drizzle. Not common for Boston in October.

I give myself another memory test. *What was the weather yesterday?* I close my eyes and think about it, feeling the tendrils of panic swipe at me as my brain freezes. Then it comes. *Cloudy. Maybe sixty degrees.* Okay, good.

The accident with Em isn't the main reason Abby and I separated, though the stress of her continuing recovery finally broke us. No, the real issue is I'm losing my goddamn mind, yet a part of me embraces the process. Abby's been trying to help, but I keep her at a distance. She's worried about my memory loss and my mood swings. I'm too young for a midlife crisis, she says, and too old for puberty. She Googles my symptoms, reporting back to me dismal potential diagnoses like *early-onset Alzheimer's*, or even *borderline personality disorder*.

Abby thinks the accident caused my behavior change, but the accident was in January. She knows this all started happening a good month before that. Besides, the accident barely hurt me, just a bloody nose from the impact of the airbag. It was my little girl who took the brunt of the damage.

*She shouldn't have been in the front seat, Jake.*

*I know. I know.*

*What were you thinking? What's wrong with you?*

*I don't know.*

*She could be dead, Jake. Dead.*

*Goddamn it, don't you think I know that?*

No, the accident isn't the cause of the things happening to me.

I look down, aware that I'm doing it again, sliding my wedding band back and forth along my finger. What'll happen if there's no longer a ring there? Maybe it will be like a phantom limb, something I've lost but can still feel. An itch of regret.

A woman standing in the aisle is talking to me. I lift the left cup of my headphones.

"Hi, that's me," she says.

My seatmate. 2A. She smiles and points to the open seat. She seems nervous.

"Of course."

I stand and let her in, and as she passes within inches of me, I catch her scent, thin traces of flowers layered within something I cannot at first identify. It's distinct, and it takes me a moment to place the other smell, and while I'm not positive, I think it smells like mosquito repellent. But it's not the actual smell that jolts me. It's the *memory* of the smell, fleeting but visceral, a déjà vu so powerful, I could be in a waking dream. I try to hold on to it, explore it until I can pinpoint the memory, but it washes away within seconds.

Isn't that something they say? Smell triggers memory more than any other sense?

As she sits, I try to look at her without staring. About my age, I'm guessing, midthirties. Perhaps younger. Kinked red-brown hair, which falls well past her shoulders. Slim and rather pale. She seems out of time, as if her looks would be better suited for a character in *Les Misérables*.

I return to my seat, buckle in, then edge up the volume on my headphones. The rumbling thunderstorms drown out the safety demonstration and the roar of the engines as we take off, but my attention is focused on 2A the entire time. I don't talk to her; she doesn't talk to me. I order whiskey; she gets water.

I reach for my drink as I remove my headphones, no longer wanting to hear the rain or anything else. The cabin lights are dimmed. My seatmate and I both have our reading lights on.

She's writing in a journal. Left-handed. I steal sideways glances from two feet away. She seems unaware of her audience.

The sense of memory slams into me a second time, more powerfully than before. This is especially jolting because memories have been sliding away rather than appearing lately.

I look at my arm, which is suddenly washed in goose bumps.

*Jesus, what is happening?*

There's something else I never would have done a year ago, and that's start a conversation with the person on the plane next to me. But the familiarity of this woman is so intense that I'm barely aware I'm speaking before I actually hear the words coming out my mouth.

"Excuse me, do I know you?"

# READING GROUP GUIDE

1. Rose insists she's different from the rest of her family, but by the end of the book, we learn that's not quite true. Do you think we have any say in what we inherit and whether we have control over it?

2. Characterize Logan Yates. What seems to be his main motivation?

3. Compare Rose's marriage and Detective Pearson's marriage. How are they different? In what ways, if any, are they similar?

4. Think about Detective Pearson's mother. How does she act at night versus during the day? What makes her spiral out of control?

5. Put yourself in Rose's shoes. If you witnessed a horrific crime committed by a family member, would you turn them in? Why or why not?

6. Describe the Yateses' position in Bury. How are they treated by people in town? How do they treat others?

7. List the ways Rose tries to cope with the memory of Caleb's murder. What activities do you turn to when trying to process something difficult?

8. Max behaves strangely throughout the story. Describe his erratic behavior. Why does he act this way?

9. It's clear that Cora is capable of incredible cruelty and violence. Why do you think she killed Caleb?

10. This story explores how far parents will go to protect their children, even if it means doing something morally wrong. To what extent is a crime justifiable if done to protect a loved one?

11. What do you think happens to Rose and Max after the story ends? Do they get away?

# A CONVERSATION WITH THE AUTHOR

**What was your inspiration for writing *The Dead Husband*?**

Unlike most of my books where I conjure an opening scene and see where it leads, all I knew about *The Dead Husband* was I wanted to write a story about two sisters. I can't tell you where that came from; it was just something that nibbled at my brain. And as I thought about the idea of two sisters, I decided it would be interesting if they were estranged and were forced into a situation where they had to reunite. That led to the idea of one of them returning to her hometown, and then I immediately visualized Rose standing at the massive front door of her childhood home. I saw Logan Yates opening the door, saw every tiny feature of his face and the tight squint he wore, and then everything took off from there.

**Like you, Rose is an author. As you wrote this book, did you find yourself drawing any other parallels between the two of you?**

Sure, it's hard not to draw some parallels when you create a character who's also a novelist, but I will say Rose has more discipline than I have. She writes gritty procedurals, a kind of thing that requires massive amounts of research (and Rose loves research!). Me? That's a lot of work, and I'm not a huge fan of spending days on end researching police procedure. I will say, however, this is my first book to feature a point of view from a detective, so perhaps I was indeed a little inspired by Rose.

**The Yates house is larger than life. It's almost a character unto itself. What made you decide to ground the narrative in this setting?**

There's a bit of a "haunted house" element to the story that I wanted to explore. I liked the idea that the Yates family had dark secrets, and those secrets involved an event that happened in the house itself. In a way, that makes the house a co-conspirator. Once I started thinking along those lines, I knew the house had to be large and looming, gorgeous but chilling, with an unmistakably malevolent energy.

**This story forces readers to confront some difficult questions about what people will do to protect their own. How did you approach these moral quandaries?**

Nearly all my characters have moral boundaries they're willing to trespass given the right circumstances, and I find that compelling to write because it's so human. But those boundaries are different for each person, and Cora's line is set very far apart from Rose's. I try to take each character and set a breaking point for them, then start throwing adversity at them to see how they react. Sometimes I'm surprised by the result, and Logan Yates is a good example of this. Although no one would call him moral in a traditional sense, some of the most terrible things he's done in his life was out of love for his children (twisted as that love may be).

**What books are on your bedside table right now?**

Stephen King's *If It Bleeds* and Joan Didion's *The Year of Magical Thinking*. Rather disparate reads, I'd wager.

**We don't know if Rose and Max get away at the end of the book. Do you know what happens to them, or did you purposely choose to leave their story open-ended, even to yourself?**

Yes, I have a pretty good idea what happens to them, which may very well be the foundation for a future story. I did want to leave it a bit fuzzy at the end, which I know can frustrate some readers, but I'm a big fan of ambiguity. I'm the person who liked the endings of *The Sopranos* and *Inception*.

# ACKNOWLEDGMENTS

So here I am, writing these acknowledgments in June 2020, and the world is blowing up. This book won't come out until 2021, and God only knows what the cultural and physical landscapes will look like then. All I know is what's happening now, and I'd like to thank all the nurses, doctors, and everyone else putting themselves at risk to help those who are sick and suffering. Also to the peaceful protesters out there who are making themselves heard, and to those who are listening, perhaps for the first time.

Also, a shout-out to my local liquor-delivery guy: you make quarantine bearable.

This book is dedicated to Drew Mosher, who, in addition to being one of my closest friends since middle school, is a former detective and was my go-to source when I was writing the character of Detective Colin Pearson. Mind you, I still took many liberties with the reality of police procedure for the purposes of the story, so that's on me, not Drew. I'm sure he rolled his eyes at a scene or two in here.

To Pam Ahearn, my agent extraordinaire, a thousand thanks for guiding me again through another book. Much gratitude to my editor, Anna Michels, and all the staff at Sourcebooks who are working from home and still feeding the world their books. You folks are impressive.

To my beautiful partner, Jessica, and Ili, Sawyer, and Henry: I couldn't think of better people with whom to spend a pandemic. Oh, the Netflix we consumed. Sole and Craig, I'm grateful for the extended family. We are all very lucky.

My critique group took a few months off, but they saw enough of this manuscript to offer excellent feedback as always. Dirk, Linda, Sean, Abe, Sam, and Lloyd: *thank you.*

A special thanks to my sister, Kristin, who is most excellent in suggesting Halloween themes, and to my mom, who offers perfect editorial notes.

I'm grateful to Tim Booth and the boys from the band James, who let me use their lyrics once again. It was great to see you all last year, and, Tim, I hope you know what a thrill it was for me to have dinner with the lead singer and lyricist from my favorite band.

Dad, I think you would have liked this one.

And to all my readers, I'm so appreciative as always. You will never know how much your support means to me, and I'm thankful for each and every one of you. Well, except for the one guy whose review of my last book included the catchy phrase *burning this book tonight*. You're kind of a dick.

# ABOUT THE AUTHOR

© Eldeen Annette Headshots

*USA Today* and #1 *Denver Post* bestselling author Carter Wilson has written seven psychological thrillers as well as numerous short stories. He is a four-time winner of the Colorado Book Award and an ITW Thriller Award finalist, and his critically acclaimed novels have received multiple starred reviews from *Publishers Weekly*, *Booklist*, and *Library Journal*. Carter lives in Erie, Colorado, in a Victorian house that is spooky but isn't haunted…yet.

To check Carter's appearance calendar, subscribe to his irreverent monthly newsletter, or to inquire about his availability for speaking events, book clubs, or media requests, please visit carterwilson.com.